"Henry is able to keep all the strands of her spiderweb woven together in a neat and concise way. . . . The end result is a complex, interesting story that maintains suspense and intrigue page after page after page."

—Sadie Hartmann, *Cemetery Dance*

*Praise for*
## LOOKING GLASS

"Mesmerizing. . . . These somber, occasionally disturbing novellas offer a mature take on the children's story but balance the horrors of the City with hope."

—*Publishers Weekly*

"Fans will delight in discovering the unknown family backgrounds and future fate of Alice and her wild and bloody Hatcher."

—*Booklist* (starred review)

*Praise for*
## THE GIRL IN RED

"An engrossing page-turner that will delight anyone who loves running through thought experiments about the apocalypse."

—Paste

"With *The Girl in Red*, Christina Henry once again proves that retellings don't necessarily lack originality."

—*Kirkus Reviews*

*Praise for*
## THE MERMAID

"Beautifully written and daringly conceived, *The Mermaid* is a fabulous story. . . . Henry's spare, muscular prose is a delight."

—Louisa Morgan, author of *The Great Witch of Brittany*

"There is a current of longing that runs through *The Mermaid*: longing for the sea, for truth, for love. It is irresistible and will sweep you away." —Ellen Herrick, author of *The Forbidden Garden*

"A captivating tale of an intriguing young woman who finds herself in the world of the greatest showman, P. T. Barnum. Original and magical, this is a novel to dive into and savor."

—Hazel Gaynor, *New York Times* bestselling author
of *The Last Lifeboat*

## Praise for
## LOST BOY

"Christina Henry shakes the fairy dust off a legend; this Peter Pan will give you chills." —Genevieve Valentine, author of *Icon*

"Never wanting to grow up, never wanting anyone else to grow up, doesn't look like such an innocent and charming ambition anymore.... *Lost Boy* is a riveting story on its own, but it gets extra force from its questioning of what we used to take for granted. Heroes and villains: It seems we got them the wrong way round."

—*The Wall Street Journal*

"Multiple twists keep the reader guessing, and the fluid writing is enthralling.... Henry immerses the reader in Neverland and genuinely shocks.... This is a fine addition to the shelves of any fan of children's classics and their modern subversions."

—*Publishers Weekly* (starred review)

"This wild, unrelenting tale, full to the brim with the freedom and violence of young boys who never want to grow up, will appeal to fans of dark fantasy." —*Booklist*

"Turns Neverland into a claustrophobic world where time is disturbingly nebulous and identity is chillingly manipulated. . . . A deeply impactful, imaginative, and haunting story of loyalty, disillusionment, and self-discovery." —RT Book Reviews (top pick)

## Praise for
## RED QUEEN

"Henry takes the best elements from Carroll's iconic world and mixes them with dark fantasy elements. . . . [Her] writing is so seamless you won't be able to stop reading."

—Pop Culture Uncovered

"Alice's ongoing struggle is to distinguish reality from illusion, and Henry excels in mingling the two for the reader as well as her characters. The darkness in this book is that of fairy tales, owing more to Grimm's matter-of-fact violence than to the underworld of the first book." —*Publishers Weekly* (starred review)

## Praise for
## ALICE

"I loved falling down the rabbit hole with this dark, gritty tale. A unique spin on a classic and one wild ride!"

—Gena Showalter, *New York Times* bestselling author of *The Phantom*

"*Alice* takes the darker elements of Lewis Carroll's original, amplifies Tim Burton's cinematic reimagining of the story, and adds a layer of grotesquery from [Henry's] own alarmingly fecund imagination to produce a novel that reads like a Jacobean revenge drama crossed with a slasher movie." —*The Guardian* (UK)

"A psychotic journey through the bowels of magic and madness. I, for one, thoroughly enjoyed the ride." —Brom, author of *Slewfoot*

# GOOD GIRLS

## GIRLS

## DON'T

## DIE

### CHRISTINA HENRY

BERKLEY

New York

BERKLEY
An imprint of Penguin Random House LLC
penguinrandomhouse.com

Copyright © 2023 by Tina Raffaele
Readers Guide copyright © 2023 by Tina Raffaele
Penguin Random House supports copyright. Copyright fuels creativity, encourages
diverse voices, promotes free speech, and creates a vibrant culture. Thank you for buying
an authorized edition of this book and for complying with copyright laws by not reproducing,
scanning, or distributing any part of it in any form without permission. You are supporting
writers and allowing Penguin Random House to continue to publish books for every reader.

BERKLEY and the BERKLEY & B colophon are registered trademarks of
Penguin Random House LLC.

Library of Congress Cataloging-in-Publication Data

Names: Henry, Christina, 1974– author.
Title: Good girls don't die / Christina Henry.
Other titles: Good girls do not die
Description: First Edition. | New York: Berkley, 2023.
Identifiers: LCCN 2023007842 (print) | LCCN 2023007843 (ebook) |
ISBN 9780593638194 (trade paperback) | ISBN 9780593638200 (ebook)
Subjects: LCGFT: Novels. | Gothic fiction. | Horror fiction.
Classification: LCC PS3608.E568 G66 2023 (print) | LCC PS3608.E568 (ebook) |
DDC 813/.6—dc23/eng/20230224
LC record available at https://lccn.loc.gov/2023007842
LC ebook record available at https://lccn.loc.gov/2023007843

First Edition: November 2023

Printed in the United States of America
1st Printing

Book design by George Towne
Interior art: Night Scary Forest © Wilqkuku/Shutterstock.com

*For my beloved aunt Berni.*
*Better than a pop-up card, right?*

# GOOD
# GIRLS
# DON'T
# DIE

# PART I

# CELIA

# CHAPTER ONE

**mysterybkluv:** who else here loves cozy mysteries best?

**poirotsgirl:** cozies are my fave, esp if they have recipes in the back

**mysterybkluv:** ngl it would be great to live in a small town where there are lots of low-stakes murders and I could solve them while working in my family restaurant

**tyz7412:** lol living the dream

"MOM."

"Earth to Mom. Come in, Mom."

"Mom, I'm going to be late for the bus!"

Celia shook her head. The small person beside her was blurry, out of focus. Did she need glasses now?

*And why was this person calling her "Mom"?*

Celia blinked hard, once, twice, and the little person came into focus. A girl—*maybe ten, eleven years old?*—staring at her expectantly, holding an open backpack.

"What?" Celia asked.

"My *lunch*," the girl said. "I need my lunch. Did you drink enough coffee this morning?"

Celia looked down. In front of her, on a white countertop, was an open cloth lunch bag. Inside it there was already a plastic bag of sliced apples, a bag of all-natural puffed corn snacks (cheese flavored), and a chocolate soy milk.

A piece of waxed paper lay unfolded on the counter. *What is all this disposable packaging? I would never buy things like this.*

"Mom!" The little person was getting really insistent now. "Sandwich!"

Celia couldn't think. She needed this small girl to leave so she could organize her thoughts.

*Why does she keep calling me "Mom"? I don't have any children.*

"Two minutes!" the girl screeched.

There was a loaf of wheat bread and a package of cheese from the deli next to the waxed paper. Celia took out two pieces of bread.

"One piece in half! Mom, what's wrong with you today?"

"Sorry," Celia said, cutting the single slice of bread in half. "How much cheese?"

"Two pieces! Come on, come on!"

*You're old enough to do this yourself,* Celia thought as she folded the bread around the cheese, wrapped the sandwich in waxed paper and shoved everything in the lunch bag. The girl grabbed it, stuffed it in her pack and sprinted toward the door.

"Bye, love you!" she said as she threw the door open, then slammed it shut behind her.

Celia walked like a sleepwalker to the window next to the door and peered out. The little girl was running down a long inclined driveway toward what appeared to be a country road. Across the street there was nothing to see except trees, tall trees that looked like older-growth maple, oak and ash.

The little girl reached the end of the drive just as a yellow school bus pulled up in front of the mailbox. She clambered onto the bus and it pulled away.

*She's gone. Now I can think.*

Footsteps sounded overhead and Celia glanced up at the ceiling in alarm. The steps moved across the floor, and a moment later Celia heard someone large coming down the stairs. She couldn't see the stairs from where she stood. The kitchen was attached to a dining room on one side and a hallway on the other. Celia peered into the hall. The bottom of the stairs was at the far end.

A strange man rounded the banister and headed toward her, frowning at his cell phone as he walked. Celia backed away from him, her heart pounding. Her butt bumped into the edge of the counter. She scrambled around it and positioned herself close to the door so she could run if she needed to do so. She looked down at her feet. Socks. Not even slippers. There was a pair of low shelves positioned next to the door with shoes neatly arranged on them. One of those pairs should be hers. But would she have time enough to figure out which pair, put them on and get out the door?

"Hey, babe, I've got a ton of meetings this morning," the man said. "I'll stop by the restaurant at lunchtime."

*Who is he?*

The man was very tall, at least six inches taller than herself, and she wasn't a small woman. He had dark hair cut in what she thought of as "millennial fund manager" style and wore a well-tailored gray suit. He had a gym-toned look about him and altogether gave the impression of someone who belonged in a city. This impression was reinforced when he pulled on an expensive-looking wool overcoat. His shoes, Celia noted, were very shiny.

He leaned close to her and kissed her cheek absently, still looking at the phone so he didn't notice the way she inched backward. She caught a whiff of his aftershave, something musky and heavy. Her nose twitched.

"See you later," he said, and disappeared out the same door as the little girl.

Celia went to the window and pulled one blind up to peek out. The man who'd called her "babe," the man who'd kissed her goodbye, had gotten into a black Audi SUV that was parked at the top of the driveway. He backed down the drive and pulled out onto the road, heading in the opposite direction of the bus.

*An Audi. City guy,* she thought again, and then wondered why she thought this.

*Because I live in a city and I see those kinds of guys all the time,* she thought, but the thought was like a stabbing pain in her head. She looked around the kitchen, then out the window once more.

Clearly, she did not live in a city. Why did she think she lived in a city?

But now, finally, all the people were gone from the house and she could stop and think.

The kitchen was large and had a white countertop that wrapped around half of the room and then extended out on the third side as a breakfast bar. There were stools lined up along that side, facing the dining room.

Celia pulled one out, sat on it and stared at the rectangular dining room table and chairs, done in some heavy dark wood that she never would have chosen for herself. She didn't like dark wood, didn't like the formality of it, and she definitely didn't like anything that looked like it would need regular polishing. Celia hated to clean, and she particularly hated to dust and polish. That dining room table represented everything she didn't want in a piece of furniture.

"I didn't buy that," she murmured. "I have a round oak table."

Again, there was a little stabbing feeling between her eyes, and she rubbed the spot with her forefinger. Obviously she didn't have a round table. The two people who'd rushed out of the house seemed to think she lived there, that she belonged there.

*And that guy, that guy who kissed me goodbye—he did look a little familiar.*

"He said he would see me at the restaurant. Do I work at a restaurant?"

She had a vague memory of her hands collecting dishes from a table, of tucking a notepad into an apron.

*Maybe I drank a lot last night. Or maybe I had a mini stroke or something.*

The only thing she knew for sure was that her first name was Celia.

She stood up again and walked into the dining room. At one side of the room there was a large cabinet with glass doors on top and drawers on the bottom. The cabinet matched the dining set, and she crinkled her nose at it.

*I hate that matchy-matchy thing. I bet all the dishes are in a matching pattern, too.*

When she opened the glass doors, she confirmed that her prediction was accurate. All the tableware and serving plates were in a matching pattern, a kind of country floral that made her think of wedding registries.

On the wall opposite the cabinet there was a large, posed photograph of three people. The background was soft gray, like they'd been in a photo studio. There was Celia, sitting next to the tall dark-haired man. They both wore white-cabled fisherman-style sweaters. The lunch-demanding little girl stood in front of them, positioned so that she was halfway between them. She, too, wore a cabled sweater, this one in pink. All three of them had the slightly glazed eyes and overly toothy smiles that came with posed photography.

*This is my family?* Celia thought, then told herself, more firmly, *This is my family.*

There was obviously something wrong with her today. Amnesia seemed unlikely. Early-onset dementia?

*It can't be dementia. I'm only thirty-four.*

"Ah!" she said, and clapped her hands together. She'd remembered something else. She was thirty-four.

*Okay, okay, you just need to walk around for a bit and then you'll remember everything. Maybe you just didn't sleep well or something.*

She paced slowly through the dining room and into the living room. Leather furniture—more yuck—a huge entertainment system, several more photographs of herself and her family caught in various activities: eating drippy ice cream cones, building sandcastles, taking a picture with a certain mouse at an amusement park. Regular family things.

There was something about the pictures that bothered her, but she looked at them for a few minutes and couldn't put her finger on it, so she moved on.

She climbed the stairs and found four rooms upstairs—two bedrooms, one office and a bathroom. The little girl's bedroom had posters of Korean pop stars and a pile of soccer gear in the corner. The carpet was pink and so were the walls. It wasn't to Celia's taste, but then it wasn't her room, so it didn't matter.

The second bedroom wasn't to her taste, either, but apparently this *was* her bedroom.

*The bedroom I share with that strange man,* she thought, with a trickle of unease.

Like the furniture downstairs, everything in the bedroom was made of heavy, dark wood, with a thick blue carpet underfoot. She didn't like wall-to-wall carpeting, and yet it was everywhere in this house. On an end table on one side of the bed there was a wedding photograph of a younger Celia smiling next to the strange man. Beside the photograph was a brown leather purse.

*Brand name, high-end. I wouldn't have bought this for myself. It's a waste of money. The Audi guy must have bought it. He seems like the type to care about stuff like this.*

Celia sat on the edge of the bed and emptied the purse onto the dark blue comforter. A large wallet fell out, along with a pack of Trident spearmint gum, a package of tissues, a bottle of hand sanitizer, a powder compact, a hairbrush, a cherry-flavored ChapStick and some business cards.

Standard purse contents, but like the photos she'd seen down-stairs, something seemed to be missing. She just couldn't think of what that something might be.

She opened the wallet and found a New York State driver's license with her photo on it. The name listed was "Celia Zinone." She said the name to herself. It seemed right, unlike everything else she'd experienced so far. There was a debit card and two credit cards in the same name, and a few more family photos—mostly the posed kind—in the photo flap. All the photos were of her immediate family. Did she have no parents? No brothers or sisters or nieces or nephews?

Celia picked up the stack of business cards. They advertised Zinone's Italian Family Restaurant next to a cartoon of a plate of spaghetti and meatballs. Her own name was listed underneath as the owner, and beneath that was the address and phone number.

*I run a restaurant. Okay.*

She again had a flash of memory—of stirring a giant pot of sauce, of folding ingredients into layers of lasagna.

"He said he would see me at the restaurant at lunch," Celia said.

She looked at the business card again. So she should probably get dressed and take herself to this restaurant. Maybe going to work would help her remember more.

Terror clutched at her for a moment. It was as though she stood beside a dizzying abyss, with no real sense of self, no memories, no knowledge of what she'd done the previous day or even that morning before the little girl started shouting about her lunch.

Black spots danced in front of her eyes and her heart seemed like it was trying to escape her chest. Her breath came in hard pants and she heard the wheezy quality of it, an inability to get the oxygen all the way to the bottom of her lungs.

She dug her fingers into the comforter on either side of her legs, feeling the material scrunch beneath her hands.

*Calm, calm, calm. Breathe, breathe, breathe. You're okay. You're not in danger.*

Hard on the heels of that thought came another one. *Why would I be in danger?*

Celia forced herself to take deep, calming breaths, and after a few moments, her heart rate slowed, though its beating still seemed unnaturally loud to her.

*I just need to go to the restaurant and then things will click into place. But how will I get there? I'm not sure where I am in relation to it.*

She glanced over the items on the bed and realized what was missing. A cell phone. Surely she had one. Where had she left it, though?

She checked all the surfaces in the bedroom and found two charging stations on top of the dresser. Assuming the strange man (*your husband*) didn't carry two cell phones, then one of the chargers was for her phone.

Why wasn't it in her purse? She always kept her phone in her purse when it wasn't on the charger. She didn't like to use it in the house.

Celia grabbed on to that thought the same way she'd done with the memory of her age. It was something concrete, something solid that she knew about herself for certain. She avoided using her phone in the house because she didn't want to be one of these people who mindlessly scrolled all day.

But she couldn't find it in the bedroom, no matter how many drawers she opened or pockets she checked. She did note the type of clothes in the closet—conservative-looking sweaters and button-down blouses in low-key colors, lots of beige and gray and black and soft pastels. The sight of them made her feel, again, that these weren't things she would have chosen for herself. She was more of a happy-print skirt and quirky T-shirt girl.

For a third time her forehead stabbed with pain, and she wondered if she needed to hydrate more, or perhaps a migraine was coming on.

A loud ringing echoed through the house, the sound of an old-fashioned rotary dial phone. The noise pulled Celia out of the bedroom and down the stairs in search of the source, and she ended up back in the kitchen, where she'd begun.

The ringing stopped before she entered the room. She stood in the doorway, irresolute, looking around for a wall unit before spotting the cell phone on the counter. The ringing must have come from the cell.

She picked up the phone—a couple of iterations out-of-date iPhone, which surprised her since the strange man seemed like the type to demand everything be top-of-the-line in his house—and tapped her finger on the bottom button to start it. A moment later, the home screen popped up, a picture of her own face mashed beside the strange man and the little girl, all of them smiling.

*This is my family,* Celia thought. *This is my family, and I don't even remember their names. I don't even recognize them. At all.*

# CHAPTER TWO

poirotsgirl: Ever notice how the person who dies in cozies is always some jerk nobody likes?

mysterybkluv: I know it's like the town is slowly killing off all the bad elements until they are perfectly serene

poirotsgirl: lol wish that was my town

THE DISCOVERY OF THE phone was a revelation. In the contacts she'd found a picture of the strange man with the name "Pete" beside it, and another of the little girl with the name "Stephanie." So she knew the names of her husband and child, at least.

She also found photos in the camera roll of herself at the restaurant—sometimes dressed in a white blouse and black pants and standing at the hostess station, sometimes in the kitchen in a T-shirt and blue jeans wearing an apron. There were also photos of her with other people—clearly staff members, who conveniently wore name tags. Celia spent several minutes carefully memorizing names and faces.

The person who'd called her was named Jennifer, and a photo of a smiling blonde was next to that name in Celia's contacts. Celia listened to the voice message.

"Hey, Ceil, I just wanted to know if you had time for a run this morning before you went into the restaurant. I'm assuming since you didn't pick up, you're either out on the road already or on your way to work. If you're at home and want to join me, I'm going to do the Cedar Creek loop. Maybe I'll see you out there."

Celia disconnected from the voice mail and stared at the phone. *Run?* She didn't like to run. At least, she didn't think she liked to run, but then everything she remembered about herself seemed to be wrong, and everything she didn't remember was all around her. Maybe she was a runner. Maybe she was the type of person who loved to train for marathons.

She looked down at her body. Slender, but was it runner-thin? She had a flash of seeing herself in a studio mirror, wearing yoga tights and a loose top, extended out into triangle pose. That seemed more her style, but it was possible that all these memories were just a dream she'd had, a dream that was causing this temporary amnesia, or whatever it was.

Celia sank to the floor in the kitchen, her arms wrapped around her knees, and stared at the phone. Whatever she thought her life was obviously wasn't true. The truth was all around her. She just needed to take a deep breath and play along with everyone until her memories came back.

*Fake it 'til you make it,* she thought, watching her hands tremble. She took deep breaths until the trembling stopped. *I am strong. I am capable. I will get through this.*

Then she went upstairs, showered, dressed, placed all the loose items on the bed back in her purse, and went downstairs again to seek out her keys, shoes and car.

The keys were hanging on a hook in the kitchen; the Nike sneakers with light blue swoops on the side fit her the best. Celia carefully locked the door and went outside to find a small Toyota Camry. She climbed into the car and turned the ignition on, setting the phone to give her directions to the restaurant.

She turned right out of the driveway and drove slowly toward town, taking in everything around her as she went. To the left, as far as she could see, was a wooded area. The tree cover was thick, and she couldn't tell if there were hiking paths inside. On the right was the occasional residence, every few hundred feet or so. Most of them looked like two-story middle-class homes, with white or blue or gray siding and reasonably priced cars in the driveways.

After a couple of miles, the houses started appearing closer together. Then the road curved away from the trees and she passed a sign that read WELCOME TO JACKSVILLE.

Her lip curled at the name. *Jacksville? Why didn't they just call it Smalltown, USA?*

Then she shook her head again. She had to stop doing that. This was her home, whether she remembered it or not. This was the place where she'd chosen to live with the strange man

*(my husband is not a strange man and his name is Pete)*

and the little girl

*(my daughter we called her Stephanie imagine how hurt she would be if she thought her own mother didn't remember her name)*

She drove onto Main Street, which had a variety of small businesses on either side of the road. All the businesses had slightly-too-cute folksy names, like Sweet Tooth Candy Shop and Melissa's Marvelous Books and Best Bread.

*Kind of like the name of my restaurant,* she thought.

There were very few cars on the street. About a dozen or so pedestrians went in and out of the shops. Some of them waved to her as she drove by and she waved back, hoping her face didn't look as frozen with fear as she felt. Nothing looked familiar to her. It was like a scene from a movie, a set designer's idea of a friendly small town where everyone knew everyone else.

Celia's restaurant was a single-story brick building on the corner of Main Street and Cherry Lane. There was a green-and-white-striped awning that extended over a large picture window

in front. The shades on the window were drawn. Above the awning, the words "Zinone's Italian Family Restaurant" were written
in fancy script.

She just stopped herself from rolling her eyes at the name of
the cross street *(Cherry Lane? Really?)* and drove around the corner
to the small parking lot attached to the back of the restaurant.
There were three spots near the back door marked "Employees
Only," and she pulled the Camry into the spot closest to the door.

The key fob she used had two parts that could disconnect from
each other. One side had a ring with her car key and house keys,
and the other side had a bunch of keys that she assumed were for
the restaurant.

A few minutes later (after trying several keys), she was inside.
Her armpits were damp and she was deeply grateful that no one
had been nearby to see her struggling to find the correct key. It
was so important that she pretend nothing was wrong, at least
until she could determine what had happened to her.

*Why don't you just tell someone—like, say, your husband—that you
have amnesia?* she thought as she clicked on the light switch.

She shook her head no at her own thought. In movies, women
who said that they couldn't remember things or were seeing
things or having weird memories were never believed and were
always locked up in psychiatric clinics.

For as long as Celia could remember, that had been her worst
fear—that she would be swept somewhere behind closed and
locked doors, that she would speak words that no one would believe, that she would have no control over the life she'd made for
herself.

*That's another memory. That's something else you know about yourself.*
She hugged these scraps of memory to her, hoping they would
spark something larger.

No, she wouldn't say anything to anybody about what was going on in her head. She'd just keep pretending everything was fine and if she slipped up, she could pass it off as a bad night's sleep.

She could pretend until her memory came back. Surely nobody would notice that she didn't know who she was or what she was doing or why she was there in the first place.

She stood in a storage room full of metal shelves, the shelves full of cans of San Marzano tomatoes and bottles of extra virgin olive oil and plastic buckets marked "flour" and "sugar." There were bins full of garlic and onions.

There was a door at the opposite wall and Celia crossed to that wall and turned on another light, this one illuminating a gleaming, whistle-clean kitchen. She nodded in approval at the sight. She always had difficulty eating out in restaurants because she was certain no one's kitchen cleanliness standards were as high as her own. The kitchen was the only place Celia cared about cleaning.

*That's another memory. See? You'll know yourself in no time.*

A door that swung in both directions led from the kitchen into the dining room. The dining room was pretty typical Italian restaurant—red leather seats, dark wood paneling, white-and-red-checked tablecloths. It didn't look too fancy, which jibed with the "family restaurant" thing. On closer inspection, the red leather seats were revealed to be imitation leather, which meant that they'd be easy to clean when little hands knocked over their milk cups.

Celia wandered toward the front of the dining room. There was a wooden hostess stand with a flat computer monitor on top next to a telephone. There was a pull-out tray underneath for a keyboard.

A portrait of an older couple hung on the wall beside the hostess stand. Celia gasped, then leaned in close to the picture. She knew these people. She *knew* them, deep down in her bones, no need to dig and scrape for their identities inside the weeds in her head. They were her parents, Sonny and Mary Zinone.

Sonny was balding in the photo, his remaining hair gray and wispy. He had thick glasses with black plastic frames over lively dark eyes. He wore a white apron over a white button-down shirt with the sleeves rolled up and black pants. His arm was around Mary, who was several inches shorter than he was.

Mary had dark brown hair that had been "done"—that is, set by a hairdresser once a week and preserved with curlers and a hairnet every night before bed. She, too, wore an apron over a white blouse and dark pants.

They stood together under the striped awning at the front of the restaurant, smiling like they couldn't stop.

Celia ran her fingers over their faces, feeling tears prick at the back of her eyes. These were her parents. She knew them. And if she knew them, then the rest of her life would come back to her, too.

*But where are they? Did they retire? Did they pass away? Why aren't their names in my list of cell phone contacts? Why are there no text messages from my mom, or photos of them on vacation or out having drinks together?*

A little spasm of grief caught her in the stomach. What if they were gone forever?

*You don't know that. You don't know anything for sure, so don't borrow trouble.*

She walked back through the dining room and the kitchen. This time she noticed a second door off the kitchen that she hadn't caught the first time through. It was marked "Office."

Another key was required to open this door, and again Celia was glad there was no witness to her struggle as she went through every key on the ring to find the correct one. Inside she found a tiny wooden desk and a shiny, new-looking file cabinet. On the desk was a yellow legal pad with a neatly written to-do list and a large calendar that had various things written in on each day—"bread delivery" was marked three days a week, for example. She didn't know why she would need to mark that down when it happened every other day, but she had.

*Okay, I'm conscientious and detail oriented. That's good, right?*

She hung up her coat and purse on the rack in the corner and sat down to go over the to-do list and the papers on her desk. Maybe it would spark a memory like the portrait.

She came across an invoice for an exterminator. At the bottom of the bill there was a handwritten note: *Sorry there was nothing to actually remove, but I have to charge you for the visit. Maybe Mrs. C would pay for it?—Nick*

Celia was puzzling over this as she heard the sound of a key turning in the back door, and then a female voice called, "Hello!"

Panic tripped through Celia again. Then she took a deep breath. *(I'm turning into a professional deep breather.)* Whoever had come through the door had a key. If they had a key, then they belonged at the restaurant.

*I just hope I remember to match the name and face.* She resisted the urge to open the photos on her phone and double-check identities.

A tall, thin redhead poked her head around the doorway. "You're here early!"

"I had a few things to go over, but I'm finished now," Celia said vaguely, trying to mentally shuffle through the photos she'd looked at that morning. *Katherine. I'm pretty sure her name is Katherine.*

"Okay," Katherine said cheerfully. "Are we still doing truffled mushroom lasagna for the special today?"

"Yes," Celia said. She had no idea if that was supposed to be the special, but if this woman was going to guide her, then Celia would take it. "I'll help you."

"Thanks, boss," Katherine said. "Everything always tastes better when you cook it. That Zinone touch."

Celia smiled, but she felt uncomfortable. The compliment had been delivered in a completely sincere tone, but it seemed like dialogue from a book, not real life. She felt again the disorienting sense that everything she'd passed on the street, everything she'd seen, wasn't real.

*Get it together, Celia. This is your life.*

She pulled an apron over her clothes and joined Katherine in the kitchen. As soon as she started preparing the lasagna, she felt calmer. This was something she knew how to do—instinctively, without grasping for a memory. She wasn't completely certain where all of the ingredients were in the storeroom, but it didn't matter, as Katherine seemed to think it was her job to carry everything out to the worktable. Celia soon fell into the rhythm of making a béchamel sauce with Marsala wine, sautéing the mushrooms, making the long sheets of lasagna noodles by hand. Katherine chopped the thyme and grated the Fontina and Romano cheeses, then the two of them worked side by side to assemble several trays of lasagna that were covered and placed in the refrigerator until it was time to bake them.

"What next? Bolognese sauce?" Katherine asked. "Or should we make the gnocchi?"

"I'll start the sauce, you start the gnocchi," Celia said.

"Aww, I hate making gnocchi," Katherine said.

Celia felt a twinge of annoyance, but kept it out of her voice as she said, "Just get going."

Katherine grinned. "Still keeping that Bolognese recipe to yourself, huh? I'm always so busy I can't watch you properly to see exactly what you put in the pot and in what quantities."

Celia was saved from replying by a knock on the back door. The knock sounded aggressive, like the person on the other side was angry about something.

"Oh, no. It's going to be Mrs. Corrigan," Katherine moaned as

Celia went to the door. "Can't you just pretend she's not out there?"

Celia turned the knob with some degree of trepidation, especially since Katherine seemed to know who was out there and she definitely did not.

A sour-faced woman wearing a pink sweatshirt, neatly ironed khakis and white athletic shoes stood outside. Her hair was gray, cropped close to her head, and her hand was raised in a fist, as if she were preparing to bang on the door again.

"Good morning," Celia said.

The woman, who Celia assumed was Mrs. Corrigan, puckered her mouth like she was sucking on a lemon.

"It might be a good morning for you, but it is certainly not for me. I was up all night listening to the sound of vermin scurrying under my window. Vermin that, I might add, are only present in this neighborhood because of your *disgusting* restaurant."

Mrs. Corrigan turned and pointed in the direction of the dumpster in the far corner of the restaurant parking lot. There were large shrubs all around the perimeter of the lot. A two-story house as pink as Mrs. Corrigan's sweatshirt stood on the other side of the shrubs.

The strange note and invoice for pest removal that Celia had found earlier finally made sense.

"I'm sorry, Mrs. Corrigan. I had Nick from Gianni's Pest Removal come out and take a look, but he didn't find any evidence of vermin," Celia said. She wondered what "vermin" Mrs. Corrigan thought were running underneath her window. Mice? Cockroaches?

"Like I'd trust a report from them. They're wops like you—they'd say anything for one of their own."

Katherine sucked in her breath. Celia was shocked herself. Did Mrs. Corrigan always throw around these kinds of slurs? Celia contemplated slamming the door in the woman's face, but instead decided to take the high road.

"I'm sorry that you think that, Mrs. Corrigan. But they did investigate your claims and there's no evidence that my restaurant has anything to do with your problem."

Mrs. Corrigan stepped forward, jabbing her finger toward Celia's face.

"You never should have been allowed to keep that dumpster in a residential area. All food waste should be brought directly to the town refuse site. It's your fault that there are rats living in my basement, and I'm going to get your restaurant shut down for violating health codes. You wait and see."

Celia was willing to take the high road, but she wasn't willing to let anyone, even an old woman, threaten her. She batted Mrs. Corrigan's hand away from her face.

"You assaulted me!" Mrs. Corrigan screeched. "I'm going to report you to the police! Assault! Assault!"

"All I did was get your hand out of my personal space," Celia said, her own temper building. "And you're not welcome on my property any longer."

She slammed the door in Mrs. Corrigan's face. The other woman continued to shriek and shout and slam her fist on the door for a few more minutes. Celia turned her back on the noise and leaned against the door. Katherine's eyes were wide.

"I know she was being more obnoxious than usual, but you shouldn't have done that, boss," Katherine said, shaking her head. "You know her nephew Lyle is on the police force. If she says you assaulted her, he'll harass you for the rest of your life."

"I didn't assault her," Celia said, annoyed. "Not even close. She had her hand in my face and I batted it away—gently, I might add."

"Sure, but it's her word against yours."

"You saw what happened. You're a witness," Celia said.

"Yeah, like Lyle would trust anything I say. I work for you, and besides—he's never gotten over the fact that I kissed Steve Miller at the prom when Lyle was supposed to be my date."

Celia rubbed her temples. *Really? Mrs. Corrigan has free rein to harass me because her nephew is a police officer and my cook offended him in high school? This is like something out of one of those small-town mystery stories.*

*(just like the kind you like to read wasn't someone asking about . . .)*

Someone knocked on the front door.

"What now?" Celia said. "That better not be Mrs. Corrigan again."

"She never comes to the front door. Of course, you never 'assaulted' her before." Katherine made air quotes with her fingers around "assaulted."

"If it is her, I'm going to punch her in the mouth," Celia muttered.

"That would definitely, unequivocally be assault," Katherine said.

"A girl can dream," Celia said as she stalked through the dining room.

She unlatched the front door without shifting the blinds to see who stood outside and then yanked the door open. A young woman with springy brown curls and green eyes gave Celia a surprised glance.

"Whoa, what's with the aggression, C?" The young woman wore a white blouse and black pants under an open blue windbreaker. The name tag pinned on her blouse read "Tia."

*Thank god, I don't think I could remember her name right now*, Celia thought.

"Mrs. Corrigan," Celia said as she let Tia into the restaurant.

Tia held up her hand. "Say no more. That lady seriously needs an attitude adjustment."

"That's the understatement of the century," Katherine said. She'd clearly followed Celia out of the kitchen to see who was at the front door.

Tia cocked an eyebrow. "I'd ask what happened now, except I suspect it had something to do with the mythical rats around her house."

"Bingo," Celia said. "She basically called me a liar and said Nick's conspiring with me to keep the rats a secret."

"Any idiot can see there are no rat droppings," Tia said. "I used to live in the city, and believe me, if you have rats, then you have droppings. You don't need Gianni's to verify that."

"But I *did* have Gianni's verify that, and she's still on a rampage," Celia said.

Tia glanced at the clock. "Lunch starts in a half hour. You're going to have to put Mrs. Corrigan and her issues on the back burner for a while."

"Right," Celia said, glancing at Katherine.

"I know, I know, I gotta make the gnocchi," Katherine said, heading back into the kitchen.

Celia rubbed her temples again. Her head had been pounding most of the day, and her disorienting loss of memory made everything seem worse than it was. Mrs. Corrigan was just a noisy old sourpuss. She couldn't really cause Celia that much trouble in the long run, could she?

# CHAPTER THREE

mysterybkluv: seriously sometimes murder is super convenient

poirotsgirl: ever notice how there are always like fifteen people with a motive but the cops only pay attention to one person?

tyz7412: cops have no imagination

CELIA FORGOT, OR MOSTLY forgot, about Mrs. Corrigan in the rush to prepare and serve lunch. Pete did stop by to pick up some lasagna to go, but she didn't really have a chance to talk to him because she was busy in the kitchen. He poked his head in the door long enough to say hello and that he'd pick up Stephanie after soccer practice, then disappeared again—a good thing, since she had no idea what to say to him. She didn't remember anything about their life together, and that wasn't the kind of thing you casually mentioned over a take-out container.

She was relieved to discover that even if she didn't remember much about her identity, she did seem to have a kind of muscle memory for running a restaurant. Recipes appeared in her brain the moment she needed them; her hands moved without conscious thought, rolling out pasta dough and assembling vinaigrettes. Another server, a curvy middle-aged woman named Nancy, had joined Tia just before the lunch hour started, and the two of them moved through the dining room seamlessly, needing no direction from Celia.

At four o'clock, Tia headed out to her night classes at the local community college. Nancy stayed for an extra hour, serving early-bird senior citizen diners, then handed off the evening shift to three new people. Celia didn't have time to examine their faces or memorize their names. Around 5:00 p.m., families with small children started showing up, and the restaurant stayed busy until almost 7:00, when the hordes finally slowed to just a few twenty-something couples staring into each other's eyes. Katherine's shift was over and Celia assured her that she could manage the last hour on her own.

Celia stuffed a piece of bread into her mouth. She was ravenously hungry and hadn't taken a moment to eat all day, instead making sure that Katherine had ample breaks. Now that things had slowed down, she grabbed a piece of truffle lasagna and stood at the work counter to eat it.

One of the servers, a young man with long brown hair in a ponytail, peeked his head inside the door just as she put the first bite in her mouth. "Uh, boss?"

"Yes?" She couldn't remember his name and she couldn't see his name tag, which was annoying.

"There's, um, a police officer here to see you. Lyle Corrigan."

"Oh, for the love of—" she said, then shook her head. There was no point in getting worked up before she even talked to him, even if she knew there was only one possible reason he could be there. "It's fine. Just send him back here."

"Sure thing," he said, and disappeared.

Celia looked down at the lasagna, which had seemed so appetizing just a moment before. Now she wondered how much power this police officer had over her. Yes, it was a small town, but he wasn't a health inspector. He couldn't charge her with nonexistent violations that would threaten the restaurant.

*Could he?*

The back door swung open and Lyle Corrigan came in. Like his aunt, he had a tight, sour-faced look, one that expected the worst of the world and usually found it. He was about as tall as Celia, maybe five foot nine, and had very broad shoulders and biceps that bulged out of his short-sleeved uniform.

*The kind of guy who lifts weights and drinks protein shakes as his personal identity,* Celia thought. *He probably hasn't eaten a carbohydrate since he graduated from high school.*

"Officer Corrigan," Celia said, with a smile that felt as fake as it no doubt appeared. "Did you stop in for today's special? The truffle lasagna is a customer favorite."

"You know I wouldn't eat a thing from this place if you paid me," Corrigan said.

She'd expected some show of authority, but not the same outright hostility she'd received from Corrigan's aunt. Temper surged, but she swallowed it down. It wouldn't help her cause if she shouted at a police officer clearly bent on antagonizing her.

"How can I help you, then, if you're not here for a meal?"

"I'm here to investigate a report that you assaulted my aunt this morning," he said, taking a notebook and pen from his pocket. "I'd like to hear your version of events."

Celia really didn't like the way he said "your version of events," like anything she stated would automatically be construed as fiction. She decided that the best thing would be to state the unadorned facts as quickly as possible.

"Your aunt knocked on the back door this morning prior to the restaurant's opening. She angrily accused me—or rather, accused the dumpster in the corner of the parking lot—of causing rats to proliferate in her basement."

Corrigan paused in his writing and glared at her. She was struck, in that moment, of how strongly he resembled the police-officer-as-Neanderthal trope, right down to his oversized chest and slightly overhanging brow. "Proliferate?"

"Multiply," Celia said, and bit her lip so she wouldn't laugh at his obvious irritation. Apparently, Officer Corrigan didn't like to be confronted with words he didn't recognize. "I told her that I'd paid to have a pest remover investigate her claims. Gianni's found no evidence of rats in her basement, but she still insisted otherwise. During the conversation, she put her finger very close to my face and I *gently* batted it away. Then she began screaming that I assaulted her. I shut the door at that point. My cook witnessed the entire event, and I assure you that nothing close to assault occurred. Katherine will verify that."

Corrigan's lip curled. "Katherine. Uh-huh."

*Oh, come on,* Celia thought. *Surely he's not holding a grudge about something that happened years ago in high school?*

She waited as he scribbled in his notebook, and wondered why he took notes the old-fashioned way. Why not just use his phone to record her statement? Then she wondered if this was something as formal as a "statement." Should she be worried? Should she be looking for a lawyer?

Corrigan finished writing and very deliberately closed his notebook. "I have to tell you, Ms. Zinone, that my aunt gives a very different account. She stated that you punched her in the face and denied her medical care when she requested it."

Celia's mouth didn't drop open, but it was a near thing. "My hand didn't go anywhere near her face. If anything, I was the one in danger of having my eye jabbed out by her fingernail."

"Really," Corrigan said, and he said it in such a smug, I-know-something-you-don't-know way, that Celia wanted to throw her plate of lasagna at his head. "Then why does she have a black eye?"

Celia blinked. "A black eye?"

"Yes," he said, and pulled his phone out of his pocket.

After tapping on the screen for a moment, he held it up for Celia to see. There was a photo of Mrs. Corrigan in the same salmon-pink sweatshirt she'd worn that morning. The left side of her face was turned toward the camera, and her eye was purple and swollen.

Celia realized then just how determined the horrible woman and her clearly equally horrible nephew were to frame her for something, *anything* at all. What she didn't understand was why on earth they would want to do such a thing. Had she wronged them in the past?

The empty blank space of her memory suddenly appeared less like a slightly worrisome black hole and more like a sharp-edged box, full of teeth and monsters. *I have to remember my life. I have to remember who I am.*

"Nothing to say?" Corrigan asked.

Celia realized she'd been staring blankly at the photo. She needed to stay in the present and worry about her amnesia later. "I'm very sorry your aunt has been hurt, but that injury has nothing to do with me."

"What, she walked into a door?" Corrigan said, and again his tone was so provoking that Celia was seized by a powerful urge to start throwing food at his big, stupid head.

One of the servers came into the kitchen then, carrying a tray full of plates. He clearly hadn't been aware of Corrigan's presence in the kitchen and stopped short as he entered, glancing from Celia to the police officer and back again.

"Everything okay?" he asked. He looked a little older than the other two servers, maybe in his late twenties or early thirties, and something in his look made Celia think he didn't much like Officer Corrigan.

Celia shot a quick peek at the server's name tag. "Thanks, Will. Everything's fine. You can leave those dishes."

Will carried the dishes over to the sink and began unloading them in what appeared to be an exaggeratedly slow manner. Corrigan gave Will a look that implied later retribution, then tucked his phone away.

"I'll be speaking to you on this matter again, Ms. Zinone," he said, and exited out the kitchen door and through the dining room.

"He is such an asshole," Will said, dumping the rest of the dishes into the sink without a care once Corrigan was gone. He came to lean on the counter a few feet away from Celia. "What's his problem now?"

The way Will stood and spoke implied a familiarity that the other servers didn't have with her. They seemed like they might be close to the same age, and Celia wondered if perhaps they'd gone to school together.

*Why can't I remember?* she thought, and the thought was fast becoming a scream lodged in her throat, a scream struggling for breath. *Why can't I remember?*

Will watched her expectantly, and a little line of worry appeared between his brows. "Hey, Ceil, are you all right? What did that jerk say to you?"

*Calm, stay calm. Breathe and don't let anyone know what's wrong. No one can know. They'll think you're crazy.*

"He seems to be under the impression that I punched his aunt in the eye this morning," she said, and she was impressed with how calm her voice sounded. Nobody would know she was on the verge of a full-on anxiety attack.

"Did you?" Will asked.

Celia frowned at him, and he laughed.

"Just kidding, I know you wouldn't. Although if anyone deserves it, it's Mrs. Corrigan. Half the town would probably give you an award if you had done it, though."

"Does *anyone* like her?" Celia asked.

Will shrugged. "Not that I know of. You know how it is. Most people can't stand her, and everyone else is tolerant. I don't think anyone would choose to be in her company."

"Except Lyle."

"Yeah, and everyone knows that Lyle only does it because he's waiting for that sweet, sweet inheritance."

"She doesn't seem like she's that wealthy," Celia said, and then realized that she might have just given herself away, that perhaps she ought to know just how wealthy Mrs. Corrigan was because it was general knowledge.

"Well, nobody's *really* sure how much money she has, you know that," Will said. "But her husband did sell the cookie factory to that international conglomerate before he died, and that sale can't have been chump change."

"And yet her clothes scream 'sale rack,' and not Nordstrom Rack, either," Celia said.

"She's a penny-pincher, no doubt. Now tell me what happened this morning."

Celia explained the circumstances, making sure to add that Katherine had witnessed the whole thing.

"He hasn't got anything resembling a case, and if he tries to pursue it, I'm going to make sure to report him for harassment," Celia said. "And maybe his aunt, too."

"Sure, that will go about as well as the last time you reported him for harassment," Will said, rolling his eyes. "The police chief is halfway to retirement and doesn't care what Lyle does so long as he does it quietly."

"This is absurd," Celia said. "Why should I be held hostage by an old woman and her jerk nephew, just because that nephew happens to be a police officer?"

"This is small-town America, sweetie," Will said, lightly punching her shoulder. "You ought to be used to it by now."

He left the kitchen and Celia stood for a moment, contemplating her lasagna. She dumped the contents of the plate into the trash. She was decidedly not hungry anymore.

The last hour passed in a flurry of cleaning and prepping for the next day. The three servers cleared the dining room, washed down the tables, refilled the Parmesan cheese shakers and played "rock, paper, scissors" to determine who was going to wash and who was going to dry the serving dishes. Celia put sauce into jars, wrapped up the remainder of the lasagna and washed down all the kitchen surfaces until they gleamed.

The other three trickled out one by one as they completed their tasks. Will paused in the back door, watching Celia tie up the plastic bag full of kitchen trash.

"Listen, don't worry too much about Mrs. Corrigan or her nephew, all right? It's not worth your time and energy."

Celia just nodded. She didn't say that she had a low hum of anxiety inside her stomach, or that it was tangled up with her lack of memory and the persistent feeling that she didn't actually belong here, that this wasn't her life and these weren't her people. She didn't say any of those things because it was very important—and she wasn't really sure why but nevertheless remained convinced of this truth—to make sure that no one knew what was going on inside her. She must keep it a secret. She must keep herself safe.

Something flitted across the front of her brain, a memory moving with the speed of a darting rabbit. Tight hands around her wrists, a cruel mouth saying that nobody would believe her, nobody would believe her no matter what.

A sharp pain followed in the wake of this, a pain that shot like electricity behind her eyes and made her bend over, gasping.

"Hey!" Will said.

He was at her side, holding on to her waist. He seemed so

familiar in that moment, so much more familiar than the man who called himself her husband. She knew Will. She knew his scent and his face and even the way his hand touched very lightly at her hip, in a way that said he would catch her if she fell, but only if she wanted him to do so.

"What's the matter? Do you want a glass of water?"

"Yes." She didn't want a glass of water, but she needed him to move away because that jolt of familiarity had confused her, had made her think that maybe she was wrong and this *was* her life after all.

He half-filled a glass with water from the tap and brought it over, his brows drawn together.

"I'm okay," she said, taking the glass from him. "I just forgot to eat today and I have a headache."

"Are you okay to drive home?"

"Definitely," she said, waving him away. "Go on, I'm perfectly fine."

"You don't look perfectly fine. You look like you're about to throw up."

"Well, there's nothing in my stomach to throw up, so that won't be a problem. Really, it was just a little pain that took me by surprise. It's a short drive home and I can manage."

"If you say so."

"I say so," she said, gathering up the trash. "Go on, I have to lock up."

She followed Will out the door, flipping the kitchen lights off as she went. She locked the door as he climbed into his car. She was glad that she remembered which key to use. The last thing she needed was Will noticing anything else was wrong with her.

His car engine turned over and the headlights clicked on as Celia turned around. She waved cheerily with her free hand as he pulled out.

*Nothing to see here. Everything's just fine.*

She lugged the bag of trash across the parking lot toward the dumpster. Most of the houses on Cherry Lane had illuminated windows, their residents tucked in for the evening. There were no lights on at Mrs. Corrigan's house.

*Probably burning a candle to save on electricity.*

Celia wondered again what she could have done to earn the ire of the older woman. There didn't seem to be a real reason for such deep hostility. She dismissed the "rat problem" out of hand, especially since it appeared to be a big nothingburger. But the faked black eye . . . that was taking things a little too far. That was more than distress over an imagined nest of vermin. Maybe Mrs. Corrigan had undiagnosed mental health issues.

The trash bag seemed heavier than it ought to be, probably because Celia hadn't really eaten and she still felt a little sick from the sudden headache that had burst behind her eyes. The dumpster seemed so far away. She should have asked Will to carry the trash out, but she'd been so focused on appearing completely normal that she'd wanted him to leave as soon as possible.

*Why am I so worried about seeming normal? Why do I feel like I can't trust anyone, like I can't tell anyone what's wrong with me?*

She shook her head. Maybe all she needed was a good night's sleep, and tomorrow morning her whole life would come flooding back into her brain. There was no need to share her troubles. Not yet, anyway. Or maybe never. She might be able to go on faking it indefinitely.

Most women faked half their lives daily, pretending to have their work and their family and their health completely under control, moving through the world with just enough makeup and effortless shampoo-commercial hair. They were the ones wearing beautiful cream-colored knitted sweaters in white rooms on their Instagram pages. They were the ones spouting corny philosophical sayings and talking about their many blessings. Meanwhile, they were taking prescription drugs just to stand up straight in the morning and their husbands were on their fourth affair with someone from the workplace.

*It's deeply irritating,* Celia thought, *to remember all these meaningless things about the world in general, and nothing about my life specifically. Why do I know so much about Instagram moms and I couldn't even recall my own daughter's name?*

A shudder ran up her spine. The idea of going on day after day with only a yawning hole behind her where her memories were supposed to be was terrifying. The future was an unknowable space for everyone, and the only thing that made it bearable was having the solid footing of the past as an anchor.

The dumpster was in the darkest corner of the lot, far out of the reach of the streetlights' glare. Celia paused when she was a few feet away from it, listening hard. She could have sworn she heard something—the scrape of a shoe? The rustle of clothing? Was someone out here, lurking in the darkness?

*Or maybe it's one of Mrs. Corrigan's fictional rats. Get it together, Ceil. If anyone is standing in the shadows waiting to pounce, it's that crazy old woman. And if she is there, you can just leave. There's no rule that says you're required to engage with her if she starts yelling.*

Celia walked the last few feet to the dumpster, lifted the lid and tossed in the trash. A second later her brain registered that there was something wrong. Something very, very wrong.

There was someone in the dumpster. The pool of shadow only allowed her to see the faint outline of a person, the glow of pale clothes and pale skin.

She let the lid close with a clang that echoed around the parking lot. Celia backed away from the dumpster, her heart pounding. Had she just seen what she thought she saw? Or was it the product of her strange day, her lack of food, her overheated imagination?

*You have to look again. You have to look.*

Celia glanced around. There was no one walking on the street, no one driving by that she could flag down. It was too late to knock on someone's door, but she didn't want to do this alone. She didn't want to open up the dumpster by herself.

*Stop being a baby and do it. You're a grown woman, and if there really is someone dead inside, then they aren't going to hurt you. A dead body is only a zombie in George Romero movies.*

The thought made her still, not because she was actually worried about the possibility of zombies, but because it seemed out of character for her to even know about George Romero movies. The boring dining set and matching dishware in the house she'd left that morning did not scream "quirky horror movie fan." Yet she had a strong, clear memory of exactly that—of watching *Dawn of the Dead* in a living room that belonged to her but did not look like the one she'd walked through that day.

*Is this really my life? Did I sacrifice everything interesting about myself in order to get married, have a baby, drive a midsize sedan?*

Her head was hurting again, the pain spreading behind her eyes like seeping lava.

*Okay, enough of this. Just open the dumpster again, confirm that there's no one actually inside and go home.*

Celia pulled her cell phone out of her bag and turned on the flashlight feature. Holding her phone in her right hand, she carefully eased the lid of the dumpster open with her left and shone the light inside.

The lid clanged shut again and Celia's phone clattered to the ground.

There was definitely someone inside the dumpster.

It was Mrs. Corrigan, and someone had slit her throat.

# CHAPTER FOUR

**mysterybkluv:** it's not that they have no imagination the cops just usually have an axe to grind

**cobenfan:** depends on the kind of mystery. If it's a darker one then the officer is the main character and they're obsessed with an old case

**mysterybkluv:** that's not my style of book LOL. I'm more a fan of the bloodless body.

IN RETROSPECT CELIA REALIZED that part of her had expected something like this to happen. The whole day had felt like it had popped out of a script—even the conversations she'd had with other people felt strangely like dialogue, like they were giving information to an audience instead of talking to her like normal people do.

And Mrs. Corrigan had been almost comically horrible to her, horrible in a way that people behaved only in a story.

*That's what this feels like,* Celia thought. *A story. Like one of the many cozy mysteries I've read over the years.*

Except the body hadn't been the typical bloodless type found in those stories, where people were demurely poisoned and keeled over in their tea sets. Sometimes characters were shot or stabbed, but there was never a pool of blood or the sight of human innards. Celia had most definitely seen the split muscles and exposed bone on the inside of Mrs. Corrigan's throat, and it was not something she ever wanted to see again.

And there had been blood. A lot of blood.

She couldn't remember anything about Mrs. Corrigan other than their morning interaction, and it had not been the kind of interaction that encouraged future contact. Still, the sight of her small body—which had appeared even smaller inside the dumpster—had raised a well of pity in Celia. Nobody, not even the worst person in the world, should have to die that way.

The police officer who responded to her 911 call was, thankfully, not Lyle Corrigan but a middle-aged man called Bob Mc-Closkey. He threw up his dinner in the bushes next to the dumpster after viewing the body, but then appeared to settle down. He called for an ambulance and other personnel, and led Celia to her car so she could answer some questions.

She unlocked the car and sat in the front seat while he stood a few feet away, busily writing everything she said into his notebook.

*Again with the notebook. Does the police department have some kind of rule against twenty-first-century technology?*

She thought again about the stories she'd read, how the police officers always took notes in a notebook. The thought pinged another thought—that she'd noticed something wrong that morning when she'd walked through the house. It was something related to stories, but she couldn't quite grab the idea.

All day long she'd felt this way, that she wasn't fully grasping her situation. If she had to go through another day like this, and another and another and another, she'd never make it. She'd start screaming endlessly.

"Do you want to call Pete? Sorry, I should have asked sooner," Bob McCloskey said.

Celia gave the police officer a blank look. She was so tired. It took a long time for the meaning of his words to penetrate. Pete. Her husband. The strange man in the house.

"Oh, yeah, I should do that," Celia said.

She took out her cell phone. There was a crack across the

screen. Of course there was—she'd dropped it when she'd gotten a good look at Mrs. Corrigan's body and it managed to fall screenside down on a huge rock instead of safely on any of the bumpers that protected the rest of the phone.

*This always happens to me. I never make it through a two-year contract without destroying my phone.*

Her fingers stilled on the screen. She'd remembered something else about herself.

*Okay, okay, no need to dance a jig. It's hardly anything at all.*

But it was hers, her own memory, and it was hard not to feel like the memory was a rescue float bringing her closer to the surface.

Despite the crack on the screen, she managed to tap through to Pete's contact info. She held the phone up to her ear and listened to it ring. Bob McCloskey politely walked a little distance away while she made her call. Celia liked that about him. She didn't think Lyle Corrigan would have done the same.

"'Lo?" Pete sounded confused.

"Pete, it's me," she said.

"Celia?" She heard a rustling sound, like he was moving around. "I fell asleep on the couch watching ESPN. What time is it?"

*Of course you fell asleep on the couch watching ESPN. That's what a person like you would* do.

She was briefly startled by the vehemence of this thought, by the contempt she felt as she had it. Did she and Pete have a bad marriage? Was she unhappy with him? He started talking again, and she forced herself to pay attention.

"Jeez, it's so late. What's going on?"

"Well, I sort of . . . found a body."

Silence from Pete's end. A decidedly pregnant pause. Then he said, "Do you want to elaborate on that?"

"Someone killed Mrs. Corrigan and dumped her in the garbage bin at the corner of the restaurant lot. I found her when I brought out the kitchen trash."

"Oookay," Pete said. "Listen, I'll see if I can get someone to come over and stay in the house. Stephanie's already asleep. Do not talk to Lyle Corrigan or anyone else until I get there."

"I already talked to Bob McCloskey." Her tone was half-sheepish, half-defensive. "He seemed okay."

"Christ, Ceil. What's the point of being married to a criminal lawyer if you don't even know not to make a statement to the police without a lawyer present?"

"I didn't *make a statement*. I just told him what happened—exactly what happened. I took the trash to the dumpster, found her inside, and called the police. That was it."

As she spoke, she heard more rustling. He was obviously collecting things, maybe changing his clothes. He might have been in pajamas or sweats, ready to relax until tomorrow, until his wife inconveniently discovered a body in her restaurant's dumpster.

Rustling. She'd heard something rustle just before she opened the lid to put the trash bag in. Had somebody else been there? Had the killer been just a few feet away, disappearing through the bushes and into the night?

"Are you listening?" Pete's voice again.

"Sorry, I was thinking about something."

"Fine, think all you want. Just don't talk to anyone else. Especially not Lyle Corrigan."

"I don't know why you're getting so worked up," she said. His tone said she was a stupid little girl who couldn't be trusted without an adult around to monitor her, and it was getting her back up. "He's not even here."

"He's going to be there soon," Pete said. "He's Elena Corrigan's only living next of kin. And he's on the force. And he hates you because his aunt hates you, so he's going to take any chance he can get to try and hurt you."

"But I didn't do anything," Celia said. She did feel a little stupid for not thinking about the next-of-kin thing, but she wasn't going to admit that to Pete.

Pete sighed. "The body was found on your property and you had a long-standing disagreement with the victim. You're the number one suspect."

*Number one suspect.* The words clanged around inside Celia's brain, echoing off the vast empty chambers where her past used to be. *Number one suspect. Just like in a mystery story.*

That's when she remembered what was bothering her about the house. The books. There were no books in the house at all.

*But how can that be? I read every day. I read nonstop when I have free time.*

A lightning bolt shot across her head again, though not as bad as the last one. Celia rubbed the spot between her eyes and wondered if these pains were her dormant memory trying to wake up.

"I'll be there as soon as I can," Pete said, and hung up.

Celia stared at the phone for a minute, watching it switch from the call screen back to her lock screen photo. Herself and Pete and Stephanie, all smiling.

It seemed fake. Her eyes weren't happy in the photo. They were blank, empty. They didn't seem like a real family. They didn't seem connected.

Maybe it was her imagination.

"Celia?" Bob McCloskey again.

Other professionals had arrived, people with cameras and medical gloves and swabs, people who looked like they might belong to a forensic team.

*And the only reason I know that is because* CSI *exists.*

"How could a town this small need a crime scene investigative unit?" Celia wondered, then realized she'd said it aloud when Bob McCloskey tilted his head at her.

"They're not ours. They're from Milton. We don't see too many murders around here, as you know."

*As you know.* Three words meant to reassure Celia that she was part of the club, part of the fabric of this community. Instead, they made her feel like she was free-falling again, a diver with an empty pool beneath her.

McCloskey seemed to expect some kind of response from her—*because that's how normal people converse, one person talks and the other responds and you need to get your shit together right now Ceil and stop acting like a space case*—so she said, "Pete's on his way."

McCloskey's phone rang, and Celia saw consternation move across his face before he answered the call. He turned away from her but she still heard him clearly say, "Lyle? It's about your aunt."

Celia closed her eyes and leaned her cheek against the driver's seat. It had been an inordinately long day, even aside from her lack of memory. The altercation with Mrs. Corrigan, the threats from her nephew, the insane busyness of the restaurant. She must have dozed off, because when she opened her eyes again, Pete was crouching in front of her, his hand on her knee.

"Long day?" he asked. He seemed sympathetic, the way a husband ought to act in this situation. There was none of the irritation he'd evinced on the phone.

"The longest," she said.

"Tell me about it," he said.

What she really wanted was to go home and fall into bed, but McCloskey hadn't told her she could leave the scene yet. She didn't see any reason why she should have to stay, unless Lyle Corrigan had specifically told his fellow officer to hold her there.

*And that's exactly what Lyle did, I'm sure of it.*

Given that bed didn't seem to be an option, Celia gave Pete the play-by-play of her day. He'd frowned when she told the story about Mrs. Corrigan, but he'd frowned even more when she told him about Lyle and his accusations. After she finished up with the story of discovering Mrs. Corrigan in the dumpster, she looked at him expectantly.

"So, what do you think?"

"The assault accusation is meaningless because Katherine witnessed the incident. The only way it could be relevant is if Lyle made a case that you went after Mrs. Corrigan later in the day. Were you ever out of the kitchen or away from witnesses?"

"No, Pete, I was too busy running my restaurant to go and punch an irritating old woman," Celia said, her temper flaring.

"I'm only asking," Pete said, but his tone hardened, too, like they were boxers taking their prescribed places in the ring.

"And I don't see what the assault accusation has to do with anything, besides. Mrs. Corrigan is the only one who could possibly press charges, and she won't be doing that anytime soon, unless she's allowed to call collect from hell."

Pete glanced around to see if anyone was standing nearby. "You shouldn't say things like that. You're a suspect, or soon will be."

She knew she shouldn't have said it the second it came out of her mouth, but it annoyed her that Pete had censured her over it. Still, it seemed nonproductive to argue about it, so she simply said, "So why is the 'assault'"—she made air quotes around the word with her fingers—"relevant? Do you think Lyle will try to use it as a reason why I might have killed her?"

Pete nodded. "He'll definitely make the case that there was bad blood between the two of you."

"Yeah, but it doesn't even make sense," Celia said. "First of all, why would I kill her? Because she claimed there were nonexistent rats running around that were my responsibility? That's a profoundly stupid reason to risk jail. And second, when would I even have time to do such a thing? As we already discussed, I was in the kitchen all day. Katherine was in there with me until eight, and servers were in and out throughout the day taking orders. I didn't have time to hunt down Mrs. Corrigan, sneak up on her and slit her throat in between plating spaghetti Bolognese."

"I'm not sure how much logic will apply, but the law is definitely on your side. There's no evidence for an arrest, but Lyle can make your life difficult."

Almost as if Pete's words had summoned him, Lyle Corrigan pulled into the parking lot like he was a police officer on TV arriving at a hostage situation—in his police vehicle, lights and siren on, tires squealing.

"That's great," Celia said. "Just in case the whole neighborhood didn't already know there was a crime scene here." Then she felt a little bad about that thought, because he was about to see his dead aunt, and maybe even Lyle Corrigan had some human feeling.

*Wait. There's something wrong there.*

Celia glanced around, deliberately ignoring the sight of Lyle charging out of his car like his butt was on fire, heading straight in her direction. Pete stood up to intercept him while Celia finally noticed the thing that had been twigging her subconscious this whole time. There weren't any people from surrounding houses standing out in the street gawking.

*That's weird. That's really weird. There should be at least one person, that one nosy neighbor who always has to know what's going on. Is everyone already asleep? Does nobody really care what's going on here? At home everybody would be outside taking pictures with their phones.*

The moment Celia thought "at home," she felt the strongest surge of pain shoot through her brain yet, so strong that she leaned forward and vomited the very few contents of her stomach just as

Lyle pushed past Pete and pounded up to her. The upshot was that Lyle's shoes were spattered with puke, but Celia couldn't think of a more deserving recipient.

He looked down at his overly aggressive military-style boots and then at her in disgust. "You did that on purpose."

Pete jogged up a second later. "Oh, no. Do you have any water in your car?"

Celia shook her head. She was still in the brace position, her head hovering between her knees. Her face felt flushed while the rest of her began to shake.

"You're going to pay to have my shoes cleaned," Lyle said.

"Are you kidding me right now?" Pete said. "Look at her. She's in shock. She didn't plan to throw up on you."

Bob McCloskey joined the crowd. "I have some water in my car. I needed it myself earlier."

His tone was warm and sympathetic, and Celia clung to it like a lifeline. Pete and Lyle were bickering as she sat there shivering, wondering what on earth that thought had meant.

"At home." She'd specifically thought of the phrase "at home." And that meant this wasn't her home, that there was someplace else she considered her real home.

She eased herself up and neither her husband nor Lyle Corrigan seemed to notice. They'd moved on from arguing about Lyle's shoes to arguing about her potential culpability in Mrs. Corrigan's death.

"She assaulted my aunt this morning—"

"There's no evidence of that."

Lyle pulled out his phone and waved the picture in Pete's face. "Got your evidence right here."

"That's only evidence that your aunt had a black eye. Anything could have happened. She could have fallen and hit a table. Or someone else could have hit her, someone close to her."

Pete said this in a way that seemed deliberately provocative, and Lyle rose to the provocation immediately.

"Are you trying to imply that I punched my aunt in the face?" The blood rose in Lyle's cheeks and his fists clenched.

Celia looked from Lyle to Pete in alarm. Was Pete deliberately trying to provoke Lyle into attacking him? What would be the purpose of that?

*None of this makes sense,* she thought. *I feel like I'm watching a movie of someone else's life, a place where conflicts are invented wholesale and nobody acts like a real human.*

Bob McCloskey arrived with one of those tiny bottles of water that are sold in cases at warehouse stores and handed it to her. He seemed oblivious to the rising tension in the air, or perhaps he was pretending not to see it.

"The forensics team is done and we don't have any more questions for you right now, Celia. I think you and Pete can go home."

Lyle turned his ire on McCloskey. "I didn't say that she can leave. I have some questions for Ms. Zinone."

"I understand you're upset right now, Lyle, but the best thing you can do is go with the ambulance and make the arrangements for your aunt," McCloskey said, and his voice was mild but also firm in a way it hadn't been before.

Celia looked at him in wonder. Maybe McCloskey wasn't the bumbler he'd initially appeared to be.

Lyle seemed ready to argue, and Celia decided she didn't want to listen to him any longer. She'd had enough of this day, of everything about this day, and she wanted to go home and sleep it off and hopefully feel more like herself in the morning.

"I think that's a great idea, Bob," Celia said to McCloskey, ignoring Lyle altogether. "Pete, I'll see you at home."

"Are you okay to drive?" he asked, his eyes moving from the mess on Lyle's shoes to her face. "You still look pale."

Celia waved her hand. "It's a short drive. I'll be fine."

"If you say so," he said doubtfully. "Maybe I should—"

"I'll see you at home," she repeated, and shut the car door.

Lyle moved toward her car. Out of the corner of her eye Celia saw McCloskey grab his arm and Pete open his mouth to say something. She pretended not to notice, turned the car on and backed out of the spot. The forensics people stopped their work to watch her go, and she felt uncomfortably in the spotlight.

*Why should they care if I'm leaving?* she thought. *Sure, I found the body, and the dumpster is technically on restaurant property, but still.*

She drove slowly through the village main street. All the businesses were rolled up for the night, lights off and doors locked and curtains drawn. Most of the homes she passed had one or two lights on, but many of them had none. People went to sleep early around here.

*Not like at home, where there's always somebody awake, no matter what hour it is.*

She had an accompanying flash of pretty colored row houses on a climbing street, and people out walking their dogs or listening to their music with white earbuds stuffed in their ears or carrying yoga mats.

*Me. I'm the one carrying the yoga mat, a purple one with a white tree design on it. I'm going to the studio.*

The thoughts had arrived unbidden, like the previous one she'd had about "home," but this time Celia was braced for the wave of pain and accompanying nausea. She gripped the steering wheel hard and felt sweat running down her temples.

*As soon as I get home, I'm going to lie down and close my eyes and try to remember my life. Something's gone wrong inside my brain. Am I remembering something that doesn't exist, or am I having memories of my life before I moved here?*

She was glad that Pete wasn't in the car with her. She couldn't bear the idea of being stuck in a small space with him, with someone who felt like a stranger to her.

The car was coasting along the road that she'd followed that morning, trees on one side and single-family homes on the other. She had a moment of panic when she realized she had no idea which home was hers, but then remembered that she'd used the map app to find her way to the restaurant. All she had to do was reverse it.

An unfamiliar car was in the driveway when she pulled in. Well, if she was being fair, everything was unfamiliar, but this car hadn't been there in the morning. A shadow moved by the living room window as Celia turned off her headlights.

*This is whomever Pete got to come and babysit Stephanie while he came out to meet me. He didn't have to bother, really. He didn't do anything except cause more trouble. I wasn't the one antagonizing Lyle Corrigan. It was him.*

The kitchen door opened while Celia stood fumbling with her keys, trying to remember which one was for the house. Why did she have so many goddamned keys?

A blonde woman who looked vaguely familiar stood in the doorway. She beckoned Celia inside and immediately launched into speech before Celia could even shrug out of her coat.

"Oh my god, what happened? Are you all right? Pete said that there was a *body* in the restaurant dumpster and that you found it? Who was it? I bet that was completely horrible. You look super pale."

Celia placed her phone and purse on the counter, unsure where to start with this onslaught of questions. The sight of her phone helped her remember who the woman was, though. Jennifer, the person who called that morning asking if Celia wanted to go for a run. The woman was tall and skinny and wearing black athletic leggings and a blue zip-up sweatshirt. She looked like a runner.

"Where's Pete?" Jennifer asked, bustling to the cabinets to take out a wineglass. Next, she opened Celia's refrigerator like she belonged in Celia's kitchen *(maybe she does, she's obviously my friend and Pete trusted her enough to rush over to look after my daughter)* and pulled out a bottle of white wine. She poured out a little less than half a glass and handed it to Celia.

"Here, you look like you need this."

Celia stared at the glass in her hand. She hated white wine. She wasn't certain of a lot of things at that moment, but she was positive of that fact. She never, ever drank white wine. Red only, even if it didn't technically pair well with what she was eating.

But whoever she was now, or whoever people *thought* she was now, apparently did drink white wine. And run instead of do yoga. And wear boring suburban mom clothes.

Jennifer was staring at her expectantly. Celia took a tiny sip of wine, swallowed a shudder, and said, "Pete will probably be back soon. He was dealing with Lyle Corrigan when I left."

"Ugh, that asshole. He and his aunt deserve each other."

"Not anymore," Celia said. "His aunt is the one I found in the dumpster."

Jennifer's mouth fell open, and Celia again had the sensation that the people around her were performing for some audience she couldn't see.

"You found Mrs. Corrigan in the dumpster? I'm surprised Lyle didn't arrest you instantaneously."

"I think he wanted to, but Pete was there to stop him," Celia said.

"Handy being married to a lawyer," Jennifer said. "So, give me all the deets. What happened to her?"

"Someone slit her throat," Celia said.

She felt the bile rise again as she thought of that waxen face, the staring eyes, the sliced skin showing what had been hidden away.

"Are you going to puke?" Jennifer said, looking alarmed.

Celia breathed through her nose slowly, trying to bring her body back under control. Nothing else seemed to be in her control at the moment, and suddenly she was angry—really, really angry. All day she'd been hiding what was wrong with her, afraid for reasons she didn't really understand, and underneath that fear had been a conviction that she wasn't usually like this. She wasn't a shrinking mouse. She was a roaring lion.

"No," she said, her voice firm and strong. "No, I'm not going to puke. Listen, I appreciate you coming over—"

"There's gotta be a ton of people who wanted to kill that old bitch," Jennifer said. "Who do you think did it?"

"Jennifer," Celia said, and there was steel in her voice, enough that Jennifer gave her a startled look. "I appreciate you coming over on short notice, but I've had an exhausting day and I'm not up to speculating about the potential causes of murder at the moment. I'll talk to you tomorrow."

Jennifer looked like she might want to argue, but something about Celia's expression stopped her.

"Sure, I'll give you a call in the morning? Do you think you might want to go for a run?"

"No," Celia said with decision. "I really don't like to run."

Jennifer goggled at her. "Since when?"

"Since always," Celia said. "I hate running. I hate panting and getting super sweaty."

And as she said it, she knew it to be true, and was braced for the accompanying burst of pain that followed on any thought that contradicted her current circumstances.

The headache came, though not as strong as it had been earlier. She gripped the counter with both hands and let it pass.

*I know there's something going on here, and I'm going to get to the bottom of it.*

"Did you fall and hit your head when you found that body? You love running. You were a state champion in cross-country in high school."

Celia was paying attention this time to Jennifer's face, her eyes, the way she responded to Celia. Jennifer had been disconcerted by Celia's response, but more than that, she seemed to want to *convince* Celia of something that wasn't true.

*I don't care what she says. I hate running, and I know this deep down in my heart.*

"Sorry, not running tomorrow," Celia said. "Thanks again for your help."

Jennifer stood there for a moment, clearly unsure of what to do next. Celia was obviously supposed to behave a certain way and she wasn't doing it.

*I'm not your little monkey. I don't dance on command.*

There was a flash of headlights in the drive, and relief visibly washed over Jennifer's face.

"There's Pete. I'll head out now," Jennifer said. "Call you tomorrow?"

"Sure," Celia said. There was no harm in letting the woman call.

Jennifer put on her shoes and slipped out the back door before Pete entered the house. Celia went to the kitchen window, standing to one side so her silhouette wouldn't be visible, and lifted one of the blinds to peer out.

Jennifer and Pete stood close together in the drive next to Pete's car. Their heads were bent toward each other, and they were talking.

Celia crouched down and got her fingers underneath the window so she could push it open without detection. A moment later there was a rush of cool air, followed by snatches of murmured conversation.

". . . argued with me about running," Jennifer was saying. "That's not supposed to happen."

"I'm sure it's just a glitch," Pete said. "Maybe the dose wasn't high enough the first time."

*Dose? What dose?* Celia's fists curled into little balls. *Nobody is giving me a dose of anything.*

"She'll be back the way we want her by the morning. Just call after breakfast and pretend that conversation never happened."

"If you say so," Jennifer said.

"I say so," Pete said.

# CHAPTER FIVE

**tyz7412:** So what kind of investigator would you be if you were in a mystery?

**mysterybkluv:** oh, amateur sleuth all the way. But without all the stupid bumbling.

**poirotsgirl:** Yeah, I hate it when the sleuth just goes up to people and is like "I have no authority and you might be the killer, but did you do it?"

**mysterybkluv:** that's the worst. I love these books but I wish the authors would respect their own characters' intelligence.

**tyz7412:** you'd never be that stupid, huh?

**mysterybkluv:** definitely not

CELIA STOOD UP SLOWLY and backed away from the window. Her husband and her supposed friend were clearly conspiring against her, and she wasn't being crazy or paranoid. There was no way to misinterpret the bit of conversation she'd just heard. This wasn't Jennifer and Pete planning a surprise birthday party for her or some innocuous equivalent. They wanted to bring her to heel like a dog.

There were two ways to handle this. First, she could pretend she never heard anything, act normal (or what passed for normal at the moment) and play along until she could figure out what they were doing and why.

The second option would be to confront Pete the moment he walked in the door. This had the advantage of taking him by surprise, but she was worried about that "dose" he'd talked about. Would he overpower her, hold her down, inject her with something to change her, to make her forget who she really was?

*Someone did that before, someone held me down by the wrists. Someone said I got exactly what I deserved.*

The flash was brief, too brief for her to grasp completely, but she was pretty sure that Pete wasn't the one who'd done that to her before. The man in her memory was hazy but somehow familiar.

*Pete is not familiar to me. That's been the problem all day. He doesn't seem like someone I actually know.*

She heard Pete's footsteps approaching the door and made a quick decision. She'd play along for now, pretend that this bullshit life really belonged to her. She wanted to know who Pete was, and why he would do this to her.

*But I've got to make sure he doesn't give me whatever he thinks he's going to give me. An injection? A pill in a drink?*

Celia resolved not to accept any food or drink from him. She wasn't sure what to do about an injection, though. If he was trying to do it secretly, he'd probably give it to her while she was asleep.

Should she avoid sleeping tonight? And how could she even do that? All she wanted to do was to put her head down and sleep forever. She was certain she'd never been as tired as she was at the moment.

*I just have to avoid Pete until he's asleep, and definitely not get into the same bed as him.*

Celia felt her skin crawl at the thought. She wasn't going to sleep next to a stranger—because whatever Pete said, and no matter what the evidence inside this house seemed to indicate, he definitely was a stranger to her. He was not her husband.

*He's not my husband because I don't have a husband. And I don't have a husband because I don't need or want that kind of relationship in my life.*

Pete opened the door just as another sharp pain stabbed behind her eyes.

*This is getting old,* Celia thought as she rubbed her temples. *If I concentrate really hard on those flashes, will they break through? Will I be able to remember my life completely and these stupid headaches will go away?*

Pete took off his coat and shoes, giving her a sympathetic glance. She was paying attention so she noticed it was a shallow thing, that his eyes didn't really give a shit how she felt.

*Because he doesn't care. He's playing a part. I just need to figure out why.*

"I bet you're wiped out, huh?" he said, approaching her. "Let's get you up to bed."

"Tired but wired," Celia said, managing not to shrink away when he rubbed his hand up and down her arm. "I think I'll stay up for a little bit."

He frowned. "I don't know. I really think you should go to sleep. You have circles under your eyes."

"Still, I don't think I can settle down right now," Celia said. "I just have too much on my mind. I'll just thrash around and keep you up."

She said this with a butter-wouldn't-melt smile, like she really cared whether he had a good night's sleep or not.

His hand closed around her upper arm—not tight, not hurting, but firm in a way that told her he wanted his own way.

"Come on, Ceil," he said, giving her the same fake smile. "Dr. Pete insists."

She shook his arm off. "I think I know what's best for me, Pete."

"Sure about that?" he asked, giving her a speculative look, and that look made her stomach turn over, made her scared in a way she hadn't been before.

*Pretend not to notice. Pretend it's all a game. Never let them see you're scared.*

"Of course I'm sure," she said, stepping around him and going to the sink to dump out the wine and rinse out the glass. She deliberately showed him her back, showed him that she wasn't in the least bit concerned about anything he might do to her. It was a good thing he couldn't see the beating of her heart. That would have been a dead giveaway.

Celia felt Pete's gaze on her. She wished she could hear what he was thinking, wished she knew what he was up to. She finished rinsing the glass and put it in the dish rack to dry. When she turned around, he was standing in the same place, watching her.

"Trash TV binge, then?" he said.

*Eww, no, I hate that crap,* she thought automatically. Then it occurred to her that this was part of the programming, of whatever he was trying to do to her. He was saying something that she ought to believe, that ought to be part of her personality, just like Jennifer's insistence that she was a runner.

"Yup, *Keeping Up with the Kardashians* all the way," she said. The words felt strange in her mouth, crazy. She rarely watched any TV at all, preferring movies and books.

She braced for the accompanying wave of pain following this truth, but it didn't come. Maybe her real self was breaking through. Or maybe whatever formula Pete had given her was wearing off.

"Come on, I'll set you up, then. I know how much you hate trying to figure out which remote to use."

Celia followed him into the living room, certain this was another test.

Pete picked up the largest remote from a collection and turned on the wide-screen television.

*Obnoxious. Who needs a TV that big just to watch sports?*

Pete glanced over his shoulder. "What channel is it on?"

So this was the test. If she actually watched *Keeping Up with the Kardashians*, she would know what channel it was on. For a moment she thought she'd been caught, then remembered sitting in a nail salon having her nails buffed, the TV overhead showing Kim and Khloé and whoever else all those "K" people were. In the corner of the screen was a big "E."

"E," she said, and caught the flicker of uncertainty in his eyes as he turned back and searched for the channel.

The screen filled with a bunch of women who'd clearly had plastic surgery wearing too-tight dresses and stilettos. Two of them were arguing and all of them held glasses of wine.

"Looks like it's *Real Housewives* time," Celia said, settling in on the couch.

Pete asked, "What city is this in?"

Celia shrugged, sure that she could skip this particular test. "Who knows? There are a million of these and they're all pretty much the same. Perfect for letting my brain drain."

"Want me to stay up with you?"

"No, you go on ahead and get some sleep. I'm sure you've got something important in the morning."

He hesitated, hunting for some reason to stay up with her. *Whatever he was planning on doing, he was definitely going to do it while I was asleep.*

Finally he said, "Okay, well, good night."

"Thanks for coming to rescue me from Lyle," she said, because it seemed like the sort of thing she ought to say if she was in a real marriage and she wanted to keep that marriage happy.

"I'll always ride to your rescue," he said, and bent to kiss her cheek.

This was the ultimate test, the final exam. She had to stay still, to let his dry lips brush across her cheek, to smell his breath (minty, he must have brushed before coming out to meet her), to feel the proximity of another body so close to her own skin. She didn't feel any accompanying rush of desire, or even of intimacy. She only felt the bone-deep revulsion that she often felt when people she didn't know got close to her. She didn't like being touched by strangers, didn't even like handshakes.

It was only a moment and then it was over, but to Celia it felt like two hundred years passed in that microsecond. Then he was on his way up the stairs, and she sat, listening intently for the sounds of him getting ready for bed. He walked around the bedroom for a while, and she tried to discern if the noises were putting-on-pajamas noises or collecting-medication-for-my-intractable-wife noises. Her conclusion was pajama noises when he went into the bathroom a few minutes later. She deliberately kept the television low so she could hear the sound of the mattress springs when he climbed into bed.

After a few minutes, she felt her head nod forward. Her eyes closed, and she jerked herself back awake.

*Not good. I've got to stay awake for a while, or else he'll just zip downstairs and jab me with a needle while I nap on the couch. When I wake up tomorrow, I won't know who I am. I'll be his good little wifey, just like in Stepford.*

She stood and stretched, thinking she would go into the kitchen and get a snack. If her mouth was busy, she wouldn't pass out.

The collection of pictures on the wall caught Celia's eye and she remembered that something about the photos had been nagging at her. She crossed to the frame, filled with a collage of family snaps.

She looked carefully at each picture, trying to grab on to whatever was bugging her. Every photo was of herself, Pete and Stephanie. There were no pics of anyone on their own, none of the requisite solo child on a merry-go-round or blowing out birthday candles. There were none of just her and Pete.

*You'd think there'd be something, maybe one of us when we were younger and dating. The only photo I saw of the two of us was a posed wedding picture upstairs.*

The feeling that something wasn't right with the photos was like an eyelash in her eye, a gritty irritation that made her blink and blink and blink.

*None of Stephanie when she's younger, either. There should be a Stephanie's first birthday, Stephanie in a baby carrier, blah blah blah . . .*

Her train of thought trailed off and she eagerly examined all the photos again. She'd figured out what was wrong.

All the pictures, every single one, was of her and Pete and Stephanie at their current age.

*Because they're posed. Because they took these recently, and the reason I don't remember is because Pete—and Jennifer?—did something to me. They gave me something to make me forget, to make me passive and compliant.*

Her eyes in every photo were glazed, the pupils dilated. Even her smile seemed like it was at half-mast.

Someone had drugged her and taken these photos, and then installed those photos and her in this house with these strangers.

Celia was seized by the sudden urge to panic, to flee, to run into the night and never look back. This was not her home. These were not her people. This wasn't even her town—she was sure of that.

But what to do? Where to go? With all these gaps in her memory and no real notion of her resources, it seemed stupid to get into the car and start driving.

*Seems stupid to stay, though, too. Seems stupid to stay inside the net when I know it's tightening around me. That's the kind of thing that always pisses me off when I'm reading mysteries.*

Celia looked around the living room again. There were no books anywhere, just as she'd realized earlier. No books, no magazines, no newspapers, no reading material of any kind. Even if she hadn't already been convinced that this life was false, the lack of paper would have clinched it. She always had a book in her bag, a magazine on her bedside table, a newspaper in the kitchen. She liked the tactile feeling of real paper under her fingers and the smell of the ink. She'd tried an e-reader but it ended up gathering dust. It felt like she was not reading at all.

*Don't get distracted. You have a decision to make here. Stay and play along, try to find out what's happening to you and why, or head out and take your chances.*

A floorboard creaked overhead. While Celia had been wool-gathering, Pete had gotten out of bed. She was sure he was standing at the top of the stairs now, wondering if she had fallen asleep on the couch.

Celia hurried into the kitchen and started hunting around, looking for a snack. Her stomach turned at the sight of the pantry. Tons of prepackaged food, almost all of it processed—snack cakes, chips, cheese puffs, fake fruit bars. She'd never eat garbage like this, and she always tried to buy bulk when possible, to reduce waste.

Another floorboard creaked. Pete was on his way downstairs. Celia grabbed a snack-sized bag of Cool Ranch Doritos *(urgh, when was the last time I ate these? Junior high?)* and poured a big glass of water.

The stairway up to the bedrooms had three steps, then a small landing for a turn, then the main part of the staircase that completed the trip to the second level. Celia passed through the opposite end of the hallway on her way back to the television, but she could just make out the slightly darker shadow on the small landing.

Pete was standing just out of sight on the stairs, listening for her.

She clomped back into the living room, rustling the bag and humming, making as much noise as possible. She didn't want another confrontation at the moment, not when she was still sorting things out in her head. And she didn't want him to think he had a chance to ambush her. She was very much awake—in fact, more awake than she'd been even a few minutes before.

Her heart galloped and the blood pounded in her head. So

many things still didn't make sense but she was putting the pieces together—or rather, she was collecting pieces that didn't exactly fit, but at least she had *something*.

And, she realized as she tried to relax into the couch, she'd *remembered*. She'd remembered that she didn't like to be touched by strangers, that she bought books and magazines and newspapers, that she didn't eat junk food. There had been a whole flood of information about her own self, and it hadn't been accompanied by a headache.

*I'm breaking through,* she thought in triumph as she tore open the bag of Doritos and noisily crunched on a chip. *The real me is breaking through.*

Then the artificial flavor hit her tongue, and she nearly choked. She swallowed half the glass of water in one gulp, trying to wash away the film from the chip.

Celia tossed the bag on the table in disgust, marveling that people ate things like that on a regular basis. She wondered if Pete was still standing on the stairs. She wondered if he was contemplating his options, considering whether to overpower her or to try again to wheedle her into bed.

*You're not going to crush me,* she thought fiercely. *You're not going to turn me into your little robot.*

She turned up the volume on the television—not enough to wake Stephanie, but enough to let Pete know that she hadn't passed out on the couch.

A moment later, the floorboard creaked at the top of the stairs. Celia released her breath in a long exhale. She couldn't deny that she felt better with him farther away from her. Still, his behavior meant that she wasn't safe while he was in the house. She couldn't risk falling asleep here.

*Where can I go, though? I don't even have my parents' telephone number on my phone, or any friend that wouldn't automatically be suspect.*

She tried hard to dredge up the image of a friend who wasn't from this town, someone she could trust, but that part of her memory remained frustratingly blank. Maybe she wasn't collecting as many pieces together as she'd thought.

Celia checked the clock. Nearly 12:30 a.m. The restaurant had closed around 9:00 p.m., and she'd spent at least two hours in the lot waiting for the police to tell her she could go home. With everything that had happened since she'd gotten home, she'd barely thought about Mrs. Corrigan, and now she wondered if the murder had less to do with that horrible old woman and more to do with Celia herself.

Someone had clearly attempted to set her up for the murder, or at least to get her into temporary hot water. There was no evidence at all linking her to the crime, and of course Celia hadn't even had a spare moment to leave the kitchen, so she doubted the issue would be pushed as far as her being arrested. But it was a complication—a complication that, now that she looked at it, was meant specifically for her. This wasn't just the tragic death of a not-very-beloved town citizen. This was a two-birds-one-stone murder. Someone wanted her out of the way.

*But why?* She wasn't carrying corporate secrets. There was no part of her recovered memory that implied she'd been an office worker. She didn't collect gossip, and she hadn't witnessed a terrible crime—at least, as far as she could remember. She was just a regular person whose husband wanted to get rid of her real personality.

Could the murder be related to Pete's behavior? Celia truly hoped so, because if not, then it meant there was someone else around here with bad intentions toward her. One confusing and scary conspiracy was quite enough, thank you.

Still, whoever had plotted to have her blamed had done a pretty sloppy job of it. There was simply no way there was any physical evidence linking her to the crime, not to mention all the witnesses who worked at the restaurant and knew that she'd been in the kitchen all day.

The gears in her head started to turn. She loved a puzzle. It was her favorite part of mystery stories, trying to follow along and solve the problem before the main character. The trouble was that she didn't know enough about the town or the dynamics to solve this one. Mrs. Corrigan had hated her and that was about all she knew. She didn't even have a clear idea why.

*Well, you also know that Lyle Corrigan was set to inherit a lot of money.* Money was a very big motivator for most people. It would be easy for him to set up Celia to take the fall. He was a police officer.

Then again, if he had killed his aunt, then why had he done such an extremely bad job of framing Celia? She rubbed her hand across her eyes. Like so many things that had happened to her in the past day, it didn't make sense.

Celia needed to sleep. She needed to let her body and mind rest so she could try to extricate herself from Pete and his machinations as well as the mystery of Mrs. Corrigan's death. But she didn't want to sleep in the house. It was too risky. The trouble was that anywhere seemed too risky. She couldn't sleep out in the open—in the yard or the woods—and there didn't seem to be any friendly house nearby where she could take refuge.

She considered calling Katherine, but then worried that Katherine, too, might be part of the grand conspiracy. Celia had thought that her conversations with Katherine had been weird— like Katherine's half had been scripted and Celia wasn't properly picking up her cues. There had been something vaguely unreal about them.

The only person who hadn't felt like a total stranger all day was Will, but Celia was wary of that feeling as well. She didn't know if there was anyone around her that she could trust. Maybe Will was just a better actor than the rest.

There was only one place she could go, and that was only if she could be sure Pete couldn't follow her. Celia got up, taking the bag of uneaten chips with her, and went to the bottom of the stairs to peek up. She figured if Pete stood there, then she'd just say she thought she heard Stephanie walking around. But no one was on the stairs, and all seemed silent on the upper floor.

She went into the kitchen, threw the chips into the trash, then pulled her key ring and Pete's key ring off their storage hooks. Pete's only had four keys on it, while hers had about twenty. She'd used at least some of those keys that day at the restaurant, but she had no idea why the rest of the keys were on the ring.

*Unless the keys were put there to confuse me.* It seemed petty but not impossible, given what she'd heard Pete and Jennifer discussing earlier.

With more patience than she knew she possessed, she carefully matched any keys on Pete's ring to hers. At least one of them was for the house back door, and of course one of them was for Pete's car.

And, as she suspected, one of them matched the door to the restaurant. She assumed the last key was for his office.

Celia removed the restaurant key from Pete's key ring, pocketed it, grabbed her purse and a charger for her phone from the kitchen, and turned out the light. She picked up her sneakers and quietly slipped outside, locking the door behind her. She hastily pulled on her shoes and hurried to her car. She felt strangely terrified, worried that at any moment Pete would run out of the house after her.

She locked all the car doors and then turned on the engine. The moment it turned over, she saw the bedroom light upstairs flip on. Pete had been awake after all, playing possum while he waited for her to drop off on the couch.

She grinned fiercely as she pulled down the driveway. She'd beaten him—at least for today.

Celia coasted down the road and back into town. Everything was dark and quiet along the way, no sign of life except for herself, no night owls up burning the midnight oil. There was almost no ambient light, streetlights being few and far between on this road. The sky seemed unusually dark, though. Celia thought that with this little light pollution, there should be more stars.

*Maybe it's just overcast,* she thought, and then realized that the state of the sky was hardly her concern at the moment. Her life and everything wrong with it was the priority.

The police were gone from the restaurant parking lot, no sign that they'd been there except for the fluttering yellow tape around the dumpster. Celia darted from the car to the restaurant and then shut and locked the door firmly behind her. She made her way into her office and shut and locked that door as well.

Earlier in the day she'd discovered some spare clothes in the bottom drawer of the filing cabinet—no doubt for days when spills ruined her workwear. There were also a few toiletries tucked away in there. She'd get up tomorrow, dress in fresh clothes, wash as best she could, and no one would know she'd spent the night.

It would be nice if she had a cot to stretch out on, but it really didn't matter. All she wanted was to feel safe, and with the doors locked and a couple of miles between her and Pete, she finally did. Celia stretched out on the floor, her back pressed against the door, and fell asleep almost immediately.

# CHAPTER SIX

**tyz7412:** Seems like you have a lot of ideas about how you'd solve a mystery if you were in a book

**mysterybkluv:** don't we all LOL

**tyz7412:** I wonder if you could actually pull it off

**mysterybkluv:** it's just for fun, an opinion—isn't that why the internet was invented?

CELIA WOKE WITH A start from a very deep sleep. For a moment she wasn't sure where she was, then she realized the dark shape in front of her was her office desk. She sat up, pulled her phone out of her bag to check the time, and discovered the battery was dead. Luckily, she'd grabbed the extra phone charger before she left the house. She plugged the phone in and then went to the door to listen for the sounds of anyone moving around in the restaurant. All seemed to be quiet. She hoped it was still well before opening time. There were no windows in her office and so she couldn't gauge the time of day.

She carefully pulled the door open an inch and listened again. Nothing. She opened the door a little farther and stuck her head out. The kitchen was dark.

Celia went into the kitchen and found the clock that hung over the prep area. It said it was only 7:30, so she had plenty of time to wash up as best she could, change, and start getting things ready in the kitchen like it was a normal day.

She went back to the office, changed her clothes, then brushed her teeth and washed her face in the employee bathroom. By the time she was done, she felt semi-normal. She checked her phone. It was at 50 percent and so the cracked screen was displaying notifications again. There were fourteen—*fourteen!*—messages from Pete.

Her stomach turned over. She didn't want to talk to Pete, didn't want to hear what he had to say. She had no more clarity than she'd had the previous day. There were huge gaps in her memory that hadn't been filled by sleep. But she knew for certain that he meant her harm.

Still, it was better to know what the enemy was thinking. And she wasn't afraid, she realized. She'd outlasted and outwitted him the night before. Now that she was forewarned, she could do it again. He wasn't going to medicate her or make her forget more than she already had.

Celia tapped the first message and put the phone to her ear.

"Ceil? It's Pete. Where are you? I woke up when I heard the car pulling out of the driveway. If you wanted to go for a drive, you should have woken me up and let me know. Call me back. Love you."

There had been a pause between "call me back" and "love you," like it was a line in a script he'd nearly forgotten to say.

The next call was about fifteen minutes after the first.

"Ceil? Come on, sweetheart. I don't know what you're up to, but you could at least call me back. Unless you forgot your phone. I'm going to check downstairs and see if you did that."

The next one, a few minutes later: "Didn't see your phone anywhere, so I'm assuming you have it with you. Even if you're upset about what happened tonight, you shouldn't be out on your own. You're more tired than you realized and it's not safe for you to drive. Call me back."

*Forgot to say "Love you" that time,* Celia thought. *Starting to get annoyed that I'm not doing what you want me to do, what you expect me to do.*

Ten minutes after that call: "Celia, this is ridiculous. You could be in a ditch somewhere. I can't believe you'd make me worry like this. Just call me."

Celia skipped the next several messages, which she assumed were just gradual escalations of the first few, and jumped to the last couple. The time stamp on the second-to-last message was from an hour ago.

"Celia, I don't know what is going on with you, but if you're not in the hospital, then we are going to have a very serious discussion about your behavior when you come home."

*A very serious discussion about my behavior? What am I, twelve?*

"It's unbelievably irresponsible of you to just go off in the middle of the night and ignore my calls. What on earth am I supposed to tell Stephanie? Who's going to get her ready for school?"

*Uh, you. You have two hands. Besides, that child is not my child. I don't know where she came from but she didn't come from my body.*

This was a true fact; she was sure of it. She'd felt no connection to the small person whining for her lunch the day before. Celia thought that if she really were a mother, then she would have felt *something*, some connection to the child despite her lack of memories. But there was nothing.

"I have a deposition this morning, so I expect to hear from you in the next hour."

He hung up, and Celia thought, *You just keep expecting what you want. You're not going to get it.*

The next message started.

"You're going to pay for what you've done. Women like you always get what you deserve."

The voice wasn't Pete's—or at least, Celia wasn't sure if it was Pete's or not. It was deep and distorted, like it had been run through a voice processor. It could have been male or female, young or old. Celia checked the message list and saw that the caller was unknown.

"What's all this now?" she said to her phone screen.

She already had enough on her plate. Was this a threat related to Mrs. Corrigan's death? Or something else? Had she wronged somebody and wasn't aware of it? Should she call the police and report the message as a threat, or should she just ignore it? Maybe it was a prank. And what was that bit about "women like you"?

If she had to put money on the identity of the caller, Celia would bet that Lyle had sent that message. He definitely had it in for her, and if he hadn't actually killed his aunt himself (which Celia strongly suspected), then he seemed pretty convinced that Celia had done it. She wouldn't put it past him to try to frame her or even just to harass her about it indefinitely.

Celia went into the kitchen, pulled together something resembling breakfast by frying a couple of eggs and toasting yesterday's stale bread (normally used to make bread crumbs or croutons), and put on a pot of coffee. She didn't generally drink coffee but she felt like her body and mind needed the boost today.

Food plus the few hours of sleep she'd gotten made a big difference. After drinking half a cup of black coffee, Celia felt more like herself again. She just needed a plan of action to deal with the falling dominoes that appeared to be her life at the moment.

First thing first—she needed to call Pete back. He was a threat to her, but he was also the only criminal lawyer she knew, and if the situation with Mrs. Corrigan's murder escalated (as it was practically guaranteed to do), she would need Pete to help her out. As long as she didn't fall asleep around him, or accept any food or drink, she should be okay. *Maybe. Probably.*

Celia picked up the cracked phone and dialed Pete's number. She noticed again the general lack of names in her phone's contact bank. It seemed so weird that she had only a few people listed there. She loved to meet people, loved to talk to them and hang out. At home she—

That thought was cut off when she heard Pete's voice. "You have reached the voice mail of Peter DeSantis. Please leave a message after the tone."

*DeSantis, huh?* So Celia had kept her own name when she got married. She bet that had burned Pete's ass.

"Hi, Pete, it's Celia. Sorry to worry you. I just suddenly felt like I was jumping out of my skin and needed to take a drive. I ended up at the restaurant, thinking to do some paperwork, and conked out on my desk. No need to send out a search party. I'll see you and Stephanie later tonight."

She paused, contemplated a "love you," realized she couldn't fake it, and hung up.

At least that task was out of the way. She'd called him back, done her duty. She still didn't have any answers about these images she kept having in her head, or why Pete wanted to drug and control her.

*Christ, it sounds so goddamned melodramatic. Like the plot of one of those domestic thrillers where the stakes become ever more fantastic with each twist and the wife never seems to know that her husband is actually a secret rapist/pedophile/serial killer despite his shifty behavior.*

And yet here she was, somehow in the middle of some weird cross between a domestic thriller and a cozy small-town mystery, like someone started writing a cozy but didn't know how to do it properly. Or maybe everything felt like a thriller when you were trapped inside it.

*Wait a second. That's it. That's why this all seems so weird and fake, why people's conversations are strangely expository. I'm not in my life. I'm in . . .*

Her brain trailed off. She was in what, exactly? She wasn't a fictional character on the page of a bestseller. She was a real person, but a real person whose real life had been pulled out from under her. Was she in some kind of movie? An unwitting participant in a prank show or reality program? Was someone watching her right now?

The idea made her body go still even as her blood pumped faster through her veins. Somebody—*many* somebodies, in fact—could be watching her at that very moment for their own amusement. Some producer or writer could be somewhere, puppeteering the next scene to up the stakes and keep people watching.

Celia took a deep breath and tried to get her rampaging imagination under control. Her life wasn't *The Truman Show.* That couldn't happen in reality. It was unethical. Somebody couldn't just decide to grab her and force her to participate in a story.

She had a flash again, a flash of being held down to the floor by strong hands, of somebody laughing and saying nobody would believe her. This was accompanied by the strongest headache she'd had yet, a pain so intense and debilitating that she clutched her head and crouched to the floor, eyes squeezed shut.

*Remember, remember, remember,* she told herself over waves of pain. *Break through, remember.*

After several minutes, though, the pain subsided with no discernible change in her lack of memories. She stood, a little unsteady, and started cleaning up the breakfast dishes she'd used. Mindless, repetitive tasks always soothed her, and she realized that she couldn't force her memories to return. The few recollections she'd had came when she was doing or thinking about something else. She needed to do exactly what she'd done yesterday—play along, act normal (or what passed for normal in this life) until she figured things out.

One thing she would do, though, was stay on her guard around everyone. She didn't know if this was a vast conspiracy or what *(that would be a political thriller, and you're definitely not in one of those)* but she didn't think she could trust any of the people around her. She certainly couldn't tell anyone that her memories were gone, or that Pete and Jennifer were plotting to drug her, or that she thought maybe she was in a TV show that she hadn't agreed to star in.

*Hmm, if I am in a TV show, then there will be cameras around. The thing is, I don't want to alert whoever might be watching that I'm onto them.*

She needed to figure out a subtle way of searching. Staring around the kitchen was not subtle. It might even clue in whoever was watching.

*If anyone is actually watching. And if they are, they might already think you're onto them by your behavior last night. Pete's phone calls could have just been performance art, acting the way a husband is supposed to act when his wife leaves the house in the middle of the night.*

Celia felt suffocated, like she couldn't get in enough air. It seemed like every possible decision she made was fraught, that she was an increasingly frantic rat running in a maze.

*You're not a rat, and you're not stupid. It's not entirely clear what's going on, but you'll figure it out if you take things step by step. Use your logic. If someone wanted to watch you, and they knew you spent most of your time in the kitchen, how would they do that?*

Celia assumed the most logical option would be a high camera with a good angle on the whole kitchen. But she didn't think that kind of camera would be easy to hide. There were more likely buttonhole-type cameras in a few locations, or nanny-cam devices hidden inside other objects.

She went into the storage area, perusing the stacks of shelves, and muttered a few recipe ideas to herself as she did so whoever was watching would think she was just taking stock of her available supplies.

"I can always do a carbonara variation as a special, maybe a pesto pasta salad? I bet that would be nice with tortelloni. I'm sure Katherine will love stuffing the pasta."

Celia ran her fingers over the cans and jars, hunting for a seam, a hole, anything that would give away a spy. Nothing. She didn't see anything that looked like a camera, either.

*Maybe I'm crazy. Maybe all this stress is making my imagination go wild. Maybe I am just paranoid and exhausted and I did misunderstand or mishear what Pete said last night. Maybe I'm just a terrible wife and mother.*

She collected all the things to make a tortelloni pasta salad with pesto, roasted tomatoes and ciliegine. The restaurant still needed to be run, and answers might occur to her while she was cooking. That seemed to be when she was most relaxed and calm, when she felt most at ease with herself.

*I must do this in my real life, or have done something like it.*

There it was again—the conviction that this wasn't her real life. Pressure built behind her eyes, not exactly like the pain that had debilitated her a short time before, but a close cousin.

*Don't think about it, don't look at it directly.*

She made the pasta, cut it in sheets, filled and rolled the tortelloni together. Her hands moved automatically and her eyes drifted away from her work.

And she saw it. Her hands froze, just for a second, and she glanced back down at her worktable so she wouldn't give herself away by staring down the barrel of the camera she'd only just noticed.

Whoever put it there had been smart, had known where she spent most of her time. The camera was looking at her through a hole in the metal canister that held her spoons and spatulas, and that was placed on a shelf that was just below her eyeline. There was a tiny hole in the front of the canister that had no reason to be there unless there was a camera behind it.

She had to check and make sure, make sure that she wasn't crazy.

*"If you try to tell anyone about this, people will just think you're crazy. Nobody believes what crazy bitches say."*

That voice again, that voice in her head that was so tantalizingly familiar, but she couldn't pin it down. She'd heard it sometime in the last twenty-four hours, and it wasn't Pete's. She was certain of that.

Celia finished twisting a tortelloni together and reached for one of the spoons in the canister.

"Oh, no!" she said, as the canister was knocked over and all the utensils clattered out, spilling over the edge of the shelf. The canister rolled off the shelf and onto her worktable before falling to the floor.

*Perfect,* she thought, crouching to pick it up. She didn't even look inside the container. She felt around the interior with her fingers until they snagged on something out of place. Then she made sure the item was facing away from her and peered inside. There was a tiny, round metal item attached to the place where the hole peeked out of the canister.

*Not crazy,* she thought in triumph. *Not crazy, not crazy, not crazy.*

She picked up all the utensils and carefully placed the canister back on the shelf with the pinhole facing away from her. She hoped like hell that whoever was spying on her was really pissed.

Her euphoria faded quickly. She was right that someone was watching her, but she still didn't know who or why. And there were probably more cameras in the kitchen that she hadn't found yet.

*I'll find them all,* she thought. *Whoever is doing this, if it's Pete or someone else, I'll find out. I'm smart and I'm capable and I'm not going to let some asshole run me over.*

Celia felt, she realized, more like her real self than she had at any other time in the past day. She wasn't some simpering miss. She was always strong, always looked after herself. She didn't put up with anyone's nonsense.

"*That Italian temper*," someone had said, and they were laughing when they said it, like her anger was a little child's tantrum, like what she felt wasn't real.

*Who is that?* she wondered again. That voice in her head was connected to the mess she was in now. If only she could remember.

There was a knock at the back door. She stared at the door like it was a portal to hell. Anyone could be on the other side of it. It could be Pete, or Lyle Corrigan, or the ghost of the horrible woman who'd been unceremoniously killed and dumped in the trash the night before.

"It's Frank, Celia," a voice said.

She didn't know who Frank was, but he seemed friendly. He seemed to know her, and to assume that he was expected.

*You can't hide in the kitchen forever with all the doors locked. You have to be brave and take chances if you want answers. Besides, it can't be that everyone in this town is out to get you.*

"Unless maybe they are," Celia murmured to herself as she unlocked the back door and threw it open.

A short, skinny middle-aged man with dark hair and dark eyes stood outside in the early-morning sunshine, grinning at her. He had a cart with several loaves of bread in small pallets.

"Good morning. Was going to just drop your order outside as usual but I saw your car in the lot. Getting an early start today?" He bustled past her and into the kitchen and began unloading the plastic pallets by the storage shelves.

Celia forced a smile that she hoped appeared semi-sincere. "Yeah, I couldn't sleep and the only possible solution was to make pasta salad."

"Heard about the ruckus last night with Mrs. Corrigan," he said, giving her a sympathetic glance. "That would affect anyone's sleep."

"It wasn't conducive to peaceful rest, no," Celia said. "How'd you hear that bit of news so early in the morning?"

Frank gave her a sideways look. "You know Janet is on the overnight emergency dispatch. She told me as soon as she came home this morning."

Celia didn't know if Janet was his wife or girlfriend or daughter or roommate, and she certainly didn't know that the woman was a dispatcher. She gave herself a little *thunk* on the head with the heel of her hand and feigned stupidity.

"Of course, sorry. Like I said, not much sleep."

"I bet you have a lot of business today," he said, straightening up as he finished unloading the last pallet. "Half the town is going to be in here gawking, beyond thrilled to be near the site of a murder."

Celia shook her head. "That's macabre."

He shrugged. "Haven't had a murder in this town for thirty-five years. Some rubbernecking is to be expected. Got my empties?"

"Over there," Celia said, pointing at the stack of empty bread pallets in the corner.

Frank loaded up his cart, said goodbye, and went out whistling. *Really? A whistler? For real?* Celia didn't think she'd ever heard anybody whistle a tune except in movies. It added to the feeling of unreality, the sense that everything around her was staged.

She shut the door behind Frank and finished prepping the pasta salad. By the time she made the pesto, boiled the tortelloni, roasted the tomatoes and tossed everything together, Katherine had arrived. Katherine appeared almost indecently excited.

"I heard!" she said, pulling off her jacket and hanging it on the rack. "Someone killed that crazy old woman last night, and Lyle Corrigan thinks it was you."

"How did you hear about it already?" Celia asked.

"I had to go to the grocery this morning and everyone in there was talking about it. Don't stress about it. You know how people are in this town."

"I really don't want people thinking I'm a murderer, even casually," Celia said.

"The only one who really thinks that is Lyle. He's an idiot, so I don't think he counts," Katherine said, pulling on her apron.

"I think it counts if he can convince the police chief that it was me," Celia said, and then she wondered, *Is this the ultimate goal? To set me up as a murderer, to see me locked away? But why?*

Her frustration was reaching its boiling point, and she didn't know how she could find any answers. She just needed to keep acting normal-ish until a solution presented itself.

"So, are you going to do some poking around? Find out who really did it?" Katherine asked.

Celia frowned. "Why would I do that? It's not my job. Besides, I don't think it's smart to potentially piss off a murderer."

"I just thought if you were worried about the police messing everything up," Katherine said. "It seemed like the sort of thing you would do. You're always talking about those true-crime mystery podcasts you listen to. You're always saying you could do a better job of solving them than the real police."

*Mystery podcasts? I don't listen to mystery podcasts. I don't like true crime. I think it's gross. It's almost like Katherine—and everyone else around me—is trying to imprint some new personality on me, someone who runs for fun and watches crappy TV and likes true crime. Someone who is fundamentally not like me.*

"Let's not worry about Mrs. Corrigan's murder right now," Celia said firmly. "When Frank dropped off the bread, he said that the restaurant will probably be busy today, so we have a lot of prep to do."

"Or it will be completely empty," Katherine said. "If people think you're a murderer and decide to stay away in case you go crazy and come charging out of the kitchen with a knife."

Celia gave Katherine a sideways glance. "Do you think that's likely?"

"People staying away or you turning into Michael Myers?"

"I sincerely hope that if you were worried about the latter, you would not be working in this kitchen with me," Celia said.

"I like to live on the edge."

Celia laughed, and the sound startled her. She'd been under so much stress that she'd forgotten how to laugh, how to feel joy even for a moment. It felt good.

The work of the restaurant distracted and soothed her for the next couple of hours. Celia and Katherine made pasta and soup, sliced bread and simmered sauce. The servers came in for the lunch shift and Celia went out front to open the blinds and flip the sign to "Open."

There were already a dozen people standing on the sidewalk, ready to come in. As soon as Celia raised the blinds on the front window, several of them waved at her eagerly.

"Oh no," Celia said, turning away after a half-hearted wave in response. "Tia, will you come up here to unlock the door—after I go back into the kitchen?"

Tia, who'd been filling the salt and pepper shakers, came to stand next to Celia. "The gawkers have arrived. I'm going to make a ton of money in tips today."

"No matter what they ask, don't come into the back to get me. If they ask for the chef, I'll send Katherine out."

"I'm not sure that's going to work," Tia said. "They could just ask for you outright."

"I'm busy," Celia said firmly. There were only so many things she could deal with at the moment, and she wasn't up to a bunch of lookie-loos asking her intrusive questions.

Celia ducked back into the kitchen, feeling a little guilty that she was leaving it up to the servers to run interference for her.

Her phone buzzed in her pocket. She pulled it out and saw that it was Pete. She considered letting it go to voice mail but then decided to just take the call and get it over with. She waved at Katherine and went into her office, closing the door for some privacy.

"Hello?"

"I see you've decided to pick up your phone." His voice was icy, disapproving.

"I explained what happened," Celia said. She was not going to apologize, even though that was clearly what he expected.

Men always wanted women to apologize, even for things that weren't their fault.

*"Are you going to apologize for being a snotty little bitch?"*

The voice—the memory—in her head drowned out what Pete said next. For the millionth time, Celia felt sure she'd heard that voice sometime recently. She just couldn't remember.

"... completely inappropriate. Stephanie was crying this morning, and everything was completely disorganized because you weren't at home. Your job is to take care of your child and the household."

"What is this, the nineteen forties?" Celia said. "I'm not your little housewife, Pete. I think you're old enough to make a sandwich and put it in a lunchbox and wave at your daughter as she runs to the bus."

"That's not the point. The point is that you've always taken care of those things."

"You know, I don't think I have," Celia said.

There was a moment of silence, and then Pete said, very slowly, "You don't think you have what?"

"I don't think I have always taken care of that little girl. And the reason I don't think that is because I don't think I'm actually your wife, and that kid is not my daughter."

"Fuck!" The word seemed to explode out of Pete unbidden.

"Yeah, that's what I thought. Bye, Pete," Celia said.

"Wait, Celia—"

She hung up before he could say another word.

# CHAPTER SEVEN

**tyz7412:** So you're not actually serious. Typical woman, full of bullshit

**mysterybkluv:** wow okay thought we were just having a fun discussion here

**archieandnero:** seriously WTF dude back off

**poirotsgirl:** yeah that's totally inappropriate

**tyz7412:** I want to know if that bitch can actually do what she says or if she's all talk

**mysterybkluv:** jesus christ you can fuck right off

**tyz7412:** I wanna know if she can actually solve a mystery better than the police. I want to see you prove it.

**mysterybkluv:** I don't have to prove anything to you, and this discussion is over

**tyz7412:** oh really

CELIA STUFFED HER PHONE in her pocket again, determined to ignore any further communication from Pete. She'd confirmed what she'd suspected—that he wasn't her husband, that the kid wasn't hers. She'd confirmed that there was a camera watching her. She still didn't know *why*, though, and she was getting sick of the broken record in her brain asking the same question over and over.

She felt strangely calm as she returned to her work in the kitchen. She hadn't planned to confront Pete, hadn't planned to reveal that she knew what he was up to. It had just come out. But it felt like the right decision in the moment.

*What happens now, though? I can't go home, or rather, to the place that they told me was home.*

Maybe at the end of the day she should just take all the money out of the till, get in her car and start driving. At least she would be safer in a different town, away from a man masquerading as her life partner and a police officer determined to frame her for murder.

*Oh, yeah, and there's a murderer around, too. And the murderer always tries for the heroine of the story.*

Was she the heroine of the story, though? It seemed like she was. Why else would Pete have done this? Why else would there be a secret camera in her kitchen?

*There's probably one in your car, too. They'll be able to track you.*

"They." Celia didn't know why, but she was certain that there was a "they." It wasn't just about Pete. For a moment she felt like she couldn't breathe, like her breath had seized in her lungs. Someone was out to get her—a lot of someones, maybe—and there appeared to be no rhyme or reason to it. What could she have done that was so horrible, so offensive, that this elaborate scheme would form around her? Had she hurt someone, killed someone?

*No.* Even with her faulty memories, she thought she'd remember doing something like that. And anyway, the idea didn't *feel* right. She wasn't a killer. She couldn't deliberately harm another person. It was fundamentally not her, just like listening to true crime podcasts or running for fun was fundamentally not her.

Her body moved on autopilot, did the tasks required of her, answered Katherine's questions and comments. The servers came in and out of the kitchen, many of them complaining that the deluge of customers did not seem to be translating into a deluge of tips because people were cheap jerks.

Even as she worked and commiserated with the servers, part

of Celia's brain was working, trying to solve the mystery that surrounded her, trying to figure out how she could get out of it.

The afternoon shift changed to the evening shift. Pete left twenty-two more voice mail messages on her phone, and Celia listened to none of them.

*You can do this. You always figure out the solution before the end when you're reading a mystery novel.*

Her hands stopped their automatic motion. There was something there, something in that thought. She was a reader. She liked reading mystery novels, liked solving puzzles. She should be able to solve this one.

*No, that's not it. Somebody said I couldn't do it or something? No, that's not quite right. Somebody said . . .*

Her thought trailed off, and she gritted her teeth. These half-formed memories were getting real old real fast.

Will came into the kitchen carrying a pile of dishes, just like he had the night before. He hummed as he stacked them in the sink to be washed later.

He was humming a tune that seemed very familiar to Celia, so familiar that she heard an echo of it inside her brain, the sound of someone else humming the same song.

She had a flash of someone standing in front of a canvas holding a paintbrush, and he was humming that very tune.

"*Eine kleine Nachtmusik,*" Celia said.

"Yup, it's my favorite," Will said.

"It's someone else's favorite, too," Celia murmured, more to herself than to Will.

Will straightened up, wiping his hands on the dishcloth. Celia thought there was something in his eyes, some wariness that wasn't there before. But perhaps she had imagined it. It was hard to know what was real and what was in her head anymore. "Whose favorite?"

"I don't know," Celia said. "Maybe Lyle Corrigan's."

Will made a *pfffft* noise. "Lyle Corrigan is a cretin. He's probably never even heard of Mozart."

"He might have heard Mozart's name once, even if he doesn't know what to attach it to," Celia said. "Or maybe he'd surprise us. People often do."

Will shook his head. "That's not been my experience at all. My experience has been that people act in perfectly predictable ways, always based on the way they've acted before. People just aren't that interesting, really."

"I don't know," Celia said, looking toward the back door. She could almost see Mrs. Corrigan's ridiculous pink house on the other side of the parking lot. She was thinking about Mrs. Corrigan, about the murder that might be pinned on her, about the mysteries that she liked to solve. "I think most people are plenty interesting."

"Keep that sunshine-y optimism, okay? I think I can predict with all confidence that the family of five in my section will leave a 10 percent tip and that the kids will drop more spaghetti on the seats than ever makes it into their mouths."

"Well, it's an interesting result, isn't it?" Celia said, laughing.

"But also a predictable one," Will said, and went into the dining room.

Katherine had gone out for her dinner break to do some shopping before the stores closed. She returned through the back door, her hands loaded with bags.

"So many sales!" she said, swinging the bags around her waist. "I got a ton of great deals."

"Cool," Celia said, but Katherine's words didn't really register. She wasn't thinking about Katherine's shopping. She was thinking about Mrs. Corrigan—a person she would have said she'd never seen before yesterday, a person who seemed to have hated Celia with the fiery light of a thousand suns. Hate that was, frankly, absurd on its face. There was no way someone could have that much built-up hostility for Celia just because of a supposed rat problem. And this whole thing with Mrs. Corrigan was tied, somehow, to Celia's fake husband and her fake life, and the cameras filming her in her kitchen.

*And Mrs. Corrigan is dead. Remember that. I don't know how this is all tied together, but one woman is dead and I don't want to be the body that pops up in the middle of the book.*

Celia abruptly untied her apron and drew it over her head. "I'm going out for a little while. Can you handle things here for a half hour or so?"

Katherine gave Celia a startled look. "Sure, but where are you going?"

"Just to run an errand," Celia said vaguely. She didn't want to confide in Katherine. She wasn't certain that she *could* confide in Katherine. Katherine might be a part of the conspiracy with Pete and Jennifer and whoever was watching Celia through the cameras.

Celia felt the expectant look that Katherine gave her, but she ignored it. She put on her jacket and went out the door with a little wave, saying, "Be back soon."

Celia wondered what the person watching through the cameras in the kitchen was thinking now. Did they have cameras set up in the parking lot as well? Was there a camera in her car? She resisted the urge to look up and check the telephone poles around the lot. If there was an electronic eye following her progress through the lot, then there wasn't anything she could do about it right now.

There was one safety light in the parking lot, close to the dumpster. The remainder of the light came from the streetlights, so there were large pools of shadow to pass through. As she walked, Celia was struck again by the unnatural quiet. No one was exiting the restaurant after their meal and coming back here to get their car. There were no cars in the lot other than her own, Will's and Katherine's. Nobody was driving up Cherry Lane. There was no sound of traffic coming from Main Street, either. No dogs barked and no music blared from the bedrooms of teenagers. There was none of the ambient murmur that came from places where people congregated, like the shops and restaurants that surrounded Celia's own business. It was like no one actually lived in the town, or those that did were robots that powered down every night.

Celia stopped in front of the dumpster. The hastily wrapped crime scene tape now fluttered uselessly in front of it. Celia resisted the urge to open the dumpster again, to see if anyone else had been murdered and dropped in there for her to find.

*That would be pushing credulity too far. Besides, in mystery novels there's always a little stretch before the second body pops up. In fact, sometimes there's no second body at all. Sometimes there's just one murder that takes up everyone's time and attention. And honestly, one murder is more than enough.*

Celia turned on the flashlight on her phone and scanned it all around the dumpster. She wasn't 100 percent sure what she was looking for, especially since several people had walked around the area the previous night. If there was any evidence to collect, then the police probably already collected it.

*If Lyle Corrigan believes in evidence at all, that is. He might just try to railroad me—make up a case, plant evidence. It was what his aunt tried to do with the fake black eye.*

There were lots of footprints in the dust, scraps of old garbage, leaves that had fallen off the bushes that lined the lot. But there was nothing that screamed "PREVIOUSLY UNDISCOVERED MURDER CLUE HERE." Celia twisted her mouth. What had she expected? Real life wasn't like a neatly plotted novel.

She walked around the dumpster, remembering that the previous night she'd thought she heard someone nearby. The only place the person could have hidden—if there was anybody—was in Mrs. Corrigan's backyard. Celia figured that made sense, because whoever had killed Mrs. Corrigan would have had to bring the body from the old lady's house to the restaurant's dumpster.

*And if someone was nearby, and the sound wasn't in my imagination . . . that means the killer had probably just tossed Mrs. Corrigan's body a few moments before I came out with the trash. Which means they could have killed me, too. Except it's pretty clear—maybe?? Or maybe not—that what they want to do is set me up as a murderer.*

But maybe it had all been in her head. Maybe there had been no noise at all, no lurking murderer confirming that his diabolical plan was at work. It was hard to know anymore. It was hard to know whether she was inventing memories whole cloth or if she was seeing things that weren't really in front of her. Celia felt a strong sense of unreality, a sense that she was hardly a real person at all. She was just a character in someone else's story, the product of someone else's guiding hand.

It didn't matter, she realized. It didn't matter because she was here, in this moment, and if she wanted to take control of her life, then she needed more information. She needed to try to understand what had happened to her and who had done it and why. The only way she could do that was to find any clues about Mrs. Corrigan's killer that the police had overlooked. She pushed through the bushes behind the dumpster and stepped into Mrs. Corrigan's backyard.

Her heart slammed against her ribs, the pulse of blood thick in her mouth. Celia was not a natural rule-breaker, whatever Lyle

Corrigan thought of her. Just the fact of standing in someone's yard, in a place where she would certainly be considered a trespasser, made her a little sick.

*And what if Lyle Corrigan is here? What if he's hanging around the house hoping to catch me at exactly this sort of thing?*

Automatically Celia looked up at the house. But the windows were dark, and there didn't seem to be anyone inside. She glanced around nervously at the house across the street, but that was dark, too.

Again she noted the unnatural silence, the lack of ambient noise. There weren't even any chirping crickets or twittering birds, no skitter of squirrels and chipmunks. It was so quiet in this town. It was almost as if no one actually lived there.

Celia paused, looking around then. Could that be true? Could she be in some kind of abandoned town?

*Don't be any more ridiculous than you already are. Isn't it enough that your husband—or someone pretending to be your husband—wants to drug you? Isn't it enough that someone is watching you at work?*

She shone her cell phone flashlight around the area, looking for something, anything. Celia crouched down to the grass, frog-walking her way closer to the house. She felt vaguely stupid and not at all Holmes-like.

*No distinct footprints or bits of cigarette ash, no conveniently characteristic candy wrapper (the killer only eats pink Starburst!) or wad of gum containing the killer's DNA.*

Celia glanced up at Mrs. Corrigan's back porch, wondered if she dared go up there. Stepping on some part of the dead woman's house seemed like a more significant violation, like she was *actually* trespassing in a way that she hadn't before.

But the killer had to have offed Mrs. Corrigan in her own house, not in Celia's parking lot. There had been no blood splattered anywhere around the dumpster. And the backyard didn't show any signs of struggle or anything else that might indicate Mrs. Corrigan had died there. She had to have been murdered in her house. The killer would have been foolish to walk right out the front door under the streetlights, so he—

*(so sexist of me, it might not be a "he" at all, but it's true that I always think of killers as men because men can be dangerous, so very very dangerous to women)*

—and as she thought this, something tore inside her brain, some seam ripped apart, and the pain was beyond terrible, beyond anything she'd ever felt before. Celia fell to her knees, felt her eyes water and blood leak from her nose. The phone slipped from her hand and into the grass, the flashlight face down so that just a thin frame of light was visible around the case.

Celia could hardly think, could hardly see beyond the pain, but there was something behind that ripped seam, some face that was just out of focus, and with it, the memory of a sneering voice.

*"No one will ever believe you."*

She knew that voice. She'd heard it recently. She just couldn't match it to a face, couldn't make that last part tighten up so she could see it clearly.

*Someone did this to me. Someone stripped my life away and I can't remember who it was. If only . . . if only . . .*

She put her face in her hands, hating how helpless she felt, how small.

*He did this, whoever he is. He made me feel small.*

A surge of rebellion rose within her, a feeling that drove her to her feet. No one was going to make her small. No one was going to make her a helpless, crying maiden. She was going to solve this murder and she was going to find the killer and she was going to find who had tampered with her brain and she was going to *fix it goddamnit* because this was her life.

Celia bent to pick up the phone, ignoring the wave of dizziness that accompanied this action. She marched toward Mrs. Corrigan's porch with a determination she hadn't had before.

There were two wooden steps leading up to the covered porch. Celia had enough wherewithal to realize she shouldn't stomp up them and make a big racket. It might not seem that there was anybody around, but someone *could* be. A neighbor might suddenly decide to walk their dog, or someone might pull into the restaurant parking lot.

*Why do I have that parking lot for the restaurant, anyway? Nobody parks in it except the staff. No matter how busy the place is, there never seems to be anyone needing the back lot.*

It was ludicrous that her whole dispute with Mrs. Corrigan—or rather, Mrs. Corrigan's dispute with her—was contingent on the dumpster in a lot that was barely used.

Celia tiptoed carefully around the porch, but nothing seemed out of place. She did note that the wooden slats appeared freshly sealed and stained, but not done-since-yesterday fresh. More like they'd been updated in the last couple of weeks. The siding of the house, too, appeared new. Maybe Mrs. Corrigan had decided to update her home recently.

Celia flashed her light across the back of the house, looking for a snagged thread on the door frame, anything that might help.

That's when she noticed that the back door was open.

It wasn't much, just a centimeter or two. But the door was not shut and locked as it should be.

Celia stared at the little gap between the door and the frame, and wondered if she dared.

*There's no one around to see you, and you won't touch anything, won't do anything stupid like leave your fingerprints behind, right? But presumably the police have been through the house already, have collected any forensic evidence that they might need. So it's probably safe to enter and not worry about incriminating yourself.*

Celia reached for the doorknob, then paused. There was no crime scene tape on the back door. Maybe that meant the police had not been through the house yet. If so, then she might be walking right into the killer's trap. She might be doing exactly what he wanted. She might be making herself an easy target.

*Just commit,* she told herself. She wrapped her shirtsleeve around her hand and pushed the door open.

It opened into a kitchen. Celia scanned the flashlight through the room. The cabinets were painted pink, like the exterior of the house, and there was an old-fashioned dinette with silver piping and puffy leather seats, also pink. The woman had apparently loved pink beyond all reason.

Celia couldn't see any obvious signs of a struggle or a murder in the kitchen. Everything was neatly arranged. There wasn't a dirty coffee cup in the sink or a loaf of bread on the counter. It looked sort of like a show kitchen for a real estate open house.

She passed through the kitchen and into what seemed to be a living room. A small television—old-fashioned and bulky instead of a modern flat-screen—stood against the wall that connected to the kitchen. The rest of the room had the sort of overly fussy furnishings and knickknacks that Celia associated with the elderly— a couch covered in an uncomfortable-looking damask *(more pink!)*, a matching pair of chairs, doilies on the highly polished end tables, dried flowers and ugly porcelain dolls everywhere. No books or magazines or a basket of knitting, no sign that an actual human had lived there. No sign of murder, or any evidence that the police had been through the house looking for such signs.

Celia frowned. The house appeared strangely untouched. She leaned over one of the tables, swiped her sleeve across the surface and examined the fabric with the cell phone flashlight. There were traces of dust there, like someone needed to give the house a good wipe down.

This whole exercise was starting to seem pointless, but Celia figured she might as well head upstairs and see if anything revealed itself to her there. As she climbed the stairs, she marveled at how easily the heroines of her favorite books stumbled across physical clues after a crime. Fiction really was easier than truth.

There was a hallway with five rooms leading off it. All the doors were closed.

Celia used her sleeve again to open the closest door. The room was empty.

*That's weird,* she thought. Most people had so much stuff that they never left a room unused. They'd use a space like this as a sewing room or a place to stash their treadmill or to keep extra clothing. But then, Mrs. Corrigan did live alone. Celia supposed she didn't have any hobbies.

She opened the next room. Also empty.

*What the . . . ?*

The next room. Empty.

A cold knot had formed in the pit of Celia's stomach. She thought again of the way the living room and kitchen were so impersonal. *Did Mrs. Corrigan actually live here?*

Celia pushed open the fourth door, already certain of what she would see. Nothing. There was no furniture, no closet, just a big, bare, empty room. And now that she noticed it, the room smelled faintly of wood shavings, as if it had been built recently.

*What is this place? Where am I?* Celia thought, and now the terror was pumping through her, making her hands shake as she pushed open the final door. The room was empty, like all the others. No bed, not even for show, no end table with a glass for dentures and a neatly folded pair of reading glasses. Nothing at all.

Panic surged through her and she ran down the hall, down the stairs, through the empty house and into the yard. She stood there for a moment in the grass, out of breath, feeling the insane rush of blood in her body. What was she going to do now? She didn't know where she was on the planet, but she knew she didn't belong there. This wasn't her home. These weren't her people.

Celia started to run, not thinking about where she was going or what she would do when she got there. She just knew she had to go, go anywhere, and she didn't trust her car not to be tracked. She tossed the cell phone aside—it had to be a plant, had to be another way to follow her.

She ran down Cherry and onto Main Street, not stopping to look inside the restaurant. There was no one she could trust, no one who could help her. She ran along the road, away from the town, in the opposite direction of her house. The last thing she needed was Pete finding her. He might grab her, throw her in the car, force her to return to that house with him—the house that she knew was not her own.

*I don't know where my home is, but I'm going to find it. I'm going to remember who I am and I am going to find my place.*

She knew that anyone who saw her would think she looked crazy, but she didn't care. She *felt* crazy in that moment, unmoored, but she was running toward something, something she was sure was out there even if she couldn't remember it.

Celia reached the edge of the town. To the right, there were houses much like the one that Pete had claimed was her home—two-story, middle-class-type dwellings. To the left was an expanse of woods similar to the one she'd passed the last two mornings on her way to the restaurant. There was only one road, and it continued straight ahead.

Celia paused for a moment, glancing over her shoulder. What she saw there made her plunge into the woods with no clear plan except to get away.

Twenty or so men were lined up across the road and running slowly, methodically, after her.

She heard shouts and yells as she went into the trees. There were no clear paths, and she didn't have a clear destination. She had no purpose except to get away.

*Maybe I can climb a tree and hide,* she thought, but one glance at the trees around her showed that none of the branches were low enough for her to grasp. Besides, one of the men chasing her would probably find her and have the tree chopped down with her in it.

She heard her own breath as she panted for air, felt the muscles under her right rib contract painfully. Her legs burned and she felt her body slowing involuntarily, wanting to stop and walk. She was not in ideal shape for running for her life.

*I knew I wasn't a runner. I knew it was a lie.*

She risked a quick look over her shoulder, saw that several of the men were within sight.

*I've got to stop running in a straight line.*

Celia turned diagonally, sprinted between trees as best she could. The tree cover was getting sparser instead of thicker, which was odd. Normally the deeper one went into the woods, the harder it became to move through it, but the trees were gradually disappearing, leaving an almost open plain of dirt in front of her.

And then the dirt was gone, and her feet were pounding on a concrete pad, and there, miraculously before her, was something that she thought for a moment was an illusion.

A very tall white wall—perhaps thirty, forty feet, maybe more—and set within it, like something Alice might have found while chasing the white rabbit, a gray rectangular door with bright red letters over it.

An exit door.

Celia ran harder than she ever thought she possibly could, heard someone snarling far too close behind her, "No, you fucking *bitch*, you aren't going to get away from us!"

She slammed into the door and pushed it open.

PART II

# ALLISON

# CHAPTER ONE

**finalgirl:** hey, what's everyone's favorite horror trope—from books or movies? Mine's definitely small town with a supernatural secret.

**eatersofthedead:** Literally anything with zombies.

**ghostwife:** Obviously the haunted house 😄

**allieoop:** I'm a huge fan of the cabin in the woods.

**finalgirl:** Ooh, there's nothing like isolation to create ideal conditions for a mad slasher.

**allieoop:** Preferably one that's just escaped from a mental asylum.

**finalgirl:** LOL all you need are some teen girls in very short shorts and you've got the perfect story.

**ALLIE'S SHORTS WERE TOO** tight. They were denim shorts, which she didn't usually wear, and they were clearly at least one size too small. Her belly button felt like it was being squeezed into an unnatural shape, and the cloth stretched tight across her hips. She wondered why she'd bought the shorts in the first place. She didn't remember buying them, but then sometimes when Cam and Madison and Allie went shopping, she bought things she didn't really want, because it was important not to stand out, not to give them a chance to make fun of her for being a boring prude or whatever. They didn't usually do this, but every once in a while, Cam would get a mean streak up and Madison would go along. Allison was always the odd one out, because Allison had joined the group after Cam and Madison were already friends. She minded when this happened but didn't show it, because bleeding was something best done internally, preferably in private.

But she didn't like to wear very short shorts, or very tight tops. Yet somehow here she was, on the long-awaited and much-anticipated birthday trip, wearing shorts she hated. At least her tee shirt was loose. Allie always wore loose tees, because anything with a tiny bit of cling showed off her stupid enormous breasts. Other girls might think it was fun to be a double-D cup, to have endless attention from men, but it definitely was not. Cam, who had very small breasts, always wore padded push-up bras, trying to create the impression of volume that wasn't really there. She'd stare at Allie's chest in envy every time they went to the beach or the pool, while Allie would wince and blush and pull at her swimsuit straps.

Allie had gotten big breasts in high school, swelling to her current size when she was only fifteen, and because of it, men twice her age (and sometimes more) felt free to watch her when she walked, and to make lewd comments, and to generally make her feel like a piece of meat in front of a group of slavering diners.

She tugged at the short hems surreptitiously, but since she was sitting in a folding chair, she couldn't really get them down any farther without standing up and drawing attention to herself. Allie didn't want to draw any extra attention to herself. She was already the odd girl out, the one who'd come for the weekend without a boyfriend. To be fair, though, this was supposed to be a No Boyfriends Allowed weekend, a trip just for Allie and Cam and Madison to drink wine and play Uno and laugh about dumb shit the way they used to, before Cam and Madison became wrapped up twenty-four seven in their stupid frat boys.

Allie looked over at Cam and Brad (*Brad*, she thought with contempt. *Who named their kid Brad in the year 2000? It's like a relic from a John Hughes movie*). Cam sat in Brad's lap, her shorts (even shorter than Allie's) showing off her long legs, their summer tan fading. Cam looked like the Hollywood ideal of a college student, tall and very blonde and high-cheekboned, true to her Scandinavian roots.

Brad looked like the trust-fund baby he was: blond and muscled and with a constant twist of dissatisfaction at the corner of his mouth, like the world never could deliver what he expected from it despite always getting what he wanted.

Madison and Steve sat on a wooden bench across the campfire from Allie, their thighs pressed together. Steve whispered in Madison's ear and Madison giggled. Steve was taller and thinner than Brad, with dark hair cut short on the sides and longer on top so that it flopped in his eyes all the time. He was constantly tossing it back like a supermodel in a music video. Allie always itched to either (a) cut his bangs, or (b) offer him a bobby pin.

Madison looked like a slightly faded version of Cam—not quite as tall and slender, not quite as blonde, but still California gorgeous. She was the follower, the one who waited for Cam's lead. Steve was the same with Brad. Allie couldn't decide if it was cute or gross, the way the alphas and the betas had paired off so perfectly, recognizing their status instinctively.

*And what does that make you? An omega?*

Allie shook off the thought. There was nothing wrong with her, nothing that made her inherently less attractive or interesting. She was shorter than the other two; she had curly dark hair; she had big brown eyes and wore glasses because she couldn't bear the thought of putting in contacts (there was nothing squickier than putting her finger into her eye, in Allie's opinion). But she was perfectly cute—she saw that when she looked in the mirror. And she was smart and also funny when she wanted to be. She just didn't want to date someone whose life priorities started with keg stands. Dating wasn't that important to her, really. Getting good grades so she could go on to graduate school was more her jam.

Allie realized she should never have agreed to this trip. Once

Cam and Madison backed out on their deal and showed up with the Wonder Twins in tow, she should have said she felt sick, had to study for a test, anything to stay back in the dorm for the weekend. But she'd felt boxed in by Cam and Madison's pleading faces, by the mocking way Brad had looked at her as she hesitated before picking up her backpack and climbing into the car.

He'd looked like he could read her mind, could see right through to her reluctance (and, if she was honest with herself, anger), like he was daring her to come anyway.

Allie knew it was stupid, knew it was childish, but she could never back down from a dare.

Besides, she was the reason for this weekend in the first place. If she had decided to stay back at school, she'd never hear the end of it.

They'd all shown up in Brad's car—a BMW, of course, which Allie was sure his parents had bought for him. Cam and Madison had moved off campus that semester, and Cam was supposed to be driving her old Toyota. It was going to be Allie and Cam and Madison, the Three Musketeers back together again, off to a beach cottage that Cam's parents' friends owned and said they could use for the weekend.

Instead, there was Brad, driving his stupid rich boy car and watching her with those eyes that told Allie never to be caught alone with him. Cam and Madison had yelled from the backseat, and Allie had swallowed her annoyance and climbed in, crammed in the middle seat because "you're the smallest and legroom doesn't matter for you."

Cam and Madison had whooped and shouted, slapping a paper "Birthday Girl" crown on her head and dropping a package of Hostess Cupcakes in her lap.

"Let's get this twenty-first-birthday party started!" Cam had shouted, her arm around Allie's shoulders.

Allie had smiled, the way she was supposed to, but she didn't miss the look Brad had given her in the mirror. Something sneaky, something snakey, something that didn't bode well at all for the weekend.

They'd driven away from the campus, and almost immediately Steve had handed a thermos to Madison, shaking it meaningfully.

"A little juice for the party," he'd said.

Madison had immediately opened it and guzzled a bunch, and then passed it to Allie, who didn't want to drink alcohol at ten in the morning, and especially did not want to drink some mystery cocktail prepared by Steve. But everyone had been watching her and waiting, so she'd taken a sip and made herself not wrinkle her nose, because whatever was in there tasted like gasoline. Cam had shouted, "Yeah, girl!" and grabbed the thermos, downing a fair amount herself.

They'd passed the bottle back and forth, Allie taking only small sips, but Cam and Madison hadn't seemed to notice. Despite limiting her intake, Allie had still dropped off to sleep in the backseat, only waking when they had pulled up in front of the cabin.

"Where the hell are we?" she'd asked, sitting up straight. Cam and Madison were out cold on either side of her. Whatever Steve had put in that bottle had packed a punch. "This is not the beach."

"'This is not the beach,'" Brad had said, his voice high and mocking. "I see why your GPA is so high. Nothing gets by you, Brockman."

Cam had stirred beside her, then sat up and looked out the window. "Are we there yet?"

"Well, we're somewhere," Allie had said, trying to draw on her patience. She'd had no idea where Brad had driven them, and since he was the only one in the vicinity with a car, she needed to convince him to stop fucking around and take them to the cottage.

"Is this the woods?" Cam had said. "A cabin in the woods?"

"Just like the movie!" Madison had squealed, jumping out and slamming the door behind her. Steve had followed, chasing her around the clearing in front of the cabin's porch.

"Everyone died in that movie," Allie had muttered. "Like, actually everyone."

"Scared?" Brad had asked.

"No, I just wanted to spend the weekend at the beach with my girlfriends, not at a run-down cabin in the middle of nowhere," Allie had said. A headache was building from the drink Steve had given her, and it made her say more than she intended.

"Are there mosquitoes?" Cam had asked, looking out the window. She hadn't seemed too thrilled either, and Allie remembered that Cam hated camping.

"Nope," Brad had said.

Allie had stared at him. "There are mosquitoes everywhere outside. You can't tell her there are no mosquitoes."

"There's no mosquitoes here," Brad had said, then he'd turned around in the front seat to appeal to Cam. "I guarantee it. Look, it will be awesome. There's a hiking trail that leads to a little waterfall. We can go skinny-dipping."

Allie had sensed Cam softening. "Hey, this isn't what we planned. What about my birthday?"

She'd caught Brad rolling his eyes as he turned back into the front seat. She'd known that Cam saw it, too, because any hesitation Cam had had was suddenly gone. If Brad wanted to spend the weekend at the cabin, they were going to spend the weekend at the cabin.

"We can still have an awesome birthday for you here," Cam had said, patting Allie's shoulder dismissively and climbing out of the car.

She'd left the door open for Allie, who'd stared after Cam in disbelief. Then Allie had pulled her phone out of her pocket.

"What are you doing, birthday girl?" Brad had said.

Allie hated the way he said it, hated the current of mean underneath everything he did. She hated that Cam was going to have her heart broken by this piece of shit when he inevitably did something unforgivable. She just hoped that Cam wouldn't get physically hurt when that happened. There was something in Brad's eyes, something that told Allie he would happily hit a woman if he thought he could get away with it. And more than once there had been signs that Allie didn't like—Brad holding on to Cam's wrist hard enough to bruise, or the time he shoved Cam halfway across a barroom floor because Cam wanted to leave and he didn't. Cam always laughed off these things later, but Allie didn't.

"Calling an Uber," she had said, but the Uber app wouldn't even open. She'd stared at the gray twirling circle that indicated the phone was thinking, or processing, or whatever the fuck it did when it didn't give you what you wanted.

"No Ubers out here," Brad had said, and whistled as he got out of the car. "No Ubers and no mosquitoes."

Allie thought of the look on Brad's face as he got out of the car, the sense she'd had that he *wanted* them to be cut off. She wondered, as she sat across the campfire, trying not to watch the couples grope at each other, where he kept his car keys.

The intervening hours between arrival and campfire had been just as awful as Allie had imagined. She didn't mind camping, or hiking, but almost as soon as they'd thrown their bags in the cabin, Brad had proposed hiking to the waterfall. Allie had tried to beg off, claiming carsickness, but Cam had wheedled until Allie gave in. Allie always gave in.

She knew this was a bad trait, that she ought to assert herself more often, that she was the Jamie Lee Curtis–in–*Halloween*/good-babysitter type, always reliable, always going along with everyone else's plans, never making any of her own. But often she didn't have an alternative, just an objection, and she didn't think it was fair just to be the naysayer all the time. So she went along and hoped that her easygoing nature counted for something.

Allie wasn't certain that it did, but she hoped. She felt sometimes, though, that she was building a callus of resentment underneath, and that one day it would rip open and all the feelings she tucked away would come bleeding out.

She'd said yes to the hike to the waterfall, and the hike itself was pleasant, if weirdly sterile. There were no mosquitoes, as Brad had promised. There were also no chipmunks, or squirrels, or rabbits, or the sound of breaking branches in the distance that usually indicated the passage of deer. There were no chirping birds, no buzzing of bees or gnats or flies.

It was like they'd been dropped into a closed movie set of a forest. The light filtering through the trees was strange, too. It didn't have the warmth of the sun. But Allie couldn't get a good look at the sky through the leaf canopy to figure out exactly what was wrong. She half-wondered if there was smoke haze or something like that making the light seem wrong. If that was the case, she'd smell smoke, even faintly, but she didn't catch a whiff.

They'd arrived at the promised waterfall, where the other four had promptly stripped out of their clothes and jumped in. Allie had zero intention of taking her top off in front of Brad, who'd mocked her mercilessly for only removing her sneakers and socks and dunking her legs in the water. On this point, though, Allie remained firm. She was not going to skinny-dip.

After a while, Cam, clearly feeling a little nip of the green-eyed monster, had asked Brad if he wanted to see Allie naked that badly. Brad had been forced to lavish attention on Cam to make her feel better, and Allie had been forced to close her eyes lest she witness them actually fucking under the waterfall.

When the other four had gotten that out of their system, it was back to the cabin, which had a galley kitchen that had been stocked with food. That, more than anything, told Allie that Brad had planned this maneuver far in advance. This wasn't some spontaneous hijacking of Allie's girls-only birthday weekend.

They'd roasted hot dogs over the campfire, and Brad was careful to point out that he'd bought Beyond sausages for "the non-meat-eaters among us." Allie had been forced to be grateful, which stuck in her craw because she knew Brad hadn't done it to be thoughtful. He'd done it so she would have to thank him.

Allie glanced at her watch—an analog Timex that had belonged to her mother—and wondered how soon was too soon to go to bed. Would it be worth the sneering and the calls that she was lame, that this party weekend was all for her?

"We should do something," Brad said. "Play a game."

*Christ no,* Allie thought. Whatever game Brad wanted to play would not be something she wanted to play. It would be, Allie was certain, something profoundly childish—Spin the Bottle, Truth or Dare, strip poker. Something intended to draw her out in the open and humiliate her. She'd wondered, once upon a time, why Brad seemed to spend so much time trying to bully her, and then she realized that it was because she wasn't impressed by him. Everyone around him acted like he was the sun and they were orbiting satellites, but Allie had always thought he was a jerk from the first time they'd met.

"I brought Uno," Allie said, wishing she could take the words back as soon as she said them.

She hoped, for a desperate moment, to distract from anything Brad might suggest. Cam's eyes lit up at Allie's words. Allie prayed that Cam would chime in that she loved Uno, because Cam *did* love Uno, because Cam and Allie and Madison had whiled away far too many of their study hours freshman year playing round after round. But Cam didn't chime in, at least not before Brad had his say.

"Not some baby shit," he said. "A *real* game."

"By any standard definition, Uno is a real game," Allie said.

"Fine, it's a real game," Brad said. "A boring one."

*Aaaand any hope that we might have a sane, normal evening just went out the window,* Allie thought.

"We should do something creepy," Steve said. "Tell scary stories or something like that."

*Great, another country heard from, as my grandma used to say. It's like Steve received a psychic message from Brad's brain.*

"Yeah, this place is total serial killer central," Madison said. "Like *The Texas Chain Saw Massacre.*"

"That wasn't set in the woods," Allie said automatically. "It was in the middle of nowhere in Texas and there aren't woods like this there."

Cam rolled her eyes. "Sorry, scream queen. I forgot that you got your PhD in horror movies."

"How can you tell the difference, anyway?" Steve said. "All those movies are the same."

"Oh, no," Cam said, holding her hand up. "Don't get Allie started. I don't like that shit, anyway."

"No scary movies for you?" Brad said. "I thought all three of you were roommates once?"

"Yeah, and whenever Allie wanted to watch that shit, I went to bed. Or out to a bar. Or anywhere the crazy guys with knives were not. Besides, those movies are super misogynistic."

*Ah, the dangers of one Feminism 101 class,* Allie thought. Cam was happy to criticize horror movies but just as happy to capitulate to her dumbass boyfriend's every whim, which included conforming to his preferred beauty standard. Allie didn't bother to point out the inconsistency to Cam, though. She'd just ignore Allie anyway.

*Why am I friends with them?* Allie thought. *Is it a habit? A bad habit that I can't break?*

If she'd made other friends, maybe her relationship with Cam and Madison would have just faded away—no harm, no foul, no bitterness on anyone's part. But it wasn't natural for Allie to reach out to people, to join in. She'd made it to her junior year in college without joining any clubs or societies, without participating in study groups. She preferred the company of her own quiet mind. When she got in the mood to be social, Cam and Madison were always there, ready with a six-pack and a plan.

"Leaving aside the misogyny of horror movies," Brad said, emphasizing *misogyny* in a way that made it seem like he didn't believe it existed, "let's play a game."

"Spin the Bottle!" Steve said.

*And there we are,* Allie thought.

"No," Brad said dismissively. "We're in the middle of the woods. We should play something scary."

"I just said I don't like that shit," Cam said, narrowing her eyes at Brad. "I don't like scary movies and I don't like haunted houses where people pop out at you and chase you. I don't want to play something that's going to make me afraid to sleep."

"I'll be right next to you all night," Brad said, giving her an open-mouthed kiss. "And if you're awake, don't worry. I know how to distract you."

He punctuated this statement with a little hip thrust, which made Cam giggle.

"Okay," she said. "I guess if you're with me."

*Disgusting,* Allie thought. She didn't mind the fact of Cam having a boyfriend so much as she minded the way Cam went along with everything Brad wanted, like a little automaton.

*Are you any better?* a little voice in the back of her mind whispered. *Don't you go along with Cam and Madison like a little automaton, doing whatever they want?*

"We should play . . ." Brad paused, obviously for dramatic effect. ". . . Ghosts in the Graveyard."

Steve and Cam looked at him blankly. It was apparent they'd never heard of it. Madison had, because she appeared deeply disappointed by the suggestion. Allie definitely knew what the game was and couldn't stop herself from snorting out a derisive laugh. Brad threw a look of challenge at her.

"Don't think much of my suggestion?"

"You're making fun of Uno, calling it baby shit, when you basically want to play hide-and-seek?"

"It's not hide-and-seek," Brad said.

"It is," Allie said. "Hide-and-seek in reverse. Instead of one person being 'it' and chasing around looking for people hiding, one person pretends to be the ghost and goes to hide. Everyone else looks for the ghost, and if the seekers find that person, they shout 'ghost in the graveyard' and try to reach home base before the ghost tags them. And just like in hide-and-seek, the magical power of tagging transfers the person who's 'it'—or in this case, the ghost—to the one who's touched. That's it. That's the game."

"And you play it in the dark," Brad said, his eyes flashing.

"Yeah, and we played it in my subdivision growing up," Allie said. "It's a tiny kids' game."

"You have a better suggestion?" he said, and Allie heard that undercurrent of nasty in his voice. He hated being questioned, being second-guessed, and Allie was always the one who did it.

"Yeah, Uno," Allie said, her tone all sugar and honey.

*I'm not playing this game no matter what,* she thought. *Because if I do, Brad will find some way to get me alone.*

She didn't know if he'd try to grope her or hurt her or both, but whatever his intention, Allie wasn't stupid enough to go into the dark with him. She'd seen enough horror movies to know better, and also to know that the whole setup for this game was stupidity. This was how people died. They separated, and then they heard a noise and assumed it was one of their friends when actually it was some madman with a mask and a knife.

"I don't know if it's a great idea to run around in the woods when we don't know this area," Madison said slowly. "I mean, somebody could get hurt. Or lost."

"Don't be a chicken," Brad said, making clucking noises. "Nobody's going to get hurt or lost."

"That's not something you can guarantee," Allie said, standing up. She'd had more than enough of Brad for one evening. "If you four want to break your ankles in the woods, go for it. I'm going to bed."

"Wow, lame," Brad said.

"Wow, grow up," Allie said, climbing to the porch.

Maybe under other circumstances she would give in to his taunting, take up his obvious dare, but she was not in the mood, not even a little bit. She kept going over and over that moment when the four of them pulled up in the car and she got in, despite her reluctance, despite her feeling that the weekend was about to go sideways.

Allie opened the cabin door, then pulled off her sneakers and left them on the front porch as the other four watched her in silence. She padded into the main room of the cabin and gently closed the door behind her, careful not to show any pique. There were two windows that faced out to the porch and the campfire pit just beyond, and both windows were open. There were no screens, Allie noted, but then there hadn't been any mosquitoes, either. *Just as Brad promised.*

Allie wondered how that could be, how Brad could have known there would be no bugs of any kind. She'd never been camping anywhere that didn't have mosquitoes, or been to a cabin where there wasn't even one spider nesting in the corner of the ceiling.

She expected the two couples outside to start talking about her as soon as she left, but an unsettled silence seemed to have descended upon them. She wondered if they were doing some silent communication with eye rolls and hand gestures. Then she firmly told herself not to care. She just needed to get through the next two days.

*Or steal Brad's keys.* Allie wondered how pissed the four of them would be if she just motored off with Brad's BMW.

That would be an end-of-the-friendship decision for sure. And Allie would likely end up arrested for grand theft auto. Even if Brad passed up the opportunity to press charges—and she doubted he would—then Daddy wouldn't miss the chance. Allie didn't know Brad's father personally, but she definitely knew the type— Brad squared, or cubed, the final iteration of Rich White Asshole.

The cabin was set up with two bedrooms and one main room. The main room had a sofa and a couple of chairs, all so new that Allie could smell the chemicals off-gassing from the fabric. There was the galley-style kitchen along one wall, the cabinets freshly painted.

She hadn't had time to really take in the cabin earlier— everyone had dropped their stuff and run out to the waterfall, and Allie only had a quick look around the kitchen when it was time to prepare dinner. Now it struck her as weird, the way that everything was obviously new.

*Did Brad have this place built just for this weekend?* Allie shook her head. The idea was ridiculous. Even Brad didn't have the money to waste on such a thing. Maybe a friend of his family had recently bought a new construction and loaned it out to Brad.

*But new constructions like this are usually in bunches. There should be other cabins nearby, and a scenic lake or something to motivate buyers.*

It was a mystery that she probably couldn't solve, so she just decided to let it go.

One of the bedrooms had a king-size bed in it, and the other had a queen next to a bunk. Allie's bag had been tossed on the bunk at some point, and she recognized Madison's pink-flowered luggage standing next to the queen, along with Steve's Adidas duffel.

*Great, I get thrown into a bunk bed like a little kid rooming with Mom and Dad.*

At least she wouldn't have to listen to Brad and Cam going at it all night long. Madison and Steve were usually a little more discreet.

Allie changed into her pajamas quickly, thought about taking her bra off but decided against it. If she woke up in the middle of the night and encountered Brad on the way to the bathroom, she didn't want him to be ogling her unrestrained double-Ds.

Conversation had started up again outside, but in muted tones. Allie guessed that Ghosts in the Graveyard was no longer in the offing now that she'd left the party.

*Tomorrow,* she thought, *I'm going to find a way to hike out of here. I'll just follow the road until it meets up with another road. I don't have to stay and deal with this bullshit.*

With that in mind, she climbed into the bottom bunk, pointedly turned her back to the rest of the room, and tried to sleep. Allie lay awake for a long time, pretending that she wasn't crying, pretending that she was going to have a happy birthday the next day.

# CHAPTER TWO

**allieoop:** you forgot about the hot and stupid shirtless guys who just want to get laid

**ghostwife:** oh yeah, and the one nerdy friend who doesn't have a partner.

**eatersofthedead:** that person is always the first to be killed

**tyz7412:** yeah, people on their own don't survive these movies.

**ALLIE WASN'T SURE WHAT** woke her. She just knew that one minute she'd been asleep and the next her eyes were wide open. Her heart pounded hard in her chest, but she wasn't sure if it was because she'd heard something out of place or if it was just because she'd woken up suddenly. She rolled over and stared into the dark room, looking for shadows that didn't belong.

The curtains were drawn over the one window in the room. The window was between Allie's bunk and the queen-size bed. No light filtered in from outside at all. The window was open. She felt the night breeze blowing in and smelled the lingering scent of the campfire.

Her eyes adjusted to the deep shadow of the room. Madison and Steve had taken their place in the queen-size bed. She could make out one big lump that looked like two bodies pressed together, and she heard Madison's soft snore. She'd roomed with Madison for two years and she knew that sound. That wouldn't be what woke her.

She picked up her phone, which she'd left charging on the nightstand with a portable battery. The screen glowed 3:13 A.M.

*Maybe I just had a nightmare, even if I don't remember it,* she thought, scrubbing her face with her hands. There didn't seem to be anything out of place. Everyone was sleeping, and there were no noises outside, not even the whistle of crickets.

*That's so weird,* she thought again as she turned over and faced the wall. *Even if Brad miraculously found some mosquito-free zone, there should be crickets chirping, and raccoons scurrying, and tree branches snapping as animals pass through the forest. Something's wrong here. Something's very wrong, and I'm not sure what, but I am definitely leaving as soon as the sun comes up.*

Getting up that early wouldn't be a problem. She normally rose with the sun, put in a workout before most of the people in her dorm were stirring, and got first crack at the dorm showers before everyone else made a mess of them. Her body would wake up at 5:30 a.m., even in the dead of winter, when the sun wouldn't start lightening the sky until she was on her way back from the campus gym. She was pretty confident that she could wake up and sneak out before the rest of them realized what had happened.

Allie rolled back to face the wall, closing her eyes. She needed to get a decent night's sleep if she was going to hike out of there in the morning.

Something scraped against the wall of the cabin outside.

Allie opened her eyes and sat up, staring at the window. The curtains fluttered, but she couldn't tell if there was anything outside. She put on her glasses and stared hard.

*It was probably just an animal.*

*(except there are no animals around here which you have observed repeatedly)*

*Then it was a tree brushing against the roof or something. No need to get yourself so worked up.*

She didn't lie back down, though. She peered into the deep shadow of the room, trying to discern any kind of motion outside the window.

She felt her blood pumping in her veins, the pulse throbbing in the side of her head. A little noise like that shouldn't have her so alarmed, but she *was* alarmed. Everything had felt off since she'd climbed into the car for this trip, and now something was wrong. She knew, with deep certainty, that the noise outside the cabin was not benign.

*But I am not going to get up and look, because that's how idiots die in horror movies. They investigate a strange noise alone, or they say dumb shit like, "You go look that way and I'll go this way." There's no reason for me to invite harm upon myself. I'm just going to stay right here in bed, where I belong.*

A scrape sounded again, a long thin *skrrrrritch* that bore an uncanny resemblance to the sound of a knife being dragged across the wooden logs that made up the cabin's exterior.

*You've got to be kidding me,* Allie thought. Then: *It's nothing scary at all. It's just Brad being an asshole.*

This idea calmed her. Of course it was only Brad being a dick. He was annoyed that she hadn't wanted to play his stupid games earlier, and now he was trying to fuck with her, freak her out for no particular reason. Well, Allie would not allow herself to be fucked with. She was not going to engage.

Someone knocked on the wall of the cabin three times, then paused.

Madison snorted, took in a great gasp of air, and then muttered, "What?"

Allie just made out the shifting of shadow as Madison sat up.

Someone knocked again, three times.

*Because three is a magical number,* Allie thought, and shivered. *Three wishes from the djinn, three witches around the cauldron, three cries in the night to seal your fate.*

"What the fuck?" Madison said. "Steve, wake up."

Allie heard rustling, saw the larger shape that was Steve rise up.

"What's going on?" he said, his voice thick with sleep.

"There's someone outside," Madison said.

"What?"

"There's someone outside, fucking with us," Madison said. "They're knocking on the cabin wall."

"It's probably just Brad or Cam. Or both," Steve said. "Just go back to sleep."

He lay back down.

The knock sounded three times once more, spaced with a breath between each.

"Okay, I guess that's pretty annoying," Steve said. He threw the covers back and stalked toward the window.

"Wait," Allie said.

Steve paused in the middle of the room, his head turned toward the bunks. Allie could just make out the gleam of his eyes and the white tee shirt he slept in.

"Allie?" he said, like he'd forgotten she was in the room with them.

*He probably did forget, because he only cares about my existence if someone points it out to him.*

"Yes, Allie," she said. "Who did you think it was?"

"How long have you been awake?" he asked.

"Not sure why that's relevant, but long enough to have heard those knocks sound three times already," Allie said. She realized she sounded bitchy, but she didn't care. Sometimes it was exhausting to be polite to someone you really didn't like in the first place.

"So why do you want me to wait?" Steve said.

"Because if it is Brad or Cam, they just want attention, and you're going to give it to them by shouting out the window. And if it isn't . . ." She trailed off, not sure if she wanted to follow that line of inquiry.

"And if it isn't?" Madison said, her voice squeaky with alarm.

"Well, then it's obviously someone who means us harm," Allie said. "So I don't think you should stick your head out the window."

Steve was silent for a moment, clearly considering the wisdom of what Allie had said. Allie sensed the deep well of idiotic masculinity inside him warring with common sense. He wanted to prove he was bigger and tougher than whatever—or whoever—was outside, but he also realized that maybe Allie was right.

Idiotic masculinity won, as Allie expected it would.

"I'll go outside and check it out," he said.

"That's even dumber," Allie said. "Are you *trying* to make yourself a target?"

The scraping sound renewed, a long draw across the cabin wall. It seemed to Allie that the sound was getting closer to the window. It also occurred to her that the bedroom window was open, and if the bedroom window was open, then whoever was outside could hear everything they said.

He—and Allie felt sure it was a "he," that it wasn't Cam messing around out there—could also climb in the window, if he felt so inclined. The bottom sill was only about knee height for an average-sized person.

"Okay, that's enough," Steve said, opening the bedroom door and heading out into the main room. Madison scampered after him.

"For chrissakes," Allie said, climbing out of bed. She didn't like Steve, and sometimes she didn't like Madison very much either, but she didn't want them to get mutilated.

But she'd underestimated Steve. Instead of going straight to the front door, he went to Brad and Cam's bedroom and pounded on the door with his fist, flipping on the main room light as he went.

"Hey, are you two in there?" he said.

Madison had paused in the doorway, and Allie stood next to the bunk, watching the window and listening hard. If Brad *was* outside, she expected to hear the scrape of his shoes as he climbed back into the room next door. It would be easy for him to pretend he'd been in bed the whole time, especially since all the cabin windows were open to let in the night air.

*And there are no screens to slow him—or anyone else—down.*

Allie didn't hear anything from outside or any telltale bumps from next door, either. A second later, the other bedroom door creaked open and Brad said, "What the hell, man?"

His voice sounded sleepy, like he'd just woken up.

*That doesn't mean anything. It's easy to fake sleepiness. Brad could still have been outside this whole time. Just because you didn't hear him climb back in—*

Allie's thought stopped cold. Her breath caught in her throat.

Someone outside passed by the window, moving toward the front of the cabin.

"There's someone out there," she whispered.

"What?" Madison said, turning back toward Allie.

"I saw someone outside," Allie said, coming to the doorway to stand beside Madison. The overhead light seemed especially bright after the deep darkness of the bedroom. "They're going toward the front."

"Allie said she saw somebody," Madison said in a loud whisper in Steve's direction.

"Oh, well, if Allie says she saw somebody," Brad said, in that sneering tone that made Allie want to leap down the hall and smack him.

She didn't have to, though, because Steve unexpectedly came to her defense.

"There's someone out there for sure," he said. "They were banging and scraping on the cabin wall. Didn't you hear it?"

"No, man, my girl wore me out," Brad said.

Allie rolled her eyes. *Why do guys always, always, always have to brag about getting laid?*

"I'm going to check it out," Steve said.

"Don't," Allie said. "You don't know who's out there, or what their intentions are."

"This isn't one of your stupid movies, Allison," Brad said. "Me and Steve can handle whatever's out there."

Brad pushed out the door past Steve, and Allie noticed that he was only wearing boxer briefs.

"You might want to put on some pants," Allie said.

"Why? See something you like? Am I too much for you?"

"Gimme a fucking break," Allie said. She tried to communicate with her eyes that she wouldn't touch him if Brad were the last man on earth. He must have gotten the message, because an angry flush appeared just below his jaw.

"Brad, what's going on?" Cam said, her voice a plaintive wail coming from the next room. Allie knew Cam was a heavy sleeper, so it would take a lot of fuss and noise for her to wake.

"Nothing to worry about. Go back to sleep, baby," Brad said as he ducked back into their bedroom.

Allie heard the rustle of clothing as Brad dressed. It was so quiet that every noise was magnified. There was no distant, reassuring hum of highway traffic or the sound of other people. And as she'd already noted, there were no sounds from animals in the woods. It was like they were inside a noiseless bubble, sealed off from the outside world.

"Where are you going?" Cam asked.

"Just outside for a sec to check something out," Brad said.

"What for?"

"Because your *friend*"—Allie heard the derisive tone in "friend"—"thinks she saw someone outside."

"Hey, it's not just Allie," Madison said, indignant. "We heard the noises, too."

"You all probably just had a nightmare," Brad said from inside the room.

"That's impossible," Madison said. "You think all three of us imagined the same knocking and scraping?"

"Can't everyone just go back to bed?" Cam said, moaning. "I'm so tired."

At this point Allie, too, just wanted to go back to bed. She didn't know if the shadow she'd seen was real or not, but she strongly suspected that the noises had been caused—or arranged—by Brad somehow. Maybe Brad had a friend lurking around in the woods. Or maybe there was actually another cabin nearby, despite the seeming isolation, and Brad's coconspirator was staying there.

It would explain why Brad had wanted to play Ghosts in the Graveyard, to draw them out into the forest at night. He'd likely planned it as a practical joke. It also explained why he was so eager to head outside. He knew there was no real danger.

*Which means that the noises are all a part of that joke, so we should all just stop giving oxygen to his ridiculous ploy.*

"Yeah, maybe we should just forget it," Allie said. "Whatever caused the noise, it's gone now."

"No way," Steve said. "If there's someone out there, I'm not going to wait for them to fuck with us again."

Brad emerged from the bedroom in a gray sweatshirt and jeans. Steve already wore pajama pants and a tee shirt—a concession that Allie assumed was for her benefit, since she slept in the same room as him. It made her think more kindly of him, even if he was dumb as a post.

The two boys—*men,* Allie reminded herself, *they are technically men*—strode toward the front door.

"Wait," Madison said, hovering uncertainly in the bedroom door. "Shouldn't you take a kitchen knife or something?"

"Who do you think is out there, Michael Myers?" Brad said, laughing. "I'm not going to have a knife fight. It's probably just some jerk who wandered in this direction and decided to have a laugh. If there's anyone at all."

"Just get back in bed, Mad," Allie said, putting her hand on her friend's shoulder. Madison was trembling. The noises seemed to have really scared her. "Brad's right, it's probably nothing."

Allie had half-convinced herself that this was nothing but a prank. She'd only gotten worked up because it was so dark and silent, because she'd been asleep and had woken so suddenly. There was really nothing to worry about.

The ringing crash of shattering glass made her freeze.

"What the—?" Brad said, yanking open the front door. He flipped on the porch light, and swore. "My car! What the fuck happened to my car?"

He rushed outside, Steve following.

"No, Steve! Stay here!" Madison said, running to the doorway after them.

"No," Allie said, but not because she was worried about Steve or Brad. She was worried about Madison rushing outside, following the Two Very Manly Musketeers into who knows what peril.

She hurried after Madison, grabbing her friend's wrist before she went out the door. "Wait."

"But—" Madison said.

Whatever else Madison was going to say was drowned in a

flurry of inventive curses. Allie peeked out the doorway and saw Brad and Steve circling Brad's car.

"Goddamned motherfucking piece of shit!" Brad shouted into the night. "If you come near here again, I will beat the ever-loving shit out of you!"

The BMW's front windshield was shattered. That was bad enough, but Allie saw that the two tires facing the cabin were punctured. She suspected, from the angle of the car, that the other two tires had suffered the same fate.

"How are we supposed to get out of here?" Steve asked. "I mean, are we supposed to walk or hitchhike or what?"

"How the fuck do I know?" Brad said. "This is *bullshit*. Total *bullshit*."

Brad *seemed* like he was shocked and angry. So maybe this wasn't part of some big plan he'd cooked up. Or maybe it was, and he was just a really good performer. Allie would reserve judgment. She didn't trust Brad at all. The damaged car could have been arranged in advance, and after a weekend of messing with them, his butler or whoever would show up with the family's personal helicopter.

*Besides, you were going to hike out in the morning anyway. Now you don't have to sneak off while they're all asleep.*

*Although*, Allie reflected, *it would be a hell of a lot easier alone.*

Allie knew Cam's bitching would be legendary if they had to hike. Cam hated walking any distance longer than from the passenger seat to the door of a restaurant, and putting up with her complaints would make any long hike irritating beyond belief.

Still, Allie hoped that this event—though potentially staged— would end the farce of a weekend once and for all. And when it was over and she was safely back on campus, Allie was going to tell Cam and Madison flat out that she didn't want their boyfriends hijacking their plans anymore. If Brad and Steve showed up, then Allie was out.

Her chest felt heavy at the thought. There was nothing less comfortable than confronting those who were supposed to be your closest friends. It was, Allie reflected, so much easier to pretend everything was fine, to not join in with the excuse that she was so busy, had so many tests, had a lot of reading to get done. So many relationships in her life had fallen by the wayside in this easy, uncomplicated way—lack of proximity, schedules that wouldn't mesh. Sometimes she thought about those people, wished she'd made more of an effort with some of them. And sometimes she was glad that an argument hadn't been necessary, that everyone just quietly understood their lives were moving in a different direction.

"That's it," Brad said, jolting Allie back to the present moment. "I'm going to find out who did this."

"Yeah, me, too," Steve said. "When we find him, we can beat the shit out of him."

"Great," Allie said. "Will that magically bring the car back? Or will you both just end up arrested on assault charges, assuming you can actually track down this individual in the dark?"

"Yeah, don't go tramping off into the woods," Madison said, and her voice trembled. "It's dangerous, and you don't know where you're going, and anyway, whoever would do this to the car might hurt you."

"Aw, babe," Steve said, and climbed the porch steps to put his arms around her. "Don't worry. Whatever kind of asshole would pull a stunt like this is just some pathetic nothing. Me and Brad can take down someone like that easy."

"But you can still get hurt in the woods," Madison said, her voice muffled in Steve's chest. "You could fall into a ravine and break your leg. And you don't know anything about tracking."

Brad joined them on the steps, his lip curling at the sight of Steve comforting Madison. Allie liked him less and less every minute. Steve, she supposed, wasn't so bad. But he was a package deal with Brad, and Allie kind of hoped Brad *would* go tramping off into the woods alone and fall into a ravine.

"You don't think we can find this piece of shit?" Brad asked, his gaze on Allie.

"No, I don't," she said. *No point in lying about it.* "It's pitch-dark. You have no idea where he came from or what direction he went in. You don't know if it was a prank of opportunity or if someone came here deliberately to cause harm. If it's the latter, then you don't know what intentions they might have for us, and if you go bungling through the woods, you might end up seriously hurt."

She didn't say "killed," though she thought it. It just sounded too melodramatic to say out loud.

"'If it's the latter,'" Brad said in a mocking tone. "You don't need to impress us with your big brain every second of the day, Allison."

"You don't need to let us all know you're illiterate every second of the day, Bradley," she said in the same tone.

Allie saw something flash behind his eyes, that deep well of mean that he kept hidden from everyone else. *Except when he's telling Cam where to go and what to do and how to do it. Except when he's demanding she change her outfit or insisting she change her plans. Maybe he doesn't hide his mean. Maybe I'm the only one who notices.*

There was a noise behind her, and Allie turned around in time to see Cam, wearing only Brad's tee shirt, stumble out of the bedroom. Her hair, normally blowout smooth, stuck up in the back. She rounded the long couch that had its back to the bedroom doorways and stopped in front of it, as if the effort of going just that far had exhausted her.

"*What* is going *on*?" she said, flopping on the couch with a melodramatic huff. "Why are you all out here screaming and arguing?"

"We're not screaming," Allie said.

"You definitely are. You're all making a fuss and keeping me awake. Brad, come back to bed." Cam tilted her head back and closed her eyes.

Allie saw him hesitate. If he did what Cam wanted, then he'd be giving up his moronic revenge plot. She saw the quick calculation in his eyes, the requirement that staying behind be *his* idea, not Cam's. Allie wondered how he'd manage this.

"Can't, babe," he said. "Steve and me have to track down the fucker who wrecked the BMW."

Cam opened her eyes. "What? Someone wrecked your car?"

She stood, crossed the room, and pushed out the doorway past Allie to stand on the porch with the other three. "What the *actual fuck*?"

"Yeah, exactly," Brad said.

"But how are we supposed to get out of here?" Cam wailed. "My phone doesn't work, and neither does anyone else's! It's not like we can call a cab or an Uber."

"Need some of Matheson's new tech," Brad said. "The phones that directly receive a signal from a satellite instead of a cell tower."

"That service is still in the experimental stage," Allie said. "And Matheson is a dick; I'm not buying anything from him."

Brad opened his mouth to respond, but as he did, Cam said, "We know, Allie. You hate tech bros. That doesn't change the fact that our phones don't work right now."

"I just think we shouldn't tell rich white men that they are visionaries when all they do is piggyback on other people's accomplishments."

"Anyway," Cam said, a note of impatience in her voice. "What are we going to do?"

"We'll have to walk to the highway," Allie said.

"*You* can walk to the highway," Cam said. "I'll stay here and wait for rescue."

"By yourself?" Allie asked. "With some weirdo running around in the woods?"

Cam hesitated. "Maybe the guys should go and we should stay here."

"Not very feminist of you, Cam," Brad said. "What was all that stuff about equality that you were telling me last week?"

"This has nothing to do with being a woman," Cam said primly. "I just don't like long walks."

"And what, you three will sit here on your asses drinking wine while me and Steve flag down some local hillbilly to come and fetch you?"

"Don't be a jerk," Cam said. "The rest of us don't even know where we are. We were all passed out while you were driving. And this stupid cabin was your stupid idea."

"Yeah, well, you went along with that stupid idea," Brad said.

Allie saw that flash of mean in his eyes directed right at Cam, and her heart did a little panic-flutter in her chest. She had to get Cam away from this guy. He was going to hit Cam one day, one day after many weeks of convincing her that he was a nice guy who sometimes lost his temper, and it wasn't him, it was her, and if she could just be a little more careful then maybe he wouldn't get so angry. Even though Cam would be hurt, and crying, she'd convince herself that it was her fault, that she just needed to be a little more careful like he said, and anyway it would never happen again.

Until it did.

"Oh my god," Cam said, throwing her hands up in the air. "Fine. I agreed to come to this stupid cabin. Now let's all agree that we need to get the hell out of here, preferably in a car."

Allie stared at Cam. "You agreed to come to the cabin? You changed the plans without telling me?"

Cam's eyes darted away from Allie. "I mean, just this morning or whatever."

"Uh-huh," Allie said.

"Like right before we got in the car," Cam said. "Brad said he had this great place to go to that was way better than the beach house."

"Uh-huh," Allie said. "So all my birthday weekend plans, they just went out the window because *Brad* had this great idea to take us to the middle of nowhere, and you went along with it? And then you pretended to be surprised when we got here?"

"It wasn't like that," Cam said.

Everyone was staring at Cam now. Madison's brows were drawn together.

"You knew we were coming here?" Madison asked.

"Oh, not you, too," Cam said. "I wasn't the one who knew about this place, who drove the car. It's not *my* fault. I just—"

"Went along with Brad," Allie said. "Because that's somehow better? You were just his passive little yes-woman?"

"Wait, so that means everyone knew about this cabin except you and me?" Madison said, pointing first to Allie and then herself. Then she punched Steve in the shoulder. "Because I know that you go along with whatever this one says."

Steve frowned. "Hey, don't drag me into your little girl fight."

"It's not a *girl fight*," Allie said. "I am angry—and I think rightfully so—that Cam lied to me and to Madison."

"You're not angry that I lied to you?" Brad said, watching her closely.

"Brad, I know you think you're the sun around which all things revolve, but I really could not give a shit about you in any way," Allie said.

"Hey, don't be a bitch to my boyfriend," Cam said.

"You're the one in the wrong here, Cam. Don't try to turn this around. I expect nothing from him, but I expect better from you."

"Oh, fuck you, Allie, and your self-righteous bullshit," Cam said. "You think I can't see the way you look at me? The way you look at us? You think you're better than me and Brad, better than Madison and Steve—always studying, always working, always stiff as a board and twice as virginal. I'm not even sure why I bother to keep trying to be friends with you."

"Good question," Allie said. Of course Cam's words stung, of course they did, but it was better to know, it was better to have everything out in the open. Then they wouldn't have to pretend anymore.

"Hey, guys," Madison said tentatively. "Listen, you don't want to do this. You don't want to say things you'll be sorry for tomorrow."

"I don't think Cam *will* be sorry," Allie said, her voice steady.

"No, I won't be," Cam said, practically spitting the words at Allie. "I thought I was doing you a favor, trying to get you loosened up for one goddamned weekend, and you're pissed that it wasn't exactly the way OCD Allie planned it."

"Like I said, you're not turning this around. I'm not the one in the wrong here."

"Oh, *no*, Allie, you're never in the wrong," Cam said, pushing past Allie and Madison again in a huff. "Saint Allie, patron saint of perfect girls."

Cam stormed across the main room of the cabin to the bedroom, her blonde hair swinging in time with her angry strides. She clearly thought she'd won the night with the perfect mic drop line.

She swept into the bedroom that she shared with Brad.

And then she screamed.

# CHAPTER THREE

**allieoop:** Not only do people on their own not survive these movies, but people are always doing THE EXACT THING THEY SHOULD NOT DO.

**eatersofthedead:** They split up. "I'm just going to check out this strange noise; you stay here." The next time the other characters see them, all their insides are on the outside, as the saying goes.

**finalgirl:** Hard rule for survival—everyone stays together. Either you all go or no one does.

**allieoop:** Exactly, the killer can't pick off a packed group one by one.

**tyz7412:** Well, some killers can.

THERE WAS A SCREAM, and then a gurgle, and then a thump that sounded very much like a body hitting the floor.

"Cam?" Madison said, her voice a tiny tremble. "Cam?"

Brad muscled his way into the cabin. His face said "panic" but he still managed to "accidentally" brush his body against Allie's. *What a piece of shit,* Allie thought, and then reached out and grabbed his wrist before he went any farther. She didn't like touching him, not even for a few seconds, because he made her skin crawl. But if there was someone in the bedroom who'd just hurt Cam—and Allie thought that was a more-than-fair assumption—then it wouldn't help if Brad rushed in there and got hurt, too.

"What?" Brad said impatiently, trying to shake off Allie's hand, but she just gripped tighter.

"Don't rush in there alone," Allie said. "We should all stay together."

"Who the hell do you think is in there, Freddy Krueger?"

"Maybe," Allie said. "Or maybe just the jerk who wrecked your car and banged on the cabin wall. Maybe he's waiting for us to rush in there one by one. So let's not do that."

"Whatever," Brad said, shaking his arm again, and this time Allie let him go.

"She's right, man," Steve said, following after Brad. "Don't go in there alone."

Allie had never before realized that Steve wasn't completely stupid. This weekend was showing a new side of him.

Brad continued toward the bedroom, but much slower than Allie had anticipated. Maybe her words of caution had broken through the testosterone fence around his brain. Madison, of course, trailed after Steve like a puppy on a leash, so Allie brought up the rear—after carefully closing the front door. No need to invite anyone else inside.

*And I'm closing all the windows, too. That's how the guy—or maybe it's a girl?—got in here in the first place. Of course, we're assuming that someone attacked Cam. Maybe she just knocked herself out by tripping over the furniture or shoes on the floor.*

*Maybe,* Allie thought, but deep down she didn't believe it.

Brad crept slowly to the bedroom door, and the rest of them followed behind. He paused just outside the room, then jumped into the doorway and flipped on the light inside the bedroom, yelling "Ahhhhhh!" as he did.

Madison leapt into the air and onto Steve's back at Brad's cry. Steve made an *oof* noise and tried to grab her flailing legs. Madison wrapped her arms around Steve's shoulders and yelled, "Is she dead? Oh my god, is she dead?"

Brad seemed frozen in the doorway. At Madison's words, he dropped his raised arms and hurried into the room. Allie pushed past Steve and Madison and followed Brad.

He knelt beside Cam, who was crumpled on the floor. His

hand was pressed to the pulse on her neck, but Allie didn't need to know what he found there. She already saw Cam's back rising and falling, gently.

"She's alive," Allie said.

"Oh, thank god," Madison said, and started crying. "Thank god, thank god. I thought somebody murdered her."

Brad shook Cam's shoulder.

"Hey, don't do that," Allie said. "You don't know what happened to her. Let's try to turn her over, gently."

Allie didn't see any obvious injury on Cam's back, and there was no telltale pool of blood beneath Cam's body, so she helped Brad turn Cam to lay on her back.

At first, it didn't seem like there was an obvious injury, but then Allie noticed a faint red mark on Cam's throat.

"Look," she said. "Someone hit her."

Allie scanned the room. There was dirt and a few leaves on the hardwood floor, tracking roughly from where Cam had fallen to the open window. She stood abruptly.

"Shut the windows," she said. "Shut all of the windows, now. And turn on all the lights in every room."

"Why?" Steve said.

Allie pointed at the dirt and leaves. "Someone climbed in there, and waited in this room, and attacked Cam. And that someone could easily be waiting outside right now for us to settle down and go back to sleep so they can return. So shut the windows."

"Right," Steve said, and backed away from the doorway. Allie heard him saying, "Baby, I gotta put you down. I have to shut the windows."

Allie went straight to the bedroom window and lowered it. That's when she noticed the other strange thing about this cabin. "No locks?"

"What do you mean?" Brad said. While Allie shut the window,

he'd lifted Cam from the floor and put her in bed, pulling a sheet up to Cam's neck.

"Just what I said." Allie pointed at the window. "No locks. Are they all like this?"

Brad had gone around opening all the windows when they'd first arrived, claiming that the cabin needed to be aired out.

He joined her by the window, his eyes following where she pointed. "I dunno. I guess I didn't notice."

"You opened all the windows. How could you not notice?"

He shrugged in that careless way that always infuriated Allie. "I just didn't."

"No locks and no screens. There might as well be no windows at all."

"Hey, did you know there's no locks on these windows?" Steve called from the main room.

"You stay here with Cam," Allie said.

"Why?" Brad said. "She's fine, and the window's closed now."

"She might have a concussion or something," Allie said. She didn't want Brad to be near her anymore. He smelled like sour alcohol and sex and the remnants of yesterday's deodorant, and she was tired of the way he took every opportunity to stand too close to her chest.

"She got hit in the neck, not the head," Brad said.

"But she's unconscious. She didn't make a noise when you moved her. I'm worried that something is seriously wrong."

"She probably just needs to sleep it off."

"Do you not give a shit *at all* that your girlfriend was attacked by an unknown assailant?" Allie said. She felt like her fury was a ball of pressure behind her eyes, swelling to the point of explosion. "I saw you express more anger that your car got wrecked."

"Of course I care," Brad said.

"You could care less, you mean," Allie said. She started toward the door again but he stepped in front of her, blocking her way. She tried to step around him and he mirrored her movement. "Back off."

"What is your problem with me, Allison? You're always giving me shit," Brad said.

"*Back off*, I said. Get out of my way right now."

"No, I want you to answer my question," Brad said, and he reached for her.

Allie didn't know what Brad intended to do. She didn't know if he was going to grab her arm, or touch her face, or what. All she knew was that she had told him to back off, twice, and now his hands—which she most definitely did not wish to be on her person—were heading in her direction.

She kneed him in the balls. Hard.

"What the *ffffffff*—" he said, his face reddening. He staggered backward and Allie stepped around him, hurrying out of the room.

"I told you to back off," she said as she stepped into the main room.

Madison was on the couch. She turned as Allie emerged, and Allie saw that her face was pale and wet with tears.

"Allie, what are we going to do? What are we going to do? There's some psycho out there who wants to hurt us and the windows don't even lock and *neither does the door.*"

Steve was going around the room, placing chairs in front of the windows. He looked slightly embarrassed as he said to Allie, "It was the best idea I could come up with."

"And it was a pretty good one," Allie said, because at least Steve was *trying.* Steve seemed to grasp that there was some danger, that they should attempt to protect themselves. Then she realized the last thing Madison had said.

"There's no lock on the front door, either?" Allie said. She couldn't keep the disbelief out of her voice. *Who owns this cabin? Do they trust that no one will break into a building with no locks on the doors and windows? Just how far from civilization is this place?*

Allie helped Steve push the dining room table against the front door. She wished that they had more to use—wood to barricade the windows, or at least some kind of object that they could wedge in to keep the bottom sash of each window from opening. She started rummaging through the kitchen cabinets. Steve went to sit next to Madison, who appeared to be in the throes of a full meltdown.

"This is crazy," she said, her voice a sobbing croak. "Crazy. We're literally trapped in the middle of nowhere and someone is outside fucking with us, someone who wants to hurt us, and Brad brought us to this goddamned cabin where there are no locks and no way to keep ourselves safe."

"I'll keep you safe," Steve said, and Allie had to give him credit—he did sound sincere.

She turned from her cabinet-rummaging in time to see Madison smack him on the shoulder.

"How are you going to do that? Are you going to be a big man and take down some psycho killer all by yourself and then die right in front of me? Do you think I want to see that?"

"Well, no, I don't . . ." Steve began, then trailed off as Madison threw herself against his chest and cried even harder. Steve gave Allie a helpless look.

She sighed, very softly. In Allie's opinion, Steve ought to be able to comfort his girlfriend when she was upset. This seemed like the least a boyfriend could do. But Madison was clearly working herself up into full-blown hysteria.

*Hysteria,* Allie thought. *A word that was originally meant to describe the "disease" of women who were, by the definition of supposedly learned men, shallow and volatile and attention-seeking. But I don't think Madison is looking for attention right now. I think she's scared to death.*

*(And I am too)*

That last thought was like a little voice in the dark, a little voice that Allie didn't want to hear, so she pushed it down, deep down, where she didn't have to listen. There were many more important things to deal with at the moment besides her fear. Fear was not a productive emotion. They had to keep vigilant, make sure they were safe in the cabin overnight. They could do it, if all of them helped keep watch. Unfortunately, Cam was out cold and Madison was not in any shape to help. That left Allie and Steve (who had, at least, demonstrated the ability to follow directions) and Brad, who Allie was absolutely certain would *not* follow directions and might actively hinder any work for the greater good.

*Especially if I'm the one directing that work. He's not exactly receptive to the thoughts of women, unless they revolve around him.*

Allie sat down on the other side of Madison and took her friend's hand. Madison lifted her head from Steve's chest and stared at Allie, her eyes huge and streaming with tears.

"It's going to be okay," Allie said, and she felt the inadequacy of the words.

There was no guarantee at all that everything would be okay on any given day, much less in a potentially dangerous situation like the one in which they were caught. "It's going to be okay" was just something people said to walk their friends back from the cliff, to pretend the screaming edge of the world wasn't right there in front of them, waiting to swallow them whole.

And yet, she found herself saying those words again as Madison gripped her hand tight and Madison's eyes searched hers, looking for the truth. "It's going to be okay. We just need to calm down and work together. We'll get through this."

"Do you really think so?" Madison said, wiping her face. "I'm sorry I freaked out. I just can't stand the idea of someone coming into the cabin, hurting us for no reason."

"I don't know if whoever is doing this really wants to hurt us," Allie said, even though that was a lie. She was pretty certain whoever was outside, whoever had climbed through the window, *did* want to hurt them. "It might just be some jackass pulling a prank, trying to see how freaked out we can get."

"I don't know about that," Steve said. "Whoever smashed up Brad's car has got some major issues. That didn't seem like a prank to me."

Allie widened her eyes meaningfully at Steve as Madison turned back to him, and he seemed to realize then what he'd said and what kind of effect it had on Madison.

"But Allie's probably right," he said hastily. "It's just a prank that's gotten out of control."

"Maybe," Madison said, but it didn't seem like she believed it. She turned back to Allie. "You don't think it's like that movie with the freaky people with the masks? You know, that one you like?"

Allie liked an astonishing number of movies that featured freaky people with masks, but she thought she knew where Madison was heading.

"*The Strangers?*" Allie asked.

"Yeah, I think that was it! The couple is in the vacation house or whatever, and these three people show up in masks and spend all night fucking with them, and then at the end they stab the couple for no reason at all. That's like what's happening to us."

"Nah," Allie said. "It's not like that. This isn't a movie. People don't do those things in real life."

"I don't know," Steve said. "The Mansons and all that."

Allie let go of Madison's hand. "Steve, you're not exactly helping here."

"You're right," he said, holding up his arms in the air in surrender. "You're right, I'm sorry. I have a big dumb mouth and dumb things come out of it when I'm nervous."

"You're nervous?" Madison said.

"Sure," Steve said. "I mean, whatever is happening—it's not normal. Allie's probably right and whoever is out there is just some stupid kid getting high off watching us freak out. I don't think we're *really* in any danger or anything. But this is definitely not the way I thought the weekend would go, that's for sure."

"Aw," Madison said, and hugged him. She seemed calmer now that she knew Steve was nervous, which didn't make any sense to Allie, but if it meant Madison would stop screaming and crying, then it was all to the good.

"All right," Allie said. "We're agreed that there's no real need to freak out, but let's be cautious. We should all stay in this room the rest of the night. We can shut the bedroom doors and block them with furniture. If anyone tries to climb in the windows here in the main room, we'll know, and we'll all be together. Safety in numbers, right?"

Madison nodded. "I knew that you would know what to do. You're the smartest person I know, Allie."

Allie flushed, especially since she'd had some unkind thoughts about Madison earlier in the evening. "I'm not smart. I've just watched a lot of horror movies and I know what people definitely should *not* do."

"Don't investigate strange noises," Steve said.

"Don't go outside alone," Madison said.

"See, you guys would know what to do even without me here," Allie said lightly. "Should we take turns keeping watch? Does anyone even feel like sleeping?"

"I couldn't sleep if my life depended on it," Madison said.

"I mean, I could," Steve said. "But I don't think I should sleep right now."

"It's only a couple of hours until dawn," Allie said. "Once the

sun is up, we can all hike toward the road, try to flag down someone who can help us."

"Cam is not going to want to hike," Madison said. "You know
how she is about walking."

"She's not going to have a choice if she wants to get out of
here," Allie said, although privately she was worried about Cam's
injury. Cam might not be physically able to walk in a couple of
hours. "Speaking of Cam, I'm going to check on her and move her
and Brad out to this room. You two shut up the other room and
the bathroom door, and double-check that all the windows are as
secure as you can make them."

Steve and Madison got up to do as Allie instructed, and Allie
went to Brad and Cam's bedroom. She was a little surprised that
Brad hadn't charged out of the room already, spoiling for a fight
with Allie because she'd kicked him in the balls. It wasn't like Brad
to brood silently where no one could see him.

*Maybe he passed out from the pain,* Allie thought. If so, she was not
sorry at all.

She hesitated just for a second before entering the bedroom.

*So that's why Brad didn't come out right away,* she thought.

Brad was gone.

Allie started for the window, to check outside for him, and
then stopped. He could be waiting to grab her. Or the person
who'd banged on the cabin wall could be waiting for her. That
person could have taken Brad—although Allie was sure that there
would have been more noise, some kind of struggle if that was the
case. She didn't see any evidence of a struggle. There was nothing
disarranged, no telltale dirt on the floor or meaningful spray of
blood on the wall. The curtains blew in the breeze from outside,
showing that the window was open. It was as if Brad had just silently stepped over the window ledge and out into the night.

*That's probably what he did do. He went outside to be a hero and left his girlfriend here alone,* Allie thought furiously, checking to see if Cam was okay. Her friend felt cool to the touch, and her breathing was deep and slow. But she didn't respond at all when Allie shook her shoulder.

Allie heard Madison and Steve closing the other interior doors and walking around the main room of the cabin, checking the windows.

"Steve!" she called. "Can you come and help me for a second?"

Both Steve and Madison came to the door, as Allie had expected. She didn't think Madison wanted to be alone for even half a second.

*That's good, though. She'll be safer with other people. We all will be.*

"What's up?" Steve asked, looking around the room. "Where's Brad?"

"Who the fuck knows," Allie said. "I need you to help me get Cam into the main room. Can you carry her?"

"Sure," Steve said, but he hesitated. "But shouldn't we look for Brad? What if something bad happened to him?"

"I suspect," Allie said, trying hard not to sound impatient, "that he went outside looking for the person who wrecked his car, and he didn't say anything about it because he knew we would object. It doesn't make sense for us to follow him—it's still dark out, and we don't know which way he was headed."

"But what if he gets hurt?" Madison asked. "I know you think he's a jerk, Allie, but you can't want that."

*Guess I was never that good at hiding my contempt. Everyone's onto me regarding Brad,* Allie thought, and then said, "Of course I don't want him to be hurt. I don't want anybody to be hurt. But remember how we were joking about horror movies earlier? You know how people get picked off in horror movies? They go off to do tasks one by one. I can tell by the look on Steve's face that he's thinking about going out looking for Brad."

Steve flushed guiltily. "I was just going to take a quick walk around the cabin."

"Right," Allie said. "And the three of us wait in here, and then you don't come back, and then what? None of us know where we are except you and Brad, and you're the only ones who can get us out of here."

"I don't know how to get out of here," Steve said, looking slightly alarmed at the prospect that he might be expected to provide directions.

"What?" Allie and Madison said together.

"Yeah, I have no idea. I passed out in the car. I always sleep on long car rides."

"Great," Allie said. "Just great. Brad brings us to the middle of nowhere, none of us knows where we are except him, and now he's disappeared into the night. Steve, you are not going outside to look for him. We can hunt around for him when it's light out. Assuming he doesn't get beaten up by our creepy stalker or break his ankle on a tree root, he'll probably come stumbling back here sometime soon."

"But what if he doesn't?" Madison said. "What if this isn't a joke and Brad gets killed by some psycho?"

Allie saw the light of panic rekindling in Madison's eyes. "I don't think that's going to happen. Movies are fun and all, but that kind of stuff doesn't usually happen in real life. Usually."

"Usually," Madison repeated. "But it *could* happen."

"Okay, it could," Allie acknowledged. "But I think it's unlikely. I'm sticking with my 'stupid kid trying to mess with us' theory until I'm proven otherwise. Look, can we get Cam moved to the couch in the main room and finish this discussion there?"

Steve went to the bed and gathered Cam's limp body up in his arms, carrying her out of the room. Madison and Allie followed. Allie thought about shutting the bedroom window but decided against it. If someone *was* lurking just outside, it would give them an opportunity to grab her. If Brad had used it as an exit, he might want to use it again as an entry.

*And anyway, the stupid windows don't even lock.*

She pulled the bedroom door shut behind her, then quickly crossed the living room and grabbed the last two dining table chairs. She hooked one under the doorknob of each bedroom. If Brad returned, he wouldn't be able to get out of the bedroom easily, but they'd let him in if he called. If their prankster climbed in through one of the bedroom windows and tried to get into the main room, they'd have fair warning.

Madison had collected the blankets from the bedroom and made a little nest for herself and Steve on the floor next to the couch. She'd also pulled the blankets off the bunks so Allie would have something to keep warm. Steve was rooting around in the cabinets, pulling out bags of potato chips and other snacks. Allie wasn't sure how he could eat at a time like this. She had a knot in her stomach that felt like it was never going to go away.

Madison was folding the other bunk blanket over Cam when she stopped, frowning.

"Allie, look at this," she said, pointing at Cam's arm.

"What?" Allie said, joining her.

"There," Madison said, kneeling beside the couch to peer more closely at Cam. "There's a little bruise on the inside of her elbow."

Allie squinted, then knelt next to Madison. She saw the tiny blue bruise on the vein and sucked in her breath.

"Someone drugged her," Allie said. "That explains why she hasn't moved a muscle since she was knocked out."

"What the hell? Why would someone drug her?" Madison asked. "And who did it? That person?"

"If you mean our mystery intruder, then, yes, I think it has to be. Unless Cam's taken up some habit I don't know about?"

Madison shook her head. "No way. She would never. Nothing stronger than pot."

"Then if she didn't do this to herself, and Brad didn't do it to her—"

"If Brad didn't do what?" Steve asked, his mouth full of nacho-flavored corn chips.

Allie explained about the bruise on Cam's arm. Steve frowned at her.

"Why would Brad do something like that?"

Allie threw her hands up in the air. "Who the hell knows? Why did he bring us to this cabin in the first place? How did he even know about it? Why aren't there any locks on the windows, and why didn't he mention it? You guys act like I'm being ridiculous because I don't think Brad is a saint, but his behavior hasn't exactly been saintly."

"Are you saying he brought us here for some bad reason?" Madison asked, looking at Steve as she said it. Allie could tell that she was wondering if Steve, as Brad's best friend, was involved in such a plot. "Like he wants to scare us? Or hurt us?"

"I'm just saying I'm not real clear on his motivations," Allie said. "And now he's disappeared."

"I still don't think he could have drugged Cam," Steve said stubbornly. "I can go along with the idea that maybe he set us up for some kind of big joke, but I can't believe he'd stick a needle in his own girlfriend."

"Yeah, and to let his car get smashed up like that, too. That seems weird," Madison added. "He loves that car."

"His daddy can always replace it for him," Allie said dismissively.

The more they talked, the more a suspicion solidified in her mind. "Anyway, what about the fact that all four of us were passed out—"

But she never finished what she was going to say, because the air was filled with the sound of breaking glass. Allie, Madison and Steve spun toward the front of the cabin and saw a brick lying just underneath the window next to the front door.

Madison screamed, but Allie wasn't worried about the brick. She was worried about the shadow moving outside the window, the one just visible through the fluttering curtains.

# CHAPTER FOUR

**allieoop:** Yes, of course, a motivated killer can take out a group of people.

**tyz7412:** A gun can be a strong motivation.

**allieoop:** Distinct lack of killers carrying guns in most horror movies. Chainsaws, yes. Kitchen knives, yes. Guns, not so much.

**finalgirl:** Yeah, only the heroes carry the guns—like Ash in ARMY OF DARKNESS. Or Sidney in any SCREAM movie.

**tyz7412:** Well, every villain is the hero of his own story.


**"THERE'S SOMEONE THERE, THERE'S** someone there, there's someone there!" Madison shouted, and leapt into Steve's arms again, attaching herself to him like a baby monkey.

Steve dropped the bag of chips from his hands and grunted as he struggled to hold on to Madison. "Brad, if that's you out there, I'm going to fucking kill you!"

"It's not Brad," Allie said quietly. "He might be a part of this, he might not, but the person out there right now is not Brad."

"How do you know?" Madison said.

"Brad's not that tall," Allie said. She'd gotten a very good sense of the shadow's height and breadth, and whoever was outside menacing them was at least four inches taller than Brad and proportionately broad in the shoulders.

*Either it's a huge guy out there, or Brad is wearing huge boots. But boots like that would make noise, and we didn't hear anything.*

She strained to see through the curtains, tried to divine what the shadow outside might do next. Whoever it was had moved away from the window, so silently that Allie hadn't heard their footsteps on the cabin porch. They could be anywhere now, creeping around the cabin, looking for their next chance to strike.

"We have to stay calm," Allie said, though she didn't feel calm at all. Throughout the night, every incident had escalated, and despite her repeated self-soothing, her nerves had accordingly escalated with each one.

First there had been harmless, if frightening, knocking on the walls. Then Brad's car had been wrecked.

The destruction of Brad's car had been one thing—while violent, something about it had still struck her as an out-of-control prank. Allie started seeing things in a different light once the stalker had actually entered the cabin and knocked out Cam. That was a personal attack.

*Although maybe a personal attack facilitated by Brad?* Allie thought. Her brain was still grinding on the fact that everyone except Brad had been knocked out cold in the car. And Brad was the only one who hadn't drunk from Steve's cocktail bottle.

*Could Brad have put something in the bottle?*

Now the brick through the window, which seemed to indicate that no matter what they did or what precautions they took, the person outside could still get to them. There was no safety to be had.

*Brad brought us to this place where we would be vulnerable,* Allie thought. *A place with no locks, a place with no near neighbors. Why?*

"I'm going to get that motherfucker," Steve said, trying to put Madison down. His face was mottled with anger as he pried at Madison's hands, but she wouldn't let go.

"Don't go out there! You'll be killed," Madison said. "Brad's probably already dead."

"Brad's probably orchestrating this," Allie said. "And Steve, you aren't going outside. We already talked about this."

"We can all go outside then, if you want to stick to your stupid nobody-goes-it-alone rule," he said. "But I am going to beat the shit out of whoever's doing this, even if it is Brad. *Especially* if it's Brad. And if Brad isn't involved and whoever is out there hurt him, I'm still going to beat the shit out of him."

"This is how people die," Allie said. "For real. Look, one of our group is gone. Whether he's gone for some nefarious reason or not, he's still gone. One of us is unconscious. We can't let ourselves get picked off. We'll stay inside and stay together. Whoever is out there is trying to provoke this exact kind of behavior. They know that people respond emotionally to potentially dangerous situations, do irrational things. So we can't give in to them."

"Just because you're the only one who actually aced that fucking Psych 101 course our freshman year doesn't mean you know everything about human psychology," Steve said. "Maybe if I go outside, then whoever's running around will take off, or I'll catch them and teach them a lesson and that will be the end of it."

"Don't go outside," Madison whimpered, her fingers wrapped around Steve's neck, her legs around his waist. "Don't, don't."

"She's not going to let go of you anytime soon, so let's not argue about it."

Steve's words had stung a little, not just because they implied that she was acting like some kind of know-it-all, but because she'd thought Steve was on her side. When it came down to it, he was more inclined to follow the impulses of his hormones than his brain. She shouldn't have expected more from him. While he'd demonstrated the occasional flash of practical thinking, he was, after all, still Brad's wingman. And Brad had zero redeeming qualities, as far as Allie was concerned.

While they spoke, Allie had mostly kept her eyes on the shattered front window. She didn't know exactly what she expected— a hand reaching out of the darkness with a knife? A masked face? At this moment, it was hard not to think of all the horror movies she'd watched, all the films she loved that she'd consumed from the safety of her own couch, feeling all the thrills with none of the risk.

There was another crash, a tinkling of glass. Allie, Steve and the clinging Madison all turned to see one of the windows on the back side of the cabin had also been broken with a brick. This time Allie didn't see any shadow. The person who'd thrown the brick had stepped away quickly—or maybe they were hiding just out of sight, pressing against the cabin wall next to the window. Allie wasn't going to check.

"God*damn*it!" Steve said, trying again to pry Madison off him. "I'm going to kill this motherfucker, I swear to god."

"Stop, just stop," Allie said. Her heart was pounding harder than it ever had in her life. She could actually hear her own blood rushing in her ears, feel the out-of-control beat in her chest. She wanted to freak out and scream just like Madison, but she didn't have someone to cling to. She was alone, and she was the only one left who could even try to make a rational decision. Whatever complicated feelings she had for Cam and Madison, she didn't want them to get hurt. Allie was responsible for making sure they didn't get hurt.

*This was supposed to be a silly girls' weekend*, she thought, and suddenly she was angry. Angry at Brad for ruining her birthday, angry at whoever was outside terrorizing them.

"We are *not* going outside until morning," Allie said, her voice cold and clipped in a way that made Madison and Steve stare at her. "We are *not* going to fall for whatever game that person or people are playing. We are going to sit right here and wait for sunrise. This time of year the sun comes up around 6:30 a.m. It's a little after four now. We're going to stay close together, back-to-back, and watch the windows."

"And what if he tries to climb in?" Steve said.

"Then you can feel free to beat the shit out of him while he's climbing in. There's no clear path through any of the windows with all the furniture in front of them, and anyone who tries to get in is going to be working their way through one limb at a time," Allie said. "Don't play fair, either. This isn't a boxing match or a chance to prove yourself in front of your fraternity brothers. If someone wants to try a home invasion, then we should make them pay for it."

Her voice was louder than necessary as she gave this little speech. Anyone outside listening and waiting for a response to the thrown bricks would hear her. She wasn't going to give them the satisfaction of doing what they wanted. She wasn't going to panic and scream and run in circles, and she wasn't about to let Madison and Steve do that either.

"Okay, fair plan," Steve said. "Let's get some shit from the kitchen to fuck up anyone that tries us on. Babe, you've got to let me put you down."

Madison shook her head. "Not until you promise not to go outside."

"I just said that Allie's plan was fair," Steve said. "I'm not going to rush outside. She's right. If anyone tries to come in, then it will be easier to take them down in here. I don't give a fuck if they think I'm not tough or whatever."

Allie wasn't so sure about that, but she was grateful that Steve seemed to have seen the light. Madison's ability to stay calm hinged on Steve's mood. Allie wasn't certain that Madison would be particularly useful if someone *did* try crawling through the window, though. Madison needed a task, something to help direct her anxiety.

Steve put Madison gently on the ground and Madison reluctantly unwound her fingers from Steve's neck. Steve went into the kitchenette area and started pulling out all the kitchen knives and oversized cooking forks.

"Listen," Allie said to Madison. "If someone does try to climb through, I want you to stay close to Cam, okay? You have to protect her, because she can't protect herself."

"I don't know," Madison said, her voice shaky. "What can I do against some giant guy?"

"Steve," Allie called. "Any cast-iron pans in the cabinets?"

"Good one," Steve said, kneeling down to rummage under the sink.

"You want me to knock someone in the head with a frying pan like I'm in a cartoon?" Madison said, a little laugh breaking through her anxiety. "Does that really work?"

"It's heavy, it's relatively easy for you to lift, and even if you don't knock the guy out, it will hurt like hell. Aim for the head or his balls," Allie said. "It could be enough to slow him down. And I don't think you want to stab someone."

Madison shuddered. "No, I don't think I could do that."

Allie had never thought of herself as a violent person, but as she took one of the kitchen knives and a long serving fork from Steve, she realized she absolutely could stab someone if she had to. But only if she had to. She had not planned on spending her birthday committing manslaughter.

*It won't come to that,* she told herself as the three of them settled on the floor in the middle of the room, their backs making a triangle. Madison faced Cam and the side of the cabin with the closed bedroom doors. Allie faced the front porch side, and Steve the back. Luckily the kitchenette took up the whole fourth side of the cabin.

Every once in a while, one of them would get up and check on Cam, but she continued to sleep deeply, undisturbed by anything around her. Allie increasingly worried about the effect of whatever drug Cam had been given. Surely Cam had to wake up sometime? She couldn't sleep forever.

Nothing happened in those long hours while they waited for the sun to rise. Initially Allie felt like a taut string, ready to release at the first sign of danger. But the longer they sat, the more difficult it was to stay alert. The one thing that horror movies had not prepared her for, she realized, was boredom. In films the thrills came one after another, increasing the tension to a peak point. But real life wasn't like that.

*Real life is boring,* Allie thought. *Real life could use some better writers.* Then she caught herself, her cheeks flushing as though she'd spoken aloud. She didn't want this weekend to turn into an elimination game where the body count of her friends got higher and higher. She wanted to get out of this place, preferably with all five of them—*yes, even Brad, wherever he is*—safe and in one piece. It was just so hard to wait, to sit around trying to anticipate what might happen next.

The light outside the windows gradually increased. Madison's head bobbed against her chest and jerked back up more than once. Allie felt the tension draining out of her friend's body as Madison slumped her shoulders. Steve, to his credit, stayed right on the edge throughout. Allie felt sure that he really wanted someone to try to break in, that he wanted the release of physical conflict.

After a while, Steve said, "The sun's up. What now?"

Allie put the knife and the serving fork on the ground next to her and stretched her arms in the air. "First thing is that we all get dressed and eat something. Then, if there are no other incidents, we all go outside *together* and check around the cabin."

"What are we looking for?" Madison asked.

"Footprints," Allie said. "Any sign of the person who was outside."

"And any sign of Brad," Steve added.

"Do you think it would be safe to shower?" Madison asked. "It's hard not to think of *Psycho* right now."

"It's probably safe," Allie said.

"You don't have to shower alone, babe," Steve said.

Allie rolled her eyes, but made sure she faced away from the other two as she did. There was no reason to annoy her last two allies.

"Go ahead," Allie said. "I'll stay here and watch Cam."

The other two went off into the bedroom to gather their robes and toiletries, and Allie sat beside Cam on the couch. She checked her friend's pulse. It seemed normal to Allie, who admittedly didn't have any medical expertise. It didn't appear that Cam was in any kind of distress. She was just deeply asleep. She hadn't moved or shifted or made any kind of noise in the hours since she'd been knocked out.

*What on earth are we going to do about Cam? We can't leave her here, and we can't carry her.*

There were two possible solutions that Allie could see. First, Cam would wake up. Maybe they could put her in the shower and see if the cold water forced her awake, or if they were lucky, then Cam would open her eyes on her own without any forcing.

If Cam didn't wake, they would have to separate. One of them would stay with Cam, and the other two would hike out to the road and try to flag down help. Allie was not fond of this plan for a number of reasons. First, she didn't like the idea of separating. She knew that Steve thought she was a little silly about it, but in her (fictional) experience, the person who was alone would be the one to die. Second, Allie was 100 percent positive that she would be the one left behind. Madison wouldn't stay in the cabin on her own, and Madison wanted Steve in her sight at all times. So Allie would be left to try to defend herself and Cam alone.

Third, if whoever was fucking around with them was watching the cabin, then they would *know* that Allie was alone, and wouldn't be deterred by a little furniture at the windows and doors.

Fourth, if Brad was a part of whatever was going on, then Brad would not have good intentions for Allie. She knew that for sure, down in her bones. It was the way he talked to her and the way he looked at her. She would be in danger from him if they were alone. She would be in danger from him even if he were an innocent bystander in all this, just a dope who went out looking for the guy who smashed his car. If Brad came back and Steve and Madison were gone . . . well, Allie didn't want to think about it. She didn't have any problem defending herself from Brad, but she'd rather it not come to that. Cam, she was sure, would never believe any version of events that Allie told if Brad was involved.

*Everyone knows you hate him. Even Brad. Especially Brad.*

Allie shook her head. She didn't need to create problems when they had plenty of actual problems right in front of them. But this was one of her issues. She was always doing this, playing through potential scenarios in her head, anxiously considering all possible permutations. It was why she never put off her homework or had to spend a night cramming to write an essay due the next day. If she even thought about avoiding work, she'd imagine how she'd feel if she didn't get her assignment done. Then she'd imagine how she'd feel after the work was done—relieved, happy, free to turn on Shudder and watch scary movies until bedtime. It was why she never drank too much—she'd never had a hangover, but had seen the effects on other people and wasn't interested in them for herself.

It was why she never said yes when boys asked her out.

She always thought the worst of men, thought they would hurt her or mock her or turn her into a joke they laughed about with their friends. She assumed they had no motivations beyond sex, that they were fundamentally uninterested in her brain because they were distracted by the size of her breasts. She could not stop herself from imagining that they might drop Rohypnol in her drink, or might corner her in a basement. She could not stop her brain from seeing scenarios of doom. Allie had never been one of those girls who pictured strolling hand-in-hand with her date after a nice dinner. Her mind jumped to the part where they tried to pressure her into letting them into her dorm room, and what they might do if she said no.

It was easier to say no at the outset. It was easier to be the one everyone mocked as the goody-two-shoes. Once you got that reputation, it became a kind of armor. "Oh, don't bother asking Allie, she never says yes to anyone" was something she'd over-heard more than once on the rare occasions that she'd gone to parties with Cam and Madison.

Besides, Allie didn't think the relationships that you had at someplace as transitory as college were in any way meaningful. They were just people who were briefly in the same circum-stances as you. Then everyone went back to their hometown or on to jobs in different cities or maybe to even more college as they pursued postgraduate degrees in other places. Your freshman roommates and fraternity-boy boyfriends faded into the distance, people who were forgotten as quickly as they forgot you.

*And if you really believed that, then why are you here this weekend, wasting time with Cam and Madison?*

*(Because you want to belong just like everyone else. Stop pretending you're not human. You're just scared to be a part of the group, to take a risk, to make yourself vulnerable.)*

Allie hated that second voice in her head, the one that chided her outward personality, the one that spoke all the secrets she'd kept from everyone—including herself.

*I don't need anybody. I'm okay on my own.*

*(Liar. What are you doing right now, in this situation? You're clinging to the group, acting like a pack animal.)*

Allie heard the bathroom door open, followed by Madison's

giggle and Steve's growl. They joined Allie in the living room, smelling of Dove soap and the fancy salon shampoo that Madison couldn't live without.

Madison noticed where Allie was sitting and said, "Has Cam moved at all?"

Allie shook her head. "I'm worried about what they gave her."

"They? You don't still think Brad is involved, do you?" Steve said, a little sharper than Allie would have liked. It was clear he'd been thinking about his buddy and decided that Brad couldn't possibly be the kind of jerk who'd be a part of the previous night's events.

Allie wasn't in the mood to disabuse him. The very fact that they'd ended up in this obscure place indicated that Brad was a party to whatever plans were in store for them. She was less worried about Brad's potential involvement than what might be planned for the coming night. They couldn't get out of the cabin fast enough for Allie.

She was disappointed that Steve seemed to have had a change of heart. She'd thought she'd convinced him of the wisdom of her ideas and plans, and that the long hours they'd spent watching for danger would have cemented that feeling. Instead, it appeared the wind now blew in a different direction.

"I'm going to get dressed," she said, avoiding Steve's question. They didn't need any dissent in the ranks right now, any more excuses for arguments.

"Do you want me to stand by the shower while you get dressed?" Madison asked.

Allie felt strangely touched by the offer, especially when Madison had been in a state bordering on complete hysteria most of the night. She seemed calmer now, like the shower (and fooling around with Steve) had made her relax.

Madison still had dark circles under her eyes, and Allie

worried that one knock at the door would set her off into a spiral again.

"I'll shower when we're home," Allie said. "We're just going to get sweaty hiking around anyway."

"Oh, yeah," Madison said, like this had just occurred to her. "I keep thinking we're going to be in a car."

"That's because we're always in cars," Allie said as she went into the bedroom to dress. "Most people hardly walk anywhere. I've seen people drive two blocks to Starbucks to pick up their coffee when it would be faster to walk and not deal with trying to park their car."

Madison and Steve had left the bedroom door open, and Allie noted that the bedroom window was still shut. She cast a wary eye at the closet in the corner of the room. She hadn't put her bag in there, just tucked it underneath the bunk, so there was no need for her to open the closet door.

But her brain did that thing, that thing where it imagined every possible permutation of doom, and she found herself checking to make sure there was no one hiding in the closet before she undressed.

She opened the closet door, her heart pounding. There was no one inside, of course. Just a plain closet built out of unfinished pine with an equally plain unfinished shelf above it. Allie chided herself for being silly. There wasn't always a stalker lurking in a hidden corner, a killer waiting to burst out.

*Why does this cabin seem like it's not actually done being built, though?* Allie thought as she pulled on a sweatshirt and jeans. *There are no locks and no screens on the windows. There's untreated wood in the closets. It seems like a rush job, or a place where people walked off and never bothered to finish it properly.*

And she wondered again how Brad had known about it, and why he'd thought it was a good idea to bring them here.

Allie put on her socks and sneakers, glancing at the open door of the closet. The sense of unfinished-ness about the cabin was significant in some way, she was sure. She just couldn't put her finger on why it mattered.

*Could Brad have had this place built just for this trip?* she wondered once again. But that seemed like a ludicrous amount of expense even for a rich boy with a lot of disposable income. And if he had commissioned a private cabin, wouldn't he have built a nicer place, something to show off his money and prestige? Why was everything here so basic, so fundamentally lacking in the type of luxury that Brad preferred? Where was the hot tub and fancier furniture, sheets with high thread counts and adjustable mattresses? Where was the climate control?

Allie rejoined Steve and Madison in the main room, wondering if she ought to mention her suspicions.

*But what, exactly, is it that you suspect? That if Brad built this cabin, it would be nicer? Doesn't that just mean that he wasn't the one who arranged for its construction? There's not necessarily anything suspicious in that, and the more you push the Brad's-a-bad-guy theory, the more you'll lose Steve. And you need Steve on your side, because Madison will do whatever Steve does, and you definitely do not want this to become a two-on-one situation. Or three-on-one, if Cam ever wakes up.*

Madison stood next to the counter in the kitchenette, waiting for bread to pop out of the toaster. It was an older model of toaster, Allie noticed. A chrome two-slice type, probably picked up a few years ago at a Target or Walmart. Again, not the sort of thing Brad would pick for himself. If Brad had paid for this place, then surely he would have chosen—or had his decorator or whatever choose—the most high-end option available.

*Because Brad didn't do the choosing? Or because Brad knew he wouldn't be here for very long and therefore it didn't matter?*

She had to get off Brad, had to stop thinking about his potential sins.

Steve had pulled out a carton of eggs and was cracking them into a bowl. "Scrambled eggs?" he asked, in a much friendlier tone than he'd used earlier. Allie wondered if Madison had told him to lay off the attitude.

"Just toast for me," Allie said. "And maybe fruit, if there is any."

"Right, no animal products for you," Steve said. "Sorry, I forgot."

"No problem."

Allie disliked the very polite, careful way they were acting. It was like they were parents who'd had a big blowout argument and they were behaving nice for their kid—in this case, Madison. But there hadn't been a big argument, at least not since the sun came up. Allie wondered what might have changed Steve's mind.

She couldn't worry about it. She had to stop trying to anticipate or understand other people. She just had to make sure they all got out of here alive.

She stilled, a piece of toast in one hand and a knife covered in strawberry jam in the other. Was she really, truly worried about the four of them getting out of this place alive? Did she really think it wasn't a prank or trick, that they were actually in danger?

*Yes,* she thought, and it was a relief to acknowledge it, even if it was only to herself. *Yes, I think we're really in danger here.*

But she didn't know where the danger would come from, and as she watched Steve scrambling eggs, she wondered about the different forms that danger might take. Stupidity was sometimes just as dangerous as malice.

# CHAPTER FIVE

**allieoop:** Every villain might be the hero of his own story but that doesn't mean he's not completely wrong LOL

**tyz7412:** How do you know?

**allieoop:** Come on, you don't think killing random people is wrong?

**tyz7412:** What if the killing isn't random at all?

**THEY ATE BREAKFAST, AND** then Steve and Allie moved the furniture away from the front door while Madison sat with Cam. The morning sunshine seemed especially bright as Steve opened the door, blinding Allie for a moment until her eyes adjusted.

"I guess we know that way is east," she said. "At least we can orient ourselves generally. I wish I knew what direction we came from, though. You really were out the whole time we were in the car?"

"Pretty much." Steve shrugged, and then pointed at the barely visible track that led up to the cabin. "I don't see why it matters, anyway. We can just follow this dirt road back to a main road."

"Sure," Allie said. "But it would be nice to know where we are, especially in relation to school. How long did we drive? Four, five hours?"

"Something like that," Steve said, kneeling down to peer at the porch. "Hey, look, there are footprints here. Big ones."

There were several clearly delineated muddy footprints on the porch. Allie frowned at the prints. They were large, and that reinforced the sense she'd had of the shadow through the window. But there was something *wrong* with them, the same sense of wrongness that she associated with the untreated wood in the closets. She just needed a minute to think, to put her finger on the problem.

Madison came to the door to see what they were doing. She shivered as she watched Steve follow the footprints off the porch and into the clearing in front of the cabin. Allie watched Steve, trying to catch the butterfly in her mind that kept flitting away.

"I can't believe this is really happening," Madison said, her voice sad. "Brad gone and Cam drugged and someone smashing up Brad's car and then breaking the windows and everything. It doesn't seem real, does it?"

"That's it," Allie said, snapping her fingers. "*It doesn't seem real.* That's the thing I've been trying to figure out. This doesn't seem real. It's like it's all, I don't know, staged or something."

Steve, who'd been crouched on the ground trying to follow the pattern of footprints, stood up. "Staged?"

"Yeah," Allie said. "Isn't it weird that we were all knocked out in the car except for Brad? Isn't it weird that this cabin seems strangely unfinished—no locks on the windows, untreated wood in the closets? Isn't it convenient that we seem to be miles from anything, no lights of civilization in any direction? It's like someone set up a half-assed horror movie scenario, then sent out a performer to terrorize us—someone conveniently large and looming, who would leave muddy footprints on the porch despite the fact that there was no rain last night and the ground is dry as a bone."

Steve's eyes had sharpened when Allie first mentioned Brad, and she was sure he would have defended his buddy then, but as she went on with her little speech, he looked more and more unsure.

"You think Brad . . . ?" he asked, but it was like he couldn't bring himself to articulate what he was thinking.

"Yes," Allie said firmly. "I think Brad had something to do with it."

"But why?" Madison said. "I don't get it. Is it just some big prank?"

"What if he's watching us?" Allie said slowly, thinking it through as she spoke. "What if he, and whoever helped him set this up, are watching us to see what happens?"

"Come on," Steve said. "Like he's making his own reality show or whatever? And then he's going to pop up at the end and laugh at us for freaking out? I don't buy it."

"There's something larger going on here," Allie said. "I can feel it. It's not just a stupid prank. A stupid prank would have been over by now. But Brad's not back, laughing his ass off at us. And there's no sign of whoever was stalking around the cabin all night."

"He might be in the woods, watching us," Madison said, and Allie heard that note of panic in her friend's voice again. "He might be right out there, waiting for us to try to leave."

"Look," Steve said, rubbing his eyes with the palms of his hands. "If there is some larger plot at work—and I don't think there is, really, and I don't think Brad is a part of it if a plot exists—"

"But he brought us here, Steve," Allie said. "You can't argue with that. He brought us here, to a place none of us knew about. That shows some kind of complicity."

"His car," Steve said, as he'd said several times before. For Steve, it appeared that the destruction of the BMW was absolute proof positive that Brad couldn't be a party to whatever was happening to them.

Allie shook her head. "You have to stop thinking that Brad wouldn't let the car get wrecked if it served his purpose."

"But he loves that car."

"Fine," Allie said, holding up her hands. "Fine. You don't want to believe Brad is fucking with us. Fine. We still have to figure out how to get out of here."

"We follow the road," Steve said.

"What about Cam?" Allie asked. "Are we going to carry her the whole way? Make a travois and pull it? It's not like we have a little red wagon to put her in, and we can't leave her here."

"Well, I can follow the road and come back for you guys," Steve said.

"No way," Madison said, before Allie could. "You can't go out there alone."

"One of you could stay with Cam—"

"I knew that would be the suggestion," Allie said, rolling her eyes. "And who is going to be the one who stays behind with the unconscious woman?"

"I don't want to be here alone!" Madison said.

"Exactly," Allie said. "So I would be left here alone while the two of you wander out for god knows how many hours, and in the meantime there's still some huge guy who likes to throw bricks through windows out there in the woods."

Madison looked hesitant. "We can't leave Allie here alone. That's not fair. It's not safe."

"Well, we're going to have to make some hard decisions. Our phones don't work, there's no landline and no internet, and one of our group can't travel anywhere," Steve said. "That means splitting up."

"Maybe I should stay here with Allie," Madison said, though her voice trembled.

Allie knew Madison didn't want to stay in the cabin without Steve. It was pretty clear at this point that Steve was Madison's security blanket.

"Maybe I should go," Allie said. "To the road, I mean."

"You can't go by yourself," Madison said, in the kind of tone normally reserved for Victorian maidens who dared suggest a solo excursion to the library. "You're tiny. You'll be killed by the stalker."

"I don't want any of us to be separated at all," Allie said. "But it makes the most sense. You and Steve can protect Cam together. You'll be in the cabin and safe."

"And you won't be," Madison said. "You'll be all alone, trying to get to the road by yourself."

"I can run," Allie said. "I run almost every day. I'm sure I can run faster than some big guy in heavy boots. This isn't an actual horror movie, where the killer has endurance beyond all reason."

"That means you don't have endurance beyond all reason, either," Madison said.

Allie pulled off her glasses and rubbed her eyes in frustration. They were going in circles. Everyone wanted to have a say and Allie conceded that was fair, but it would be easier if they would just listen to her. At this point she was getting concerned that decisions wouldn't be made before midday. And if that was the case, they would all have to spend the night at the cabin again.

Allie didn't want to think about what the night would bring.

"Look, it makes the most sense for me to go. I can move the fastest and nobody is left here alone. But if I'm going to go, I have to go now. I don't want to be out wandering on a dark road in the middle of the night."

Steve and Madison looked at each other. They seemed to be communicating with their eyes. Allie wondered what it was like to trust somebody that much, to be able to talk without speaking at all.

"Okay," Steve said. "Okay. But I don't like it."

"I don't either," Madison said.

"I'm not exactly thrilled myself," Allie said. "But I'll go, and I'll be as quick as I can. If we're lucky, then there will be a main road within a few miles."

Steve shook his head. "I haven't heard the sounds of cars at all since we got here. Since there's nothing nearby—buildings and restaurants and whatever—we should be able to hear cars and trucks if the road were close."

"Yeah, you're right," Madison said. "I haven't heard any kind of engine at all—not a car or a truck or even an airplane."

Allie tilted her head up to look at the sky. The sunlight seemed overly bright, the sky a little too blue.

*It's like a summer blue,* she thought. *The way the sky looks in July, not in late September.*

"It is weird that we haven't heard any planes," Allie said. "I'm not sure there's anywhere in America where planes don't pass overhead."

"I guess there must be some places," Madison said. "We must really, really be in the middle of nowhere. And that means you'll be walking a long way by yourself."

Allie held up her hands. "Don't start again. We can't keep talking in circles. I'll go; you two stay. I'll pack a bag with water and food and keep track of the time. If I'm gone for two hours and I haven't reached the road, I'll turn around and come back and we can formulate a new plan for tomorrow. Fair?"

"I guess," Madison said. Then she rushed at Allie and threw her arms around her, hugging her tight. "I just don't want to lose you. I already kind of feel like I have."

Tears pricked at Allie's eyes. She shouldn't be so mistrustful. She shouldn't have put the distance between herself and the other two. She could have moved off campus with them—they'd asked, after all—but she'd thought it would be better to be on her own. She'd used some of her summer savings to get a single room on campus so she wouldn't have to deal with a roommate, so she wouldn't have to make accommodations for anyone else. She wouldn't have to deal with being interrupted late at night when she was studying, or tolerate the company of anyone else's boyfriend or girlfriend.

*You did it so you could feel superior, so you could keep yourself above it all. But even you need people. Even you need friends, sometimes.*

"You haven't lost me," Allie whispered into Madison's ear. "It's okay. You haven't lost me."

"We need to hang out more," Madison said, sniffling. "This weekend was supposed to be for us."

"Yeah, it was," Allie said, sighing.

"I'm sorry about all this," Madison said. "I knew you wouldn't like it when Brad convinced Cam to let them come along."

"No use crying over it now," Allie said, a heavy weight in her chest. *Cam should have told Brad no, it was a girls-only weekend. We'd be waking up around now, stumbling out to find somewhere for brunch. We wouldn't be terrified and exhausted and isolated. We wouldn't be contemplating our mortality.*

"Hey," Madison said, and leaned back to look into Allie's eyes. "Happy birthday."

Allie choked out a laugh. "Best birthday ever."

"I'll make it up to you. Both of us will—me and Cam. When Cam wakes up. If Cam wakes up."

"She's going to wake up," Allie said. "Whatever she's been given will wear off eventually."

"But what if it doesn't?"

"Don't worry, I'm going to return with an ambulance," Allie said. "If she hasn't woken up on her own, then the EMTs or a doctor at a hospital will know what to do. She hasn't been placed in a permanent coma."

But Allie worried that whatever drug had been given to Cam

*had* done permanent damage. Cam's deep, untroubled sleep was concerning in itself. It implied, to Allie's way of thinking, a concussion. But they'd already established that Cam hadn't been hit on the head.

*Or maybe she was and you just didn't know? You're not a doctor, after all.*

"Okay, I've got to go," Allie said. She couldn't stay here talking while the day wore on.

Steve had continued to root around in the clearing while Allie and Madison talked. He'd followed the footprints around the edge of the cabin.

"They just keep going around," he called.

"Yes, we know," Allie said, and tried not to sound impatient. They'd seen the evidence of that with their own eyes, and she didn't want to go back inside the cabin without Steve. She wanted to make sure that he stayed with Madison while she was gone, that he didn't get caught up following some line of inquiry of his own.

"Well, I'm trying to see where he goes after he circles the cabin," Steve said, a little defensively. "We might be able to track him to . . ."

"To where?" Allie asked.

"I don't know. Wherever he came from. And Brad might be there. Or he might not be."

Allie couldn't believe that Steve was still trying to prove Brad was an innocent party, but she supposed that it was hard to think of your best friend as the kind of guy who would put them all in this position.

"You can't go haring off after footprints," Allie said. "You have to stay with Madison and Cam while I'm gone."

Steve's mouth twisted. "But—"

"You have to stay with me," Madison said. "Or I'll lock you out."

"You wouldn't," Steve said. "Besides, there's no locks, anyway."

"That's not the point," Madison said. "I could block the door and leave you outside."

"With a psycho?" Steve said. "Some girlfriend you are."

"Okay, look, just come back up here," Allie said, trying and failing to keep a note of impatience out of her voice. "We all need to stay together."

"Except you," Steve said. "You're going off on your own."

Allie opened her mouth to retort, but before she could, Madison crossed the porch, grabbed Steve's arm and pulled him toward the front door.

"The sooner Allie goes, the sooner she can come back," Madison said, yanking him through the door. "Stop fucking around trying to be a hero and let her . . ."

Madison paused a few feet inside the door, still holding Steve's arm. Allie crowded in behind them. She wanted to shut the door. She'd felt ridiculously exposed while they were outside, and she tried not to think too hard about how much she would *really* be exposed once she left the cabin and started off on her own.

"Cam?" Madison's voice was a wavy, receding line in the air.

"What the fuck?" Steve said.

Allie pushed around them, wanting to see what they were seeing. The world receded to a narrow point, like a focusing telescope in a film. The edges of the room went dark, and all she could see was the blood.

There was blood everywhere, so much blood, more blood than there should be in one small body, for Cam did look small, so much smaller than she'd been in life. There was blood pooling on the couch and running onto the floor and blood smeared in long streaks that looked like footprints.

*It's not supposed to happen this way,* Allie thought. *The killer is supposed to come at night, supposed to terrorize in the dark. He's not supposed to walk up in the bright light of day with the rest of us a few feet away, clueless.*

And then she thought, *He's not afraid of us at all. He's not worried about us at all.*

She took another step closer to Cam, to Cam's staring dead eyes, to the long red smile cut into her throat, and wondered if Brad really was behind this. There were easier ways to get rid of your girlfriend if you didn't want to date her anymore. Killing wasn't usually the top option. And there was no doubt that Cam was dead. Allie didn't need to check her pulse to know that. She could see the exposed cords of Cam's throat underneath the cut.

"Brad couldn't have," Steve said, his voice faint and echoing Allie's own thoughts. "Brad wouldn't have done this."

Allie glanced over and saw that Steve was pale, his lips bloodless. He swayed on his feet.

"He's going to faint," Allie said, but her words were drowned out as Madison started screaming.

Steve tumbled to the floor, all the bones in his body seemingly turned to rubber. At the exact same moment, Madison turned and fled out the door, her scream trailing behind her.

"Shit!" Allie shouted, looking from the unconscious Steve to the open door where Madison had disappeared. "Shit, shit, fuck! Madison!"

But Madison didn't reply. Her scream receded into the distance, getting farther away with each second.

Allie didn't want Madison to get too far away, to potentially get lost in the woods as she panicked. But Allie also didn't want to leave Steve here alone and vulnerable, passed out and easy prey for a stalker who was clearly close by.

*Yes, he's close by. He's very close, hidden somewhere in the woods, or even . . .*

Her thought trailed away as she looked at the streaks of blood on the floor that led away from Cam's body, the ones that went into the bedroom that Allie and Steve and Madison had shared.

The bedroom door was closed, the way Allie had left it, but that didn't mean there wasn't someone behind it. That didn't mean the person who'd killed Cam wasn't waiting for them to panic, to run in every direction so he could pounce.

*In other words, waiting for exactly what happened. Anyone with rudimentary observational skills would have known that Madison, at least, was about to crack.*

Allie hesitated, because she felt Madison's need was probably greater than Steve's, but that closed bedroom door felt more ominous than before. She could almost hear someone breathing behind it, someone waiting.

*He could just as easily have popped out a window and gone around to the porch. He could come in that way, especially since Madison left the door open in invitation.*

The back of Allie's neck prickled. She didn't want to turn her back to any potential opening, to any source of egress that might assist a killer's transit. But there were windows and doors everywhere, windows and doors with no locks, almost as if they were designed to make it easier for outsiders to enter.

*Staged,* she thought again as she knelt beside Steve and rolled him onto his back. He didn't appear to have any injuries. Allie shook his shoulder, a little harder than she might have normally. Madison's screaming had not stopped, but it seemed very far away now. Allie hoped like hell that Madison had followed the road and not gone haring blindly into the woods.

"Steve," she said, and as she shook him, she couldn't stop herself from looking all around, from making certain they were actually alone. "Steve, come on. Wake up."

Steve moaned a little, but didn't open his eyes. In movies people always slapped someone who'd fallen unconscious, or poured cold water on their face, or (in certain period pieces) waved smelling salts under their nose. Allie didn't have smelling salts *(what are smelling salts, anyway? Are they even made anymore?)*, but she did have cold water. She stood and ran for the sink.

The bedroom door opened behind her.

Allie stopped, as still as a child playing freeze tag. She didn't want to turn around. She didn't want to see.

*You have to look, you idiot. Are you going to stand here and let him kill you, too?*

The large chef's knife was lying on the counter, just a few feet from where Allie stood. Steve had left it there while making breakfast. They hadn't been as worried about the stalker after the sun came up. They'd thought they were safe in the light.

She took a huge step forward, grabbed the knife and spun around to face the bedroom door.

Nobody was there. There was just an open door, moving a little as the wind sailed through the open window beyond.

*That might mean the killer has gone out the window. Or it might mean he's standing behind the bedroom door, waiting for me to investigate like a dumbass.*

Allie listened hard, hoping for some indication one way or another—a creak of the hardwood floor, the rustle of clothing. But she couldn't hear anything, not even Madison's scream.

*She's gone too far away. Or something has happened to her. I should have followed after her right away. I should have left Steve here. I care more about Madison than I do about Steve, and that's the truth, even if it makes me a bad person.*

Allie's eyes darted to all the windows, looking for the huge shadow looming on the other side of the glass. There was nothing.

*He could be just out of sight, leaning against the cabin wall between the windows. He's waiting for me to scream, to run, to do something foolish.*

Allie backed slowly toward the sink, the knife gripped in her right hand. She stopped when she felt the counter bang against her back. She switched the knife to her left hand and fumbled with her right to get a glass and fill it while still watching the room.

There was Cam and her blank dead stare, and the pool of blood on the couch. There was Steve, face up on the floor a few feet from the front door.

There was the open bedroom door, a watching eye.

She moved slowly toward Steve, the glass trembling a little in her hand, the water dripping on the floor as she walked. She poured the glass of water onto Steve's face without kneeling down, her eyes fixed on the bedroom door. Allie was certain that any second now the stalker would appear in the open doorway.

*Any second now,* she thought, as Steve spluttered and sat up.

"What happened?" he asked, wiping water from his eyes.

"You fainted," she said, not looking at him. *Any second now.* "And Madison went crazy and ran out into the woods. We have to go after her."

"I fainted?" he said, and sounded disbelieving. "*I* fainted?"

"Yes, you fainted. Men faint," Allie said, a little impatient with his macho bullshit. She did not take her eyes from the bedroom door. *Any second now.* "Can you stand? Can you walk?"

"Yes," he said, and pushed to his feet and immediately wobbled. "Shit, I don't feel right."

Allie grabbed him around the waist, trying to support him. It wasn't easy when he was about a foot taller than she was. "Do you need a glass of water?"

Steve looked down at his damp shirt. "Looks like you already gave me one."

"To drink," Allie said, trying to keep her eyes on the bedroom door and a good grip on the knife even as she helped Steve stand. "This really isn't a time for jokes. Cam is dead. Brad is missing.

Madison went off somewhere on her own. Even without the presence of a psychopath, I'm worried that she'll hurt herself."

"Right," Steve said, straightening up and pushing away from Allie to stand on his own. "Right. I know. Okay, yeah, I need some water and then we can go after her."

"I'll get it," Allie said, backing away toward the kitchen area again.

The open bedroom door watched her as she went. Her fingers tightened on the knife. Now was the moment, she was sure, that the killer would appear. She hadn't taken the bait and gone through the door to investigate the way she was supposed to, so he would pop out now. She had to be ready. She had to be prepared. She knew what would happen. She spent almost all her free time watching horror movies. She was smarter than any killer.

Allie felt around for another glass. Steve gave her a quizzical look.

"What are you doing? Why don't you just turn around and get a glass?"

"Because I think that someone is—"

But Allie never got to finish what she was saying, because a huge man wearing a red shirt stepped through the open front door, slashed Steve across the throat, and stepped out again almost before she could blink.

# CHAPTER SIX

**allieoop:** Yeah, I guess in some movies the killer's motivations are personal.

**eatersofthedead:** Whether the motivations are personal or not the characters would probably survive more often if they weren't so stupid.

**allieoop:** I know, there are a million things I would never do if I were in a horror movie. As Nancy says in NIGHTMARE ON ELM STREET, "I'm into survival."

**tyz7412:** All right, then. Prove it.

ALLIE WATCHED STEVE FALL to the ground, blood spurting from the artery in his neck. His hands clutched the place where his life was draining away. There was nothing she could do, no help she could give. Putting pressure on the wound would not save him now.

*I should have known,* she thought. *I should have known the opening bedroom door was a misdirection. That always happens. I should have known. I could have kept Steve alive. Why didn't I shut the front door? Why did I make it easy for the killer?*

She stood stock-still, the handle of the knife in her hand pressing into the palm hard enough to bruise. If that man—and all Allie remembered about him was his shirt and the impression of size, of breadth and height and strength—tried to come at her, she would make sure he regretted it.

Her eyes were blurry. For a moment, Allie thought she needed to clean her glasses, but then she realized she was crying, tears that fell thick but silent. She couldn't release the sob in her throat, or the scream that was caught next to it. She couldn't show any weakness, couldn't crack up and fall apart like Madison. She had to keep it together.

She was the only one left.

Steve stopped moving, and the smell of shit and piss suddenly filled the air.

*He's dead now,* Allie thought, wiping at her eyes with her free hand. *He's dead and I'm all alone.*

She'd thought she'd known better; thought she could do everything right. What was the use of a mind that ran through every doomsday scenario, every possible permutation of disaster, if she couldn't even keep her friends alive?

*You forgot to account for human nature. You forgot that not everyone would be coolheaded. You didn't think that one of you would disappear in the night, that one would be drugged, that one would just start running and screaming like a crazy person.*

There was a great heavy weight somewhere in the center of her body, something that held her in place, something that made her feel like she couldn't run or think or move at all. She waited, and waited, because she didn't know what else to do. If the man came for her, she would hurt him. That was all she knew.

*This isn't you. This isn't how you always said you'd react if you were in those movies you love*

*(the movies I'll never watch those movies again it's not a joke it's not funny it's not make-believe)*

*You always said you'd be the smart one, the one who survives. You wouldn't be stupid or panicky or stand still, trembling, like you are now*

*(my friends are dead they're dead)*

Allie took a deep breath, choked on her tears, tried again.

*I can do this. I'm not alone. I just need to find Madison.*

She glanced at the front door, the door through which the giant man had materialized like Leatherface in *The Texas Chain Saw Massacre.*

*Why can't I remember his face? All I can picture is how huge he was, and that he was wearing a red shirt.*

A memory twanged deep in her subconscious, a story she'd read many years before in which bank robbers had worn brightly colored or patterned clothing to distract the eye of witnesses, so that all they remembered about the perpetrators was that they had worn polka-dot bandannas or some such thing. That was what had just happened to her, she realized. All she'd seen was the red shirt.

*And the knife. I saw the knife, too.*

One thing she was pretty sure of, though—she'd never met that man before. She'd remember someone that large.

*Which means that if Brad is a part of all this—and he still might be; I haven't seen any evidence to the contrary—then he's working with someone. But you knew that already, because someone had to be outside the house tapping on the wall while Brad was inside pretending to sleep.*

Allie realized that if she didn't get moving, she would get caught in a kind of feedback loop in her head, worrying about things that didn't matter, gnawing at mysteries that could stay unsolved. The identity of the killer was hardly the point at the moment. She could worry about identification after she found Madison and they got away to someone who could help.

*But he's somewhere outside. He's moving silently. He could be climbing through the window in Brad and Cam's bedroom right now. Or he could be waiting for me to rush out the door. What should I do? What should I do?*

Allie had never panicked before, never thought of herself as the sort who would. But she recognized panic's edges creeping up on her, seeping at the corners of her mind.

*Pull yourself together RIGHT NOW.*

Her eyes darted from the open bedroom door to the open front door to the sticky blood underneath Cam to the spreading pool around Steve.

*No flies. Why are there no flies in here, zooming through the open win-*

*dows, landing in the mess around Cam and now Steve? Isn't that what's supposed to happen? Wouldn't that be normal?*

There were no flies and there were no curious animals nosing through the door, and Allie felt sure that there should be. There was something so wrong about the cabin, not just the cabin itself but the area around it, and so many things she didn't understand.

*Staged,* she thought for the third time that day. *But I don't understand how, or why.*

She glanced at the open front door, wondering if she dared go out that way. It would be more dangerous to go through a window—what if she got stuck while climbing out, or fell awkwardly? Going straight through an open door seemed the most sensible thing. People in horror movies, especially big-breasted girls

*(and you are a big-breasted girl, you're practically a walking trope)*

were always getting stuck in places that they shouldn't have tried to go through. She thought of Tatum getting stuck in the cat door in *Scream,* her head crushed as Ghostface raised the garage door while she struggled to break free. Allie didn't want to stick a limb out one of the windows only to find it lopped off by a waiting murderer.

She knew she had to go through the front door. She just had to suck it up and run fast and hope that he wasn't lurking on the other side of the frame. She had to hope that if she ran fast enough, she'd take him by surprise and he wouldn't be able to catch up. She had to hope that she'd find Madison, and that Madison would be alive and okay, and that the two of them could make it to the main road.

Allie slid her foot forward, trying not to make a sound. Her rubber-soled sneakers only whispered against the hardwood floor but seemed unnaturally loud in the silence. Nothing rustled outside. The wind didn't move the trees or shift the dried leaves that were scattered over the clearing in front of the cabin.

She moved slowly toward the front door, stepping carefully around Steve, not wanting to tread in his blood. It seemed disrespectful, somehow, especially since she was leaving him behind. She was leaving Steve and Cam behind because there was nothing she could do for them, but it still felt wrong.

*You're into survival. You have to survive.*

Allie looked through the open doorway, a narrow frame enclosing the world outside. There was the wooden porch, and the two steps down. There was the clearing and the artfully scattered leaves.

*Artfully scattered?*

She shook her head. She couldn't think about all the things that were off about this place right now. But it wasn't hard to imagine someone walking through the clearing with a black trash bag full of leaves, dropping them here and there for effect.

*Especially since all the trees around here are evergreens.*

Her eyes widened as she realized this, as one of the not-quite-right sensations fell neatly into a defined box. The leaves on the ground couldn't have come from the trees around the cabin.

*They made a mistake. They thought nobody would notice, or care.*

Allie didn't have a clue who the mysterious "they" might be, or what Brad's connection to them was (because she wasn't giving up on her idea that Brad was involved), but she felt secure in the notion that there was a "they." This *was* an elaborate conspiracy to— what? To get rid of all of them? To terrorize Allie specifically? What was the endgame?

*You sound insane. You know the whole idea sounds insane.*

And yet Allie couldn't shake the sense that she was right, and more importantly, that she wasn't supposed to figure it out. But enough details had been off that she almost *had* to be suspicious. She'd be inexcusably stupid if she weren't.

She tried to see if the man *(hunter, stalker, killer)* was standing just outside the door. There should be a shadow. It wasn't so late in the day that the sun would be directly overhead.

*Of course, if he's sensible (and he does seem to be), he'll stand on the side where his shadow is cast away from the doorway so you can't judge anything from that.*

Allie knew she was standing there thinking instead of moving, that she should have pushed herself out the door several minutes before, that she was scared to move, scared to make the wrong decision. This wasn't a multiple-choice test, where the worst result for choosing incorrectly would be a lower grade. This was her life she was playing with here, throwing the dice and hoping they didn't come up snake eyes.

*If you stand here until it gets dark, he* will *come back. You'll be all alone in here with two dead bodies, and he will come back.*

Allie ran.

She burst out through the door, looking left and right as she went, and found she was alone. She slammed down the steps and through the clearing and ran along the dirt track that had led them to this place, following the faint trace of the car's wheels in the dirt.

Allie ran regularly as part of her exercise routine, and she knew that she was running too fast, that she couldn't maintain this pace. If she didn't slow down soon, her body would force her to stop. She was already sucking air, the rasp of her breath telling her that she was working too hard. A stitch pinched under her right ribs, sending pain shooting through her. She tried to fix her form, to stretch the cramp, but she couldn't, because she was running too fast to think about all the things she normally thought about, like keeping her core engaged and her shoulders over her hips and all the other stupid shit that she did when she ran for fun and not for her life.

After about a half mile of almost blind sprinting where she registered nothing except the pounding of her heart and the screaming of her lungs, Allie felt herself slow involuntarily. She couldn't keep up the pace any longer. She looked behind her, saw that she was alone on the road. Her feet stopped moving of their own accord and she bent over her legs, pressing her hands into her thighs, trying to slow the frantic rabbit that wanted to escape out of her chest. Her right hand still gripped the knife and her fingers felt like they'd attached to the handle permanently.

She had to think. She was away from the cabin, and that was all to the good. If she was lucky, the killer had been lurking around behind the cabin, looking for an excuse to terrorize her some more, and hadn't realized right away that she'd escaped. Once he did realize, though, he would certainly come after her. There was no way he could let her get away. That wasn't how these things worked.

*And you left your footprints in the dirt for him to follow, dumbass.*

It didn't really matter if she left a trail or not, she realized. There was only one logical path for her to follow—the road—and he would assume that was the way she'd gone. It was senseless to berate herself for leaving tracks behind.

*He'll know these woods better than you, so don't even think about trying to hide yourself there and potentially get turned around. Just follow the road.*

Her breath had returned to something resembling normal inhalations and exhalations, though her heart didn't seem to want to stop racing. The surge of adrenaline was still pumping through her.

She started again at a jogging pace, glancing over her shoulder frequently, expecting every time to see a looming figure silhouetted on the road. But every time she looked, he wasn't there.

While she wasn't exactly disappointed, his nonappearance made her more sharply aware of everything around her, reminded her of the way he'd tricked her in the cabin. What if he *had* followed and was just pacing along inside the cover of the trees, lulling her into a false sense of security?

The sun shone down on her, but it seemed only to cast light without heat. The wind wasn't blowing, but she shivered a little as the rivulets of sweat dried on her body. The air felt strange, tasted almost metallic in her mouth. Everything was bright and still and chilly, but not the kind of chill that came from crisp fall air. It was more artificial than that, she realized. It almost felt like a climate-controlled room.

Allie stopped then, looking all around from the sky to the trees to the dirt she walked on. She felt like she was on the verge of something, of all the clues finally clicking together.

"Allie?"

A tiny, shaky voice came from Allie's right, and a second later there was Madison, stumbling out of the trees and throwing herself at Allie.

"Allie, Allie, Cam's dead," she said, sobbing into Allie's sweatshirt. "She's dead. Someone just came and killed her while we were all standing right there."

"Madison," Allie said, sighing in relief. At least she didn't have to run around looking for her friend. "Come on, we have to keep moving."

"But Cam," Madison said, crying harder. "She's really dead. She's really gone."

Allie wondered if this was the moment to tell Madison that her boyfriend was dead, too. She decided against it. The important thing was to get Madison walking, to keep making progress away from the cabin. If Allie mentioned Steve's fate right now, then Madison might just come unglued completely, might sit down in the middle of the road and wail endlessly. They couldn't afford that. Just because the killer hadn't yet reappeared didn't mean their luck would last forever.

"We've got to go, Madison. We've got to find someone to help us." Allie unraveled Madison's tight hug and took her friend's arm, leading her away from the direction of the cabin.

"But what will we say? Some crazy killer is out in the woods?" Madison said, her voice breaking as she sobbed. "It sounds nuts. We'll sound nuts."

"I don't really think a stranger's impression of us should be our priority," Allie said. "We just need someone with a car to pick us up and take us to a police station."

"W-what if the person with the car is the killer?" Madison said. "How will we even know?"

"Well, if it's a huge guy wearing a red shirt, we won't get in the car," Allie said, tugging at Madison to keep her moving.

"What do you mean?" Madison said. "Did you see him?"

"Yes," Allie said, not wanting to go into the details, as that would stray dangerously close to the circumstances of Steve's death. She wasn't trying to hide the information from Madison exactly—she just didn't want to tell Madison at the moment. It was better to wait until they were out of danger, preferably when they were in a police station surrounded by walls and officers with guns.

*Although police officers don't have a great track record in horror movies. A lot of them die, or get hurt, or just flat out don't believe the people reporting what happened to them.*

She had to stop thinking this was a movie. It wasn't. They just needed to act normally, act logically—find their way to a main road, hitch a ride, get to the police. Once Allie and Madison brought the police back to the cabin, it wouldn't matter if the officers believed them or not. They'd have to see the truth. The bodies of Cam and Steve would be right in front of them.

"But no Brad," Allie murmured.

"What?" Madison said. Tears leaked out of her eyes continuously. She wasn't actively sobbing, and she stumbled along more or less at Allie's pace. But she kept crying, almost as if she were unaware of it happening, and she kept one hand on Allie's sleeve, like a little kid holding on to their parent so they wouldn't get lost in a crowd.

"Brad," Allie said. "What the hell happened to Brad? Did he go off in the middle of the night on his own or did someone take him? And was he involved with all this?"

"I can't believe he'd hurt Cam, or let someone else hurt her," Madison said. "I can't believe that."

"As Randy says in *Scream*, 'There's always some stupid bullshit reason to kill your girlfriend,'" Allie said. "Besides, I always thought Brad might hurt Cam. There was just something about the way he talked to her, the way he treated her."

"Cam would have left him," Madison said. Allie noted that Madison didn't say she was wrong about Brad. That meant that Madison had sensed the same quality that Allie had, the same undercurrent of mean, even if she hadn't identified it as such.

"Maybe," Allie said. She knew how easy it was for women to pretend that there was nothing wrong, to believe a man when he said it would never happen again. She'd spent years watching her mother and her stepfather perform the same dreadful dance. But she wasn't going to talk about that. She didn't ever talk about that. "I think that Brad would definitely hurt Cam if he thought he'd get something out of it."

"But what?" Madison said. Her voice was shaky, like she was barely holding on. "What could he possibly get out of it? If he didn't want to be with her anymore, he could have just broken up with her. That's what normal people do. They don't have their girlfriends murdered."

"Maybe it's for his own amusement or something," Allie said. "I don't really know. I just know that he brought us here in the first place and that he disappeared. Jesus, doesn't this road have an end? I still don't hear the sound of a highway."

Allie paused and Madison stopped a half second later. Madison seemed to get tangled up in her own feet, clutching Allie's arm for balance before she was able to right herself.

"I can't hear anything, either," Madison said. "What if it's farther away than we thought? I mean, we were all asleep in the car basically right up until we arrived at the cabin."

"Except for Brad," Allie said. She wished she could figure out Brad's role in all of this. He was culpable in some way; of that she was certain.

*And you want him to be the bad guy because you never liked him in the first place.*

Allie looked at the dirt road stretching out before them. It went straight into the horizon, running neatly in between the thick forest on either side. There was no movement ahead on the road, nor sound or sign of any person or animal in the woods.

"How can the road be this straight and flat?" Allie asked.

Madison looked confused, then shrugged. "Who cares?"

"It's not how dirt roads are, usually. They're rutted and pitted and full of rocks and they weave all over the place because they're just old cart tracks or something. They aren't smooth and straight and *groomed.*"

Because the road *was* groomed, Allie realized. She could see the marks of a rake or some similar implement on the edges of the road. She tugged Madison over to point out the marks.

"So?" Madison said again. Her tears were still falling, though less rapidly. "I don't get why this is important. I thought we were running away from someone who wanted to kill us. Someone from highway maintenance or whatever they're called came here and raked the dirt. Isn't that what they're supposed to do? Make sure that the roads are passable?"

"Yeah, they're supposed to make sure the *highways* are passable. This isn't a highway. It's probably not even a marked road on a county map. It's basically a driveway that leads to one place—that cabin back there. So why would someone come out here and smooth the dirt away? Why would the road be this flat and straight in the first place?" Allie said.

Madison shook her head, and Allie could tell that Madison didn't get it, didn't understand why Allie was making such a big fuss over this.

She felt a deep-seated frustration that she couldn't explain. It was important that the road was straight and flat and that all the dirt was neatly arranged over the top of it. It was all part of the growing certainty Allie had that all of this was staged, even if she didn't know why.

She looked up at the sky, at the light that didn't seem quite like sunlight. She thought about the straight road and the freshly built closets in the cabin and the lack of flies and mosquitoes and other buzzing things. She tasted the air, felt the recirculated smoothness slide over her tongue, and it all clicked together.

"We're inside," Allie said, and dropped to her knees, scrabbling at the dirt with her fingers.

"What are you doing?" Madison said. "Allie, have you lost it?"

"We're not outside at all," Allie said. "We're in a big, I don't know, some kind of warehouse maybe or indoor park. This is all a setup."

"A setup for what?"

"I don't *know*," Allie said, and she heard the frustration in her own voice, heard the longing for answers, for understanding. "I don't know why Brad brought us here or why Steve and Cam are dead—"

"Steve's *dead*?" Madison said, her voice rising into a howl on the last word. "Steve's dead and you didn't even tell me?"

"—but this has all been arranged for some reason. We're like players in a play, but nobody told us our lines. Like *The Blair Witch Project* or something. The actors in that weren't really told what would happen. They were just supposed to act natural and the filmmakers kept fucking with them, basically. But no one died. No one really died. Not like here. Not like us. So it can't be like *The Blair Witch Project*."

"Steve's dead and you're still talking about some goddamned horror movie? What is wrong with you? Is your heart made of stone?" Her tears fell thicker and faster now.

Allie's heart wasn't made of stone. Her emotions just wouldn't engage when there was a problem to be solved. Her whole intellect, her whole self, was wrapped up in the mystery of their circumstances. She wanted to comfort Madison. She really did. But that impulse was underneath the other one, the one that made her dig into the dirt beneath them, push her fingers down until she found the thing she expected to find.

"Concrete," she said triumphantly, brushing the last of the dust aside so Madison could see. "Look. Concrete."

"So?" Madison said, scrubbing at her eyes. "Steve's dead. I don't give a shit that there's a road under the road."

"You don't use concrete for roads, at least not this kind. There's no asphalt in this," Allie said. "This is proof that we're inside. We're in some kind of huge structure."

"I don't understand," Madison said, her brain seeming to move away from Steve and to their current problem. "We're, what, in a movie or something? Like you said, like *Blair Witch*?"

"No, I don't think it's a movie."

"Then what? Is it a game? Like that old movie with Michael Douglas, where he thought he was in this big life-threatening conspiracy but really it was all fake, some weird present from his brother or whatever?"

Allie stared at Madison. "A game. A great big game."

"I always thought that was a pretty shitty present, to terrorize your brother, but everyone was smiling at the end, so I guess it was all okay? At least that's what I remember."

"Mad, that's genius! A game. We're in some kind of game, like a survival game."

"For real? You think something *I* said was genius?"

"Well, yeah," Allie said, frowning. "Why wouldn't I think that?"

"I don't know," Madison said, shrugging. "Everyone knows that you think everyone else but you is stupid."

"I don't think that," Allie said automatically, but it wasn't true. She *did* look down on most people, did think almost everyone else was dumber than she. "Okay, maybe I do think that. A lot. And I'm sorry."

Madison shook her head. "I mean, don't be sorry, because it's true that you're smarter than me."

"But that doesn't mean you're stupid. And I'm sorry that I made you feel that way."

"We haven't always been the greatest friends to each other, huh?" Madison said. "Because I know me and Cam make you feel bad because you don't want to be a party girl all the time."

"Let's be better, then," Allie said, and put out her hand so Madison could hook it in a pinky promise like they were little kids.

Madison smiled a very watery smile. "Stamp it."

They hooked their fingers and then stamped their thumbs together, then looked at the patch of dirt Allie had cleared away.

"So, a game?" Madison said. "But whose game? And does it mean that Cam and Steve are really all right, that it's all fake, like in the movie?"

Allie thought back to the moment when the killer stepped through the door, saw again the arterial spurt pulsing out of Steve's body.

"It's not fake," Allie said, her voice grim. "We don't get a reset button if we die in here."

"You think Brad organized all this, don't you?"

"It's not looking good for him," Allie said. She faced Madison, hands on hips. "So, what do you think we should do th—"

Madison's eyes widened and she screamed, "Allie, no!"

A second later Allie was on the ground, shoved there by Madison's frantic movement. Then Madison was on the ground, too, a great gash in the left side of her neck, and her blood was pooling under Allie's hands and her mouth fell open but no sound came out.

Allie rolled away from Madison and saw the man, the man who'd come out of the woods behind her to ambush them while she was worrying about the goddamned road and now Madison was *dead*, dead like Steve and dead like Cam and dead like Allie was going to be if she didn't get her ass up and get moving.

The man stood above her, and she saw that he'd added a mask to the proceedings, a Lone Ranger–type half mask that would have made Allie laugh except that his stupid mask didn't matter, just the knife that he held in his hand. She saw the gleam in his eyes, the gleam that said he was enjoying this, that he wanted to feel her fear first, that he wanted her to know that she was completely alone.

Allie took a moment, calculated her chances.

She launched herself at him from the ground, keeping herself low like a football player pushing an exercise sled across the field. She took him by surprise, felt the whoosh of air rush out of him as she shouldered him in the solar plexus. He fell backward and the knife spun out of his grip, landing a few feet away.

Before he could really register what had happened or what she'd done, Allie stomped hard on his balls. Again she heard the rush of air in his lungs, but this time it was the sharp inhale that follows intense pain. He grabbed at his crotch while Allie ran to the knife, picked it up *(don't think about Madison's blood on it, don't think about it, don't don't don't)* and sprinted into the woods.

She heard the man's hoarse voice follow after her. "I'm going to *kill* you, you bitch! Do you hear me? I'm going to fucking *kill you!*"

*Can't kill me if you can't catch me,* Allie thought, and she ran harder than she'd ever run in her life, and she knew that if she stopped running, that life would be over, just another ignominious death in a world full of them.

*I don't want to die because of someone else's game. I don't want to die because Brad is the world's biggest asshole. I'm going to find that piece of shit and he is going to pay for this.*

Allie knew this was the kind of thing you told yourself when you were scared and the future was bleak, knew that Brad had never paid for a thing in his goddamned life and that he wasn't about to start now.

But she wanted him to pay. She really, really wanted that.

Allie wasn't looking at where she was running, knew that in some sense it didn't matter because she was inside, not really in a forest at all.

*If I just keep running, I'll get to a wall or a door. Even if this place is huge, there will be an end to it, and when I find the end to it, I'll probably find Brad.*

Allie didn't want to think about what would happen then, because if Brad had planned all this, then he was responsible for three murders. And someone who was willing to let that happen wouldn't balk at killing her, too.

She couldn't think about that, couldn't worry about what might happen later. She had to concentrate on getting away now, getting away from the man who was crashing through the woods behind her now, the man who kept shouting that he was going to rip her from end to end.

*Whoever Brad hired to play this part really seems to enjoy it,* Allie thought in a distant part of her brain, the part that wasn't gibbering with fear. She wondered if the order of deaths had been planned, or if it was just coincidental that she was the lone survivor—so far.

*You always wanted to be the final girl. You always said you could survive a horror movie, that you would be smarter, faster, better than anyone. So prove it.*

"Prove it," she murmured to herself even as her arms pumped and her legs propelled her forward, even as she heard the man crashing behind her getting closer and closer and closer.

"You *bitch*! I'm going to kill you, you bitch!"

*Get an original line, why don't you?* she thought, and she ran and ran, but part of her was stuck on two words.

*Prove it. Someone said that to me before. Just recently. Who was it?*

Allie crashed through the trees and found herself in a kind of open lane, a stretch of concrete flooring that nobody had bothered to hide.

On the other side of the lane, there was a wall. A huge white wall with a door cut into it, and above the door, four letters highlighted in red.

"Bitch! Bitch! I'm going to gut you when I catch you!"

Allie ran, ran, ran for the exit.

She slammed into the door, and pushed it open.

PART III

MAGGIE

# CHAPTER ONE

**apocalypseya:** I know they kind of got overdone a few years ago but I love those ya books with the dystopic future and dangerous killing games and their painfully obvious love triangles

**mags13:** agreed they're a total weakness. Pretty disappointed that you don't see as many of those kinds of books anymore

**apocalypseya:** maybe you should write your own!

**MAGGIE LOOKED DOWN AT** her hands, then glanced at the women on either side of her. The woman on her right was sobbing, her face pressed into her knees. On her left was another woman, staring at the opposite wall. It wasn't a stoic kind of stare, though. It was the thousand-yard stare of the exhausted and disbelieving, or maybe the woman's body hadn't yet shaken off the effects of the sedative they'd all been given. Another woman stood by the double doors, banging ceaselessly and energetically, shouting, "Let me out! Let me out! Let me out!"

*So her sedative has definitely worn off, then.*

Nobody tried to stop the screaming woman. Nobody tried to comfort the sobbing woman. Most of the women were like Maggie, their body language saying that they were resigned to their immediate future.

All the women were dressed the same way, in black leggings and gray tee shirts and white sneakers. The backs of their tee shirts had bright orange numbers on them. Maggie's was number three—she'd pulled it away from her body and peered over her shoulder to look at it.

She had not dressed herself in this stupid outfit, and that upset her a lot. It meant that someone else—possibly more than one someone else—had pawed at her, had taken her pajamas off her, had looked at her body without her permission. Maybe they'd laughed. Maybe they'd grabbed at her breasts or her thighs and she'd been completely out cold, unable to do anything about it.

Maggie wasn't as resigned as she pretended to be. She was angry. And she knew exactly who to be angry at—Noah.

Noah, her ex-husband, was a piece of shit, and when Maggie saw him again (assuming she survived the next twelve hours), she was going to kick his ass from here to kingdom come.

She wouldn't be in this situation if it wasn't for him. She was 100 percent certain of that. Most of the bad shit in her life had come down because of Noah. It was hard to remember now why she'd ever loved him in the first place, how she ever thought she could be happy with him. She sometimes thought of when they were younger, when they laughed together instead of screaming at one another all day, and it was like remembering somebody who wasn't her, remembering a character in a TV show that she'd watched long, long ago.

Now she was in a big metal room—a shipping container, if she wasn't mistaken—with nine other women who'd been equally fucked by life.

*No, not fucked by life. Fucked by the men in our lives, and not in the fun way.*

Maggie didn't know their stories, didn't know their names, but she was sure they'd all experienced the same thing—the terror of waking up in a strange place, groggy from the sedative, followed by a bright light shone in their faces.

Maggie had tried to speak, but her tongue had felt like it was rolling uselessly around her mouth. It didn't matter, anyway. A few moments after she had opened her eyes, a man came into the small room where she was being held. That was when she had realized she was tied to the chair, and she began to struggle to get free of the cords.

The man had laughed. "Well, he said you were a fighter. Glad you won't be a disappointment. Some of them are, you know. They just cry and cry."

Maggie couldn't see the man's face as he stayed out of the pool of light that shone directly on her. Her brain felt scrambled. "Wh-what are you—"

That was all she had managed to eke out because the man cut her off.

"You will not talk. You will listen. Your daughter, Paige, is in our custody. If you ever wish to see your daughter again, you will do exactly as we say, when we say it, and you will not ask questions."

Maggie stilled the moment the stranger had mentioned Paige. This monster had kidnapped her daughter? Was Paige hurt? Was she scared? Did they mean to hurt her?

"She is not hurt," the man had continued. "And we have no intention of hurting her, unless you become a problem. Are you going to become a problem? Shake your head yes or no."

Maggie shook her head no. She had to get out of this, whatever *this* was. She had to find Paige.

"Good. Now, listen carefully, because these instructions will only be given once. You are here to participate in a survival game. At the appointed time, you and nine other participants will be released into the Maze."

Maggie could hear the capitalization in his voice as he said this—"the Maze." *What the fuck is the Maze? Am I stuck in some kind of goddamned Dashner fan's fantasy?*

"In the Maze, there will be various obstacles to your completion of the course. You will attempt to conquer these obstacles. You will not refuse to participate at any time, no matter what the obstacles entail."

That sounded ominous. Maggie had squinted, trying to catch a glimpse of the man's face. She wanted to be able to describe him to the police later, when she got out of the situation.

*I'm going to get out of this. I'm going to get you, Paige.*

"You will have twelve hours to complete the Maze. Anyone who does not complete the Maze in the required time will be eliminated. Anyone who does not follow all rules and directions at all times will be eliminated."

"Eliminated?"

The hand had appeared out of the darkness, and a second later, Maggie's ears were ringing.

"You will not speak unless you are given permission to speak."

Maggie's teeth had ground together. She didn't know who this man was, but she was going to find out and make him pay for this. After she got free. After she found Paige.

"Any player who completes the Maze in the required time and under the required circumstances will be allowed to go. We would like to make sure you understand the gravity of your situation."

The man held up a phone with a video playing on the screen. There was no sound, but the video showed Paige in a big white room. She wasn't restrained, but she was hunched over her knees, and tears ran down her face. She wore the pajamas that she'd picked out the night before, mint green with little ice cream cones patterned all over.

*I'm going to kill this man,* Maggie thought. She could take any amount of abuse to herself, but anyone who made her baby cry could drop dead, do not pass Go, do not collect two hundred dollars.

"We don't wish to hurt your daughter," the man repeated. "But we will if we have to."

Those words had rung in Maggie's ears as she was untied by two other men, both of whom wore full balaclavas and sunglasses that covered their eyes. The men had blindfolded her, dragged her some unknown distance, and then yanked off the blindfold just before tossing her into this metal room. There had only been four other women in there then, and none of them had spoken to her. Maggie had waited with the others as their ranks grew, one by one.

Now there were ten of them waiting, waiting for a sign or a signal that their nightmare would shift, that they would have some chance to try to regain control of their fate.

Maggie's stomach rumbled, and her throat felt parched. She supposed it was purposeful that they—whoever *they* were—had left all the women hungry and thirsty. Suffering seemed to be the point of this exercise. And there was no person on this earth who wanted her to suffer more than Noah. He was the only one who would have arranged for her to be in this situation. The man had mentioned a "he" who had said Maggie was a "fighter." So it had to be Noah. He was the only person who hated her that much.

And it was all because Noah was angry about the custody decision at the hearing. It wasn't Maggie's fault that he was a coke addict who terrified the shit out of their ten-year-old daughter.

Paige had told the judge at the hearing that she didn't want to live with her dad, that she was scared of him, and even though she was a minor and Noah's lawyer had argued strenuously that Noah's income and lifestyle were far more advantageous to Paige's future *(as if the only thing that mattered was money)*, the judge had still awarded sole custody to Maggie.

Maggie knew that Noah couldn't give a shit about Paige. He was only interested in her as a weapon, as leverage he could use against Maggie.

The proof was in the pudding. If Noah cared about Paige at all, then he wouldn't allow his daughter to be used for this sick game. He wouldn't mind if Maggie were dropped into a pit of alligators, she knew that, but if he was any kind of decent dad, he wouldn't want Paige to be hurt or scared.

*But what if it isn't Noah? What if I've just been randomly selected by a bunch of weirdos?*

Maggie shook that thought away. It was definitely Noah. He had the money to arrange for something like this, and he hated her guts.

*I'm going to get out of here. I'm going to find Paige. I'm going to make sure that Noah never sees her ever again, not even for a supervised custody visit.*

Her mother must be worried sick right now. Maggie's widowed mother lived in the attached town house next to the one that she and Paige lived in, and Mom usually stopped by every morning to check in.

*How did they even get us?* Maggie wondered. *It must have been sometime last night, because Paige is still wearing her pajamas. And I know I set the security system before I went to bed. I double-checked it. I triple-checked it.*

Maggie always double- and triple-checked the security system because Noah had tried to break into the town house more than once. Infuriatingly, he somehow always managed to wiggle out of jail time even though Maggie always pressed charges.

*Because he's a rich white guy, and rich white guys get what they want. And rich white guys who pal around with the police in town really get what they want.*

But he hadn't gotten custody of Paige. He hadn't gotten custody of Paige because family court judges were not the same as criminal judges, and the family court judge had taken Maggie's— and Paige's—fear of Noah seriously and didn't care if Maggie was a middle-class Latina and Noah was a rich white guy.

The screeching sound that indicated the metal doors were being unlocked filled the container. The screaming woman, the one who'd been banging on the doors this whole time, increased her volume and frequency.

The doors swung open, and several men—dressed in black, wearing balaclavas and dark glasses—stood outside. One of them extended a long silver tube with a U-shaped end in the direction of the screaming woman. Maggie realized what it was a second before the man applied it to the woman's neck—a cattle prod. The woman screamed louder, for a brief and terrible moment. Then she keeled over backward. The air filled with the smell of burnt flesh.

"Oh my god," the crying woman beside Maggie whispered. "Is she dead?"

"You have been told not to speak unless spoken to, or you will be eliminated," the man who'd used the cattle prod said to the group at large. "This is your final warning."

The screaming woman wasn't moving. Maggie stared at her, hoping to see the rise and fall of her chest, hoping for some proof that she hadn't just seen a murder occur right in front of her.

The screaming woman still didn't move.

The crying woman began to sob again in earnest, holding her hand over her mouth to cover the sound. The men—there were about twenty of them—stepped back and lined up to face one another, leaving about four feet of space between the lines. The cattle-prod guy—who Maggie assumed was the leader—gestured at the remaining women.

"File out," he said.

The majority of the women looked around uncertainly.

Maggie stepped to the front of the line. She wanted to see what was coming. She gave the cattle-prod guy a hard look as she stepped down from the shipping container. He stared back at her—or at least she thought he did, since his glasses were pointed in her direction. His hand twitched on the cattle prod and she figured he must want to shock her on principle, but technically she hadn't done anything to violate his rules. She was pretty certain that he was the one who'd given her that little speech when she woke up tied to the chair.

Whoever he was, Maggie was coming back for him. She'd remember his voice. He had a slightly raspy undertone, like a lifelong smoker. And he smelled like smoke, too, now that she thought about it. She had a pretty clear idea of his height and build, despite his keeping to the shadows. She'd find him.

*First get through this goddamned nightmare,* she thought. *Then you can take your revenge or bring the authorities or whatever.*

Maggie walked down the line of men, who all stood impassively as the women passed by. She kept her chin up and her eyes straight ahead. She was not going to let a bunch of role-playing misogynistic assholes think they had broken her in any way.

The shipping container opened onto a wide grassy area, maybe four or five acres across, and faced a high white wall with double doors. The wall curved around left and right, away from the grass. Other than the grass and the wall, Maggie couldn't see anything but trees.

*So we're in the middle of a forest. I guess we're not in Arizona anymore, because there are no trees like that at home.*

That scared her, because it meant that she—and Paige—had been knocked out for a serious length of time and likely taken on a plane somewhere. Even if she managed to break out of this facility and away from these paramilitary yahoos, she didn't know where she would go. Was she even still in the US? What if she'd been taken to Canada, or even farther from home?

Once all of the women were out of the shipping container, the cattle-prod jerk shouted, "Stop!"

Maggie stopped walking. The woman behind her bumped into her back, treading on the back of Maggie's sneaker.

"Sorry," the other woman murmured.

Maggie turned to tell the woman it was all right. Before she could, one of the men in the line stepped out, grabbed the accidental bumper by the shoulder and slapped her across the face.

"Do not speak unless spoken to," he said. He then roughly released the woman so that she stumbled backward into Maggie and stepped back into the line.

Maggie put her arm around the other woman's shoulders—her number was six—and steadied her. #6 looked at Maggie, her eyes full of shock and fury.

Maggie nodded back at her to show that she understood exactly what #6 felt. Then cattle-prod guy strode past them until he reached the head of the line.

"Players!" he called, and Maggie confirmed that this was the same man who'd spoken to her inside. It was the same raspy smoker's voice. "You are about to enter the Maze. In the Maze, there are only two rules. You must complete all obstacles in the Maze or you will be eliminated. There will be no Katniss-ing this shit. You may not abstain from participation."

Maggie thought it notable that the man knew *The Hunger Games* well enough to reference it, and that he also assumed that everyone else there knew it, too. She supposed it had been a cultural phenomenon, but still . . . he didn't seem to be the reading type.

"The second rule is that you must complete the Maze in twelve hours or less, or you will be eliminated. This is also non-negotiable. When these doors behind me open up, you will enter the Maze. Once the doors close, the clock will begin running. Once the doors close, you may speak to one another, though at no time will you be permitted to speak to any male. Women are to be seen and not heard."

He said this like it was a joke, and all the men in the lines chuckled. Maggie wanted to run at the fucker and tackle him and stick him with that cattle prod several times. It was bad enough that they were all in this unbelievable situation to begin with. It was somehow worse that the leader spewed bad sexist dialogue like a cartoon villain.

*It doesn't matter if he acts like a character in a bad movie. He—or this organization or whatever—has your daughter. She's the only thing that matters, and you need to get through this and get her out.*

"You have all been told what is at stake for you. Remember that if you cease participation, your hostage will be eliminated as well."

That wasn't what the guy had told her in the room. He'd threatened Paige with harm, but he hadn't said he'd kill her. Was this really what was going on here? These pricks would kill a child if her mother didn't jump through their hoops?

Maggie felt #6 shift beside her and wondered who they were using to force the other woman to play their stupid game.

"Let the game begin," the man said, and the white double doors behind him swung open.

He stepped to one side as the women filed past, but not very far. If Maggie wanted to, she could have reached out and grabbed the cattle prod, or at least reached out and grabbed his balls and squeezed until he screamed. But she didn't, because this fucker had Paige somewhere. She stared death daggers at him until she passed by and entered through the double doors. Maggie couldn't see his mouth under the balaclava, but she was sure he was smirking. Men always smirked when they thought they'd gotten one over on you. She was going to wipe that smirk off his face.

*Count on it, fucker.*

The doors swung closed behind the ninth woman. Maggie didn't want to think about the screaming woman, who lay so still and quiet on the floor of the shipping container. She couldn't help that woman, couldn't do anything that might change her fate. All she could do was try to get through whatever was ahead.

A few seconds after the door closed, almost every woman started talking at once, most of them in various degrees of panic.

"Oh my god! They took my sister."

"What's happening? What are we doing here?"

"I have to get out of here. I have to get home. I have a business to run."

"They have my mom. My mom. She has a heart condition. What if she has a heart attack and dies?"

Maggie thought about telling them all to be quiet and focus, but she didn't want to be anybody's leader. She didn't want the responsibility of all these women and their hostages. She had to save Paige.

Maggie noticed that #6 stood beside her. She didn't want to be a leader, but it couldn't hurt to have an ally. She stuck her hand out.

"Maggie," she said.

"Sanya," the other woman said. She was a very slender African American woman with beautiful light brown eyes, almost golden. "They took my daughter."

"Mine, too," Maggie said.

"Any idea who set up this playland for assholes?"

"Nope. But I'm pretty sure it was my ex who got me roped into this."

"That's what I thought, too," Sanya said. "He's always trying to get me for something. I committed the grave crime of daring to divorce him after he cheated on me. This is a little, uh, extreme though. Compared to nonpayment of child support, which is his usual gambit."

"Not just extreme. Elaborate," Maggie said, gesturing around. "Who could have built all of this?"

They stood in an open grassy area, similar to the one outside the walls. Ahead of them, the walls narrowed into a passage maybe fifteen feet across. The walls were white, smooth and very high—too high to climb, even if she could find a handhold. Maggie liked to rock climb in her spare time—what she had of it after spending all her time fighting Noah—and she wasn't afraid of heights. But it looked like the organizers had eliminated climbing as an option. She'd have to inspect the walls more closely.

A blinking light overhead caught Maggie's attention. She glanced to the left and noticed a large digital clock on the wall, counting down the time from twelve hours.

Sanya followed her gaze. "Looks like we should get started with this shitshow."

"Yeah," Maggie said.

The two of them jogged in unison toward the entrance to the Maze.

"Hey!" one of the women behind them shouted. "Where are you going?"

"Where do you think we're going?" Maggie shouted back over her shoulder.

"Seriously," Sanya muttered beside her. "That jerk with the cattle prod made it very clear that participation was not optional. What part of 'not optional' do they not understand? I've got to get my girl out of here."

Maggie snorted, then sobered. "Yeah, but I don't want anyone else getting hurt. Do you think she's dead?"

"Number eight?" Sanya asked.

Maggie nodded. The screaming woman's tee had a large orange eight on the back.

"It didn't look like she was alive," Sanya said. "But I find it hard to believe that this group, whatever it is, would kill a woman right in front of us."

"They seem perfectly willing to kidnap a bunch of women and

throw them into their gladiator arena," Maggie said. "Why not kill people?"

"I guess. Kidnapping would already be a felony charge, and the penalties are sometimes higher than for murder. It depends on the state and whether or not the charge is first degree or aggravated or if the charge is second degree. First degree or aggravated can result in a life sentence, again depending on the state. Of course, if they crossed state lines with us, that could result in a federal felony charge." Sanya said all of this with almost automatic recitation, like she didn't have to think about what she said.

"Because of the Lindbergh baby, right?"

Sanya nodded. "Right, that law was put in place to allow federal officers to pursue kidnappers over state lines."

"Are you a lawyer?"

Sanya nodded again. "Division attorney for the great city of Chicago, which is nobody's second city. It's not as glamorous as it sounds, though. Mostly I prosecute municipal ordinance violations, and the bulk of them are misdemeanors. What do you do when you're not running through some freak's maze?"

Maggie laughed, a little out of breath because she was jogging while talking. "I'm a school librarian in Tucson, which means I've read a lot of young adult apocalypse fiction."

"Hopefully that means you have lots of knowledge that will get us and our girls out of this mess," Sanya said.

"Only if these dumbasses read the same books as me and follow the same formula," Maggie said. It felt strangely soothing to have a semi-normal conversation, even if the circumstances didn't warrant it. She wondered if Sanya felt the same way, that she was grasping at something normal in a very abnormal situation.

"Yeah, you're right," Sanya said. "They didn't seem like they spent a lot of time in the library. Which means that everything we encounter will be from some movie one of them saw once."

"It's funny that you say that, because when cattle-prod guy talked about Katniss, I thought he didn't look like a big reader. I guess it wouldn't matter, though, if he saw the movie. I kind of forgot about the movie."

"Jennifer Lawrence is Jennifer Lawrence Superstar because of that movie," Sanya said.

"Yeah, but I'm not a big movie watcher. I'd rather read."

"Unsurprising in a librarian. I'm more of a reader myself."

They entered the first passage. Maggie smoothed her hand along one of the walls as she passed, trying to see if there were any potential handholds.

"What are you looking for? Secret doors?" Sanya asked.

"Handholds," Maggie said. "I'm a rock climber. I thought maybe I could climb up to the top and see how big the maze is, or see a clear path out."

"I thought you had impressive biceps for a librarian," Sanya said. "No go?"

Maggie shook her head. "Not here, anyway. I'll keep checking."

"I don't think they'll make it that easy," Sanya said.

"Probably not," Maggie said. "I have the distinct impression that they want to make us suffer."

There was a rustling behind them. Maggie looked back and saw that the rest of the women were approaching, strung out in twos and threes.

Maggie and Sanya reached the end of the first passage. The maze came to a T-intersection there, extending off to the left and right. In front of them was a long white table covered in a thick white tablecloth like at a fancy restaurant. On top of the table were six cloth bags in neon colors—yellow and pink and orange and green. Each bag had a blank tag tied to a string that was wrapped around the bag's opening.

"Is this an obstacle?" Maggie said.

"I don't think they put this here for fun," Sanya said.

They both stared at the table for a minute. Maggie wondered if Sanya felt as reluctant as she did to open the bags.

"They did say that the obstacles were required," Sanya said.

"Yeah, I know," Maggie said. "I just have a bad feeling that the bags have scorpions in them, or bombs or something."

The other seven women caught up with Maggie and Sanya while they stood there.

"What's going on?" one of them asked.

Maggie glanced over at the speaker—medium height, professional blonde highlights, twisted mouth. Maggie didn't want to make assumptions about the woman because they were all in this shitshow together, but the blonde had a whiff of privilege about her, like she was used to asking for what she wanted and getting it. Maggie had a strong feeling that this woman drove a BMW crossover and wore overpriced yoga pants and always had something to say at the school board meeting. She felt her back molars grinding. This was a type that made Maggie crazy.

*You've got to stop being so judgmental. Maybe she's not like that at all.*

"Jesus Christ, what are all of you standing around for?" The blonde pushed through the crowd and strode toward the table. Maggie saw a two on the back of her shirt. "I don't know about the rest of you, but the sooner I get through this, the sooner I can get back to my real life. I have a multimillion-dollar company that can't wait."

*Yep, she's definitely that type. Probably asked to see the manager the second she woke up tied to a chair.*

#2 grabbed a neon pink bag and yanked at the string. She didn't even look inside the bag before dumping the contents on the table.

A bottle of water and an off-brand granola bar fell out.

"Thank god," she said. "I'm so thirsty I could die."

She opened the bottle of water and tipped her head back, swallowing it as fast as she could.

The rest of the women moved forward. Maggie took one of the bags and opened it cautiously, because she didn't trust that every bag would have the same contents. Beside her, Sanya did the same thing. They both peered into their bags before looking at each other.

"Water and goldfish crackers," Maggie said.

"Water and a Nutri-Grain bar," Sanya said, making a face. "I hate Nutri-Grain bars."

"I don't mind them," Maggie said. "Swap?"

"Hey, I didn't get anything," one of the women said, her voice full of outrage.

"Me, neither," said another, in a very small voice.

#2 had crammed most of the granola bar into her mouth already. Now she spoke around a mouthful of toasted oats.

"You snooze, you lose. These are obstacles for a reason."

"Hey," Maggie said. "There's no reason why we can't share what we have. Just because they put us in this maze like animals doesn't mean we have to act like it."

A couple of the other women murmured their agreement, but two of them clutched their bags to their chests.

"I'm not giving up any of mine," #4 said.

#9 nodded beside her. "Who knows if this is the only water we'll get for the next twelve hours?"

"If it is, then all the more reason to share," Maggie said. "We don't want anyone else to end up like number eight."

"I'm not giving up anything I've got," #9 said, and moved to stand closer to #4 and #2.

"Swap," Maggie said to Sanya. "You can have the crackers."

"No worries," Sanya said, beckoning to #1 and #7, the two who'd been left out. "We can pool with them."

#5 had opened her granola bar and started eating it already, but now she stepped forward with a slightly guilty look. "Sorry I already bit into it. Anybody can share what I have left."

"Cool," Maggie said, opening the package of crackers. "Let's put what we have on the table and divide it up between the five of us. I'm sorry to say that we're all going to have to share the same bottles of water, so I hope none of you are the backwash type."

#7 laughed, and #1 gave a timid smile.

*She's a little mouse,* Maggie thought. *If she's not careful, she's going to get eaten up in here.*

#10 looked between Maggie's group and the two women standing close to #2. She appeared torn.

"Nobody's making you do anything you don't want to do," Maggie said to her. "I just think we all stand a better chance of getting out of here if we help each other."

"And I think that kumbaya shit is going to get you killed," #2 said. "You can all stand around here having a picnic together, but time's running out, and I'm not going to be stuck here with a bunch of losers."

# CHAPTER TWO

**mags13:** LOL I'm more of a reader than a writer, although I will admit that I've fantasized about how I would handle one of those dystopian games

**apocalypseya:** who among us hasn't been convinced that they could do a better job than Katniss?

**mags13:** to be fair she was distracted by her hot teammate. That wouldn't happen to me. I'm too old to be distracted by men's bullshit, hot or not

**battleroyale:** tell me about it, sister

**#2 POINTED TO THE** clock on the wall overhead.

"I'm going to get out of here even if you don't," she said, swallowing the last of her water and tossing the bottle on the ground. She gave a derisive look at the small piles of food on the table. "Have fun with that."

#2 jogged away to the left of the T-junction. Maggie watched her go. *Yep, she's definitely that type.* It made Maggie feel marginally better about making snap judgments.

"Since we don't know if we're going to get any more water, I think maybe we should all just take a swig off the one bottle and save the other," Sanya said.

"Good idea," #5 said.

"But I'm so thirsty," #7 said.

"We all are," Maggie said, trying not to be annoyed. #7 had a petulant look about her, not quite as high-tone as #2, but definitely up there on the Karen scale. "But let's try to think long-term if we can."

#4, #9, and #10 were all hastily finishing their own snack bags, though Maggie noticed that #10 only drank half of her water. Then the three of them took off in the direction of #2.

"How do they know that's the right way to go?" #1 murmured.

"They don't," Maggie said. "It's a maze, which means that you have to make choices, and sometimes those choices will be wrong."

"How big do you think it could be?" #5 asked, stuffing a few crackers into her mouth. She was a short Asian woman with a cute pixie cut that was dyed electric blue at the tips. Maggie loved that cut, but her own face was too broad to pull it off. "I'm Natalie, by the way."

They all introduced themselves. #1 was Elizabeth ("but you can just call me Beth") and #7 was Roni.

"So what do you think? About the size of the maze, I mean," Natalie said again.

All the women looked at her, and Maggie realized she'd become their de facto leader. She felt a little tug of nervousness. She didn't want to be in charge of all these women, all these lives. To have an ally was one thing, but if any of them didn't make it through the maze because of a decision she made, Maggie didn't think she could live with herself.

"Well," Maggie said slowly, because she was thinking as she talked, and she didn't want to say anything that someone might decide to use against her later. "They gave us twelve hours to get through. So either the maze is very big, or the obstacles are much more difficult than this one. Or both."

Natalie nodded. "That's what I was thinking, too. And if it's big, we don't want to have to double back if we can avoid it, so rushing through doesn't make a lot of sense."

"But we do have to go fast enough not to fall too far behind on time," Sanya said. "We've already eaten up a half hour."

"Oh god," Roni moaned. "How are we going to do this? How did this happen?"

Maggie clapped her hands together three times, a librarian habit she used at story time when the kids were getting squirrelly.

"Look, this is hard on all of us. If we work together, we're going to get through. So let's get moving."

*Not the world's most inspiring speech, Mags,* she told herself as they jogged along in the opposite direction from the other group. *Could you be any more clichéd?*

It wasn't her job to give inspiring speeches to the troops. The only priority she had at this moment was to get through the maze and get Paige.

*But you don't want any of these others to get hurt, either.*

Maggie let a little sigh escape her lips. No, she couldn't let anyone else get hurt. It was fundamentally against her nature to allow anyone to be harmed if she could avoid it.

*Although maybe I wouldn't mind letting #2 fall into a Pit of Despair, or whatever else they might have set up in here.*

They went along for about fifteen minutes. Natalie and Sanya and Maggie conferred at each turn before deciding which way to go. Beth went along with whatever they decided, and Roni spent most of the time complaining.

"This is impossible. Impossible," Roni said.

In between complaints, Roni told everyone about her mother, who lived with her and had a very serious heart condition. She also told them all about her job as an insurance underwriter, her shitty ex-husband who'd taken their house and most of their assets in the divorce, and the general misery of her life.

Maggie did her best to tune Roni out, thinking only of Paige. She had to get to Paige.

It soon became clear that only Maggie and Sanya and Natalie were in any shape to move at a decent clip. Beth tried her best but was continuously out of breath, and Roni didn't seem to want to try at all.

"I can't do this," Roni moaned. "I'll never make it. I can't run like this."

Sweat poured over Roni's temples, and the front of her shirt stuck to her chest, which was not small.

"You have to," Natalie said. "If you don't try to get through, they'll kill you and your hostage."

"My mom," Roni said. "They took my mom. She has a heart condition."

Maggie exchanged a glance with Sanya. She knew they were both thinking the same thing—should they try to help Roni along, or should they just leave her behind? Every second was precious, and Roni could potentially jeopardize the whole group.

Maggie shook her head no once, and Sanya looked resigned. They couldn't leave Roni behind even if they wanted to. They couldn't let the woman's poor mother die because her daughter didn't have the physical strength to save them both.

Beth had fallen several paces behind the group, and Maggie dropped back to jog next to her. As she did, she saw Sanya move next to Roni and murmur words of encouragement. Natalie glanced at both pairs and said, "I'm going to scout out the next turn."

Maggie nodded. Natalie had revealed that she was a regular marathoner, and a fast one, too. She'd already scouted some of the turns for them, making sure they didn't accidentally walk into something terrible.

Beth gave Maggie an apologetic look. Her small pale face was coated in a thin sheen of perspiration, and her chest heaved with every step.

Maggie said, "Maybe you should walk for a few minutes, catch your breath."

Beth shook her head. "I . . . have . . . asthma," she managed to choke out. "They . . . took . . . my . . . inhaler."

"Shit," Maggie said. "What can we do to help you?"

"Nothing," Beth said. "Unless . . . there's . . . a . . . coffee . . . pot . . . somewhere. Caffeine."

"Well, at least you can joke about it," Maggie said. "But seriously, you need to walk for a bit. Maybe sit down and take some deep breaths."

Beth shook her head, and Maggie knew she was thinking of her hostage. Beth had said the least of all of them, hadn't revealed anything about why she thought she was there or about her life or hobbies or job. Maggie couldn't rid herself of the initial impression she'd had of Beth as a mouse, a little mouse trying to scurry along the baseboards until she could dart into a hole.

"Look," Maggie said. "Asthma attacks can kill you, right? If you don't get your breathing under control, you're not going to make it through. We still have a long way to go."

The skin around Beth's eyes tightened. Maggie could tell she didn't want to stop, but Beth's breathing was getting more labored by the second.

"Okay, enough," Maggie said, putting her arm in front of the other woman. "You've got to stop for a little bit and get this under control."

Beth tried for a second to push past Maggie, but Maggie gave her the "quiet in the library" look that brooked no disagreement. Beth stumbled to a halt and sat down with her back against the high, smooth wall, her breath a thin wheeze.

"Sanya!" Maggie called, for the other two had gotten farther ahead as Beth struggled.

Sanya glanced back, said something to Roni, who also looked over her shoulder and then shouted, "Thank Christ!" before sitting down herself. Sanya jogged back to Maggie.

"You do not look good," Sanya said to Beth.

"She has asthma," Maggie said. "She's got to sit for a while and catch her breath. And then I think we're going to need to walk for a while."

Beth shook her head and opened her mouth, but Maggie held up her hand to still her.

"Don't try to talk. Just calm down and try to take long, deep breaths if you can. I know what you're going to say, anyway. You're going to say that the rest of us shouldn't stay just for you, that we should leave you behind because you can't keep up."

Beth just stared at her with huge brown eyes, looking like a puppy waiting for the inevitable kick of a cruel master.

"But we're not going to do that," Maggie said. "Or at least I'm not. I don't want to speak for anyone else."

"I won't, either," Sanya promised. "Women should look out for each other, and I'm not going to be like that bitch number two. I am definitely better than her."

Maggie laughed. "Yeah, me, too."

Beth gave them both a little smile, and Maggie thought that Beth's smiles were probably rare and wonderful gifts, earned by only the fewest.

"Hey," Natalie called, jogging back.

She went right past Roni without a look, which let Maggie know that Natalie, at least, would leave Roni behind without regret. She stopped when she reached their huddle of three. Maggie noticed the wrinkle of worry between her eyes.

"Are you okay?" Natalie asked Beth.

Beth held up her hand and flapped it loosely. Maggie wasn't sure, but Beth's breathing seemed to be smoothing out.

"You're not going to believe what's up ahead," Natalie said. "I'm not even sure how to describe it."

"Try," Sanya said.

"Well, it kind of looks like a jungle?" Natalie said, her voice turning up at the end to make it a question.

"You're not sure?" Maggie asked.

Half of her attention was on Beth, making sure the other woman was breathing normally. Maggie didn't know what they would do if Beth's airways constricted past the point of no return. She couldn't believe those fuckers had taken Beth's inhaler. It was like they wanted her to fail.

*That's exactly it. They want her, and you, and everyone else here to fail while claiming they gave you a fair shot. But they've stacked the deck so that a fair shot doesn't really exist.*

"Well, it's extremely weird to see a jungle in the middle of a man-made maze," Natalie said, responding to Maggie's question.

"It's extremely weird to be in the middle of a man-made maze," Sanya said. "I'm not sure anything could surprise me after this."

"It will," Natalie said.

"How are you feeling now?" Maggie asked Beth.

"Better," she said, and then her eyes darted nervously around the circle of women. "But I don't think I can run anymore."

"It's okay," Maggie said, coming to her feet and offering Beth a hand to help her up. "It seems we're going to have to cross a jungle, anyway. I don't think there will be much running."

The group of four started toward the next turn of the maze. As they passed Roni, she heaved a melodramatic sigh.

"I'm so tired," she said. "And hungry."

"So's everyone else," Maggie said.

Roni huffed out an insulted breath, but Maggie kept walking.

She didn't want to leave the other woman to her own devices, but the whining was getting pretty old pretty quick. It was also hard to feel sympathy for Roni when Beth had an actual medical condition and Beth was trying her hardest not to be a burden on everyone. Roni seemed to relish the idea of being a burden.

The group made it up to the turn in a few minutes, and Natalie pointed right.

"It's there."

They stepped out into the middle of the maze, and all of them stared.

"You're right," Maggie said after a few stunned moments. "It's definitely a jungle."

The stretch of maze before them was covered with climbing greenery from the top of the walls on both sides and down to the ground. In between, there were trees and thick, lush plants with huge leaves.

"How did they put this here?" Sanya asked. "It looks like it was properly grown. Look."

She pointed at the ground underneath the plants.

"There's actually soil," she said.

"How long were they planning this?" Natalie asked. "Long enough to grow a goddamn jungle?"

"They could have had the plants shipped in from somewhere else and just deposited them in the soil here," Maggie said. "Let's not make this conspiracy any bigger than it needs to be."

"You mean bigger than a strange organization kidnapping ten women and their family members and dropping them into some sick game? Which they are no doubt observing right now?" Sanya said.

"Yes, that's what I mean," Maggie said.

She hadn't thought about the men watching until Sanya said it, but of course, they must be. What was the fun of forcing people to participate in a game if you didn't get to watch the game? She imagined the bastard with the cattle prod in one of those rolling office chairs, his feet up on a counter, a bank of monitors before him. Maybe he was eating pizza or French fries, the cattle prod propped up beside him. Maybe he was laughing.

"So what do we do?" Beth asked in her smallest voice. She'd shrunk back when she saw the jungle before them.

"We go through it," Maggie said. "Carefully. It's probably filled with traps and tricks."

"Do you think there are spiders?" Beth said, her voice even tinier than it had been a moment before.

Maggie glanced at her. Beth's face was bloodless.

"You don't like spiders?"

Beth shook her head.

"If it means anything, I'm not too fond of them myself," Natalie said.

Spiders didn't bother Maggie. She lived in the Southwest, and there were tarantulas everywhere. Natalie was clearly trying to make Beth feel better. It seemed, though, that Natalie just disliked spiders. Beth appeared bone-deep terrified.

"There might be spiders," Maggie said. She didn't think it would be a good idea to lie to the other woman. "But we'll all be together. We'll be with you, and you can get through this."

*Ugh, more stupid platitudes.* But she didn't know what else to say, really. Maggie wasn't worried about spiders, in any case. Or snakes, or any other fauna that might be crawling through the greenery in front of them. What worried her was the possibility of traps—hidden holes that might break someone's leg, say, or trip wires. That seemed like the sort of thing that might amuse the guy with the cattle prod and his giggling little buddies.

"What the hell is all this shit?"

The voice was behind them. The group turned as one to see the second gang, led by #2, come jogging up. Maggie noticed that they all looked sweaty and out of sorts. Seemed like #2's path had been longer than their own, though they were clearly keeping up a faster clip. #4 and #9 stopped on either side of #2, but #10 hung back a step, like she wasn't sure she wanted to associate with the other three.

"As you can see," Sanya said (in a voice that Maggie imagined she used in court), "it's a jungle."

"We're supposed to go through it or what?" #2 said.

"What do you think?" Maggie said.

"Then why the hell are you dumbasses just standing around?" #2 tapped her wrist, as if there were a watch there. "Time's ticking."

She charged ahead, deliberately pushing through their group instead of going around. #4 and #9 stayed on her heels, but #10 went around the group, throwing them an apologetic glance.

"Hey!" Roni said. "What's your problem?"

"Get going or get out of my way," #2 said. "I don't have time for your bullshit."

"And yet you took longer to get here than we did," Maggie said. "Despite all of our kumbaya crap."

Sanya and Natalie grinned as #2 looked momentarily flustered. Then she put her armor back up, the hardness back in her eyes and jaw.

"Let's just see who gets to the end first," #2 said. "I never lose."

"It's not a race," Maggie said.

"That's what you think," #2 said. "What if they decide to only let out the first three that arrive at the end or something like that? I'm not going to be left behind."

"Do you think they would do that?" Sanya asked in a low voice so only Maggie could hear.

"I think that there are no real rules and they can do whatever they want," Maggie responded in the same tone. Then slightly louder, "But we're not there yet. We're here, and we have to get through what's in front of us."

"Good luck with that," #2 said.

Maggie could hardly believe such a walking stereotype existed in real life. #2 was hardly a person at all—more like someone dreamed up in a writer's room.

#2 moved toward the mass of plants before them. #4, #9 and #10 followed behind, even though #2 didn't give any indication that she noticed or cared what happened to them. The four of them quickly disappeared into the thick growth. Maggie heard the rustle of leaves and the crack of branches, but it faded swiftly. She didn't know if it was because the other group was moving so fast or because the plants were so thick that they muffled any noise.

Sanya and Natalie started forward, but Maggie held up her hand. "Wait. Wait and see for a minute."

Sanya gave her a sideways look, and Maggie flushed. It was incredibly cruel, what she was doing. She was letting the other group go ahead so that they could trigger any traps, but only Sanya seemed to realize it.

"Are we really doing this?" Sanya murmured.

"I don't *want* anyone to get hurt," Maggie said. "But if it has to happen, then my priority is making sure it doesn't happen to you guys."

"I have to pee," Roni said. "Like, really bad."

"So pee," Maggie said.

"Right out here in the open?" Roni said, obviously aghast. "I thought maybe I could go hide under a tree or a leaf or whatever."

"I kind of had the same idea," Natalie admitted. "I've been holding on to it for a while. I didn't want to give those pricks a thrill by letting them see my ass hanging out."

"They already saw your ass when they put you in that stupid uniform," Maggie said.

Natalie appeared disconcerted. "I forgot. It's been one thing after another since I woke up, and I forgot. They saw me. They touched me."

Natalie ran her hands up and down her arms like she could wipe away what had happened. Maggie's stomach gave a guilty little twist. She hadn't meant to be so blunt, to make anyone else feel worse about their situation.

"I'm sorry," she said. "I didn't mean to remind you."

"No, it's okay," Natalie said. "I mean, it's not okay that it happened, but it's okay that you reminded me. Because it happened to all of us, right? So we can help each other, like you said. We can make it better for us, let them know that what they did won't hurt us."

Maggie nodded. So did Beth and Sanya.

"Okay, so what we should do now—" Maggie began, but Roni pushed past, her hands flapping in a panic.

"I have to *pee right now*," Roni shouted, running toward the jungle's entrance.

"Wait, Roni, don't!" Maggie said.

But it was too late. Roni plowed into the trees, just a little to the left of where #2 and her gang had entered.

Just a little to the left, and then something exploded, and someone was screaming, but it wasn't Roni, because Roni was gone. Roni was a spray of blood and flesh and bone, and Roni's mother with the heart condition wasn't going to make it, because even if the men didn't kill Roni's mother, she'd probably die from the shock.

Maggie's ears rang. She felt her breath heaving in her chest, like she couldn't get enough oxygen. Beth sobbed beside her, her hand clinging to Maggie's sleeve like a child's.

"I told her not to go," Maggie said. Her voice sounded far away to her own ears, like it was coming from somewhere outside her body. "I told her. You heard me."

"It wasn't your fault," Sanya said. "Not your fault at all. Someone like her, she probably wasn't going to make it anyway."

"That's harsh," Natalie said. A tear ran down each of her cheeks, like she'd been shocked into crying.

"It's true, though," Sanya said. "You know it even if you don't want to say it."

Natalie pressed her lips together but didn't say anything else. Maggie noticed her glance at Beth, though, and realized that the other woman was thinking the same thing about Beth that Sanya had said about Roni.

*She's probably not going to make it,* Maggie thought. *I have to get used to the idea now.*

"We should get moving," Maggie said.

"Into the minefield?" Sanya said.

"All roads lead this way. We don't have a choice if we want to get through," Maggie said.

As she said this, they heard another explosion, deeper into the jungle, followed by a scream of terror.

"Maybe that bitch number two got blown up," Natalie said, then gave everyone a sideways look. "Don't try to tell me you weren't thinking it."

"Oh, no, I definitely was thinking it," Maggie said. "But I was also thinking about how to get through this without all of us being blown to smithereens one by one."

Maggie's eyes moved toward the gory splat that used to be Roni, and the others did the same.

"So what was your idea, fearless leader?" Sanya asked.

"Don't call me that," Maggie said.

"It's already happened, whether you want it to or not," Sanya said.

"Just . . . don't call me that," Maggie said. She felt again the tremendous burden of responsibility, of the feeling that it was on her to get all of them through the maze. She'd already failed Roni.

*No, I didn't fail her,* Maggie told herself firmly. *Roni charged ahead. Roni didn't listen.*

But it was still difficult for Maggie to think about Roni's mother. Roni's mother was going to hear something that no mother ever wanted to hear—that her daughter was dead.

And then, according to the cattle-prod prick, Roni's mother would die, too.

Maggie thought about her own daughter, thought about her daughter all alone and scared, and she stiffened her spine. Roni was the past now. Maggie couldn't do anything about Roni anymore, couldn't help her or her mother in any way. Maggie had to go forward. She had to think about the living.

"Okay, so what I was thinking is that we each get something like a long stick and make the end pointy," Maggie said. "And then we stay in a tight group, two by two, and use the sticks to prod the ground in front of us."

"So that we'll be able to feel the explosive with the stick and then avoid it," Sanya said. "That could work. I think I saw that in a World War Two movie once, except they used their bayonets."

"Right," Maggie said. "I was thinking of the same movie."

"Isn't that funny?" Sanya said, shaking her head. "Especially since we both just said we'd rather read."

"Movies stick in your head," Maggie said. "The power of visual media."

"What if the bombs are so pressurized that even the touch of a stick will set them off?" Natalie asked, and then gestured at the remains of Roni. "Mines in World War Two didn't usually vaporize people."

"Well, we can use really long sticks," Maggie said. "Hopefully we'll be out of range if one of the explosives goes off."

"Hopefully?" Natalie said.

"You have a better idea?" Sanya asked. "Because if so, you can feel free to tiptoe wherever you want without us."

"No," Natalie said. "I just . . . I'm scared."

Her words seemed to run around the group. Beth's hand, still holding Maggie's sleeve, trembled.

"I'm scared, too," Maggie said. "But we don't really have a choice, do we? We have to go forward."

"What if we didn't?" Natalie said. "What if we just sat down and refused to participate?"

"We know what would happen," Maggie said. "We all saw what happened to her, at the beginning."

The cattle prod pressing into flesh, the body falling backward.

"What if it wasn't real?" Natalie said. "What if she's not really dead, and it was just an act to convince us we have to play this game?"

"It could have been a performance," Maggie said. "But I don't think so. And anyway, we all saw what happened to Roni. Whatever this is and whoever is running it—they're deadly serious. It doesn't matter what we want right now. We have to play the game, and if we want to save our hostages, we have to win."

Sanya nodded, and so did Beth.

"Okay," Natalie said. "Let's play."

# CHAPTER THREE

**mags13:** I think I'd be okay in a hunger games–style scenario

**battleroyale:** are you in the military or something? Because I don't think I could kill other people.

**mags13:** oh no I'm not killing anyone. Not on purpose anyway.

**tyz7412:** if those are the rules of the game you don't have a choice

**MAGGIE BROKE OFF ONE** of the branches from a nearby tree to use as a prod. She was careful not to step onto the dirt of the jungle area at all, since Roni had been killed by a mine that was very close to the edge. She didn't have any tools to sharpen the point, but she did tear off the large, floppy green leaves and any smaller branches. Sanya did the same with another branch, and they huddled up into a two-by-two formation near the place where #2 and her cronies had entered the jungle.

Maggie and Sanya carefully inserted the tips of each stick into the dirt before them, feeling for anything that might be just under the surface. It was slow, frustrating work, and Maggie sensed both Natalie and Sanya getting impatient with her caution.

"We can follow the other group's footsteps," Sanya said.

The first set of women had clearly plowed through the jungle with no regard for any danger. There were broken leaves and branches in a clear path ahead, as well as the marks of their sneakers on the ground.

"We can use them as a guide," Maggie said. "But one of their group got blown up, too. We heard the explosion, heard the scream. It might have just been luck that they missed some of the other mines."

"We're just going so slow," Sanya said.

"Slow or dead," Maggie said. "I know which one I'd rather be."

When they'd entered the jungle, Maggie had noticed the lack of sound right away. There hadn't been much sound in the main part of the maze, but she'd still heard the distant echoes of the men outside shouting to each other or doing maneuvers or whatever they were up to. The greenery of the space seemed to block all that out, to blanket the area in a deceptive quiet.

Beth held on to the back of Maggie's shirt like a child trying not to lose their parent in a crowd. Maggie wondered again what her story was, how she'd gotten there. Maggie herself was still pretty convinced that her own kidnapping was Noah's doing, but Beth didn't seem like the kind of person who would piss anybody off at all, much less to the degree that Maggie had done for Noah. It made her sad sometimes, to think about how once they'd been happy, how they'd laughed together, how they couldn't wait to see one another at the end of the day. Then Noah started doing cocaine with his coworkers after work instead of—sometimes in addition to—having a few beers. He became paranoid, frightening, and often violent, and Maggie had to forget the person he'd been, the person she'd fallen in love with. That man was gone.

But Noah was so angry when she said that, when she defied him, when she took Paige and ran.

He was so angry.

And then she'd filed for divorce, and gotten custody of Paige, and he was even angrier than before—angry because he'd lost, angry because, as he put it, "that bitch judge sided with you." Angry because he was a man and he expected the world to fall into line for him the way it always had.

Maggie could definitely see him encountering something like the group that had kidnapped her and agreeing with their base philosophy, which seemed to be "punish women." She imagined it as some online group, a private chat that became reality.

*But this reality is pretty elaborate. Who pays for this? How did they set up some giant maze without newspapers or local TV stations catching on? How do they keep it a secret?*

She shook away her questions. She needed to pay attention to the here and now, to focus on what was in front of her. If she didn't, they could all die.

A few minutes later, Sanya inserted the tip of the stick into the dirt, and Maggie heard a tiny metallic ping.

"Shit," Sanya said. "I found one."

"Oh god," Natalie said. "What now?"

"Stay calm," Maggie said. "Don't take the stick out yet. Nobody move your feet at all. I'm going to get something to mark the spot, and then you can all come single file behind me for a few feet. We don't know how big these mines are."

Maggie took a few steps off the path they'd been following, careful to prod the ground before her, and grabbed a handful of hot pink flowers with oversized petals. They were so bright that they looked almost fake, like someone had painted them.

A tune rose up from the depths of her memory, an animated film she'd watched with Paige when her daughter was three or four.

*Painting the roses red, we're painting the roses red . . .*

She moved carefully back to the group, stepping into the foot marks she'd made already, and dropped the flowers over the spot where Sanya stood, trembling, holding the stick into the ground.

"What if I set it off when I pull the stick out?" Sanya whispered.

Maggie thought about this for a moment. "I think it's probably set off by pressure, but more pressure than you're applying at the moment."

A bead of sweat dripped over the bridge of Sanya's nose and fell onto the ground. "Better safe than sorry. All of you get ahead of me."

"Sanya—" Maggie began.

"No," Sanya said. "If this thing goes off, then I want all of you out of harm's way. It doesn't make any sense for all of us to get blown into little bits."

Maggie did not like this idea at all. She'd already lost one member of the group, and if she was completely honest, the last person she wanted to lose was Sanya. The other woman was smart, strong and practical, and Maggie liked her on top of everything else.

"You know you'd do the exact same thing," Sanya said, holding Maggie's gaze. "You know you would."

"Please, let's do what she wants," Natalie said.

Maggie felt a little flare of anger. Of course Natalie wanted to go ahead. Then she would be safe, and it wouldn't matter what happened to Sanya.

*She's scared. She can't help it,* Maggie told herself.

But Maggie was scared, too, and she wasn't thinking only of her own safety. She was thinking about everyone's safety, including—especially—the hostages.

"My little girl's name is Joy," Sanya said. "You'll find her for me, won't you, if something happens?"

"You're going to find her yourself," Maggie said. "Because you're going to pull that stick up and nothing's going to happen. You're going to be just fine."

"Move ahead of me," Sanya said. "The longer we stand here talking about it, the less time we have to get through the maze."

Maggie stared at Sanya. "No. I'm going to stand right here because you're not going to die."

"Look, if you want to be a hero, you can do that," Natalie said. "But give me the other stick so I can go ahead of you."

"No one's getting blown up," Maggie said. "I promise."

"I never thought I'd meet someone more stubborn than me," Sanya said, her voice shaky.

"It's one of my best qualities," Maggie said.

Sanya gave a little laugh. "If you say so. I'm not loving it right at this moment."

"Count of three," Maggie said.

"Let me get by you!" Natalie said, her voice reaching its shrieking point. "This isn't fair. You can't play Russian roulette with all of our lives."

"One," Maggie said. "Stay still, Natalie. You don't want to accidentally push Sanya forward. Two."

Natalie put her hand over her mouth, like she was trying to hold in a scream.

Sweat ran down the back of Maggie's neck, over her spine, pooled in the small of her back. "Three."

Sanya pulled out the stick.

Nothing happened.

For a second, they all stared at the place where the stick had been. Then Maggie said, "See? I told you it would be fine."

Sanya looked like she was about to collapse, and Natalie bent over, holding her stomach like she was about to throw up.

Beth didn't say anything. She just gave Maggie a tiny smile, like she had known everything was going to be okay all along.

Maggie gave everyone a few minutes to breathe, then said, "We've got to keep going. We can't see the clocks in here with all of the foliage overhead. We don't know how much time has passed."

"A ton, I bet," Natalie said. "We're moving super slow."

"For a reason," Maggie reminded her, trying not to be as short with Natalie as she wanted to be. "Which was just illustrated for us in living color."

Natalie looked mutinous for a minute, then subsided. "I get it. I do. It's just hard to feel like we're making progress. Number two and her mean girls are probably miles ahead of us already."

"We don't know that," Maggie said. "Anyway, their race is not ours. Don't let number two convince you to endanger yourself just because she's happy to do it."

They moved ahead, slow and careful as before. Maggie heard everyone's breathing clearly in the still air, and heard the soft thump of their sneakers on the ground. Everything smelled like wet greens, like someone had been in to water the plants just before the game started. Then she noticed something she'd been too distracted to notice before.

"There's no wind," she said.

"Yeah, it's hot as hell in here," Sanya said.

"No, I mean, there's no wind *at all*. No air movement of any kind."

"So?" Natalie said.

"So when we were outside the maze, did you notice anything about the sky?"

"It was fake." Beth's voice, very low behind Maggie, almost like she was a student afraid to give the correct answer in class. "The light was weird."

Maggie nodded. "Exactly. The light didn't seem like natural light. And there's no wind. We're inside some bigger structure."

"Why does it matter?" Natalie said. "That knowledge isn't going to help us get through this."

"You know, you're just incredibly negative," Sanya said. "And it's starting to piss me off."

"I'm just saying," Natalie said, her tone defensive, "I don't get why it matters."

"Because," Maggie said, "it explains a little bit of how they've been able to keep a place like this under wraps. No helicopters or planes flying overhead wondering what they're getting up to."

"It also means it's going to be harder to get out," Sanya said. "We can't just grab our hostages and escape into the wilderness or whatever."

"Yeah," Maggie said. She knew that Sanya had been thinking what she'd been thinking—that escape was the only real solution. If they were indoors, maybe inside some big complex—it would be harder. A lot harder. They didn't know how big this organization was, or how many personnel they had, but surely there would be guards everywhere. And locked doors.

"What do you mean, escape?" Natalie asked, her eyes wide. "If we get through the maze, they'll let us go. That's the deal."

"Uh-huh," Sanya said in the tone of someone talking to an idiot.

"What do you mean, 'uh-huh,' like that?" Natalie said. "They told us. Get through the maze and they'll let us and our hostages go. They told us."

"Do you always believe everything you're told?" Sanya said.

"They can't just let us go," Maggie said, cutting in before the two of them started arguing. She sensed that Sanya was beginning to lose patience with Natalie. "What's the first thing that you'll do when you get home?"

"Go to the police," Natalie said promptly. "Report all of this."

"Right. And assuming that the police take you seriously—they might not, you know—then there will be an investigation. And then the investigation might find this place, and these men. Do you think they're just going to give up their fun when they've gone to such lengths to get it?"

Natalie's face had gone slack. "But, but . . . they said! They said we'd go free! They can't just lie like that."

"They kidnapped us," Sanya reminded her. "And our children, or parents, or siblings. They have weapons, and we're essentially imprisoned. Why can't they lie?"

"Because it's not fair!" Natalie said. "They set out the rules. If we follow the rules, we get what we want."

Maggie resisted the urge to explain to the other woman that life was not fair, that it had never been fair, that terrible things happened all the time that nobody planned on, that even when you tried your hardest, you didn't always get what you wanted. Natalie should have been old enough to know that already, but apparently not.

Natalie seemed like the kind of person who'd always been a quiet rule follower, and she'd probably been rewarded throughout her life for that—by parents, teachers, employers. Society in general liked those who colored inside the lines, who didn't raise a fuss, who handed in their reports on time. Those people who were good little cogs all their life got straight As and entry into the best colleges and jobs with high starting salaries and paid vacation. And as long as you kept doing what you were "supposed" to do, as long as you didn't take too many days off and avoided conflict in the break room, you got your raises in pay at the correct intervals and could afford that nice little house, the one that made you an upright property-tax-paying American. Maggie could see the course of Natalie's life in her eyes, see all dotted i's and crossed t's, see the self-satisfaction that came with knowing she'd done everything right and everything well.

And yet she'd ended up here in the maze, and the people who put her there were not going to let her—or any of them—go when this was over. There would be another task, another hill to climb, another obstacle to scale. There would always be more, because they could change the rules whenever they wanted.

So Maggie had already been thinking about escape, and what might be needed, and what might be involved in order to be successful. She needed to get through the maze first, or maybe find an escape route out. She knew that Sanya had been thinking of it, too. Maybe Beth had considered it—Maggie couldn't tell, because Beth was an enigma. But Natalie hadn't contemplated the possibility at all.

"You're all looking at me like I'm stupid," Natalie said, tears running down her cheeks. "I'm not stupid. I'm not. I just believed them. That's not stupid. I wanted to, you know, be hopeful. I wanted to think there was an end to the nightmare."

Beth tugged on Maggie's shirt as Natalie continued to rant and cry. "Maggie, there's something."

"What?" Maggie said, leaning close to hear Beth's soft voice.

"There's something. A noise. Listen."

Maggie strained to hear over the sound of Natalie's voice. There was *something*, as Beth had put it. A humming kind of sound, or was it clicking? Something soft that was gradually getting louder.

Maggie tuned in to what Natalie was saying. ". . . don't think that you should treat me like a moron just because—"

"Stop," Maggie said, holding up her hand. "Listen."

Natalie looked outraged. "These other two might have made you their unofficial captain, but you don't have the right to tell me—"

"No, I mean really listen," Maggie said, and Natalie finally stopped.

Sanya turned her head to look behind them. "Something's coming."

"I know," Maggie said.

"We have to move," Sanya said.

"If we run, we could step on a mine."

"If we don't, then whatever is behind us is going to get us," Sanya said.

Despite the collective sense of urgency, none of them moved a muscle. Maggie felt paralyzed, compelled to find out what was approaching before she went another step.

*Come on,* her brain shouted at her. *Go, go, go! This is the stupid shit that people always do in the movies, just stand there waiting for their doom to fall down on their heads.*

"Let's go," she said, and started poking the ground in front of her with the stick again. Sanya copied her. Beth kept hold of Maggie's shirt, and Natalie walked so close to Sanya that Sanya had to tell her to back off.

"Faster," Natalie moaned. "We have to go faster."

The clicking noise was louder, getting louder every second. It sounded like a mass of something, a hive that had been opened up and set loose. Maggie glanced over her shoulder and Beth stared up at Maggie, her eyes wide and fearful.

"Spiders," Beth said. Her breath was coming in ragged, shallow gasps.

"How do you know it's—" Maggie began, but then she saw them.

Spiders. Lots of spiders, big spiders and small spiders, spiders surging toward them in one massive, undulating, alien wave.

Maggie didn't mind spiders, generally. But the sight of so many of them, charging directly toward her, twanged some primal chord of fear deep in her soul. These creatures did not seem to come from the same earth as she.

"Oh my god, run, run!" Natalie shouted, pushing past Sanya and barreling through the jungle, batting leaves and branches away.

"No, don't!" Maggie said, but she couldn't stop them, they were all running now, and then she was running, too, heedless of the traps that might be set or the mines that might explode, because it wasn't *natural*; it wasn't right. Spiders didn't hurtle toward people like an invading army; they didn't move at the speeds that they were moving now.

*Those guys did something to the spiders, or maybe they created them whole cloth and they're just robots or something. Whatever they are—fake or chemically altered—they were obviously sent to get us moving, to stop us from crawling carefully through the jungle. They're watching us and they want entertainment, and we weren't providing it.*

Maggie wished she could stop wondering about everything all the time, wished she could turn her brain off and run without trying to solve for *x*. She was always like this, somehow incapable of letting things go once her brain snagged on a question. The other three women were well ahead of her now. Beth was the farthest from Maggie, sprinting hard. Maggie wondered how she could even run that fast, if her airways were so constricted that she would fall down at any moment.

*She's really scared of spiders. Really, really scared. Maybe the adrenaline is opening up her airways. Does it work like that?*

Sanya was behind Beth, and Natalie was closest to Maggie, maybe ten feet in front of her. Maggie felt something tickle the back of her neck. She brushed it away and felt hairy legs trying to cling to her hand.

*Don't look, don't look, keep going.*

"Help," a voice said, somewhere ahead of Maggie. "Help me."

Maggie slowed, her eyes searching for the woman who'd called out for help. Several spiders scuttled up her legs, and Maggie used the stick she still held to bat them off, but it was fruitless. If she didn't run, they'd catch up to her, overwhelm her, crawl all over her and spin their webs until she was mummified.

"Help," the voice said again. It was the last gasp of a desperate person.

Maggie saw her then. It was #9, one of the women who'd refused to share food with anyone else at the first obstacle. The bottom of her right leg was missing and she was lying in a pool of sticky blood. She'd obviously stepped on one of the mines, but maybe only the edge of one, because she wasn't entirely blown to smithereens like Roni.

Her group had abandoned her, though, left her there to die slowly. Maggie was amazed she was still awake, considering the amount of blood loss. But then people generally did show a remarkable desire to stay alive.

#9 saw Maggie staring at her. Her eyes widened in hope and she said, "Help. Please help me."

Maggie was rooted to the spot, spiders crawling freely up her body now. She tried not to think about them, beating at her legs as best she could to keep them off. She didn't know what to do. She didn't think she could help this woman on her own. The other three had disappeared. And even if Maggie somehow managed to pick up #9, what could she do for the woman? She didn't have a way to stop the blood loss, or to replace the blood that was gone.

#9 reached toward Maggie, beseeching. "Help. Don't leave me alone."

"I can't," Maggie began, but then it didn't matter anymore.

The spiders swarmed #9, and she began to scream.

"Oh, god," Maggie said, running in the same direction as the others, #9's screams echoing behind her. "Oh, god. Oh, god. Oh, god."

*What have I done? What should I have done?*

She ran and she beat at the spiders that had crawled up her chest and over her shoulders, that were trying to nest in her hair. She ran and she screamed and she cried and she prayed that she didn't step on a land mine because she couldn't see, she didn't know how to be careful anymore and she couldn't shake the feeling that she'd done something terrible, something irreversible, something she shouldn't have done.

*I should have helped her. I shouldn't have left her there.*

And then somehow, all of a sudden, she was out of the jungle. There was no more foliage, just the walls of the maze around her and the hard ground beneath her and the fake sky above her. And there were Sanya and Beth and Natalie standing huddled together before her.

They turned toward Maggie as one, their faces relieved, but then Beth turned white and fell to the ground.

"Beth!" Natalie shouted, and knelt beside her.

Sanya strode toward Maggie, still holding the stick she'd used to prod the ground for mines. She lifted it up in the air like a baseball bat and swung it toward Maggie's head.

Maggie didn't even have a chance to think as the stick whooshed above her. She saw a very large spider fly through the air out of the corner of her eye.

"Thanks," she said to Sanya, but Sanya didn't say anything, only circled behind Maggie and methodically began removing any visible spiders with the stick. All the spiders ran back into the jungle, like they were afraid to be in the light, and the rest of the arachnid army had stopped at the border.

Sanya finished up, but Maggie still felt like there were minute feet moving over her skin. She yanked her tee shirt over her head, turned it inside out and saw several tiny spiders clinging to the cloth. Maggie shook and beat at the shirt until they were all gone, but she couldn't shake the creepy-crawly feeling. Her hands kept going up to her scalp, running through her hair, feeling for something that didn't belong there.

"What happened?" Sanya said. "I thought you were right behind us."

Maggie realized her heart was pounding like she was still running. She couldn't shake the terrible image of #9, part of her leg gone, the pool of blood beneath her, her open, screaming mouth as the spiders ran over her.

"The other group, they left someone behind. Number nine," Maggie said. "She called out."

"So?" Sanya said. "You know that none of them would spit on you if you were on fire. They made that very clear."

"Well, I'm not like them," Maggie said, irritated at Sanya's dismissal. "I can't just pass by someone bleeding and asking for help without trying to do something."

Sanya said, "So where is she?"

"I couldn't help her. Part of her leg had been blown off by one of the mines."

"And as soon as you saw that, you should have kept going," Sanya said.

Maggie stared. "You saw her, too."

"Sure did," Sanya said. "And I could tell right away that I couldn't do anything for her, so I kept moving."

"But you couldn't tell that from a glance," Maggie said.

"The woman's leg was missing," Sanya said, her tone hard. "I could tell."

"But—"

"Listen," Sanya said. "I can tell you're one of those people who wants to help everybody, who wants to do their best for their community. But you're not going to be able to help everyone in here. You're just not. They didn't set up the game that way."

"They set it up so we would fail," Maggie murmured.

"They set it up so we would hurt each other, and then we would fail," Sanya said. "As we have heard so often, the cruelty is the point."

Maggie swiped at her arms, shivering. She didn't know if she would ever be able to shake the feeling of spiders crawling all over her.

Sanya and Maggie walked over to Beth and Natalie. Beth was sitting up, leaning on Natalie's arm, bleary-eyed.

"Are the spiders gone?" she asked.

"Yes," Maggie said.

"Time's running down," Sanya said, pointing at the clock overhead that was visible now that they were out of the jungle. "We've got to move faster."

Two hours had already gone by.

Maggie thought about Paige—maybe cold, maybe hungry, definitely scared. Maybe almost as scared as Maggie herself was feeling, wondering if she could make it through the maze.

*I can. I will.*

She looked down the seemingly innocuous channel of the maze in front of her, at the T-junction ahead.

"Let's move, ladies," she said, and gave Beth a hand up.

# CHAPTER FOUR

**mags13:** rules LOL

**battleroyale:** yeah, the one who always wins those games in the books is the one who doesn't follow the rules

**tyz7412:** they should have let that bitch Katniss kill herself. Otherwise dumb bitches like you would know that rules are there to be followed

**mags13:** whoa dude chill. We're just having some made-up fun here.

**tyz7412:** no, I'm sick of bitches like you who think they can do whatever they want

**mags13:** muted

**THEY CAME TO THE** T-junction and peered in both directions. There was no obvious obstacle.

"Which way?" Sanya asked.

"I'm not sure it matters," Maggie said. "At some point they make sure we're all funneled to the same obstacles. Damn, I meant to try to use one of the trees in that jungle, but I got distracted by the problem of the mines."

"And the spiders," Beth said, her voice quavering. She was still too pale.

"Yes, and the spiders," Maggie agreed.

"What were you going to do with the trees?" Natalie asked.

"Climb one of them to see if I could get to the top of the maze and maybe scope out an efficient exit."

"Not sure it would make a difference," Natalie said. "Since they're going to make sure we're all killed anyway."

Maggie and Sanya exchanged looks, and silently agreed not to engage. Natalie was still holding on to the argument they'd had before the spiders arrived. She had a broody look, especially whenever she looked at Maggie. It was pretty clear Natalie blamed Maggie for something.

Maggie couldn't worry about Natalie, or about Natalie's issues. It wasn't Maggie's fault if they were stuck in a game where the rules could change at any minute. But she knew that Natalie felt helpless, and sometimes when people feel helpless, they lash out. They look for someone to blame. As Maggie had become the de facto leader, she was the obvious recipient of any emotional sludge Natalie wanted to throw around.

"I wonder where the other group is," Beth said.

"Wherever they are, they're down to three," Maggie said. "I just hope that somewhere soon there's another food drop. I'm starving."

"And I peed myself," Natalie said. "Because I wanted to go underneath a bush or something in that jungle, but you scared us to death with the mines."

"I didn't put the mines there," Maggie said in as mild a tone as she could manage.

"No, but you acted like they were the worst thing in the world, and we lost a ton of time because of it. And I peed myself."

"Guess you've never been pregnant," Sanya said. "In the last trimester, I peed myself in my sleep at least three times."

"I never made it to the last month," Maggie said. "Paige was in a hurry and broke out four and a half weeks early. I thought I peed myself, though. I woke up because my underpants were wet. I went to the bathroom and I remember I was crying because I thought I wet myself in my sleep and Noah was telling me it was all right, that they told us at the parenting class it might happen."

She remembered how he'd come into the bathroom with dry underwear for her, and she was sitting on the toilet, and she'd suddenly realized that it wasn't pee at all; that her water had broken. She'd looked at Noah and told him that they were going to have the baby that day, and she remembered how panicked he'd looked because he hadn't packed their hospital bag yet. He'd thought they'd have more time—another month, maybe more, because first babies don't usually show up on time. But Paige had been in a big hurry, a big hurry to get out and see the world. She was still like that—always rushing, always running, always jumping, always wanting to go faster, do more, see everything.

And now she was in a locked room, waiting for her mother to find her.

"Yeah, they do tell you that, because the baby starts pressing on your bladder *nonstop*," Sanya said, picking up the thread of Maggie's story. "Like they've got their little feet on your bladder and they're watching it squirt for fun or something."

"Well, some of us have never had children," Natalie said. "And some of us think it's humiliating to wet ourselves."

Maggie opened her mouth—she wasn't sure what she was going to say, but she was losing patience with Natalie's attitude—but Beth cut in.

"Some of us don't give a shit," she said. Then she slapped her hand over her mouth, clearly appalled at herself.

Sanya started laughing. "Now that's what I call a Freudian slip."

"I'm sorry," Beth said to Natalie. "I just— It just kind of came out."

Maggie started laughing, too, and Beth giggled, like it was catching and she'd been infected. Sanya's laugh got bigger then, and she bent over slightly, clutching her stomach.

"It's not funny," Natalie said.

"It is," Maggie said, gasping. "It's really funny."

"It really, really is," Sanya said.

"I'm s-s-s-sorry," Beth said again, through a mouthful of giggles.

Natalie's mouth turned up at the corners, like she couldn't help herself.

"Okay, I guess it is a little funny," she said.

Maggie knew that they were all a little hysterical, all on the verge of screaming or crying or running headlong into a wall over and over, and that's why they were laughing so hard. If they didn't laugh, they'd have to think, have to think about what they'd already been through and what was up ahead, and none of them wanted to do that.

*Just think about Paige. She's the light at the end of the tunnel, and she's waiting for you.*

"Okay, okay," Maggie said, holding one hand up and wheezing through her laughter. "We've got to get it together here."

"Yeah," Sanya said, trying to straighten out her expression and failing.

"And the next time somebody has to go to the bathroom, three of us will surround that person while they go," Maggie said. "With our backs to you, obviously. I don't know if it will actually make a difference in your privacy, because I'm assuming that there are cameras everywhere, but hopefully it will help you feel more comfortable."

A blush crept up Natalie's cheeks, and Maggie thought she looked a little ashamed that she'd given Maggie such a hard time.

"Thanks," Natalie said. "It *will* help."

"You never think about this stuff when you're watching a movie or reading a book," Sanya said as they started forward again, the four of them lined up shoulder to shoulder. "The main characters never seem to need the bathroom. I'm telling you right now, I would have shit my pants immediately if I were in those Hunger Games."

"I don't know about that. You seem to be doing pretty well right now," Maggie said.

"Yeah, but in the book, those were teenagers, right? And in that Japanese one, too." Sanya snapped her fingers like she was trying to remember the title.

"*Battle Royale*," Maggie said. "And lots of others, too. Even if there isn't a killing game, there's always some kind of apocalyptic scenario that requires adolescents to put themselves in extreme physical danger."

"*The 5th Wave*," Natalie said.

"*The Maze Runner*," Beth added.

"Right," Sanya said. "The point is that these are always kids in these stories, and kids don't have the same sense of caution that adults do. They don't think they're actually going to die, even if they see other people die around them. Teenagers think they're immortal."

"Okay," Maggie said, wondering where Sanya was going with this.

"Therefore," Sanya said, with the air of someone presenting an inevitable conclusion, "they aren't going to shit their pants when dropped into some killing game."

Maggie shook her head, laughing. "I feel like you went a long way around for that."

It also did not escape her notice that every woman present had more than a passing familiarity with young adult dystopic fiction. There was something in that fact, she was sure. She just didn't know exactly what.

"And I'm not 100 percent sure how it's currently relevant?" Natalie said, grinning at Sanya.

"What I'm trying to say is—" Sanya began, but whatever point she was trying to make was lost in the sound of screams from up ahead.

"Oh god, what now?" Maggie said.

They all started running except Beth. Maggie looked at Beth and saw her wave them forward.

"I'll walk as fast as I can," Beth called.

Maggie figured the other woman didn't want to have another asthma attack, and she understood. Beth was at risk in here just because she didn't have her inhaler, and heavy exercise seemed to set off her attacks.

Maggie, Sanya and Natalie followed the sound of screaming to the right turn of the maze. They rounded the corner and all three of them stopped.

Before them was an obstacle course, a big solid-built wooden and metal and plastic structure that spanned the whole width of the maze. There was no going around it or, Maggie noticed, above it. Some kind of thin, tight wire had been strung from the top of the obstacle course to various points along the wall, and it was crisscrossed so densely that squeezing through wasn't an option.

*They thought of everything. There's no cheat code, no getting around their requirements. Ever.*

The obstacle course started, Maggie observed, with a plastic tube tunnel that was close to the ground. It reminded her of the inflatable obstacle courses that Paige liked when she was younger, the ones they had at those bounce house businesses. Maggie loved those places when Paige was small, because her daughter had more energy than your average toddler, and for ten bucks, Maggie could sit on a bench and watch her daughter go berserk jumping on inflatables until it was time for lunch. Paige was still high-energy, still the type of kid who ran instead of walked, who wanted to take her bike everywhere.

*She's probably banging off the walls of whatever cell they've hidden her in. I hope they don't hurt her because of it.*

The bounce house obstacle courses always had a little tunnel for the kids. The kids would scoot through the tunnel, then come out and have to climb up a short wall. On the other side of the wall would be a slide, and then more objects to climb over or bounce off. Maggie had a strong feeling that whatever was at the end of the tunnel in front of them would not be so benign. They couldn't see what the other obstacle might be, though, because there was a high wall, maybe fifteen feet or so, blocking the view of the obstacles ahead.

*And the obstacles will be ridiculous,* Maggie thought. *There will be swinging axes and walls designed to make you fall and break your leg. They want us to get hurt. They want us to fail.*

They'd have to crawl inside and through to whatever waited farther along, sight unseen. And whatever waited farther along was clearly not great, because the screams were echoing through the tunnel and out into the maze. Maggie also heard two people arguing, but couldn't make out their words over the screaming.

"Sounds like number two's group is coming apart at the seams," Natalie said.

"Yeah," Maggie said. The screams were making her feel sick. Whatever had happened inside the course, the woman was clearly suffering. Couldn't the other two help her instead of arguing?

Sanya gave Maggie a sideways glance. "Even if they wanted to help her—and I'm not sure they do—they don't have any medical gear. It's the same problem we have. We don't even have bandages."

"Yeah," Maggie said, but the knowledge didn't make her feel any better.

The screams had faded away by the time Beth caught up with the rest of the group. She gazed apprehensively at the plastic tunnel in front of them.

"Do we have to go in there?" Her voice was tiny and mouse-like again. Any confidence she'd gained from telling Natalie off had disappeared.

"There's no way to go around it," Maggie said.

"And we have to do every task," Sanya reminded them. "At least until we find a way to break out of here. We have to play their game until we find a way to figuratively shove the game up their ass."

"It's just . . . It's just . . ." Beth said, but she didn't finish her thought.

"Are you claustrophobic?" Natalie asked, with more compassion in her tone than Maggie had heard from her yet.

Beth nodded.

*Claustrophobic, arachnophobic, asthmatic, and her arms look like limp noodles, so if there's any climbing in there, she's going to have a hard time.*

Maggie worried again that Beth wasn't going to survive this game at all.

*But she's not as weak as she looks, not on the inside. She's trying. She's determined. She doesn't want to be a burden.*

"We'll help you get through it," Maggie said. "The tunnel might not even be that long. It will be like we're at the playground, crawling through one of those little climbing set tunnels."

"I never went through those," Beth said. "I never went inside anybody's playhouse, either. I had some friends who had an actual cupboard under the stairs—"

"Like in *Harry Potter*?" Sanya asked.

Beth nodded. "And they used it as a little playroom. They loved it in there, but I hated it. Whenever they closed the door, I felt like I was suffocating."

Natalie went to the tunnel, crouched down and peered inside. "The stretch I can see is pretty short, but it turns, so I can't tell how far it goes on."

"Of course it does," Maggie muttered. "They want us to be afraid every second, scared of whatever's around the corner."

"Well, job well done, because I am," Natalie said.

"Me, too," Beth said.

Maggie wasn't scared—not the way the other two were, anyway. She wasn't scared for herself, or scared of what might be ahead of them. She was scared that she would fail, and that her daughter would pay the price for her failure.

She already worried that Paige had paid too high a price for Maggie's hesitance to leave her marriage, for her stubborn conviction to try to work it out with a man who'd changed so utterly that he literally bore no resemblance, physically or emotionally, to the man she'd married. Coke made him thin and twitchy, carved long lines in his cheeks and forehead, made him sniffle constantly. It made him quick to argue and to anger, to always find fault in whoever was present. Paige would skirt around him if they were in the same space, giving him the kind of wide berth one generally reserved for snarling animals. Or she'd quietly exit the room if he came into it. Maggie worried every single day that she'd done something unforgivable, that she'd hurt Paige just by not leaving sooner.

So Maggie couldn't lose, couldn't let this sick game take her down or out. She had to get through, had to save her daughter, had to prove to Paige that she was worthy of being her mother.

"How do you want to do this?" Sanya said.

"I'll go first," Maggie said. "Beth, you behind me. Once we get through the tunnel part, we'll call back to you to come through."

Sanya nodded, and pointed at the sign overhead. "We'll time you, though. If it's been ten minutes and you haven't called back, we're coming after you."

Maggie crouched in front of the tunnel and took a deep breath. The odor of new plastic was overwhelming, and just underneath it, fresh sawdust. This construction, whatever it was, had clearly just been built.

*So we're the first, then? The first group to be dropped into this game? Or maybe we're the only ones. But that doesn't make sense. Why build this elaborate maze if you're only going to use it one time?*

She had to stop thinking about the whys and wherefores. There was a task in front of her that needed to be completed. Paige was counting on her. She could worry about logistics later.

Her stomach churned. Her mouth felt like it had too much saliva in it. There could be anything inside the tunnel, anything at all. These fuckers could have put in falling blades or triggers to release snakes or . . .

*Or there could be nothing, and you're letting yourself get psyched out when you're supposed to be helping Beth get through this.*

Maggie crawled into the tunnel.

The fit was tight. She couldn't move forward on her hands and knees. The only way to move was on her stomach, using her forearms to pull herself along. Behind her, she heard Beth enter the tunnel. The other woman's breath was already shallow and terrified.

*Please don't let her have an asthma attack in here,* Maggie thought. *I have no idea how I would pull her out if she did.*

Maggie crawled forward to the turn. This wasn't a junction, like in the maze, but a left turn clearly meant to make the participants anxious about what might be on the other side of the bend. Maggie peeked around the corner and saw nothing except more tunnel, and another turn maybe ten or so feet away, this one turning right.

"Looks okay up ahead," she said. "How are you doing, Beth?"

"All right," Beth said, her breath ragged. She was so close to Maggie that Maggie felt the other woman breathing on her ankles. She wanted to tell Beth to back off a little bit, but she realized that might make Beth more anxious, so she kept her mouth shut and concentrated on pulling her body through the tunnel as fast as possible. The plastic chafed her skin as she crawled, and the strong chemical smell made Maggie feel a little nauseous.

"How are you doing?" Sanya called.

"It smells gross in here," Maggie called back.

"Can't wait for my turn," Sanya said.

Maggie reached the next corner, peeked around, saw daylight ahead.

"Okay, there's just this one turn here, and then the exit is a little farther away," Maggie said to Beth.

"O-okay," Beth said. She sounded completely spent.

Maggie was glad they would be out of the tunnel soon, and grateful that it didn't seem to be booby-trapped, as she expected. It was just a psychological barrier, though not an insignificant one for someone like Beth. Maggie felt weirdly proud of the other woman for sticking it out. She wondered if Beth could have managed the tunnel on her own if she hadn't been with a larger group.

When she reached the end of the tunnel, Maggie paused. It would be pure stupidity to clamber out without taking a look around first. Directly in front of her was a doorway cut into a wooden wall. A cheap plastic shower curtain was pulled across the doorway so she couldn't get a glimpse of what was beyond—the next obstacle, she assumed. She inched forward, only sticking out her head far enough to see to the left and to the right.

To the right there was nothing special—just more wooden wall, so that the space before her was like a rectangular box with an open top. Up above she saw the gleam of the wire that had been strung to prevent them from climbing over obstacles.

Maggie looked to the left, and then she wished she hadn't.

There was a woman there, pinned to the wall by what appeared to be a giant blade, like a scythe but with two sharp and equally sized ends. Maggie followed the path of the blade's handle to a rod directly above the tunnel. It appeared that the blade swung back and forth on the rod, almost like one of those Viking ship–style rides at the amusement park. Except this ship had gleaming razor points and no one was supposed to scream with happiness and delight.

*There was screaming, though. We heard the screams.*

Blood had pooled beneath the pinned woman—Maggie was pretty certain it was #4, although she couldn't see the back of her shirt. Her eyes were blank and lifeless.

Maggie thought that the blade was supposed to swing continuously, so that whoever left the tunnel would be risking their life just to get out. But the blade had gotten caught in the wood behind #4, and so Maggie and Beth and Natalie and Sanya would be safer because of #4's accidental sacrifice.

*I bet it wasn't accidental, though. I bet #2 made sure someone else was in front of her and someone else behind, so that she would be perfectly safe throughout. What's she going to do when she runs out of bodies to throw around her?*

"Maggie?" Beth said. Maggie heard the edge of panic in her voice. "Can we get out now?"

"Yeah," Maggie said, crawling forward. "But just don't look around yet, all right?"

She felt almost motherly toward Beth, like she was a child who couldn't be allowed to see the horror.

*I've got to stop thinking that way. She's a grown woman, and even if she's a little timid, she's not a child.*

Still, she couldn't stop herself from blocking the view as she climbed out and then helped Beth out of the tunnel. It didn't help, though. Beth crinkled her nose and said, "What's that smell?" and then immediately peeked around Maggie's shoulder. Beth closed her eyes and looked like she might be sick.

"We're through," Maggie called. Then she said to Beth, "You'd better go over there by the curtain, make sure you're out of the path of that blade in case it loosens."

"You should, too," Beth said.

"I'm going to, believe me," Maggie said. First, she bent over and called through the tunnel again. "Listen, don't rush out when you get here. There might be an obstacle. But hopefully there won't be."

She heard the slide of cloth over plastic, heard it pause. "So which is it?" Natalie said. "An obstacle or not?"

"You'll see when you get here," Maggie said.

"Great," Sanya said.

The sound of crawling resumed. Maggie went over near Beth, out of the potential path of the blade. Beth stood nervously near the plastic curtain.

"Did you look?" Maggie asked.

Beth shook her head. "Too scared. I almost don't want to know."

Maggie swallowed. Her mouth was so dry, and they only had a little bit of water left in the bottle to be shared around with everyone. She hoped that there were more food drops somewhere along the way, although she had a feeling there wouldn't be. The comfort and safety of the participants didn't seem to be high on the organizers' priority list.

Maggie twitched the curtain aside, peering through the doorway. On the other side she saw what appeared to be a standard obstacle course, like the kind you sometimes saw at outdoor races. There was a climbing wall and a pretty brackish-looking body of water that might be generously termed "a pond." There were even rubber tires lined up in two rows, like they had to run in and out of the tires. She could see all the way to the end. It all appeared fairly straightforward, but Maggie did not trust the evidence of her eyes in this place. It couldn't be that easy, that they would just have to complete a bunch of tasks like they were in PE class.

A sliding, squeaking noise drew her attention back to the tunnel, and Natalie's face appeared in the opening.

"Is it safe?" she asked.

Maggie looked at the blade, still firmly embedded through a woman's body and into the wall. "Sure."

Natalie clambered out, saw #4, blanched, and hurried to Maggie's side. A few seconds later, Sanya was out and they were all surveying the obstacle course together.

"It can't be that easy," Sanya murmured.

"That's what I thought, too," Maggie said.

"You mean there's probably bombs inside the tires or the wall will collapse when we try to climb it?" Natalie said. "It seems like that would be the case, but wouldn't we see evidence of triggered traps, then? Like the swinging axe."

"Yeah, okay," Maggie said slowly. "But what if not all the traps are triggered on the first go? What if they're set for the third person, or the eighth person? They're trying to take out as many of us as possible. It would be too easy if every trap went off when the first person went through."

"Number two would just sit back and watch her minions get blown up and then stroll through," Sanya said. She jerked a finger over her shoulder, in the direction of #4's body. "Looks like what she did back there."

"She's already established that she does not give a flying fuck about anybody in here except herself," Maggie said.

"Yeah, but she's so horrible, she's almost not real," Sanya said. "You know what I mean? She's like a bad caricature from a TV show about high school life. People don't act like that. Not really."

"Oh, they do," Natalie said. "I've met plenty of assholes in my time."

"Yeah, but not in such a clearly cartoony villain kind of way," Sanya said. "A lot of people are hateful, but they keep that hate under their breath. They only show it to certain other people. They're passive-aggressive. That lady, she's all aggressive."

Maggie looked at Sanya, trying to figure out the point of all this. "What are you saying?"

"I think that she's a ringer," Sanya said. "I think that her job is to get as many of us killed as efficiently as possible. And look—her group is down to just her and one other person."

"A ringer," Maggie said. For some reason, this idea bothered her more than the notion of the men who'd kidnapped them. She expected terrible behavior from men. She didn't expect women to be just as bad. "That would be awful. Just unbelievably awful."

"Because women are all saints?" Sanya said, smirking. "What kind of sheltered life have you led, librarian?"

"That's not what I mean," Maggie said, stung. "I just . . . It's hard to believe that a woman would be complicit in something like this. In kidnapping other women. In killing them."

"Women serial killers exist," Natalie said. "There was that movie, you know, the one with Charlize Theron?"

"She was so good in that movie," Sanya said.

"That's not really germane to this conversation," Maggie said, frowning. "Do you really think number two is a ringer?"

Sanya shrugged. "I'm just saying that it's possible. I think we should be prepared for anything, including that one of the supposed victims is actually a perpetrator."

# CHAPTER FIVE

**mazernning:** well that got toxic real fast

**mags13:** why do men have to act so insane online? We're just trying to have a fun book conversation here.

**tyz7513:** how do you know it was a man? They didn't have an avatar.

**mags13:** (eyeroll) women don't usually start calling other women bitches for no discernible reason. Also avatars are pretty meaningless.

**tyz7513:** I'll keep that in mind

**MAGGIE VOLUNTEERED TO GO** through the tires first.

"Uh-uh," Sanya said, shaking her finger. "You think I can't see that thing you keep doing, the one where you put yourself in front, trying to protect the rest of us? I'll go first this time."

"Maybe I wasn't trying to protect you," Maggie said. "Maybe I was trying to protect myself because I think that the traps might be triggered by the second person through."

"Don't expect us to believe that," Natalie said, and grabbed Sanya's arm. "Listen, I'll go first this time. You and Maggie have been doing the hard work through here, and all I've done is complain."

"No, you haven't," Maggie said automatically.

"Yes, I have," Natalie said. "But it's okay. I'm going to do my part, pull my own weight. So let me go first."

Maggie noticed Natalie's hands were shaking, a fine trembling that seemed to emanate up her arms and into the pulse in her neck.

"Are you sure?" Maggie said.

"Yes," Natalie said. "Anyway, I think I'll be good at this. I've run Spartan races before—you know, those big obstacle races where you end up covered in mud? I know how to handle these courses."

"Okay," Maggie said. "This is what we'll do. One of us will go every minute. Sound good?"

"Assuming I don't get blown up. Or get sliced by a falling blade," Natalie said.

"Ha," Maggie said. She understood the point of gallows humor, but it was hard to laugh right now. The image of #4 embedded in the wall was hard to shake.

Natalie took a deep breath, blew it out, then started running the course.

Maggie looked up at the clock hanging on the wall to the right, high above their heads. These clocks were omnipresent throughout the maze.

*Guess we can't complain that they aren't being clear about how much time remains.*

Almost four hours had ticked down already. Maggie wondered what would happen if they didn't make it through the maze in time. Would the cattle-prod guy send his little toy shock troops into the maze to find them, line them up against the wall for a firing squad? Or would they wait and see if the women managed to stagger through to the end, and then finish them off? How many men were in this place, anyway? Maggie had seen maybe twenty of them in the line outside of the maze. That wasn't a lot, all things considered. If that was the maximum size of their force, and the men were dispersed throughout the complex . . . well, maybe they would have a shot at escaping.

"That's a minute," Sanya said. "I'm off."

"Wait," Maggie said, but Sanya was already jogging through the tires. Maggie had thought she would go next—she was still thinking about how to protect the others, even when she knew she shouldn't, even when she knew she ought to be thinking only of herself and Paige.

*I'm bad at this,* she thought. *I'm bad at being selfish.*

It was funny, though, how Noah had accused her of being selfish when she said she wanted a divorce, when she said she'd had enough, when she couldn't carry the burden of his addiction anymore. She'd wrestled with guilt for a long time, wondering if she could have done more, if she should have done more. If she'd actually been selfish.

"Okay, me next," Beth said.

Maggie realized she'd been woolgathering. She needed to stop thinking about the past and get her head in the present, otherwise she and everyone else there might get killed.

Natalie was pretty far ahead. She'd already cleared the brackish pond and was on to what appeared to be the sixth obstacle. Green slime dripped down her legs as she steadily pulled herself up a rope that had a bell at the top. There were five ropes in a row, meaning that the men who'd organized this had thought it unlikely that all ten of the starting racers would make it this far.

In an obstacle race, the racer was supposed to climb up the rope, ring the bell and get back down as fast as possible to move on to the next hurdle. Maggie meant to watch Beth, to make sure she was okay and that she was progressing at a decent pace, but she was mesmerized by the sight of Natalie moving so strong and steady, hand over hand, as she went up the rope. The ropes went extremely high—maybe twenty, twenty-five feet. That wouldn't be a big deal in a gym with padded mats underneath, but there were no padded mats underneath these ropes. There was only hard wood. Natalie's hand reached out for the bellpull.

"No," Maggie said. "Don't!"

Natalie yanked on the cord, and the rope disconnected from the plank. Maggie saw the look of confusion on Natalie's face, the flailing of her arms as she tried to grab one of the other ropes. Then Natalie was falling, falling, falling, and there was nothing Maggie could do except watch, and listen.

Natalie screamed, and then there was a thud and a sickening crunch, and no more screaming.

Sanya and Beth were standing still in the middle of their respective obstacles.

"Go," Maggie shouted at them, and began running the tires behind Beth. "Go, go, we have to see if she's okay."

But Natalie wasn't crying out, wasn't calling for help, and Maggie knew that there was likely no chance at all. But she had to hope, had to pray that Natalie had just had the breath knocked out of her or was unconscious from the fall. That crunch couldn't mean that she was dead.

*But she fell a long way,* Maggie thought as she hurried Beth through the obstacles to reach Natalie. She heard Beth's ragged breath, could tell that she was pushing the other woman too hard, but she couldn't help herself.

She couldn't bear the thought that Natalie had died alone, baffled, betrayed by what amounted to a deadly prank.

*We keep expecting the men who arranged this to play by the rules, for the tasks to be straightforward. But they aren't. They'll do anything, literally anything, to make sure we get hurt.*

Maggie waded through the pond, her fingers on Beth's wrist, pulling her along. The pond was disgusting, filled with thick green slime and things that wriggled around Maggie's ankles. She heard Beth say, "Leeches," but she couldn't stop to acknowledge this, couldn't even take a second to be horrified or grossed out. Of course there were leeches in the pond, because some man in the group had probably seen *Stand By Me* when he was young and was traumatized by the sight of Gordie pulling a leech off his penis.

But Maggie wasn't a man, and she wasn't afraid of leeches—

she was afraid of losing people, afraid of making mistakes that would hurt somebody else. Leeches were nothing because Natalie had fallen.

She saw Sanya ahead, crouched next to Natalie, green slime dripping from her legs. Sanya glanced back as Maggie struggled out of the pool, finally releasing Beth's wrist. The blood roared in Maggie's ears and black spots danced in front of her eyes, but she held on, she held on until she reached Sanya's side and finally saw Natalie.

Maggie stared down at Natalie's body, at the angle of her neck. *At least she didn't suffer. There is that, right? No suffering, no slow dying like being pinned to the wall by a scythe and bleeding out slowly, or having hundreds of spiders cover your body while you screamed. At least it wasn't like that. At least she just fell and she died and she wasn't hurting.*

Maggie tried to tell herself that this made it better, but she remembered that Natalie had a sister, and Natalie's sister was in a room just like Paige was, and just like Roni's mother, and just like all the other hostages of the women who'd already died. Maggie wondered if those hostages had been eliminated already, or if the game organizers were waiting to see if any of the women made it through. It had to be more efficient to kill all the hostages at once.

*Shame on you, Maggie,* she thought. *Those are people's lives, people that were loved.*

She realized she was getting slightly hysterical, even if she'd done a good job of suppressing it thus far. And then she realized the danger of the maze, of all of those dystopic worlds that she'd carelessly read about and let herself be entertained by, was not the danger itself, per se. The danger was in watching the bodies pile up around you, in letting yourself drown in grief, or worse— becoming inured to it.

There were only three of them left in her little group, and maybe two in the other group if nothing else had happened. A third of the total time had passed, and half of them were already dead.

She didn't know how she got through the rest of the obstacle course. She moved through it mechanically, barely acknowledging Sanya or Beth. It wasn't that she'd been particularly attached to Natalie. It was that Natalie's death had seemed one too many, and Maggie's fierce determination to reach Paige was starting to seem like a willfully ignorant fantasy. The men who'd kidnapped them were not going to let them go. Somehow, some way, they would make certain that all the participants failed.

*At least in the Hunger Games there could be one winner. There are no winners here.*

But that wasn't quite right, either. In those books Maggie had loved (she didn't think she'd ever be able to read them again), the main character might *technically* win, but they always seemed to lose at the same time. They'd lose somebody they loved, or compromise their principles. They'd do something that anyone else might just consider survival, but that the protagonist would think was personally unforgivable.

*What will I have to sacrifice in order to get me and my daughter out of here?*

It was the first time she'd thought about it, the first time she'd considered the possibility that she might have to abandon the others, or potentially hurt them, in order to escape. She didn't know if she could actually do it.

They moved forward, all of them quiet after Natalie's death. There was no more sense of "we're all in this together, let's try to lift each other up." There was nothing but furrowed brows and grim silence and the acrid smell of sweat.

They went through another obstacle, and another and another. Each was dangerous, difficult and potentially deadly—a swinging bridge over an actual pit of crocodiles, a stop where they had to put their hand inside a mysterious box and hope nothing happened (Maggie suspected that there were poisonous insects inside, but none of the women were stung), a challenge where they had to choose berries to eat and hope the berries weren't poisonous. Maggie went through each one in a fog, and somehow all three of them survived each time. They came upon another food-and-water drop but discovered that the group ahead of them had eaten everything.

"Assholes," Sanya said, crumpling up the empty wrappers that were left behind and dropping them on the ground in disgust.

"There are only two of them left," Maggie said tiredly. "I believe number two would act like this, but not number ten. I thought that maybe she was all right, that she would come around."

"Why would you think that?" Beth said, staring sadly at the empty water bottles.

Maggie shrugged. "She hesitated before joining the other group. She seemed like she wasn't certain about them. And then I thought after the others were killed, number ten would give up on number two for sure, because it's pretty clear that number two is only interested in using everyone around her as a body shield."

"Maybe number ten is planning on doing the same thing to number two," Sanya said. "Maybe she's going to throw number two in the fire and get herself out of here without any strings to hold her down."

"Maybe," Maggie said.

She had trouble caring about what happened to #2 and #10. She was so hungry, so tired, so run-down. She wanted to take a nap, or just a rest. But the clock kept ticking down, relentlessly, and she couldn't escape the sight of it. There were clocks everywhere they turned, always showing the inevitable march of time in the wrong direction, always showing how Maggie had fewer hours, fewer minutes, fewer seconds to find Paige, to keep her safe.

They kept going forward through the maze, connected now only by the most tenuous of threads—by the simple expediency of staying together while they could all maintain the same pace. Maggie noticed that Beth was having an easier time keeping up now. She wondered if Beth had acclimated to their speed, or if Maggie and Sanya had slowed down so significantly that it was easier for Beth to keep up. Regardless, Beth's breathing seemed to be a lot smoother than it had been at the beginning of the maze, and she hadn't clung to Maggie's shirt or arm since they lost Natalie.

*Maybe she's realized she has to toughen up in order to make it. I'm glad.*

She looked over at Beth, who was a pace or two ahead of her, just enough so that Maggie could see her face in profile. Beth's face was blank, and she was breathing smooth and easy, like she was a long-distance runner and she did this all the time.

Maggie frowned. Beth couldn't have improved that much, couldn't have had such a dramatic turnaround, especially under the stress of the maze. People with asthma didn't see their conditions magically improve without inhalers. Or maybe they did? Maggie didn't really know a lot about asthma.

*But what if her condition* didn't *improve?* Maggie thought. *What if she—?*

Maggie didn't have the opportunity to finish that thought, to follow it to its conclusion. They rounded another corner and discovered yet another obstacle.

In front of them was what appeared to be a boxing ring. And in the ring, #2 and #10 were hitting each other with all the savagery of an MMA cage fight. Maggie hated seeing even short clips of those fights, seeing people attacking one another with bare fists and feet, seeing the brutality and the blood. Noah used to make fun of her because she hated when he stopped on one of those fights as he was clicking through the channels. He'd say it was ridiculous that she could read books about teenagers murdering each other and not watch a few minutes of fighting.

*"It's different,"* Maggie had insisted. *"In the books, no matter how much the author describes, I can put a limit on what I imagine. I don't have to see it unless I want to. But something like this, you can't escape it. It's all blood and viciousness, and it's completely in your face."*

Noah had laughed at her, and kept the channel on even when she asked him to change it. She should have known then what he would become, that the kind of man who couldn't even respect such a simple boundary would turn out to be an asshole.

Maggie, Sanya and Beth approached the ring slowly. #2 and #10 didn't seem to be remotely aware of their presence. #10's arms and face were scratched, and she weaved on her feet, but #2 was in much worse shape. Her scalp bled, her left wrist hung at a terribly wrong angle, and one of her eyes was, if not missing completely, then certainly damaged beyond repair. Blood and jelly ran over #2's cheekbone.

As they watched, #2 kicked out at #10's ribs and Maggie heard a solid *crack*. #10 cried out, but it was a puffy, barely oxygenated cry. She didn't seem to have the breath to speak her pain.

Then Maggie noticed something on the other side of the ring, and she sucked in a hard breath. She wondered if she was hallucinating, if her desperate brain was creating an out where there was none.

"What is it?" Sanya asked.

"Look," Maggie said, pointing. "There's an exit."

A bright red exit sign hung over a plain white door set in the wall, almost invisible except for the presence of the sign. The door was several feet past the ring where #2 and #10 were presently trying to kill each other.

There was a way out. They just had to get to it.

"That door will be locked, for sure. Or it will be a trick, not a door at all," Sanya said, but Maggie heard the spark of hope in her voice nonetheless.

It was the same spark that surged in Maggie's own chest, a surge of energy that she thought she'd exhausted. There was a way out. This wasn't just an endless nightmare where they had to keep going through the maze until they all fell down, meaningless dominoes in some sadist's game.

"We can try it," Maggie said. "The door is right there. We'd be stupid not to try."

Some part of her wondered, though, if the exit was just a trap, just a trick to keep the men who were watching them amused. Would they laugh when Maggie and Sanya and Beth tried to get through it? Or would the door be temptingly unlocked, just another opportunity for death and horror in a different place?

*What if the door is all part of their plan?*

Maggie knew that it was a possibility. She also knew that she still had to try, had to make the attempt to get out of this place. She'd lost herself for a little while there, unable to get the sight of Natalie falling, flailing for the rope that couldn't save her, out of her mind. The exit sign gave her hope again, shot a jolt of energy into her veins. She could do this. They could do this. They could get away.

"But the obstacle," Beth said.

"What about it?" Maggie said.

"We have to, you know, do the obstacle," Beth said, pointing at the ring.

#2 looked like she was on her last legs, reeling around the ring like a drunk. #10 watched #2 with narrowed fox eyes, waiting for her chance.

"Looks to me like the obstacle's currently occupied," Sanya said. "And I don't see any instructions, either, that say we have to fight like those two idiots are doing. I think it would count as completing the obstacle if we just climbed over it."

Beth shook her head. "No, I don't think that's right. I think we're supposed to . . ."

Her voice trailed off, and Maggie gave her a hard look.

"We're supposed to fight each other, that's what you think?"

Beth gestured toward the ring again. "I mean, it's a fighting ring. So I think we're supposed to fight."

"Do you see any indication of that?" Maggie said. She had a suspicion about Beth, a suspicion that was growing stronger by the second. "Any sign that says we have to fight, have to be cruel to each other or hurt each other?"

Beth stared at Maggie with wide eyes. "No, I just thought—"

"I'm not going to fight anyone unless I have to," Maggie said, and thought, *Don't try to give me those big Bambi eyes now. Not when I'm onto you.*

"Looks like number two isn't doing so great," Sanya said. "Guess she wasn't a ringer after all."

"Yeah, but I think there's still a ringer here," Maggie said, looking at Beth. "I think there's someone whose job it was to make sure we all end up shredded into little pieces so we don't make it to the end of the maze. Someone who was always making sure we went in front of her. If there is an end of the maze at all, and I'm not convinced of that."

Sanya followed Maggie's gaze to Beth. "Really? You think it's her? She can barely get through this without collapsing."

"Sure about that?" Maggie asked. "Because I noticed that she hasn't had any trouble breathing for a while, no matter how fast we ran or how much stress she was supposedly under."

Beth grabbed Sanya's shirtsleeve. Maggie realized how purposeful the gesture was, how childlike, how it made you think that Beth was someone small and delicate who needed to be protected.

"Sanya," Beth said, and her voice wobbled convincingly. "You don't believe this, do you? Maggie, I think you're just really tired and really sad because of Natalie. I mean, you barely got through the last few obstacles. I had to help you a couple of times because you were really out of it."

"But not so out of it that I couldn't have made it on my own," Maggie said, and as she said it, she realized it was true. She'd been in a fog, but not so badly that she couldn't move her body or get through the tasks that had been set for them. Beth hadn't really helped her.

If anything, Maggie now realized, Beth had been a hindrance. It had been carefully done, not obvious unless you were looking for it, but Beth's supposed physical weakness and clumsiness had almost gotten Maggie seriously hurt more than once. She'd dragged the whole group down, made them go slower than they had to, made Maggie feel like she had to look out for her. And every time Beth would say, "I'm so sorry, I'm so sorry," or, "I was just trying to help."

*Uh-huh,* Maggie thought. *Just trying to help. Just trying to help me get killed before we got to this obstacle so she could take out Sanya and then waltz out that exit, free and clear.*

Sanya said, "I don't know, Maggie. It doesn't seem like she's been, you know, actively trying to get us killed. Both of us made it this far."

"But Roni and Natalie didn't."

"Yeah, and half of number two's group died before they got here as well," Sanya said. "I don't think that is really an indicator. Maybe you're, you know, just getting a little . . ."

"Paranoid?" Maggie said. "I'm not paranoid."

She tried to keep her voice steady and even, because that was what Noah had told her when she said he was acting weird and different and not like himself, when he was keeping secrets from her.

*"You're just being paranoid, Maggie. I think those books you read are making you a little cuckoo. There isn't a vast conspiracy out there, waiting to get you."*

But Maggie had known something was wrong from the start, had let him convince her to second-guess herself and all the red flags. She'd known he was becoming someone other than the man she'd married. She'd just wanted to believe the best in him, to believe that she could still love him and that he could love her the way he used to. That mistake, that naïve belief, had almost cost Paige her life.

Maggie wasn't going to let that happen this time. Nothing mattered anymore except Paige, except getting her daughter out of this hellhole safely.

"Did you notice," Maggie said, "that when all those spiders came up on us in the jungle, Beth got out way ahead of everyone? She was like a sprinter then, no trouble with her 'asthma' at all."

Maggie made air quotes with her fingers around "asthma."

Tears welled up in Beth's eyes, but didn't spill over.

*She's good. I wonder how you do that, how you almost cry without letting it actually happen.*

"I'm scared of spiders," Beth said, in a tiny, wispy voice. "I told you I'm scared of them."

"Yeah, and that was funny, too," Maggie said. "Weird coincidence, that the thing you're supposedly most scared of just happened to come after us."

"I didn't know that was going to happen. I don't even know how I got out of there," Beth insisted. "My body just took over, but in my brain, I was screaming and screaming."

Maggie heard a grunt, followed by another, and looked back at the ring. #2 and #10 toppled simultaneously, crashing onto the mat. #2 didn't appear to be breathing. #10 lay on the mat with her face mangled, her mouth open. She didn't seem able to move at all.

*Who are you fighting for?* Maggie wondered. *Who did they take from you? Who did they threaten you with?*

Even #2 had to have someone, or else she wouldn't have pushed so hard. Underneath that mean-girl exterior, she cared about someone.

*People are never what you see on the surface. There's always a secret heart with a fortress around it, a hideout for their smallest and truest selves, the piece that they never show anybody else.*

Inside her secret heart, #2 loved somebody enough to beat #10 almost to death.

Inside her secret heart, Beth cared so little about Sanya and Maggie that she would side with their captors, that she would work to ensure that all the other participants were hurt.

And she did it all while looking so sweet, so helpless, so innocent. But Maggie saw what was underneath. She saw that Beth was a traitor.

Sanya had taken a couple of steps toward the ring when #2 and #10 fell down, but stopped and looked back at Maggie. "I figured you'd be rushing to help anyone who got hurt, like usual."

"It's not safe to turn your back on a snake," Maggie said.

Maggie and Beth stared at each other. Sanya looked like she wanted to intervene but wasn't sure what to do. Maggie knew that Sanya thought she'd been pushed off the deep end by the maze.

"Stop pretending," Maggie said to Beth.

Maggie saw the shift, the calculation in Beth's eyes the second before Beth smiled.

"All right, bitch. Let's dance."

# CHAPTER SIX

**mags13:** wait, didn't I just mute you? WTF?

**tyz7513:** no, that wasn't me. That person had "7412" at the end of their name.

**mags13:** that's ... pretty weird though. That you would have such a similar ID.

**tyz7513:** Coincidences happen.

**mags13:** do they tho?

**tyz7513:** Let's go back to the beginning. Do you really think you'd be able to survive one of those dystopic games like in all of those books?

**mags13:** Sure. I'm a mom. I can do anything 😄

**tyz7513:** All right then. Prove it.

SANYA'S MOUTH DROPPED. "WAIT, you're *actually* a bad guy and Maggie isn't just having a paranoid hunger hallucination?"

Beth smirked. "I can't believe how easily you all fell for the 'poor little me' routine. Especially you, Maggie. You just can't stop yourself from helping people."

"I don't consider it a character flaw," Maggie said tightly. "Although in retrospect, I do wish that scythe had swung as you were exiting the crawl tunnel."

"So mean, Magdalena," Beth said, using Maggie's full name instead of her nickname. That, more than anything else, convinced Maggie that she was right, that Beth was part of the group that kidnapped women and threw them into some sick gladiator game. "What happened to your compassion for humanity?"

"I find it's lacking at the moment. Maybe I'll get it back. After I kick your ass into the stratosphere."

"What happened to 'I'm not going to fight anyone unless I have to'?" Beth said, her voice high and mocking.

"Oh, I have to," Maggie said. "I definitely have to."

Sanya looked like she was struggling to keep up. She glanced at Maggie. "Does she know you? Like, personally? Seems like there's a lot of hostility all of a sudden."

"Nope," Maggie said. "She's probably cattle-prod guy's handmaiden or something. His little side piece."

"I'm nobody's accessory," Beth said, snarling. "And Clark knows I wouldn't fuck him if he were the last man on earth."

"Clark," Maggie said thoughtfully. "He didn't really seem like a Clark to me. More like a Chad. A petulant little frat boy trying to prove he doesn't have a micro-penis."

"Chad, Clark—I mean, they're all rich white boy names," Sanya said.

"Yeah, but when I think of Clark, I think of Superman," Maggie said. "Morality, nobility, self-sacrifice. It doesn't seem like the kind of name you give to a little shit."

"I guess his parents couldn't have known when he was born that he would end up being a little shit," Sanya said. "That's not really predictable."

"There's probably at least one Brandon in that group," Maggie said.

"Ooh, and a Landon, too."

"I bet your name is not really Beth," Maggie said. "Is it McKayla? You look like a McKayla."

"Total sorority girl name," Sanya agreed. "Was Chad your college boyfriend? Did you meet at the kegs-and-eggs breakfast?"

"It's Beth," she said, her face mottled with fury. "And you're not going to be joking soon enough. Just as soon as we clear the ring of those useless cunts, you're going to be in there with me, and you're not going to like what you discover."

"You know," Maggie said, "if you want to trick somebody into thinking you're weaker than you actually are, then maybe you shouldn't give away the game before we even start. I revise my opinion of you. I thought you were pretty good at deception at first, but when it comes down to it, you are a crap hustler."

Maggie didn't want to fight Beth. It would be emotionally satisfying, sure, but she didn't want to risk injury or death at the hands of this woman. Maggie had already concluded that despite her slight appearance, Beth probably knew five separate martial arts disciplines or something, otherwise the group wouldn't have sent her into the maze. Maggie hoped that if she ran her mouth long enough, Beth would get angry and charge, and Maggie would be able to take advantage of her mistake.

Maggie wasn't a fighter. The only time she'd fought anyone was when Noah broke into her house after she'd moved out of his, and it wasn't some Queensberry boxing rules match. She'd tried to run, grabbed vases and wine bottles and anything else she could reach to slam into his head, had kicked him in the balls and slammed a door into his nose. She'd fought dirty because he'd been high as a kite and intent on killing her for taking Paige away.

Maggie didn't like her chances in an open ring, with no heavy objects to throw.

*But I'll fight dirty. I'll do whatever I have to do to take her down and get to that exit.*

Maggie's eyes went to the bright red sign, glowing in the artificial light of the maze.

"It's open, you know," Beth said, giving Maggie a sly smile. "Because I'm supposed to be the only one left after this obstacle."

"You won't be," Maggie said.

Her heart thrummed wildly. The door was open, unlocked. If she could just get there, then she might be able to find Paige.

"I will be," Beth said. "Because none of you are supposed to survive. That's my job."

"And what do you get out of it?" Maggie said. "They're a bunch of misogynists, anyone can see that. And they're probably the types that like to cosplay as military and pretend that it means something. But you? Why would you want to do this to other women?"

Beth sneered. "I don't believe in all of that sisterhood shit. I like manipulating people. I like hurting people."

Maggie knew there were those who enjoyed seeing others in pain, knew there were those who got a sadistic thrill out of that. But she'd never heard it stated so baldly, so honestly. Beth wanted to see the women around her suffer. Maggie couldn't grasp it. It was fundamentally not in her nature to be cruel.

"This group gave me the chance to do it on a large scale. Of course, I hardly had to do anything because you were all so *earnest* and *helpful*. Now, clear them out of the ring."

Beth flicked her fingers at #2 and #10. Maggie noticed that while she argued with Beth, #10 had stopped moving. Her eyes were closed, and Maggie couldn't tell if #10 was breathing anymore.

"No," Maggie said.

"I said, clear them out," Beth said. "You have to do every obstacle, and this obstacle is a fight to see who's still standing."

"Why should I do every obstacle?" Maggie said. "You've made it clear that we were going to be killed anyway. They never intended to keep their promise to let us go at all."

She said this with a fair amount of bravado, but inside, her heart was crumbling into pieces. *Paige, Paige, Paige.* Maybe they wouldn't really kill the hostages. Maybe Paige would be all right even if Maggie wasn't.

"Well, who knows?" Beth said, her look so smug that Maggie had a hard time resisting the urge to punch her in the face right there. "Maybe they'll change their minds if you're good enough."

*Good enough.* It was always like this, always a quest to prove herself to some man, to work three times as hard for half the recognition. She didn't want to play by their rules anymore. She was tired of feeling like she'd been shoved inside a box and permitted to bounce off the walls but never allowed to open the top and climb out.

*But they're making you follow their rules because they're holding Paige over your head. They can make you dance because it's not just about you.*

"There's nothing that says we have to go into the ring to fight," Maggie said.

"I just explained, dumbass, that you have to complete *every obstacle,*" Beth said.

"And what I am saying, dumbass, is that I don't have to be inside that ring to fight *you.*"

Maggie ran at Beth, tackled her before Beth realized what was happening. She slammed Beth into the ground with all the force she had in her body. Then she grabbed Beth's hair, close and tight to the scalp, and slammed Beth's head into the ground. Repeatedly.

Maggie knew her strengths. Her arms and legs were strong from climbing, but she didn't know the first thing about punching and didn't think she'd have the wherewithal to put a sufficient amount of force behind any blow. So she'd use what was available to assist her—the ground, the walls, whatever.

Beth bucked, tried to throw Maggie off her. Maggie was flat on top of Beth and she tried to move, to dig in her knees on either side of the smaller woman. As she'd suspected, Beth was much stronger than she looked. Despite the disorientation she must have felt, Beth managed to dig in her heels and heave Maggie off to the side. Maggie kept her grip on Beth's hair, though, and Beth screamed as some of her hair and scalp tore away.

Maggie spread her fingers and shook her hand, repulsed by what she'd just done. The moment of disgust was all Beth needed. She leapt on top of Maggie and did what Maggie should have done in the first place—sat on Maggie's hips and pounded her fists into Maggie's face.

Beth's hands were bony, her knuckles sharp, and she punched like someone who'd been trained to punch as hard as possible. After a few seconds, Maggie wondered if Beth would hit her until there was nothing left of her face, until she looked like she'd been shredded in a meat grinder. She felt something shift in her cheek, heard a crack, and there seemed to be a lot of salt in her mouth, salt and liquid and copper, and Maggie knew she'd lost at least one tooth. Agonizing pain coursed through her, and it dawned that her cheekbone was probably broken.

Then suddenly the pain stopped, the weight on Beth's body was gone, and Beth screamed out in fury. Maggie took a breath, discovered that breathing hurt. She turned to one side and spit out all the liquid in her mouth. The cracked pieces of tooth came out with the blood and saliva, and she thought, strangely, despairingly, of the dentist's bill. Her dental insurance was not so great.

*The dentist is the least of your problems. Get out of this mess first.*

Maggie pushed herself up to a crouch, saw Sanya had managed to get Beth on her back on the ground. Sanya was kicking Beth hard in the ribs, the face, whatever she could hit. Beth tried to roll away but Sanya stomped on her hand.

*I should have done that,* Maggie thought dazedly. *I should have used my legs and kept my face away from Beth's hands.*

She stood, wobbled, righted herself. She wanted so badly to lie back down and have a rest, but Sanya needed help. Maggie went to the other side of Beth and added her own kicks.

Soon Sanya and Maggie fell into a rhythm, a rhythm that meant that Beth was continuously receiving blows. It didn't take long before Beth's eyes closed, before she stopped trying to roll away, before she lay still and silent.

Maggie stopped, stepped back, peered down at Beth from a few feet away, half-convinced that Beth would pop back up like the killer in a slasher film.

Sanya said, "She's still breathing. Don't worry."

Maggie and Sanya looked at each other, both of them sucking air like they'd just run a hard race.

"I'm not fighting you," Maggie said.

"Same," Sanya said. "I've had enough of this shit. And by the way, your face does not look okay."

Maggie laughed, or tried to, because it hurt to smile. Her laugh came out like a strange little puffed grunt. It hurt to talk and stand and do anything, really.

"My face does not feel okay," Maggie said, and gave in to the driving need to sit down, just for a minute. She leaned her head forward between her knees and gagged, dry heaved, spit out some more saliva.

"Got nothing in there to throw up," Sanya said. "I would kill someone for a sandwich right now."

"God, I love sandwiches," Maggie said, gasping and holding her hand over her stomach, willing the dry heaves to stop. "That's my favorite food."

"What kind?" Sanya said, giving Maggie a hand up.

They walked toward the ring, because the ring was set up so that it covered the maze from wall to wall. There was no way around it; you could only go over it.

"Any kind," Maggie said. "I like all the sandwiches. I like cold-cut sandwiches and hot sandwiches. I like banh mi and Italian subs and short rib torta and Cubanos. I'll take a turkey and Swiss over a slice of pizza any day of the week. I even like—*gasp!*—tuna sandwiches."

"I like tuna," Sanya said. "I don't see why liking a tuna melt is such a controversial opinion."

"Right?" Maggie said as they pulled themselves through the ropes surrounding the ring. "A tuna melt and a cup of soup is just comfort food."

"I could go for a tuna melt right now. Hell, I could go for a goddamned Nutri-Grain bar right now," Sanya said. "I can't remember ever being so hungry, not even when I was a broke undergrad. At least I could afford cornflakes and ramen."

They paused in the middle of the ring. Maggie knelt down beside #2, and Sanya beside #10. Maggie reached a shaky hand to check #2's pulse, and Sanya did the same for #10. Maggie jerked her hand back from #2 right away.

"She's already cold," Maggie said. "Does it really happen that fast?"

"It's been longer than it seems, I guess. I wasn't really watching the clock, what with the shocking revelations and all," Sanya said, holding her fingers to #10's neck.

After a minute, Sanya said, "Nothing."

"So it's just the two of us," Maggie said.

"Just the two of us and a bunch of guys with guns and cattle prods," Sanya said. "And Lord knows what else."

"Seems totally safe and straightforward," Maggie said, standing and looking toward the door built into the wall of the maze.

Alice went through a door, after she grew and then shrank, after she ate and drank things that maybe she shouldn't have. On the other side of the door, she had an adventure with flowers and grinning cats and very unhinged tea parties, an adventure that was sometimes wondrous and sometimes dangerous. Despite all of this, she made it home, wondering if it was all just a dream.

Lucy went through a door, one that was built into a wardrobe, and she came out by a lamppost and had tea with a faun. Later, her adventure got more wondrous and also much more dangerous, but she and her siblings all made it home safely.

Beauty went through a door in a castle, and had tea with a beast, but only after he shouted and pretended to be angry. Later, her adventure became more wondrous but somehow less dangerous, for that beast was all bark and no bite.

Maggie always thought this was irresponsible storytelling, because beasts don't stop being dangerous as long as they have teeth.

She didn't think she was going to find a cup of tea on the other side of the door, nor any adventure strange and wondrous. Maybe she would find her daughter. That was her hope.

Maybe she would find death, and that seemed more likely.

"What's going on in your head?" Sanya asked, standing beside Maggie and staring at the same door Maggie was staring at.

"The same thing that's going on in yours," Maggie said. "Is it a trick? Is it a trap? Will we just get shot on the other side? Will I be able to find my daughter?"

Sanya looked up at the running clock. "There's only one way to find out."

Maggie climbed over the other side of the ring, half-expecting a voice to boom out over a loudspeaker, telling them that they had to fight one another. But nothing happened. There was only the sound of her own breath, and Sanya's, and the thump of their sneakers on the ground outside the ring.

"Okay," Maggie said, and they started walking toward the door.

Maggie again expected something, some exhale of breath—an announcement, an outpouring of tin solders through the door. But there was nothing, and no one, and she wondered why. It seemed wrong, like the story wasn't following the preordained plot.

*It can't be this easy,* Maggie thought. *After all of this, it can't be this easy.*

Her feet began to move faster of their own volition, and the bright red exit sign bobbed up and down in her vision.

*Let it be open. Please let it be open. Paige, I'm coming.*

Maggie ran, ran, ran for the exit.

She slammed into the door, and pushed it open.

PART IV

# ALL
# TOGETHER
# NOW

*There's daggers in men's smiles.*

—William Shakespeare

# CELIA

CELIA SLAMMED THE DOOR open, fully expecting there to be someone on the other side—some kind of guard, or even some office dweeb watching a monitor. Something. But there was only an empty hallway that was painted white like the wall outside. The end where Celia stood was set at a strange angle—her own door and another directly across, and then a third to the right where the hallway narrowed, almost but not quite making the point of a triangle.

The floor was covered in industrial gray carpeting, and there were two more doors like the one she'd just come through—blank and white, though she noticed that the two doors set opposite hers had deadbolt locks on them. The locks were not thrown.

She turned around and saw the door she'd come through had the same lock. Celia threw the bolt and then took a step back, wondering if the lock would work or if the faceless men chasing her would be able to break through. There were a lot of them. She didn't want to think about how many there were, or what they might do to her if they caught her.

*They can't pretend anymore that I belong in that place, though. I know now. I know.*

She was almost comically out of breath, clutching a stitch in her side. Celia couldn't believe that anyone would ever think they could convince her that she was a runner. She hunched over a little, trying to catch her breath. One of these doors had to be a way out. And the locked door behind her wouldn't stop those men for long. They would have another way in.

A moment later, someone tried to pull the door open. This was followed by the pounding of a heavy fist. "Bitch! You fucking bitch! Open the goddamned door now or you'll be sorry!"

Celia backed away from the door, staring at it as if it were a hovering cobra. The door shook in its frame, and there was a cacophony of yelling voices.

"What the hell is going on?"

"Bitch locked the fucking door, that's what!"

"How did she get this far anyway? I thought Pete was supposed to inject her again last night?"

Celia was about three feet away from the door, almost in the dead center of the hall, but she stepped a little closer. Maybe she would get some useful information.

"We're not going to be able to break the fucking door down." This man's voice sounded wearier than the others. "We're going to have to go around to the other exit."

There was a rumble of protest, and Celia heard someone say, "That's almost three miles in the other direction, and that's where the actors are supposed to go! I told Ray that this design was stupid. There should be more access points for us. How are we supposed to run this place properly without enough people and with everything going to one central hub?"

"You hear that, Ray? Stupid fucking design!"

Celia had the distinct impression that this person was shouting up into the sky. *Probably to whoever planted those cameras. The person who was watching me in the kitchen, watching me in the fake life they set up for me. But everything comes into this hub. Okay. That's good to know.*

"Ray, get off your goddamned ass and unlock this door!"

The door was pushed again, the lock rattling a little. But it looked like it was going to hold.

Then one of the doors behind Celia flew open. She spun around, her fist raised in the air like she was going to punch whoever came through.

*Which is ridiculous, because I don't know the first thing about hitting people.*

She'd assumed it would be another one of the men in black, but instead it was a tiny brunette woman. She was splattered with blood—blood on her face and her glasses and her clothes. She was younger than Celia, maybe college-age. The brunette slammed the door behind her, the same as Celia, but she noticed the lock a lot sooner. The bolt had just clicked home when that door also began to shake from pounding.

"Bitch! Goddamned bitch! I will gut you! I will fucking kill you!"

The brunette turned her back to the wall and leaned against it. She looked as exhausted as Celia felt.

"Typical," the brunette said, rolling her eyes at the door. "Some man doesn't get his way and suddenly I'm the bitch for not standing still when he wanted to stab me."

An involuntary giggle escaped Celia's mouth and she covered it with her hand. The door behind her shook, and the men on the other side of it continued to shout at Ray (for being stupid) and Celia (for being a bitch).

"Looks like you're having the same kind of day I am," the brunette said. She held out her hand, seemed to register that it was covered in sticky blood and dirt, and then withdrew it with a chastened look. "Allison. Allie."

"Celia. At least, I'm pretty sure I'm Celia."

Allie raised her eyebrow at that but didn't ask any questions. "Well, Celia, I'd like to know your life story up to this point, but I think there's a more pressing need at the moment. We both seem to have arrived here while being chased by shouty men."

"We've got to get out of this place," Celia said, nodding in agreement. "Whatever this place is."

"No idea, either? Or where we might be?" Allie asked hopefully.

Celia shook her head. "I mean, my driver's license says something, but it's a fake, because I'm not married to Pete and I don't have a daughter either, and the whole town was a set, so . . ."

"Maybe I *should* hear your life story," Allie said. "Yours seems a lot more complicated than mine. I just had all my friends murdered by a crazy slasher. The one shouting behind this door, in point of fact."

Allie's eyes welled up behind her glasses, but she sniffed hard and seemed determined to squash the tears down. Celia didn't know if she should express sympathy or not. Something in Allie's face told Celia that the younger woman wouldn't want sympathy from a stranger.

"I don't remember anything before yesterday, so my life story will be short," Celia said.

Allie opened her mouth to respond, but as she did, yet another door flew open. This time, two women came through—a tall, slender Black woman and a fit-looking Latina, both wearing the same type of gray tee and black leggings. The Black woman slammed the door shut behind them, then locked it. The left side of the Latina's face was swollen and blood had run out of her mouth and over her chin.

"Jesus!" Celia said. "What happened to you two?"

"Somebody's idea of a funny game," the Latina said, then put her hand to her cheek. "Ow. It hurts to talk."

"Don't talk, then. If we come across any kind of ice, we'll put it on your face, but I think your cheekbone might be broken," the Black woman said. "It doesn't look right."

"It doesn't feel right," the Latina said, wincing as she spoke.

"I'm Sanya. This is Maggie. And if you two are ringers like Beth, you ought to go outside and see what we did to her before you even think about taking us on."

"I don't know who Beth is," Celia said. "I'm not even 100 percent sure who I am."

Sanya raised her eyebrow. "Well, that's a thing. Where did you two come from? Another part of the game?"

"What game?" Allie asked.

Sanya quickly explained that she and Maggie had been forced to participate in a sick survival game, and they were the last two survivors.

Celia shook her head. "There was a town, and they told me I was married and I lived there, but they were drugging me so I would forget who I really was."

As she said this, Celia felt the same resurgent well of despair rise up in her that she'd felt over and over in the last day. Would she ever remember who she really was? Or was she broken forever by what they'd done to her?

"I was supposedly camping in the woods with my friends, and now they're all dead. Except for one, that is. And he wasn't really my friend. I think he was responsible, anyway. Sorry, I'm not really making sense. My brain is racing a hundred miles an hour, and all I can think is that I've got to get out of here," Allie said.

Just then, the man on the other side of Allie's door slammed against it, and it shook so hard that Celia thought it would actually buckle. He seemed to have taken a run at the door and tried to tackle it.

All four of them stared at the door for a moment, and then without another word they all started down the long corridor, away from the doors.

"How come the two of you didn't have a shouting guy calling you a bitch trying to follow through your door?" Allie asked.

"The shouting guys were at the beginning," Maggie said.

"Yeah, some wannabe militia types," Sanya said. "But we haven't seen them in a while."

"Men in black? With balaclavas? And guns?" Celia asked, trying not to let the tremor she felt show.

"Yeah, did you get a look at them, too? I thought for sure they'd come pouring down the hall here," Sanya said, pointing in front of them.

The hall seemed very, very long to Celia. It didn't escape her that their only means of egress were behind them if the men did appear. And they'd all run through those doors, desperate to escape what had been following them. She wanted to run again, to pelt through the halls until she reached the outside world, the real world, but she knew that was foolish. She needed to keep calm, keep herself smart and safe until she was free. Then she could break down all she wanted once she was home.

*But I don't know where my home is. I don't know where to go, where I belong.*

Then she realized what Sanya had just said. "All those men who were following me, I locked them out. And I heard them shouting at someone called Ray to let them in, or else they were going to have to go a long way around. To where the actors come in, he said. The town must have been filled with actors, people who probably didn't know what was going on." *But some of them had known, for sure. Jennifer, my "best friend." Pete, my "husband." I heard them talking about drugging me. So they knew for sure what had happened to me.*

"How many men were chasing you?" Sanya asked.

"Maybe twenty?"

Sanya and Maggie exchanged a look.

"That's about how many were outside our maze when they forced us in," Maggie said. She spoke very slowly, every word obviously painful.

"But this can't all be run by twenty guys," Allie said. "Look at the size of this place. Look at the size of the . . . I don't know what you would call them. Scenarios, maybe? They were huge. You'd need a lot of people to build and maintain all this."

"Build it, yes," Maggie said. "Maintain it . . . they probably have a cleaning crew or whatever that comes in to take care of certain things, a crew that doesn't really know what goes on here. But otherwise they probably have a certain degree of automation controlling the climate and whatnot."

"How long could this have been going on?" Celia said. "I mean, without people finding out about it? It can't be that women go missing in huge numbers and nobody cares."

"If you're a blonde white woman, somebody will care, especially the major news networks," Sanya said.

"They do love a missing white girl. Especially a young pretty one," Allie said. "But everyone else—well, let's just say that aside from their family and some close community members, there are varying degrees of concern."

"Particularly from police," Maggie said.

"And anyway," Sanya said. "We're all from different places. At least, we were in the maze. Maggie is from Arizona. I'm from Chicago. There were women from Florida and Virginia and Wyoming. So it's not like these fuckers are scooping up a huge group of women from one area. They picked and chose. It wouldn't look like a vast conspiracy of kidnappings. It would look like, well, the regular sort of girls-gone-missing stories that happen every day."

Celia wasn't stupid, she *wasn't*, but it felt crazy to her that all of this could happen. She'd thought the worst of it was being drugged, or having a parade of people trying to convince her that the wrong life was hers. But the stories that Sanya and Maggie had told, about a kind of culling game, and Allie talking about all her friends being killed . . . How could this happen? How could so many women be kidnapped by one organization? How could authorities not be aware of it? She didn't say any of this, though, because she still felt a little shaky and a little unsure of her ground. And if she was completely honest . . . she didn't know if she could or should trust these women. They might be a part of the organization. This might still be part of the game, or the story, or whatever. Celia would just keep her mouth shut as much as possible, and watch and wait for her chance. And she would see if these women were the real thing, if they were what they said they were.

"But still," Celia said, going back to the original topic. "Twenty guys to control three scenarios? To keep us from escaping?"

"Why not?" Sanya said. "As long as they have weapons and we don't, as long as they outnumber us . . ."

She trailed off.

"It does seem crazy," Allie said. "So many things could go wrong."

"So many things did go wrong," Maggie said. "We're all here, inside the complex, instead of out there in their stories for us."

"Besides, is the idea of twenty guys running all this crazier than being dropped into a survival game? Or being forced to live out a slasher movie? And I don't even know what happened to her yet, but it sounds like some Stepford wife shit." Sanya gestured at Celia.

"Stepford wife," Celia murmured. "In that story, all the wives were replaced by robots, right?"

"Sounds kind of like what they wanted to do to you. Drug you, gaslight you, make you a robot that did what they wanted," Allie said.

"But *why?*" Celia said. The word broke out of her almost involuntarily, the chorus to the song that had been playing in her head almost nonstop for two days. *Why? Why? Why?* "What did I do to deserve this? What did any of us do?"

"I'm not sure I care," Maggie said. "I just want to find my daughter and get out of here."

"Your daughter is here?" Allie asked.

"Yeah, they used hostages to force us to participate," Maggie said. "They claimed that our hostages would be killed if we didn't make it through the game."

"But who *built* this place?" Celia asked. "It's enormous. The town I just came from—there are two or three miles of road around it, and woods, and houses everywhere. And you say that you were in a maze, a maze big enough to send you running around for hours."

"And the place where Brad brought us—Brad was my friend Cam's boyfriend, and he disappeared in the night, and by the way, I definitely think he was responsible for what happened, and when I see him, I'm going to kick his balls into his throat," Allie said. She took a deep breath. "Anyway, that place was a cabin in the middle of trees, and there was at least two miles of road leading up to it. And somehow all of this is *inside.*"

"Yeah, we noticed the fake light, too," Sanya said.

"What fake light?" Celia asked.

"Like the sunlight wasn't quite right," Allie said. "You can tell we're under a big dome or something. They did a pretty good job faking it, but once you notice it, you can tell that the sun isn't like the real sun."

"I didn't notice. I mean, I kind of noticed there was something weird about the night sky, not enough stars, but I didn't figure it out," Celia said, feeling stupid. "I hardly noticed anything, because all I could think about was remembering who I was. Who I really was, not the me they told me I was. And they tried to set me up for a murder, too, and that was pretty distracting."

"Damn," Sanya said. "They went all out for you."

"Seems unnecessarily complicated," Maggie said. "To set up a whole storyline and force you to live in it."

"Maybe that's why they only put one woman in that position," Allie said. "Just to test it out, like. To see if it would take."

"But you had all your friends with you, and you thought it was just a regular trip," Maggie said. "How did they get you inside here without you noticing, though?"

"Drugged," Allie said. "All of us, except Brad. He drove the car. We were drinking from a cocktail that this guy Steve supposedly made for us, and then we all passed out."

"And we were drugged and woke up in here," Sanya said. "Somebody's got a pharmacist on staff."

"Yeah, the last thing I remember is going to bed," Maggie said.

"Me, too," Sanya said. "And then waking up here. Which means they must have . . . what? Come for us in the night? Drugged our mouthwash?"

Maggie shook her head. "I have no idea. I don't remember anything after shutting off the light."

As she talked, Maggie held her hand to her cheek and her eyes streamed. Celia had no idea how Maggie was dealing with the obviously profound amount of pain she was in.

They reached the end of the corridor. It only turned in one direction, so they followed it. Celia half-expected those twenty men that they'd just been discussing to be waiting for them, smug and secure in their conviction that they could overwhelm four women. But there was no one at all, and it was so strange. Almost as strange as finding a camera in the kitchen, or an empty house instead of a furnished one.

This complex was clearly enormous, and yet there was no hum of activity, no rush of people shouting, "Hey, you don't belong here!" Was it all another trick? Another trap? Were the four of them being lured into some further game? Or was it another trick just for Celia? What if Maggie and Sanya and Allie were just really good actors, like Katherine or Jennifer in the town that had been made up for Celia?

At the end of the corridor, another door waited for them. Celia watched the door come closer and closer, closer and closer, and wondered what would happen to them on the other side. She wondered what she would do if none of these women were who they seemed to be.

# MAGGIE

MAGGIE'S FACE HURT SO bad she could barely think. She sincerely hoped that she'd broken a few of Beth's ribs. Her left eye was blurry, too. She knew that if she didn't get to a doctor soon, she'd be running the risk of complications and infections, and she did not need any more complications or infections in her life. She needed to find Paige and GTFO.

The tall woman, Celia, seemed really shaky. If what she claimed had happened to her was true, then she had reason to be shaky.

*No, don't think that way,* she told herself. *Don't be like, "Oh, she claimed this happened." We need to believe each other. We need to trust each other. Just because Beth turned out to be terrible doesn't mean that everyone is out to get you.*

Maggie knew she could trust Sanya, at least. Sanya had helped her take down Beth. If Sanya had been a part of the group, a part of the system that had imprisoned Maggie and killed Roni and Natalie and all those other women she only knew by number and not name . . . well, if Sanya had been a part of that group, then Sanya wouldn't have helped Maggie. Sanya would have helped Beth instead. So Sanya was safe. Sanya was on her side.

Maggie knew she shouldn't feel bad about what happened to Beth, but part of her did. It didn't feel right to hurt somebody that way. It *shouldn't* feel right.

That same part of her knew that Beth would have killed her, and that was unacceptable. Not for her own sake, but because who would rescue Paige if Maggie died? Noah wouldn't, that was for sure. Maggie was still convinced that Noah had gotten her into this shitshow in the first place.

The four of them stopped in front of the door at the end of the corridor. They all looked at each other.

"So, we should go through," Allie said. Her brows were pushed together and her hands were curled into fists.

"Yeah, I think we have to," Maggie said.

"It's go through here or go back the way we came," Sanya said.

"No, thank you," Celia said.

Maggie grabbed the doorknob, turned it and pushed.

They were in a large room, maybe the size of one of those floor-sized offices one might see in a downtown building in an urban area. The room was painted a flat white and the floor was covered in the same serviceable industrial carpeting as the hall-way. It looked like it might be big enough to accommodate ninety or one hundred people in cubicles, but there were no cubicles. There was, again, no hustle and bustle of people. It seemed unbelievably strange to Maggie to have all this space and nobody to administer it.

Along the wall in front of them, there was a huge bank of television screens—about thirty, by Maggie's calculation. Each set of ten screens seemed to accord with one section of this complex. Maggie recognized different areas of the maze she and Sanya had just run through. The second section showed a cabin, and inside the cabin were two dead people, a boy and a girl in Allie's age range.

*So that part is true,* Maggie thought.

The third bank of TVs showed scenes from what looked like a restaurant kitchen, a suburban house, a parking lot, and a few other places.

Underneath the monitors, there was a long counter. There were three computers set directly in the middle, each with its own flatscreen, keyboard and tower. In front of the middle computer was one rolling office chair. The chair was empty.

At the far corner of the room from where Maggie, Sanya, Allie and Celia stood, there was another door.

Celia and Allie approached the monitors. Maggie turned around to see if the door they'd just come through had a bolt like the others. It did, and Maggie threw it.

Sanya nodded. "So they can't sneak up on us."

"They probably have another way of entering this part of the building anyway," Maggie said. "But just in case."

"Why make it easy on them?"

"Exactly."

"Look!" Celia said, pointing at one of the monitors. "They're all in a truck."

One of the monitors seemed to be following the progress of a truck down a winding country road. Maggie assumed there must be several cameras, triggered by motion.

The truck was some kind of large pickup. The camera showed three men sitting in the front cab—one driving, one in the passenger seat, and one on the secondary bench behind them. Maggie only saw that guy because he leaned forward between the other two.

Several men were jammed into the back of the pickup. Maggie did a quick head count.

"There's only eight of them in the back of the truck, and three in front," Maggie said. "That means the rest of them are probably trying to get through the door you came through, Celia."

"Or they have another way around," Allie said, scanning all the televisions. "I don't see the doors on any of these screens, though."

"I think the cameras are triggered by motion," Maggie said.

"Right, so we should be able to see the rest of the group moving around, but I don't. Could they have shut off the cameras so we won't know what they're doing?"

Sanya shook her head. "Presumably someone would have to do that from this room. Unless they deliberately wrecked their own cameras, which seems shortsighted."

"How come nobody is actually watching the televisions?" Celia asked. "They can't all be out there, can they?"

"That would be amazingly stupid," Allie said. "Even if they do think that we're all under their control. It would be foolish not to assume that at least one of us wouldn't follow their set narratives. I can't believe they didn't prepare for the possibility that there might be a breakout."

"Men always underestimate women," Celia said with an eye roll.

"And four of us got fucking out," Sanya said.

Allie tapped the keyboard of the central computer. The monitor sprang to life, and it showed the area just outside the door where Maggie and Sanya had left the maze.

Allie tapped the second keyboard and said, "That's the door I came in. You can see my personal psychopath is still there trying to break down the door."

All four women watched in silence for a moment as a very large man wearing a black half-mask and a blood-spattered flannel shirt over jeans ran at the door with his shoulder down, like he was trying to make a football tackle.

"I used that move on him," Allie said idly.

"You tackled that guy?" Celia said, startled. "He looks like he's about three times your size."

"I caught him off guard," Allie said. "And then I didn't hang around. I ran."

"Good thinking," Sanya said.

"Which is what we should be doing now," Maggie said. "I have to find Paige and get out of here. Who knows when those guys will find their way back into this building."

"Hang on a second," Allie said, tapping the third keyboard to wake up the last computer. "It makes sense to try to gather as much information as we can before we go barreling forward."

Maggie knew this was the smart thing to do, the right thing to do. She'd just run through a killer maze and she wanted to make it out of here alive. If they could find a way to the hostages using the cameras on these computers, then she would reach Paige even faster. But it was hard not to feel like she was wasting time in this room, like every second they stayed there, they were in more danger.

The third computer monitor showed the nine men who'd been missing from the truck. They had collected a big piece of wood, almost like a tree trunk, from somewhere and were using it to rush and slam against the door that Celia had come through.

"Okay," Allie said. "So they're all accounted for, at least all the men we know about. Some of them are in a truck trying to reach another way into this area, but it appears to be a long way around. The rest are trying to get through the doors."

"Is there any way to see the rest of the facility?" Maggie asked. "I need to find my daughter, and so does Sanya."

The door in the corner of the room swung open, and a man who looked like a Hollywood nerd stereotype stood there holding an armful of Dorito snack bags. He was almost painfully thin, his jeans and white polo shirt hanging off his body. He wore plastic glasses with those pretentious clear frames that Maggie hated, and gray Allbirds, which marked him as Silicon Valley basic. His mouth gaped.

Before Maggie realized her feet were in motion, she'd rushed at him, knocking the Doritos from his arms and pushing him to the floor.

"Where's Paige?" she shouted as she kneeled on his arms, pinning them to the sides of his body. She grabbed hold of his polo collar and lifted his face closer to hers for a second before slamming his head to the floor. "Where's my daughter?"

"Ow! I don't understand—what are you doing here?" he said. He had very pale blue eyes behind the glasses.

"Where's my daughter?" Maggie shouted again as the other three rushed over to join her. "Where are you keeping the hostages?"

"How did you get in?" he asked. He seemed strangely unfazed by the fact that Maggie was holding him on the floor. "It shouldn't have been possible."

"You mean, it shouldn't have been possible that we would read an 'exit' sign and go through the door?" Allie said, her voice dripping with sarcasm.

He shook his head. "No, it shouldn't have been possible for any of you to outrun your pursuers. Women are slower runners than men, statistically speaking. Some member of the group should have caught you. Except for you and you."

He used his head to indicate Maggie and Sanya. "It was Beth's job to ensure none of you made it to the exit. Why didn't she kill you in the ring?"

He said all of this like he was a robot caught on a "does not compute" cycle, like his expected programming had a bug in it.

"I'm not here to answer your questions. You're here to answer mine," Maggie said, slamming his head back on the floor again.

"Watch with the head slams," Sanya said. "If he has a concussion, he can't tell us anything."

"A concussion is going to be the least of his problems if he doesn't tell me where Paige is right the fuck now."

He must have seen the deadly intent in Maggie's eyes, because he said quickly, "She's not here."

"Don't *lie* to me," Maggie said. "I saw that video of her."

He shook his head. "I swear, she's not here. There are no hostages here. Those were tricks, deepfakes. We knew some of you wouldn't participate if you thought only your own lives were at stake."

"Deepfakes?"

Allie said, "It's a video of a person who's been digitally altered so that they appear to be someone else. The technology is getting better all the time. Some of the videos really seem to be the person they are portraying."

Maggie stared at the man. "You're telling me my daughter isn't even here?"

"No, she isn't," he said. "It would have been impractical to bring ten additional hostages along with the players. None of you were expected to survive."

"Thought so," Sanya said. "Number two was out there trying

to run us over just because she thought she could win. But they didn't intend for any of us to win."

"Why would any of you win?" the man said. "I designed the game with the weaknesses of women in mind. You shouldn't have had the strength or the stamina to make it as far as the exit, and if you did—well, there were safeguards put in place. Safeguards which seem to have failed."

He frowned, but it seemed like an inward-looking expression, like he was contemplating the ways in which he would improve his system in the future.

"As I just said, men always underestimate women. Always," Celia said.

"So we don't have to worry about our girls," Sanya said. "That's good. That's the important thing. Now we just need to get ourselves out of here and to the closest police station."

The man gave a little barking laugh, and Maggie slammed his head down once more.

"Would you please stop doing that?" the man said, his voice strained.

"No." Maggie slammed his head down again just on principle. "What's so freaking funny?"

He gave a little shrug, and Maggie was struck by how blasé he seemed. He wasn't enjoying the head slams, but otherwise he didn't appear very concerned about their presence—more annoyed, really, like they were a calculation he'd figured wrong.

"There's no escaping here, and there are no police to be found," he said. "You're on an island. My island."

# ALLIE

AT THAT MOMENT, ALLIE remembered a short story she'd read a while ago—maybe her senior year in high school or freshman year in college; she couldn't recall exactly. It was called "The Most Dangerous Game," and it was about a weird big-game hunter who called himself General Something. He had a private island where he lured people to be the prey in a sick hunting game.

"General," she murmured, trying to remember his name.

"General what?" Celia asked.

"From the story," Allie said, then snapped her fingers before pointing them at the man on the ground. "General Zaroff!"

The man gave another of his strange barking laughs. "Ah, no. If you'll recall, in that story it was *man* that was the most dangerous animal. And none of you are men. Especially not you."

He leered a little at Allie's breasts. Nothing made her angrier than men gawping at her over a physical trait she could not control. It was one of the things that always pissed her off about Brad, the way his eyes always flickered down from her face. She slammed her sneakered foot into the man's nose, and he screamed as blood spurted out.

Maggie had started when Allie moved next to her, but then she nodded up at Allie in approval.

"Bitch!" he shouted, and now he began thrashing underneath Maggie, trying to get out of her grip. "Fucking bitch! I'll kill you for that!"

"How many times today have I heard that?" Allie said in a bored voice. "I outran your personal Michael Myers, and I'm pretty sure I can take down your skinny ass."

"Fucking cunt," he said, his voice full of venom. The malfunctioning robot was all gone now. "You'll get what's coming to you."

"Try to catch me, asshole." Allie peered more closely at the man. There was something about him that seemed familiar, like she'd seen his face before. He was older than her, and she didn't think she'd seen him around campus. But there was something, something about his pale eyes and his stupid clear plastic glasses, something she'd seen pretty recently . . .

"So my daughter isn't here?" Maggie said, her voice breaking into Allie's thoughts. "You're not lying about that?"

"No," he said impatiently. His voice was thick, and the blood coming out of his nose was running back along his cheeks. "Why would I lie about it? It's impractical, like I said. The logistics of transporting fourteen of you were enough."

"Fourteen?" Sanya said. "There were only ten players in the maze. And one of them was yours."

"First her," he said, pointing his bloodied nose toward Celia. "Then the nine players. That was a lot of work on our part. We had to pick our times to grab you, keep you drugged until you were in the scenario."

"And Brad brought me and Cam and Madison and Steve," Allie said, her brows knitted together as she stared at his face. She knew him. She *knew* him, and the knowledge danced just out of reach. "Which means we can't be too far off the West Coast, because we arrived here in his car."

"Well, if they brought us here, then there has to be a way off," Maggie said. "A boat or something. We can find the boat and get out of here while the rest of the dipshits are scrambling around trying to break down locked doors. We can flag down the Coast Guard on the way."

"What do we do with him?" Sanya said. "There's no duct tape around to wrap him up."

"Wrapping him in duct tape seems awfully humane," Celia said, practically spitting the words. "Maybe we should tie him up and drag him behind the boat. Then, if he's still alive, we can hand him over to the police right away."

"You're not going to get anywhere," he said, with a tone of such unbearable smugness that Allie wanted to stomp on his face again. "The others will be back soon, and they know that there aren't supposed to be any survivors. Except for you."

He frowned up at Celia.

"Why me?" Celia said.

"Well, Pete wanted to fuck you first," he said. "But you shook off your dose a lot sooner than we expected, and he didn't get his chance. We'll have to re-dose you and drop you back into the scenario."

"You did all this," Celia said, her voice shaking, "all this, because some guy wanted to *fuck me* and he wanted me drugged so I would play along?"

He shook his head, and the blood from his nose sprayed from side to side.

"I mean, Will wanted to kill you, but Pete wanted to fuck you first, so we arranged a story where they could both get what they wanted."

"Will," Celia said faintly. She crouched down, her head in her hands. "Will, from the restaurant? What did I do to him? Why would he want to kill me?"

The man gave his strange barking laugh for a third time. "He was pretty angry when you reported him for assault. All this could have been avoided if you'd just taken your lumps and kept your mouth shut."

"Assault," Celia said. Allie heard the agony in the other woman's voice. "I can't remember. I can't *remember*. Every time I think I can, it slips away from me."

"Troy did a pretty good job with his formula, then," the man said. "We were hoping for a complete memory wipe and personality replacement, and it looks like he didn't quite succeed there, because your original self started to resurface a lot sooner than we expected. We could almost tell when it was happening because you seemed to be getting headaches. I don't think we anticipated that your personality would be that strong. I think he'll make some changes for next time, tweak some of the dosages."

"Next time?" Celia said, and she stood up, glaring down at the man. "There won't be a next time. I'm leaving, and this place, whatever it is, is going to be shut down. You can't play with people's lives this way. You can't just do whatever the hell you want."

The man didn't say anything, just stared up at the four of them with the kind of smug certainty that Brad always had, stuffed with the knowledge that he was white and male and privileged, and that all ways would be smoothed for him. And it was that look, the ridiculously smug look that made Allie want to kick his face, that finally twigged Allie's memory.

"Raymond Matheson," Allie said. "You're Raymond Matheson."

"Who the fuck is Raymond Matheson?" Sanya said.

"One of these Silicon Valley assholes who made a zillion dollars on a tech startup and now spends all his time giving shitty TED talks and spending his money on idiosyncratic personal bullshit instead of helping the world."

"Oh, I'm helping the world," Matheson said, and Allie was sure all four of them heard the unsaid thought that followed—*by getting rid of bitches like you.*

"Are you one of these guys who builds rockets for your rich friends to fly in?" Sanya said. "I saw something about one of those guys. And another one who drank blood to stay young or something?"

"No, that's not him," Allie said. "I heard that you'd bought a private island off the Washington coast, and that you'd built a huge secret complex on it. The media couldn't stop speculating about how many bathrooms you had in here, how many bedrooms, what you might do with all the extra space. But you wouldn't let anyone in to see it, and all the workers who helped build the project had to sign NDAs. Everyone, down to the guy who swept up the sawdust. Apparently, you put the fear of god in them. Nobody would talk, not even anonymously."

"Well, at least the fear of the legal system," Matheson said with a little smirk. He jerked his head at Celia. "All those actors who performed for her scenario had to sign the same thing. Nobody will talk unless they want to get sued into oblivion."

"But you killed someone! Mrs. Corrigan was killed," Celia said.

Matheson gave Celia a dismissive look. "She wasn't killed. You didn't actually get close to the body, did you? You didn't check it."

"No, because I could see the cords in her throat, for god's sake. There was blood everywhere."

"Just like Cam. Exactly like Cam," Allie murmured.

"Who is also not dead," Matheson said. "I anticipated that if the bodies were gory enough, you wouldn't actually get close to them, wouldn't check to see if they were dead because it would be obvious. I hired a special effects makeup artist to create fakes. He did an incredible job, by the way. Both were astounding works of art."

"Just a fake body," Celia said, almost in an undertone. "All pretend."

"Are you fucking kidding me?" Allie shouted. She was torn between fury and relief. "You made me think my friends were dead and it was all makeup?"

"Oh, Madison and Steve are dead," Matheson said, with the same tone he might use to report that there was no milk in the fridge. "But Cam isn't. Why would Brad want to kill her?"

"Why would he want to kill any of us?" Allie said. She wanted to pull on her own hair or start screaming endlessly. None of this made sense. None of it.

Matheson shrugged. "He didn't want his girlfriend hanging around the two of you anymore. Said you were a bad influence. And Steve was an accident, I guess. Luke got a little overexcited. Brad was irritated about it at first, but he decided Steve would have been annoyingly mopey if his girlfriend was killed, so he's not that upset about it."

"Bad influence?" Allie said, her voice dangerous. It seemed to confirm everything she'd ever thought about Brad, and now here he was, in abuser fashion, isolating his girlfriend from anyone who might help her. Except that he'd gone way farther than isolating Cam. He'd tried to have Allie and Madison killed. He'd succeeded in one case, and Allie's stomach felt sick and sore.

"Those actors have to get here every day," Maggie said, cutting into Allie's thoughts. "Right? They don't live here?"

"Of course not," Matheson said. "I don't want that rabble poking around. People always get curious."

"So there's probably a ferry or something," Maggie said. "We can go there and leave with the performers."

"That exit is through Celia's village," Allie said. "We'd have to go back a long way, right? That's what it sounded like when they were all shouting. That was one of the reasons they were mad."

"All shouting?" Matheson said. "When was this?"

"Were you taking the world's longest shit or something?" Celia asked. "When all your little fake militia friends chased me up to the door and I locked them out."

Matheson's cheeks reddened, and a muscle in his jaw twitched.

"You *were* in the bathroom," Allie said, laughing. "You're all pissed off that we made it in here, and you don't even know how we got here, because you were supposed to be watching the cameras, monitoring what happened, but you weren't."

"I would have thought that the rest of them could handle a few women," he said through gritted teeth. "They're carrying Tasers. They're all larger and stronger than you four."

"But not smarter," Maggie said.

"*Definitely* not smarter," Sanya said.

"Why haven't they made it back here yet, though?" Allie wondered. "It's been a while now."

"I bet the only access from the performers' entrance is from the water, right?" Celia said. "So they have to get a boat and come around to this side of the island."

"He's not answering, which means you're right," Allie said. "And he can't stand it."

"You're not as smart as you think you are, you little bitch," Matheson snarled. "It doesn't matter what you try to do. You can't get away from here. None of you can. I know you can't. I planned this place so that nobody could leave unless I wanted them to leave. Besides, women are inferior to men. They talk big but they can never prove that they can actually do what they say."

"Prove . . ." Allie said. Just before she'd found the exit out of her personal Nightmare Forest, she'd been thinking *prove it*. Somebody had said those words to her recently. "Prove it. That was you. The guy who was being a dick online."

"Prove it," Maggie repeated. "It sounds familiar."

Sanya snapped her fingers. "There was some guy on a message board I was on. He said that to me! We were talking about books, about YA dystopias . . ."

"Wait, I remember that, too!" Maggie said. "The conversation took a real turn after some guy insisted that I prove that I could do what I said in the chat. I remember that I blocked him."

Maggie stared down at Matheson's face.

Allie shook her head. "That was you? You took what some people said online, just messing around, having a conversation with like-minded folks, and turned it into some kind of real game? You built this complex just so you could fuck with people who pissed you off in a chat?"

Celia had her hands around her head again, like she was trying to shake something loose. "Prove it, prove it—I remember! I remember this. I was on a message board and we were all chatting about how much we love mysteries, especially cozy mysteries. And then there was some guy who just went off completely, totally lost his mind."

"This guy," Allie said, nudging Matheson's head with her foot. He glared up at her. "Right? You have no actual life, so you just lurk around on message boards, looking for people to fuck over?"

"But how did you find out who we were? There are privacy settings, and I know that I, at least, have a username that's not my full name," Maggie said.

Matheson blew a raspberry. "Please. I can't believe anyone thinks their information is private online. It's literally the easiest thing in the world to track someone back to their real identity."

"And, what? Once you found out who we were, you put a target on us?" Celia asked.

"Not everyone. I don't have that kind of time. There are dozens of bitches like you everywhere, running their mouths off because they know there are no consequences," Matheson said. "I selected women who had someone in their lives willing to pay for their punishment."

"Willing to pay?" Sanya said.

"Like my shitty ex-husband, I'm sure," Maggie said. "I knew he was a part of this."

"Brad," Allie said. "Brad paid you to set up that horror-movie story, because he knew that I liked those kinds of movies and it would be the perfect way to get rid of me and Madison."

Matheson didn't say anything, just gave them a self-satisfied look. Allie actually felt her leg twitch, felt the longing to smash his face with the heel of her shoe some more.

Allie felt very vindicated at that moment, remembering how she'd insisted that Brad was a part of the terror at the cabin. Steve had scoffed, and Madison hadn't wanted to believe it. But she'd been right.

*You were right, but you lost your friends. The only real friends you had.*

Allie felt her eyes welling up, felt tears choking her throat. She turned her face away so that Matheson wouldn't see, so that he couldn't get any satisfaction from her pain. But it was too late.

"Aww, missing your widdle girlfriend Madison?" he said in a mock-baby voice. "I don't know why. She was only good for one thing, and you don't swing that way, as far as I can tell."

"All right, that's enough," Maggie said, hauling Matheson to his feet. "Celia, Allie, search his pockets. See if he has a cell phone, maybe a badge or something to get through doors in this complex."

Allie had already noticed the bulge of the cell phone in Matheson's left pants pocket. She pulled it out, noticed that it required facial recognition to work, and stuck it in front of Matheson's face before he realized what had happened.

"Bitch! That's a violation of my privacy! There is important company information on that device, and you have no right to take it," he shouted, and he really struggled for the first time in Maggie's grip.

Maggie kneed him in the balls so hard that Allie swore she saw them come out his ass. Matheson's face purpled and his knees buckled. Maggie released him and let him fall to the ground, where he moaned, putting his hands over his crotch.

Allie looked at the phone. She noticed that the recorder was on, and that it had been recording for the last fifteen minutes or so. "Oh-ho! What is this? A recorded confession of all of your misdeeds?"

"Fucking cunt," Matheson wheezed. "You are going to be destroyed, I swear to Christ."

"When did he turn on the recorder?" Maggie wondered.

"Asshole was probably recording a voice memo or something in the hallway before he came in here," Allie said. "And lucky for us, the phone was still recording the whole time we were talking. I wonder what the world will think when this is released online. I bet the police will be more interested in your little misogynist's playland then."

For the first time, Allie noticed a flicker of concern in Matheson's eyes, quickly swallowed by rage.

"I'm going to get you. I'm going to get all of you. You will pay for this, you—"

"Fucking bitch," Allie said in a bored voice. "Mix it up, why don't you?"

"All right, let's take this piece of shit with us," Maggie said. "If we run into any members of the goon squad, we can throw his body in front of us if they shoot."

"Do you think they have guns?" Celia asked in a small voice.

"I'm sure," Maggie said. Despite her obvious pain, she seemed to have gotten a surge of energy from manhandling Matheson. "Whether or not they'll actually use them on us is another story. Maybe some of them, at least, won't be able to kill a woman when she's looking him in the eyes. It's really easy to kill us when you're just watching and laughing through the screen, though, huh? Real easy to set off your little tricks and traps."

Sanya ran back to the monitors. "I can't see the truck anymore, so I'm assuming those men are either on a boat or boarding it. But the ones who followed Celia and Allie here are still outside—Allie's psycho killer and the group that was trying to bust down the door with a tree like they're in *The Lord of the Rings*."

"Great. It's time to get out of here before any of them work out how to find us," Maggie said.

# MAGGIE

**"OKAY, LET'S GO," MAGGIE** said, indicating to Matheson that he should get up.

Matheson shook his head. "You can't make me."

"Seriously? How old are you, five?" Allie asked.

"Get up now or I'll break every bone in your right hand," Maggie said. Before today she would have said that she abhorred violence, that she could never hurt someone unless in self-defense. But Ray Matheson and what Ray Matheson had done to her and Sanya and Celia and Allie, what he had done to all the other women in the maze—that seemed to more than justify any amount of violence. "I am absolutely goddamned *done* with you and your bullshit."

Matheson must have seen the truth of it in Maggie's eyes. After all, she had slammed his head to the ground enough times to give him a concussion and had kneed him in the balls hard enough to prevent future generations of Mathesons. She couldn't take credit for his swelling nose, though. Allie had done a good job there.

Matheson stood, his movements slow and careful. His eyes weren't on Maggie, though. They were on Allie and the phone she had in her hand.

"You're lucky you outran Luke, you dumb bitch. Luke and Brad and a couple of others were planning on reenacting that scene from *I Spit on Your Grave.*"

Maggie didn't know what this meant, but she knew it was a

barb meant to hurt Allie. Instead of responding to the provocation, Allie very deliberately slid Matheson's cell phone into her front pants pocket and covered the top with her sweatshirt, so it couldn't be seen.

"Trying to piss me off so that you can grab your phone back?" Allie said. "Try again. You're pathetic."

Matheson's face reddened again. "I am not pathetic. I am a goddamned billionaire. I have more power than you could ever dream of."

"Yet you'll be going to jail for murder all the same," Allie said. "And none of you watched that movie closely enough. She got her revenge on all of them in the end."

"We should move," Celia said. "He's probably just trying to delay us at this point, hoping his little buddies show up in time."

"Move it, rich boy," Maggie said, spinning Matheson around and pointing him at the door.

"Wait, let me go out first so that he can't sprint down the hall," Sanya said. "Then when he's through the door, we can both hold him."

Sanya went out, Maggie pushed Matheson out after Sanya, and the rest followed after Maggie. They were in another white-walled, gray-carpeted hallway. This one had many more doors off it.

"Bet some of these lead to the residence," Allie said.

"I sincerely hope you have a better decorator for your living space," Sanya said. "This color scheme is a little too 'doctor's office' for me."

Matheson had started muttering under his breath. Maggie curled her fingers into his skinny bicep and squeezed.

"What are you saying, rich boy?"

"He's saying he's going to get us all later, that we're a bunch of bitches," Allie said. "You don't actually need to hear the words to know what he's saying."

"Should we just try all of these doors?" Celia asked.

"Nah, we can just go right out the one marked 'exit,'" Allie said, pointing at the door at the farthest end. "Bet Ray-Ray here didn't want any of the dipshits accidentally poking around in his stuff, so he marked all the doors they're allowed to walk through."

They were halfway down the hall when the exit door swung open. Maggie's stomach turned over. They were here. The rest of the men were here.

But it wasn't a large group carrying Tasers and butterfly nets to capture the escapees. It was one man, his black clothes soaked to the skin like he'd swum all the way around the island.

Maggie recognized him immediately. It was cattle-prod guy. And he didn't have his cattle prod.

"You!" she shouted, releasing Matheson's arm. She sprinted down the hall, the other women shouting after her, and tackled him right out the door before he realized what was happening.

Maggie landed on top of him, but he bucked her off and she rolled away. The sun blared down on them—the real sun, and it was absolutely blinding after the fake sun of Matheson's maze. Cattle-prod guy—*Clark, Beth said his name was Clark*—grabbed Maggie's ankles and yanked her so that she was underneath him. He grabbed her by the face and pressed onto her broken cheekbone, and Maggie howled.

"I told you women are to be seen and not heard," Clark said. "I think you need to be taught a lesson."

His hand closed around her throat. Maggie's eyes were blurry, her vision covered in black dots. After all of this, after all she'd gone through—would she die on the shore of this island, far from home and her daughter?

Then Clark's hands loosened, and he was the one howling,

because Sanya and Allie had descended upon him. Sanya grabbed a handful of his hair and pulled so hard that his head was bent backward, and Allie pressed her thumbs into his eyes.

Clark screamed, and the pressure of his legs loosened around Maggie. She wriggled out, gasping for air.

"Don't . . . pop . . . his . . . eyes . . . out," Maggie said, wheezing. "I want him to see me when I testify in court against him."

Sanya slammed Clark's head down to the ground and Allie released him. When he fell, Allie and Sanya each stomped on one of his hands, almost as if it were a planned, coordinated movement. Maggie heard the sound of crunching bone.

"You're not going to be strangling any more women, motherfucker," Allie said, stomping again and again. "You'll be lucky if you can pick up a sandwich."

Clark had stopped howling and now whimpered for them to stop.

"All right, ease up, cowgirl," Sanya said. "You've got some unfocused rage issues, huh?"

"They're not unfocused," Allie said, but she eased back. "They're very, very focused on a certain type of person."

Maggie noticed that Celia was holding on tight to Matheson by the door. She looked around. They were on a small stretch of grass that led down to a little rocky beach and a rather unassuming wooden dock. There was a small speedboat tied to the dock. On the other side was a Jet Ski. Clark must have used the Jet Ski to beat the rest of the gang to this side of the island.

"Where are all of your little buddies?" Sanya asked. "Did they all drown in the bay?"

"Fuck you," Clark said.

"Such terrible language when speaking to a lady," Allie said, and stomped on his hand again.

"They're . . . they're stuck. The ferry wasn't running right now because of engine trouble at the other end. It's delayed."

Maggie laughed. Her laugh sounded a little wheezy, a little crazy. "Saved by mechanical trouble. All right, let's get into the speedboat with rich boy there."

"What about him?" Allie asked. "Should we take him with us, too?"

Maggie stood up, and stared down at Clark, and thought about him using the cattle prod on the screaming woman. For a moment, she felt the same murderous rage that Allie had expressed a moment before. Then it ran out of her, leaving her exhausted.

"Leave him," she said. "We don't need any more shit stinking up the boat. We have Matheson, and that's enough."

# CELIA

CELIA PUSHED MATHESON IN front of her, guiding him toward the boat. The fight seemed to have gone out of him as he watched Allie and Sanya kicking the shit out of the man in black. Celia had watched his shoulders droop, his body become boneless with shock. He stumbled toward the speedboat with the air of a man who didn't know quite where he was.

"Watch him," Maggie said. Sanya had slung her arm under Maggie's and was helping Maggie walk. "He might break and run."

Allie hurried to join Celia. She grabbed Matheson's arm and dug in her nails, causing him to cry out.

"Don't try anything funny," Allie warned. "Remember, I've got your phone."

"You beat the shit out of Clark," Matheson said. "Just . . . beat the shit out of him. Without mercy."

"We used just as much mercy as you showed to us," Allie said. "Now get in the boat."

They all climbed in. Sanya carefully settled Maggie next to her in the front. Allie and Celia sat in the back with Matheson between them.

"Do you know how to drive one of these things?" Maggie asked.

"Oh, yeah," Sanya said. "I live on Lake Michigan. I pretty much spend every summer on a boat. And Genius back there left his keys."

Sanya started up the boat and pointed its nose toward the coast, just visible in the distance.

Celia leaned her head back against the seat. She still couldn't remember all of her life. She wasn't sure if she ever would. But she was ready to put this chapter behind her. She'd never read another mystery again.

"You know, when we get to the other side, no one is going to believe you," Matheson said.

Celia opened her eyes and stared at him. Sanya and Maggie appeared not to have heard him. Allie had her eyes closed and Celia thought she might have fallen asleep already.

"We have the recording of you," Celia said. "And there are all the dead bodies on your island."

"You don't think the police will arrest me just on your say-so, do you? If anything, they'll think you kidnapped me instead of the other way around. A bunch of crazy-looking women with a crazy story, and one of the country's wealthiest, most influential men? Whose side do you think they'll be on?"

Matheson seemed to have gotten his swagger back. He'd been shaken up by their attack on Clark, but now he was thinking about how easily he'd shake them off, how he'd literally get away with murder.

"Bitches like you never win. You know that. The world was made for men. Men like me never pay. I'll get what I want, and you'll get nothing."

Celia stared in front of her for a few minutes, thinking about what he'd said. She didn't need all of her memories to know that what he said was probably true, that his money and his gender would protect him, that she and Allie and Sanya and Maggie would seem insane, that he'd never pay the way he ought to.

She was moving before she knew what she was doing, yanking him backward, pulling his body over her own, letting his torso dangle over the water. Matheson began screaming and thrashing. Allie shouted something, and out of the corner of her eye, Celia noticed Maggie turning around to see what was going on.

"I'll get nothing, right?" Celia said. "No matter what I do, you'll never be punished, you'll always win, is that right?"

Matheson screamed incoherently as Celia pushed him out of the boat. She heard the thud of his head against the side, and thought, with no small amount of satisfaction, that it was probably awfully hard to swim with a concussion.

"All right then," Celia whispered. "Prove it."

# GOOD GIRLS DON'T DIE

## CHRISTINA HENRY

---

# Discussion Questions

1. Who was your favorite character in the novel, and why?

2. How do the three women differ in their reactions to finding themselves in their scenarios? How does each woman surprise herself? How do you think you would react to the challenges these characters face, and why?

3. Celia's biggest fear is that "she would speak words that no one would believe." In constructing his trap, how does Matheson take advantage of the fact that women are often not believed?

4. What did you think the story was about at the end of Celia's section? At the end of Allie's? At the end of Maggie's? Did you see the ending coming? Why or why not?

5. While they are dramatized for fictional purposes here, do any of the women's experiences online match up with your experiences of cyberbullying and toxic internet culture?

6. How did the online conversations running throughout the book guide your expectations for each section?

7. If you had to cast this book as a film, who would you envision playing Allie, Celia and Maggie?

Photo by *Kathryn McCallum Osgood*

**Christina Henry** is a horror and dark fantasy author whose works include *Horseman*, *Near the Bone*, *The Ghost Tree*, *Looking Glass*, *The Girl in Red*, *The Mermaid*, *Lost Boy*, *Red Queen*, *Alice* and the seven-book urban fantasy Black Wings series.

She enjoys running long distances, reading anything she can get her hands on and watching movies with samurai, zombies and/or subtitles in her spare time. She lives in Chicago with her husband and son.